Miles grabbed her at the wrist. Alison tried to pull herself free but his powerful arm caught her slender waist and held fast.

"Unhand me this instant," she hissed, angrily. "Why have you kept me waiting this long?"

Miles grinned lazily, "Ah, you long for me so quickly?"

But before she could answer, Miles crushed her to his body, his mouth covering hers with savage insistence. A surge of sensuous warmth overwhelmed her as his hand brushed the swell of her breast. Her senses were reeling from desire. *Yes, yes,* she said to herself, over and over again. And she let her traitorous body yield to his tantalizing touch. . . .

WYNDFELL

◯ SIGNET (0451)

Sagas of Love, Danger, and Destiny

- ☐ **CHANDRA by Catherine Coulter.** Lovely, golden-haired Chandra, raised by her noble father, in the time of the Crusades to handle weapons as well as any man, was prepared to defend herself against everything but love.... (142012—$3.95)

- ☐ **ROSEHAVEN by Lynda Trent.** Aflame with passion, Abigail McGee surrendered to the bold rebel as he unlaced the ribbons of her tattered gown. He was like no man she had ever known, and Abigail knew she would be willing to relinquish her fortune, her fate—everything—to follow this daring, sensual man to the end of time....(139097—$3.95)

- ☐ **WINTER MASQUERADE by Kathleen Maxwell.** Lovely Kimberly Barrow was enthralled by the glorious winter splendor of William and Mary's court and the two devastatingly attractive men vying for her attentions. But her hidden secret thrust her into a dangerous game of desire.... (129547—$2.95)

- ☐ **BEWARE, MY LOVE by Lee Karr.** In a mountain mansion, lovely Allison Lacey scales the peaks of passion and learns that love is another word for terror ... as she follows a labyrinth of murderous secrets about handsome Kipp Halstead who touched her heart—even as he chilled her with fear. (147413—$2.95)

- ☐ **WYNDFELL by Lynda Trent.** She was caught between the tides of war and passion. Alison Wakefield, beautiful illegitimate daughter of Henry VIII swore she would bend to no man's will—until she met Miles Garret, as handsome and charming as he was loyal to the Protestant Crown. Against all her loyalties she willingly surrendered to the flame of desire between them ... (400607—$3.95)

Prices slightly higher in Canada

Buy them at your local bookstore or use this convenient coupon for ordering.
NEW AMERICAN LIBRARY,
P.O. Box 999, Bergenfield, New Jersey 07621

Please send me the books I have checked above. I am enclosing $_____
(please add $1.00 to this order to cover postage and handling). Send check or money order—no cash or C.O.D.'s. Prices and numbers are subject to change without notice.

Name_____

Address_____

City_____State_____Zip Code_____

Allow 4-6 weeks for delivery.
This offer is subject to withdrawal without notice.

WYNDFELL

Lynda Trent

AN ONYX BOOK

NEW AMERICAN LIBRARY

NAL BOOKS ARE AVAILABLE AT QUANTITY DISCOUNTS WHEN USED TO PROMOTE PRODUCTS OR SERVICES. FOR INFORMATION PLEASE WRITE TO PREMIUM MARKETING DIVISION, NEW AMERICAN LIBRARY, 1633 BROADWAY, NEW YORK, NEW YORK 10019.

Copyright © 1987 by Dan and Lynda Trent

All rights reserved

Onyx is a trademark of New American Library.

SIGNET, SIGNET CLASSIC, MENTOR, ONYX, PLUME, MERIDIAN and NAL BOOKS are published by NAL PENGUIN INC., 1633 Broadway, New York, New York 10019

First Printing, January, 1988

1 2 3 4 5 6 7 8 9

PRINTED IN THE UNITED STATES OF AMERICA

*To Dolores and Art Johnston,
for friendship*

For herein may be seen noble chivalry, courtesy, humanity, friendliness, hardiness, love, friendship, cowardice, murder, hate, virtue, and sin. Do after the good and leave the evil, and it shall bring you to good fame and renown.

Le Morte d'Arthur
—Sir Thomas Malory
(From preface by William Caxton)

Prologue

Alison Wakefield gazed fondly across the firelit hearth at her husband, Charles. Although he was almost twenty years her senior, his light brown hair was scarcely touched with silver, his long face virtually unlined by the passing years or by concern. Theirs had been a love match—a rarity for the time—and for the past three years she had been happy as his wife and was certain she still pleased him. Charles was not a man to lust after a pretty face or a flashing ankle. His masculine urges were, as was Charles himself, subject to the control of his brilliant mind.

A log shifted in the fire, sending a spray of glowing embers arching up the chimney. Charles glanced up from the religious treatise he was studying. He caught Alison's gaze and returned her smile, his green eyes joining her brown ones in shared but unspoken intimacy.

Alison looked back down at her embroidery, her lips still holding a gentle smile. The fire reflected the deep red highlights in her auburn hair, a legacy from her illustrious father. There had been news of him lately. Disturbing news. Alison's smile faded with the recollection. She did not want to think of him. During all her eighteen years he had merely been a name whispered in awe or shouted in allegiance, but of late his name had become synonymous with much darker subjects: a faithful wife put aside, a younger and more vivacious wife beheaded at his command, and two daughters declared illegitimate at his whim. Now there was talk of his taking yet another wife—Jane Seymour. But King Henry, the eighth sovereign of that name, had had no such bent toward marriage where Alison's own mother was concerned.

How strange, Alison mused, that she had two half-sisters, both royal princesses in spite of the king's decree, and she was merely a by-blow, a bastard daughter not even formally recognized.

Alison looked toward her mother, who was seated nearby, and curiously studied her for a moment. At one time those cheeks had been rounded with youth and flushed with the pleasure of a royal lover, but now her mother's skin had the waxen transparency of one not far from the grave. The rattling cough that had shaken her for months was now accompanied by a fever that never quite abated. Alison stared frankly at her mother as she tried to determine what in so frail a body and so retiring a spirit had attracted the most powerful ruler in Christendom. Whatever Eleanor Mendal's physical charms had been, they were long since faded. Yet perhaps the spark was not entirely gone, for when her mother spoke of King Henry, it was with a reverence another might reserve for a saint.

Chiding herself for such a blasphemous thought, Alison looked back to her handiwork and tried to busy herself, but her mind would not leave the subject. After her mother's brief but fruitful affair with the king, Eleanor was married to a man of title and some note, but not of her own choosing. Their years together were not happy, and according to her mother, fate intervened to release her from the match when the man died after falling from his horse. Her mother seldom spoke of her husband, but rather persisted in her old and hopeless love of the king. Even though King Henry had never officially acknowledged Alison as his child, when she reached a suitable age he had seen to it that she was properly wed to a viscount, Lord Charles Wakefield. Once the arranged courtship began, Alison quickly fell in love with Lord Charles, and he with her. Whether this love match was the result of her royal father's benevolence or whether it was mere chance, Alison didn't know. Aside from his refusal to acknowledge her, Alison's real grievance with her royal father was their difference in religion.

Hoping to block her unpleasant thoughts with conversation, Alison turned to her husband. "What are you reading, Charles?"

Her husband's hand caressed the thin book he held in an unconscious manner much akin to that of a lover for a woman he cherishes. "The life of St. Thomas," he replied in a calm, matter-of-fact tone. "Would you like for me to read it aloud?"

Eleanor glanced cautiously about as she pressed a bit of linen to her pale lips in a futile effort to suppress a cough. The reading of Catholic literature was expressly forbidden by royal edict, as Charles well knew.

"Yes, please do," Alison prompted. They were alone and their servants were to be trusted. On occasion, Charles had even invited his steward, Walter Landon, to sit with them during such readings. Since the Roman churches had been closed and the holy orders scattered, there were few opportunities to hear the words of their religion.

Charles began to read, his words rising and falling in an accustomed rhythm in the calm of the room. Though a winter gale howled outside, within the security of Wyndfell Castle's massive walls was only peace. Alison sighed with contentment; she could wish for no more than she already had. Under Charles's serene guidance she was even learning to conquer her fiery temper—one of her father's traits—and had every reason to compliment herself on becoming a sweet and dutiful wife.

Suddenly a loud knocking on the chamber door drew everyone's attention. Eleanor nervously jumped, startling Alison. Charles stopped reading but his long fingers marked his place on the page.

" 'Tis the king's men!" Eleanor hissed in fear. "Hide the book!"

"The king's men? Here in Yorkshire? I think not," Charles replied evenly.

Alison's round eyes flicked back to her husband. Surely it would be more prudent to assume her mother was right and put the book out of sight. Having reading material such as this was a serious crime and could be construed as treason.

Answering Charles's summons to enter, his aging steward, Sir Walter Landon, hurried into the chamber, his plump jowls quivering from exertion. "Lord Wakefield, there are men here to see you!"

"Show them in, Landon." Charles turned to the women and said, "You'll excuse me, ladies?" Eleanor hurried to her feet and left the room by way of the side door, but Alison paused in front of Charles. Although she greatly admired Charles's courage, she often wished he would exercise a bit more caution. He had not even asked who these visitors were before telling the steward to bring them in. And he still held the book on St. Thomas in clear view.

Her natural inclination was to demand that he give her the book so she could hide it, but she had struggled hard to overcome such improper behavior and wouldn't let her temper best her now. Her mother had warned her that a willful wife would forever regret her actions. In their three years of marriage, she had never crossed Charles, and now was no time to start. The only important thing was to get the book out of the room. With a sweet smile on her lips, Alison said, "I'll do as you have asked and leave you to your business, but may I take the readings on St. Thomas with me?"

When he failed to answer immediately, Alison quickly added, "It's for Mother. As you could see, she is quite nervous and upset. Perhaps if I read to her, it will calm her."

"Yes, yes. If you think it will help, then please do so. I don't understand her concern for safety. Our own St. Ruan has protected us and our ancestors for many generations, not to mention the strength we get from our faith in the teachings of the church. Take the book and read to her from those passages that have given you courage. Perhaps she, too, will find reassurance."

Alison forced herself to smile, and clutching the book, walked quickly from the room. At times he was exasperating. Didn't he realize the danger in being so vocal about his religious convictions? The servants had been full of news gleaned from various peddlers and travelers that the entire country was in a state of unrest. She was sure he had heard, but he seemed not to care. Granted, Wyndfell was a veritable fortress, but Charles seemed to be flirting with disaster.

Gliding through the doorway, Alison tugged the heavy wooden door behind her, but stopped it short of completely closing. Curiosity having gotten the better of her, she put her eye to the crack and watched as several travel-stained men strode briskly into the room. Charles rose to greet them, calling the leader Hallam and asking after a man called Bigod. Alison strained to catch the rise and fall of their hushed words. A rebellion was under way, Hallam said. A righteous rebellion, to set England straight again. Robert Aske was its leader, and he had been lured to London by the king's man Norfolk, doubtless to be jailed and martyred.

"We'll not stand for it!" Hallam spit out. "King Henry cannot get away with such heresy forever. We must stop him!"

"But he is our king," Charles protested as if by rote, his voice lacking the sincerity of a truly loyal subject.

"If ye had a bowl of my blood and a bowl of his, there would be naught difference," one of the others said.

Alison's eyes widened as she heard Charles respond, "Such is true." Charles might speak of treason in private with his wife and mother-in-law, but this was too foolhardy! What if these men reported his words in order to claim the reward that Cromwell was offering for information on traitors? Once money had been offered, some had become spies in an attempt to line their pockets with gold.

"We have our rights as Englishmen," a man with a squint eye spoke up. "There's been too much injustice to the common man!"

Charles, who was a viscount, merely smiled. "The true Catholic Church must be returned to England. As a nation we are in dire threat of heresy."

"If we don't do something, England may not survive," Hallam rasped out. "We can't afford to be weakened by this heretic raving. The king has taken a third wife, and it's said he joyously celebrated the anniversary of Queen Catherine's death, may she rest in peace."

Automatically Charles crossed himself. "So he's wed again?"

"Aye. Jane Seymour, it is," a rough man said from the rear of the room. "I'd not rest easy in her place."

Charles let his calm gaze rest for a moment on the man, then said to Hallam, "What can we do?"

"We can fight, my lord. Norfolk has been sent to put us down, just as Suffolk put down the rebellion in Lincolnshire. Yorkshiremen are made of sterner stuff. We'll fight and we'll win!"

Charles paused contemplatively. "Fight the king? 'Tis treason."

"No more than to speak of it. Even doddering old graybeards are hauled to the gallows for muttering against the king."

" 'Tis said he will tax us yet again," the rough man added. "I've heard he will go on until he owns even our oxen and all our crops."

"What would the king want with your oxen?" Charles asked incredulously. "I think these are exaggerations. However, on the matter of religion I am in agreement with you. There have been rumors of pulling down our parish church."

"It's already happened in my parish," Hallam affirmed. "It wasn't enough for the king to disband the larger churches in London and send the poor monks and nuns to live on the road. He means to raze the church buildings as well."

"Soon there'll be no Masses at all, only heathen sermons." The rough man nodded decisively.

"We cannot allow that! We must be true to ourselves and defend our faith," Charles boldly responded.

"Then you and your men will ride with us?" Hallam demanded.

After a brief hesitation Charles said, "We will."

"Good! Good. We ride tonight."

Alison wanted to shriek with terror when she heard Charles agree to take up arms against the king, but she was unable either to move or to speak.

"I'll give the order to my men." Charles motioned to his steward. "Have the men made ready to ride. We leave within the hour."

"My lord, I beg to go also," the old man said. "Young Walt can see to the castle and the ladies."

"No doubt we will conquer and be home in a fortnight," Hallam said.

"Then come with us, Landon," Charles agreed. "The more men we have, the sooner we'll be home." He clapped the steward on the shoulder. "In the meantime, have Cook set out food and drink for our comrades in arms. I'll go tell my womenfolk the news."

Forcing herself from the door, Alison retreated along the frosty corridor to the ladies' solar where Eleanor waited.

"Where have you been?" her mother asked. "I was worried about you."

Alison went to the brazier of coals and warmed her icy fingers. "It's a rebellion, Mother. Charles . . ."

The door opened and Alison turned to see Charles enter the room. He seemed as composed as if they had had no visitors at all. She studied his face as he told them all she had overheard from the doorway. When he announced his decision to ride with the rebellion, it was as if he proposed nothing more daring than a canter down to the village.

"You cannot ride with them!" Alison vehemently objected, no longer able to remain meek and submissive. "You might be killed!"

"Or I might not be." Charles's expression clearly showed his surprise and amazement at Alison's temper.

"Even if you aren't killed in battle, if your cause fails you'll be executed as a traitor!"

"*Our* cause, wife. But we cannot fail. God is on our side. If it so happens that I die in battle, it will be a martyr's death and will no doubt speed me through purgatory."

"But you'll be dead!"

"Now, now. Don't fash so. See how your lady mother is taking the news? You must bear up."

Eleanor straightened herself as well as she could and put her arm around her daughter. Alison felt the familiar fever-heat of her mother's palm on her shoulder. "It's the way of the world, sweeting," her mother began stoically. "Men must fight for what they believe in, and we must sit at home and pray for their safe return."

Pulling away from her mother, Alison retorted, "I care not to sit and wait for news of my beloved husband's death! Especially when I see no hope of the cause succeeding."

Charles Wakefield studied his young wife for a moment, obviously perplexed by the return of her outspokenness, but not angered by her outburst. Calmly he continued with his attempt to reassure her. "Of course we will succeed. Our cause is just. I've heard news of this rebellion. It's called the Pilgrimage of Grace. Robert Aske is an able leader. This is a crusade of sorts. After it is all over, we will again be able to hear Mass in the village church."

Alison faced her husband with tears in her eyes. "But how will that avail me if you are dead?"

He sighed in a rare show of exasperation. "Calm yourself, Alison. Follow the good example of your lady mother. Would you send your husband to battle with tears and railings?"

She lifted her chin proudly. "I can do naught else if you insist upon this foolhardy venture."

"Alison!" her mother reprimanded sharply. "You forget yourself!"

Forcing herself into submission, Alison managed to say, "Forgive me, my lord husband. I have a woman's foolish fears." She lowered her head so he couldn't detect the frustrated anger that paled her cheeks.

"That's better, sweeting," Charles said in approval. He touched her arm in the way he had of showing tender affection. "I have things to attend to. Wait for me in the winter parlor and I will come there to bid you farewell."

Eleanor bowed her head in agreement and took Alison's hand to escort her from the room. Alison allowed herself to be led, but her thoughts were seething. Charles was leaving them virtually unprotected while he rode about the countryside in a hopeless cause. Why was it always a woman's place to sit around and nod in agreement with everything her husband said? She had as keen a mind as he did, so why couldn't she use it? She struggled to accept her lot in life, but it was for naught.

Why did she feel so afraid? It wasn't that she feared being left unprotected. Since her father had never been present to shield her, and her stepfather had been a weak man, she had developed an independence uncommon for most of her gender. Wyndfell was a strong castle, and Alison felt confident that she could hold out through a siege. She would almost welcome one, rather than meekly wait for Charles to return.

But if he didn't return, she would be alone, and perhaps that was what she feared most.

She looked back to see Charles walking briskly in the direction of their bedchamber. Servants passed her in the cold corridor, each hurrying to perform some task in preparation for the men's departure. Because they would travel quickly, no carts would be taken, no extra clothing carried. Alison tried to picture her fastidious husband sleeping on the ground and wearing the same clothes day after day. Surely no man in all of England was less suited to be a rebel than Charles.

Within the hour Charles came to them in the winter parlor. After a brief farewell to Eleanor, he stood before Alison and took both her hands in his. "You'll see to things while I'm away?"

"Of course, Charles." Her voice was husky with suppressed emotion but she held her head high.

"Don't worry, sweeting. The rebellion will soon be over and I'll return to you safe and sound."

A deep dread swept through Alison. She put her arms around him, inhaling his fragrance of tobacco and rosewater, and clung to him fiercely, not trusting herself to speak.

Charles carefully disengaged her and held her at arm's length. Alison knew he hated to be touched and abhorred any show of physical affection before others, but she hadn't been able to control herself. "I'll miss you so," she whispered brokenly.

Charles gave her his gentle, rather absentminded smile. As usual, his thoughts were racing ahead of his actions. Patting Alison's arm, he nodded again to Eleanor and left.

To keep herself from running after him, Alison gripped the doorframe until her fingers were pale and trembling. As she stared at his retreating back, wave after wave of apprehension flooded over her. With the dread came the disquieting yet undeniable knowledge that Charles would never see Wyndfell again. Something of the same premonition must have touched him, for he paused and looked about the hall, then walked resolutely out, and the castle was quiet once more.

Days crept into weeks, and then into months. Christmas came and passed with little note; then the new year began. Letters arrived sporadically, first telling Alison of the rebels' progress, later their lack of it. Finally the letters stopped coming.

Alison and her mother, as well as the women who made up their ladies-in-waiting, sewed and tried to pretend all was well. They indulged themselves in the fancy that Charles had stopped writing only because he was too busy or too tired. Then one morning young Walt ushered in the rough man that had come with the others the night Charles left.

He stood uneasily before her, his bravado gone. She found her mouth dry and had to force her tongue to form her words. "What news have you?" she demanded.

"Ill news, my lady," the man mumbled. "We've met defeat. Norfolk has put down the rebellion. All who survived the fighting are being held captive in York."

"Charles?" Alison whispered. When he didn't respond, she asked more loudly, "What of my lord husband?"

"He be captured, my lady, and imprisoned in York Castle. Most of his men were killed, including Walt Landon, but Lord Wakefield was not hurt. The ones that got away as I did will likely make it home before long. They be hiding out on the way to save their skins. I come here myself so you would know what come of us."

Alison found she was holding her breath. The chamber seemed close and stuffy; her head was reeling. Forcing herself to breathe, she said briskly, "Thank you for telling me." When she turned to the son of her steward, who had done his best to manage the castle in his father's absence, she noticed tears creeping down the young man's face at the news of his father's death. "Walt, bring me pen and paper, then you may go to your mother and give her the sad news."

"What will we do?" Eleanor wailed.

"I'm going to write to the king and plead clemency for Charles."

One of her waiting-women blurted out, "He'll never listen, my lady. His heart is surely hardened against us after this."

Eleanor buried her face in her hands. "To think of it. A wife having to beg her father not to kill her husband! What hard times these are."

Alison motioned for the rebel to follow Walt out. Angrily she resented him for his freedom and leapt to the conclusion that he must have avoided capture by running away before the battle began. At any rate she didn't want to see him. He was a reminder of all that had turned her world upside down. "Surely the king will listen to me." She seldom referred to the English sovereign as her father, stubbornly affirming that since he would not acknowledge his relationship to her, neither would she.

"Mention my name," Eleanor suggested hopefully. "Ask him this in remembrance of me."

Although Alison nodded her agreement, she doubted that the reminder would affect the king one way or the other. Quickly her pen moved across the page in the literate hand Charles had taught her. How much easier it was, she reflected, to be submissive on paper. Inside she was frightened for Charles, confused at what was happening, and angry that her husband had not heeded her protests. Yet in her letter she was as meek and humble as any woman could be. Anything else would surely prejudice the king against granting her request.

When the letter was sealed with the unicorn emblem of the Wakefield family, she gave orders for her horse to be saddled and for a guard of men to accompany her.

"Where are you going?" Eleanor asked with great surprise and concern. "Surely not to London!"

"I'm going to York. There must be something I can

do to free Charles." She glanced over her shoulder at the retainer who was staring at her in confusion. "Go to my husband's closet and bring me all the gold ryals and angels we have on hand." To Eleanor she said, "Mayhap I can bribe his jailers to let him escape."

"But the king, surely—"

"I put little faith in the king. If news comes of Charles's pardon, send a rider by post to tell me. Time may be terribly important." Alison hurried to dress for travel and to order clothing to be sent after her to York. For a woman to set out on such a journey was dangerous in the extreme, but she had no other choice. She had been meek and submissive, and this was the result. She couldn't bear the thought of Charles being hanged, drawn, and quartered which was typically the traitor's fate. Each time fear assaulted her, she resolved to be strong for Charles.

In the waning hours of the next afternoon, Alison and her small band of guards entered the city of York through Bishopgate and began making their way through the press of humanity that lived within York's protective walls. As she had heard, the streets were overhung with houses and shops, and towering above it all was the cathedral of York Minster. They crossed the Ouse River, and found themselves before the enormity of York Castle. Its lime-washed walls were immense and appeared impregnable, and Alison felt fainthearted over what she was about to attempt. Surely no prisoner could escape from so impressive a fortress.

She hid her doubts and turned to the man nearest her. "Sir James, find us a lodging as near the castle as possible."

The knight took his leave and departed. With her remaining men, Alison rode into the gatehouse of the castle. She dismounted and purposefully strode up to the sentry and announced that she was there to see a prisoner.

"No, my lady, I've orders from the bailiff to show the traitors to no one."

At the word "traitor," Alison's heart sank, but she kept her mask of fearlessness in place. "In that case, I insist that you take me to your bailiff. I'll speak with him."

The sentry led her into the castle, leaving her men to await her return. Its furnishings and tapestries were much superior to those at Wyndfell, but Alison was too troubled even to notice them. The bailiff was a short, swarthy man with a beard on his lower jaw. With narrow, untrusting eyes he inspected this woman who had demanded to see him.

Putting on her most beguiling smile, Alison said, "I fear there has been a most grievous mistake. My husband, Lord Charles Wakefield, has been imprisoned. He is no traitor but rather was journeying through the area and was arrested by mistake."

"That he was not, my lady. I know Lord Wakefield and was there at his capture. He was riding with the traitors and will die with them."

"But I assure you, he is innocent," she protested demurely, casting her almond-shaped eyes at him. "If I could but see him, I—"

"That's impossible," the man interrupted.

"Perhaps you know not who I am. My name is Lady Alison Wakefield and my father is the king. Surely my husband is above suspicion."

The bailiff paused, stroking his beard thoughtfully while he considered what Alison had said. "Our king has many children from the wrong side of the blanket, I wager. If it mattered to him that you were sprung from his loins, I daresay all of England would know your name. If there was a mistake in your husband's arrest, I'm sure he will free Lord Wakefield." After another brief pause he smugly added, "Perhaps you should take your request directly to the king."

Alison's eyes glinted with anger as she demanded, "What is your name? I'm sure the king, my father, will want to know who imprisoned his son-in-law."

The man's eyes widened in amazement at her outburst. A frown puckered his forehead, and he shifted his weight as if he had been thrown off balance by her forcefulness. "I'm Sir Hubert Stone, my lady. But I'm only doing my duty. I meant not to offend you. Sir Emmitt Grayson is actually the bailiff here, but because he's ill, I'm taking his place."

Alison was pleasantly surprised by the man's sudden change of attitude and his apology. Deciding to press her advantage, she drew a gold angel from the purse that hung at her waist and held it up for him to see. "I'd like to see my husband," she stated firmly.

Sir Hubert had once seen the king while in London, and while the woman did not resemble him, neither did the two royal princesses. She might well be one of the royal bastards, and he could be in trouble for his insult. His eyes darted about the room to be sure that no one was watching; then he pocketed the coin. "I suppose a wife should be allowed to see her husband, and I can arrange that, but whether he is pardoned or not, I cannot say."

Anxiously Alison followed the man through the castle and down a flight of steps cut into the side of a wall, then down another, even more narrow one. Only the bailiff's torch cut through the damp darkness, though it was sunny outside.

As she cautiously made her way down the steps, with her heart pounding in apprehension, she asked, "Are there no windows?"

"The dungeons weren't designed for the prisoners' comfort," Sir Hubert retorted nervously. He was going against orders in allowing her down here and was beginning to worry that he had made a mistake.

The stone walls were damp with seepage from the nearby river and slimed with centuries of accumulated scum. Alison drew her skirts near about her and tried not to touch either wall.

As they entered a narrow corridor at the bottom of the steps, Sir Hubert began to walk much more swiftly. Both sides were lined with heavy wooden doors, one of which was open. As Sir Hubert hurried her past the open doorway, she looked inside and saw several soldiers lounging about. Sir Hubert moved quickly for he didn't want the guards to know what he was doing. Nearby she heard the drip of water and a scurrying of rats. She tried to keep the fear and revulsion from her face. Surely her Charles wasn't really in this dreadful place.

Sir Hubert stopped at the farthest door and put a large key into the lock. The sound of metal turning metal was replaced by low moans and hushed murmurings as he pushed the door open.

As his torch flooded the room with light, she stepped in and found herself in a large cellarlike room. The floor was of paving stone and the walls were hewn of the same wet rock as the stairway. As the stench nearly took her breath away, her eyes found the dim shapes of the prisoners, and horror dispelled her nausea.

The men were chained to the walls by iron cuffs on their wrists and ankles which prevented movement. Most lay or sat on the floor, oblivious of the filth and wetness. Some were so still that she assumed them to be dead or dying. Others stared at her as if they couldn't believe she was real. Sir Hubert led her to a thin and dirty man, indistinguishable from the rest. His head was bowed in resignation; his hollow chest moving almost imperceptibly with his shallow breathing. For a moment Alison didn't recognize him.

"Charles!" she cried out in alarm.

"Alison? Can it really be you?" He lifted his bony arm toward her, but the chain stopped him short.

As she reached out for him, the bailiff stepped between them. She glared unflinchingly into the man's narrow eyes, then angrily commanded, "Out of my way. I paid you handsomely for a visit with my husband. Leave us so that we may talk."

"That I'll not do, my lady. I agreed only to show you your husband."

"Charles," Alison said as the bailiff motioned for

her to go, "I'm working to free you. I've written to the king. Surely your pardon will arrive any day."

His lips stirred in a ghost of his sweet smile. "You've been a good wife, Alison, but you shouldn't have come."

She slapped away the bailiff's hand and reached out to lace her fingers with her husband's. "I'll have you free. Trust me."

"If all fails, Lord Roger Bainbridge will look after you. I spoke with him before we left for York. You can depend on him." He gave her a look that said much more.

Alison was taken aback. Charles expected to die! He had already given her into the keeping of their neighbor, a viscount who had been his closest friend and a staunch Catholic who, but for an untimely illness, would have joined the rebels. "Despair not. I'll set you free!"

"Farewell, Alison. I do not fear a martyr's death. What more could I wish but to die for my faith?"

Alison bit back her cry and let the bailiff lead her to the dank corridor. Charles had not only given up hope, but actually seemed to have accepted his fate. As soon as the heavy door was locked, she said to Sir Hubert, "Why is he chained there like a common felon? He is a viscount!"

"I don't make the decisions, but in the eyes of the law he is a traitor and a heretic. He's lucky to be fed and watered."

Angrily Alison held out another gold angel. "Move him to a drier cell."

"I cannot. I've risked too much already."

She lowered her voice as they passed the guardroom and ascended the stairs. "I have gold. What will it take to set him free?"

"You ask too much of me."

"You answer me too quickly. I'm a very wealthy woman."

"I *will* not."

"I have thirty ryals in this bag."

Sir Hubert's eyes nervously darted about. "Thirty?"

"If you free my husband, they are yours." She held her breath. "I'll give you half now and the rest when he stands free beside me on the street."

"I would need more than thirty ryals to put myself in so much danger. Say four hundred."

"Four hundred!"

"And fifty light sovereigns when the matter is done."

Alison stared at him. The man's greed was appalling. That was more money than she had ever seen. Finally she said, "Done. But it will take me some time to raise it."

Sir Hubert smiled thinly. "Don't tarry, my lady. His death orders could come at any moment."

Alison glared at him, then brushed past him and hurried toward the door that led outside. Gulping in deep breaths of cold, clean air, she waited for her men to join her. After the stench of the dungeon, she felt dirty inside and out. And Charles was imprisoned in that hell!

Retaining two of her men as guards, Alison said to another, "Sir Francis, go at once to Wyndfell. Tell young Walt that the price for my lord's freedom is four hundred ryals and fifty light sovereigns." When the man's eyes widened but he didn't move, she commanded, "Go at once, and make all the speed you can. Sell whatever is necessary, but do it quickly and return at once. Do you understand? And tell Lord Bainbridge of all that's happened."

She dismissed the men and let the two guardsmen accompany her to her rooms in a nearby inn. She didn't know if Walt could raise the money, but their neighbor was wealthy and she felt certain he would help with the gold.

For the next week Alison alternately paced her quarters and haunted York Castle, but the bailiff refused to allow her to see Charles again. In an effort to stall Charles's execution, she lied that she had received word that the money was on the way. Sir Hubert promised to wait another week if possible.

Eight days after her visit with Charles, Alison heard a clamor outside the window of her room in the inn. She rushed to see what was going on just as several carts loaded with prisoners were being hauled from York Castle, obviously on their way to the gallows. From the commotion, it appeared that the procession would be passing on the narrow street below. Calling for her men, Alison grabbed her wool cloak and ran the length of the uneven hallway and down the steep stairs.

As she stepped out onto the street, the first carts were passing by, the prisoners squinting against the bright sunlight and huddling together against the harsh cold. Charles passed, his face haggard, his hair matted and almost totally silver after his months of privation and his weeks of imprisonment. She clapped her hand over her mouth in horror.

Alison fought her way through the gathering crush of curiosity seekers in order to keep pace with the carts, but Charles never looked her way. She wanted to call out to him, but couldn't. His pale lips were moving in prayer, and from the expression on his face Alison concluded that he was in such a state that he had little idea what was going on about him. Perhaps his brilliant mind was insulating him from the horror that awaited him. At least she hoped so.

Alison looked about frantically, and saw Sir Hubert walking behind the cart that carried her poor Charles. When she managed to get near enough to him to speak, she asked where the prisoners were going and why.

"The execution orders came. We're taking them to the green."

"But you promised to wait!" she protested frantically. "You promised!"

Sir Hubert glanced around fearfully. "Quiet, woman! I have no power to countermand the king's orders."

"The king?" she gasped. Henry had had ample time

to receive her letter and pardon Charles. "*All* of them were condemned?"

"All."

A chill struck Alison and she began to tremble with the realization that the end had come for Charles. With the small dagger she always carried, she cut her purse from her belt and tossed it to Sir Hubert. "Be merciful, I beg you. Hang him until he's dead," she pleaded. "At least do this. I can't bear the thought of him being drawn and quartered."

Quickly the man stuffed the prize under his coat and gruffly nodded to her.

Alison quit trotting and her guardsmen helped shield her from the crowd that followed the prisoners. Soon she and her guards stood alone on the street. Her mind raced over all the events that had led to this moment, and with each recollection she asked herself if she could have prevented this from happening. But the answer was always no. Charles lived his life by his faith, and risked his life in an attempt to preserve it. For him, death would be a victory. But had her father pardoned him, Charles would also have been victorious and would have lived to continue sharing life and happiness with her. A shout went up on the green, and she knew it had started. A cold sickness gripped her middle and she reached blindly for a guardsman's arm. "Take me away," she murmured. "Take me away quickly. Tonight, after it's dark, get my husband's body. I'll not leave it for the crows."

Turning her back on the roaring crowd, she numbly walked toward the inn.

1

Alison walked reverently through the empty church. Beneath the sweep of her skirts were slabs engraved with names, dates of birth and death, and solemn inscriptions. The only sounds were the swish of the hem of her gown brushing over the stones and the faint echo of her footsteps. She turned into a small alcove on her right and approached the nearest tomb.

The visage of a knight, carved from the same gray stone as the tomb itself, lay stretched upon it, a sword by its side and a stone hunting dog at its feet. The features looked younger than Alison had ever seen them and the shoulders seemed broader. Charles had been a smaller man, she mused, but the village stone carver had only known him in his youth and had carved his likeness from that recollection.

She placed her hand on the unyielding stone and asked herself again why it had to be this way. Charles had been a scholar, not a warrior. And he certainly was not a traitor except in his religious beliefs. So why had he died a traitor's death? Although nearly three years had passed since that dreadful day in York, Alison still grew mournful when she visited the tomb. The sharp pain she had known at first had dulled to an ache and finally had faded into regret and an abiding resentment toward the king. What man could send his son-in-law to death? Her only comfort, if it could be termed such, was the notion that Henry might never have seen the letter she wrote or have been told the names of the rebels. Thomas Cromwell was said to rule the land, just as old Cardinal Wolsey had before him. Perhaps Cromwell had ordered the executions at York on behalf of the king. She might never know for sure.

Alison passed Charles's tomb and went to a newer one. Her mother had died the previous spring and her effigy still looked freshly hewn. How odd, Alison thought, that stone seems to die, too, after a time. The older tombs were darker and stained with time, while the more recent ones were pale and seemed too new for the ancient church.

She sat on a marble bench, spread her voluminous skirts about her, and clasped her hands together. "What should I do?" she asked the two carved figures. Of late she had formed the habit of talking to them in the solitude of the alcove. "Roger Bainbridge has asked me to marry him and professes great love for me. I care for him, but I don't love him. Perhaps I will never love again," she said as she gazed at Charles's lifelike features. "Yet a woman cannot live alone. I must have a protector or the king may marry me to whomever he wishes." Her voice grew cold at the thought of the king. "Thus I have written to him and asked his royal permission that I might wed Lord Roger. I expect his reply soon.

"I seem to have at last learned to curb my temper, Mother," she said to Eleanor. "I know you'll be pleased to hear that. Lord Roger doesn't provoke me." She sighed. "In truth I find him a bit dull. He doesn't read or have long discourses with me. But you know how quiet he is. It's just his way. I'm sure we'll be happy together and that I'll learn to regard him with more affection." She paused, waiting for an indication that the benediction she wanted from her mother's spirit would come. But only the cool dampness of the alcove surrounded her.

With another sigh, she got to her feet. She was terribly lonely and wished for someone to talk to—someone who would listen to her deepest needs and secrets. She never confided these to Roger because she knew he would pass them off as female prattle. Her marriage with Roger might be felicitous, but it wouldn't be one of deep sharing. Even Charles had wanted her to curb her deepest emotions. Perhaps all men were like that.

She walked out of the church and mounted her horse. Touching her heels to the jennet's side, she galloped around the outskirts of the village and up the grassy slope to Wyndfell.

The castle was large and well-proportioned, with crenellated battlements and five towers. The curtain wall, built from a pale gray stone that had been left its natural color, unlike Roger's whitewashed castle, reared proudly over the glassy waters of Wyndfell's moat. Alison let her horse drop back to a trot as she crossed the heavy drawbridge. On the side of the moat three of the young pages were fishing in the spring-fed water. She smiled. They rarely caught fish there, but they never tired of trying.

The courtyard, which was unusually spacious, was lined with the typical outbuildings: smithy, dovecote, weaving room, and the like. Alison made a practice of visiting each one during the course of a week. With no master of the castle, she had to strive harder to keep the servants and hirelings working.

She dismounted at the block nearest the entrance to the great hall and tossed her reins to a waiting stableboy. This was Thursday and she was to oversee the soapmaking and check on the progress of the preserving of food for the winter. The hall was quiet and well-ordered, she noted with satisfaction. Servants were polishing the long tables and scouring sand on the candle sconces. Her life was serene and calm, if lonely, but her approaching marriage would change that. Again she congratulated herself on conquering her lamentable temper.

"Begging your pardon, my lady?" young Walt said as he entered the room.

"Yes, Walt. What is it?" Alison watched the young man scratch where his jerkin was belted to his waist. Since his father's death in the rebellion, he had been struggling to perform the duties of castle steward as his father had, but as yet he was still somewhat of a failure. Alison wanted him to succeed although overlooking his shortcomings was difficult. The job of steward was a demanding one, and often Alison was the one who had to attend to responsibilities.

Within weeks after the execution, the king had sent a man named Sir Cecil West, ostensibly to serve as Alison's steward, but she knew he was there to determine whether she was conspiring with the rebels. The man performed neither task, but instead whiled away his time sampling Wyndfell's wines in the buttery. Less than six months after his arrival, Walt reported seeing him leaving Wyndfell on foot in a drunken stupor, and he was never seen or heard from again. Alison had been glad to see him gone and saw no reason to report his disappearance to the king.

"There is a messenger from London, my lady. Also there's another man who has not said what he wants. They're both waiting in the winter parlor."

"Thank you, Walt." No doubt the messenger was bringing approval for her marriage. The other man was likely the messenger's guardsman. Walt could never get anything straight.

As Alison entered the winter parlor, she removed her kid riding gloves and looped them over the silver-gilt chain she wore at her waist. Her mulberry kirtle brushed the rushes, and she made a mental note to have new grasses brought in before the fields became bare. A man somewhat younger than Walt was admiring the enormous stained-glass window that made up most of the north wall of the room.

"Greetings," Alison said as she swept into the room. "Were you sent by the king?"

"Aye, my lady." His eyes widened at her unexpected beauty and he handed her a roll of paper.

Alison broke the seal and her eyes scanned the page once, then went back and read more closely. Blood drained from her face and her mouth dropped open as she understood. "Permission refused . . . a wedding has been set . . . *Lord Miles Garrett!*" She turned to the messenger. "Who is Miles Garrett!"

"A man at court, my lady." The young man shrank back at the fire in her eyes. "His father is a confidant of the king's."

"His father a confidant! That tells me naught!"

"Lord Garrett is the heir of Llanduff and Clwd castles in Wales. He's a baron, my lady."

"A Welshman! And a baron? I am a viscountess!"

"Yes, my lady."

"My father, the king, thinks to wed me beneath my station to a Welshman?" Her tone clearly showed her outrage. "How dare he!"

"He's the king," the hapless messenger began.

"A pox on the king! And you can tell him I said so!"

At her raised voice, Alison's lady-in-waiting, Leatrice Fletcher, hurried into the chamber. "What's amiss, my lady?"

"This! Just look at this!" She thrust the foolscap at Leatrice.

"I cannot read, Lady Alison. What does it say?"

Alison's eyes narrowed with fury, and she took back the paper and rerolled it as she advanced on the messenger. "It says I may not marry Lord Bainbridge." Her voice was menacing, and her pantherlike stalking was threatening. The messenger retreated before her. "It says I'm to be given to a Welshman named Lord Miles Garrett! And a baron! Whose father is a confidant of the king!" With each exclamation Alison jabbed the air with the roll of paper.

"Forgive me, my lady," the man begged as he maneuvered toward the door. "I but delivered the message."

"A pox on the message! And on you too!" Alison swatted him across the shoulder, and he stumbled in his hurry toward the door.

Over his shoulder he called back, "The king bade me give you his greetings . . . and to tell you of his fond wishes for the approaching wedding."

"He did, did he?" Alison hit him again.

"Lord Garrett's duties will prevent him from riding north, so he will be unable to meet you before the wedding."

"So I'm not to even get a look at this groom until it's too late?"

The man took to his heels and sprinted the remaining distance to the door.

"Lady Alison," Leatrice ventured cautiously, "what does it mean?"

"Mean! It means I must marry this . . . this Welshman!"

"His name doesn't sound Welsh. Perhaps . . ."

"I care not what his name may be. All Welshmen are alike. Find Walt and have him send a man to tell Lord Bainbridge to come at once."

Leatrice curtsied and hurried away as Alison reread the message. A noise startled her, and she jumped when she saw the other man standing in the far corner. She had completely forgotten him in her rage over the king's message. Assuming a defensive stance, she demanded, "Who are you? Have you a message as well?"

He came forward cautiously and bowed. "My name is Sir Edmund Campbell. His highness has sent me to replace Sir Cecil West as steward of your castle. I would have a word with him, at your convenience."

"You may speak with him all you like, if you can

find him. He wandered off only a few months after his arrival. We have not seen him since."

"His majesty was unaware of this."

"I saw no reason to tell him. The man served no useful purpose while he was here, and I had not requested he come in the first place!"

"I assure you that I will be of service to you."

Alison took note of the older man's confident manner. He appeared to be well-trained in his address, and if he could do the job at all he would be better suited than Walt. He wasn't an ugly man; in fact his features would be pleasing except for a certain craftiness that lingered in his black eyes. His hair was also black and hung just below his ears in a style that had lost favor. His jerkin and doublet were soiled from his travel, but he was otherwise presentable. Alison couldn't deny she needed a steward, but she was still angry. "I gather I have no say in this matter either?"

"If I don't please you in the performance of my duties, you may complain to the king." Edmund watched her pace the chamber in a way reminiscent of the sovereign. She was a beauty despite her temper, and for a fleeting moment he wished he could have her for his own. Such, of course, was impossible. He had to serve as her steward, as the king had instructed him, or answer to the royal wrath. He had been sent to do a job, not to dally with the viscountess.

"Indeed I will! Just as I intend to complain of his disposal of me." Her eyes flashed fire and the red in her hair seemed to crackle. "This Lord Garrett! Do you know him?"

"Aye, my lady. Lord Garrett is well-known to all at court. The ladies seem to find him pleasing."

Alison snorted. "As his father seems to be so close to the king, I don't doubt his popularity."

"He may be only a baron, but he is heir to a considerable fortune from his mother. She was Welsh," he added. "However, his father is as English as you and I. I should also tell you that his father's health is very poor. No doubt Lord Garrett will soon inherit his family's fortune and estates, as well as his father's title."

"I care not for that," Alison replied haughtily. "I have wealth in my own right."

"I meant only that it is a good match. Most women would be pleased."

"I am not most women," she retorted. "And I am definitely not pleased."

Again she paced the chamber, her movements as fluid as a jungle cat's. Sir Edmund watched her in fascination. When King Henry had ordered him to Wyndfell, Edmund had been reluctant to leave court for this rural castle, though naturally he hadn't shown it. His job was an important one: to reassure the king of Lady Alison's allegiance to the crown.

"I will refuse to marry this man," Alison affirmed. "If I will not repeat the vows, no man can force me."

"Forgive me for differing with you, my lady, but the king did not request that you marry Lord Garrett, he commanded it. He might view your failure to obey as an act of treason, with all that implies. Besides, this castle with all its lands belongs to the king until you remarry. If you disobey, he might cast you out on the road penniless."

"What?"

"Were you not aware? When your late husband was sentenced for treason, all his belongings became the property of the crown."

"I wasn't informed of that!"

"An oversight, I suppose, but nonetheless true."

Alison stopped at the window and leaned against the frame, her face bathed in hues of red and blue from light that filtered through the stained-glass depiction of St. George battling a dragon.

"I suppose I have no choice. Even if the king were benevolent, I haven't any other relatives to turn to. He is my only living kin, though he won't publicly admit it." Her words were tinged with bitterness. She hated that she still cared, but a part of her stubbornly clung to the hope that someday he would admit, if only to her, that he was her father. "I don't suppose he mentioned to you that I am his daughter?"

"No, my lady, he made no mention of that, but he did ask me to give you the glad news of his new marriage."

"Again?"

"When he divorced Anne of Cleves, he took Catherine Howard as his wife. She has not yet been coronated, but will be soon. The wedding was in late July."

"His fifth wife." Alison's tone was indictable. "No wonder he marries me off with so little compunction. He obviously has no regard for the sanctity of marriage, and no consideration for love. My mother loved him, but he spurned her affection. And he had my husband executed for merely expressing his support of his lifelong faith." Alison gazed at St. George, lost in thought.

Edmund's eyes narrowed, but he took care that she didn't notice. The king had told him that Lady Alison had at one time been a devout Catholic but that Cecil West had reported to him that she appeared not to have been in league with her husband's rebel activities. However, Alison's request to marry Lord Roger Bainbridge had brought her situation fresh to his mind, particularly so because Bainbridge had recently been unconvincing when he had disavowed his faith and pledged his allegiance to the king. When Henry had asked to see the recent reports from West, he learned that nothing had been received for over two years. He had no way of knowing if things had changed. Immediately Edmund had been assigned to go there. If the viscountess's feelings about the old faith were shared by others in the Wyndfell district, the king's suspicion of disloyalty might have a basis in truth. But then, this might be just another of the king's unwarranted apprehensions. Only time and careful attention would tell.

Alison turned back to Sir Edmund after a moment, somewhat more composed. "You said his new wife is a Howard. Is she perhaps a cousin of Anne Boleyn?"

"Yes, my lady, she is."

A wry smile lifted Alison's lips. If what she had heard of the Howard family was true, her father would likely find this match no more satisfactory than the one to Anne Boleyn. He deserved no better. "You may go, Sir Edmund. Find the young man named Walt Landon who escorted you in here and tell him the king has sent you to replace him as my steward. Inform him that I have agreed only on the stipulation that he serve as your assistant. You will find him somewhat slow-witted, but he knows this castle well and will be able to answer most of your questions. Have him move your things into the upstairs chamber in the gatehouse. He is to move into the one below."

"Thank you, my lady." Sir Edmund's bow went unnoticed, as Alison was still looking out the window. Quietly he took his leave.

Alison was still in the winter parlor when Roger Bainbridge arrived almost an hour later. At the sound of his entrance, she turned toward the door.

"Is something wrong?" he asked. "I was on my way here when one of your men told me to ride over with all haste."

"The king has forbidden us to wed," she said bluntly.

"Forbidden! With what reason?"

"He has promised me to another. A Welsh baron named Lord Miles Garrett."

Roger stared at her as if he hadn't understood her words.

"It seems the baron's father is close to the king, and I'm to be given to him as if I were royal bounty."

"He can't do that!"

"Oh, but he can. Not only is he the king, but he's my natural father. Besides, I learned today that he confiscated Wyndfell and its lands when Charles was convicted of treason. In truth, I have nothing of my own."

Roger arched his eyebrows and drew back as if he were more shocked at the suggestion she might be destitute than the fact that they could not marry. Alison noticed this and, not for the first time, considered that the love he professed might be based more upon her wealth than his emotional attachment to her. She brushed aside the thought and in a gentler voice said, "I'm sorry that we cannot marry, Roger. I know you must be as surprised and disappointed as I am."

"Yes," he said absently as he contemplatively stroked his beard. As Alison watched for any further reaction she took stock of her own feelings and was surprised by what she found. Her indignation resulted from her lack of choice as to whom she would wed, not from the fact that she could not marry Roger. Admittedly she had never felt the depth of love for Roger that she had for Charles, and she had no expectation that she ever would. But still, they had made the decision to marry and now that would never be. Shouldn't the disappointment be keener? Alison's introspection was interrupted by Roger's voice as he broke the silence. "If the Garrett family is indeed close to the king, I suppose they are all heretics as well."

At the reference to heretics, Alison stiffened and made a silencing gesture toward Roger. "The king also sent me another steward, a man named Sir Edmund Campbell."

"Protestant?" Roger whispered.

"What else could he be?"

Roger moved nearer. "We must be careful and alert the others. This may no longer be a safe place to meet."

"Everything happened so fast today. I hadn't thought of our meetings. Perhaps I could send Sir Edmund on errands when we want him gone, or mayhap we could meet under the guise of another purpose? Otherwise, we could ride out into the forest to discuss our plans. Do you think Sir Edmund may be a spy?"

"Who can tell? Cromwell's men are everywhere. Until we get to know this Campbell, I think we should be cautious."

Alison nodded, but she was perturbed by the course the conversation was taking. They had schemed for years on ways to restore or preserve the old faith, to no avail. But at the moment, she felt their personal matters were more important. In a smaller voice she said, "I don't want to marry this Welshman."

"I know you'll hate having a Protestant heretic under your roof," Roger commiserated. "His presence will greatly interfere with our secret Masses."

"More important, I will hate having a Welshman in my bed," she retorted. "I don't even know what he looks like! Until an hour ago, I had never heard his name!"

"Love matches are very rare. We do what we must. I never met my Minerva, God rest her, until our wedding day."

Alison rested her head on the cool glass and closed her eyes. "I suppose I had expected you to rant and rave and somehow defend me."

"Against the king? Open defiance? Impossible." He put his arms around her waist. "If I could have you, I would."

With greater objectivity than ever before, Alison looked at the man she had thought would be her husband. He wasn't tall, for his eyes were nearly on a level with hers. His hair was brown and cut close to his head. His narrow mustache and pointed beard gave him an air of sophistication. His eyes were gray, and even though she looked hard, she found no indication of pain over losing her. Alison was hurt as she realized he must indeed have been marrying her in order to combine Wyndfell with his own neighboring estate, or as a last favor to Charles.

Chiding herself for being overly sentimental, she

made mental notes of all her transgressions for the day that she would have to confide in secret to the abbess who lived in the anchorage attached to Wyndfell's back wall. Alison had given the holy woman a place to hide when her convent was closed by royal edict, and with no other place for her to go, the abbess had taken up permanent residence. Soon afterward, the only priest in the area was arrested and taken away, leaving no one but the abbess to hear the confessions of those who faithfully clung to the Catholic tenets. Alison reminded herself that she must think how best to explain the holy woman's presence to the new steward and this man who was to be her husband, if she decided to tell them at all.

Miles Garrett leaned his forearm on the rail that bordered the jousting list. "Closer, man, closer!" he bellowed to the squire he was training, as the man thundered on his charger toward the target. The man thrust, but missed his mark, causing the sandbag to swing squarely into him, toppling him to the ground.

"Pah!" Miles snorted. "That's the fourth time you've been knocked down. Can you not get it right?"

The man frowned as he rolled to a sitting position. "It's not easy, my lord."

"Of course it's not," Miles said as he ducked under the rail and went to the man. "If it were, any peasant could do it and there would be no honor in becoming a knight." Miles clasped the man's forearm and hauled him to his feet. "Watch me, and I'll show you again."

He vaulted into the saddle and sent the huge horse back into position. Taking a lance from the page, Miles kicked the horse into a gallop. His deep blue eyes narrowed in concentration as he leveled the shaft at the target. The point never wavered as the charger raced forward. The tip of the lance hit the target dead center, pushing it away from him, and Miles was gone before the pivoting sandbag could reach him. "There! You see? Try it again."

"Well done, Lord Garrett," a familiar voice said.

Miles dismounted and bowed to his sovereign. "Thank you, your majesty."

"By Saint George," Henry boomed, "how I wish I were riding in the tourney."

"You'd best us all," Miles said good-naturedly.

"I might at that," Henry agreed with a complete lack of humility. He slapped his rounded belly. "They don't make horses big enough these days," he said with a booming laugh.

Miles matched the king's smile, but he knew better than to comment on Henry's weight. The king had been moody lately and everyone around him was being more cautious than usual not to offend him.

"How is your father today?"

"Not well, your majesty. I fear he's sinking."

"At his age? Why, he's scarcely older than I am!"

Again Miles prudently skirted another sensitive issue—the king's age—by saying, "He never quite recovered from that winter campaign in France."

"Yes, we lost many a good man that winter. Well, give him my regards and tell him to recover with all speed. I miss his face and cunning strategy over my draught board."

"I'll tell him, your majesty."

"I have a bit of a surprise for you," Henry said, clapping his hamlike hand on Miles's shoulder and steering him toward the palace.

"Oh? A surprise?"

"A bride!" Henry boomed jovially. "Ha! There! You are surprised. Admit it!"

"I'm stunned, your majesty."

"As well you should be. I haven't met the woman myself, but I knew her mother well. Quite well, if you follow my meaning." He winked broadly. "They say she has my hair, but darker. About the same shade as that of my daughter Mary."

Miles paused. "Are you saying you're marrying me to one of your daughters?"

"Some say she is," Henry hedged. "Only her mother knows for sure, I always tell them. I've never recognized her as such. God's bones! If I acknowledged all of them, I'd have time for little else!"

Miles tried to look pleased, for he knew the king expected him to be, but this was all so sudden. "Why are you doing this for me?"

"Why? As a sign of appreciation toward your father. Lord Edward has been my loyal companion for years. As for your bride, she's named Lady Alison Wakefield of Wyndfell Castle. I confiscated her castle and lands as a measure of protection for her and the crown when her husband turned traitor, but I have allowed her to continue living there and will give them to you after your marriage." Henry's blue eyes looked icy as he recalled the circumstances surrounding that unpleasant time. "Lord Wakefield died with the others after the Pilgrimage of Grace was brought to an end."

"Was she Catholic?"

"Her husband was, as was she. But I assume she has renounced the old faith as I have ordered all my subjects to do." His jovial mood returned, and he smiled at Miles with the old charisma of his youth. "Wyndfell is a fine castle. I've seen sketches of it. It's in Yorkshire."

"Yorkshire?" Miles repeated doubtfully. Yorkshire folk were known for their independent thinking and rebellious ways.

"I expect you to live there at least part of the year. There's need for a firm hand in that area. Several of the rebels hailed from the Wyndfell lands, and I've heard rumors of unrest again. The time to stop a rebellion is before it starts." Henry inclined his massive head toward Miles, who matched the king's great stature as few did. The king had a rare gift of making those he talked with feel as if they had been singled out for importance. "I want you to write to me from time to time and tell me how things are."

"Of course, your majesty." Miles still couldn't believe his ears. True, he had no bride in mind for himself, but this had come like a bolt from the blue. "Does my father know of this?"

"Naturally I mentioned it to him first. He's honored. Not every man is given so wealthy a bride! Ha!" Henry belted out his loud laugh and again slapped Miles on the shoulder. "Away with you now. I see my fair bride and would speak with her." Henry's hawklike gaze fastened to a short, plump woman, elegantly attired in garnet velvet, who walked on a nearby path.

Miles bid the king farewell and watched the massive man limp over to Queen Catherine. Would Henry's daughter resemble her hulking father? He had met the royal princesses and found the elder, Mary Tudor, to be rather plain and fanatically religious. The younger princess, Elizabeth, was also no beauty, though she had a vivaciousness and a quick mind that made up for her lack of good looks. He studied the king's heavily jowled face and rotund belly and hoped the daughter resembled her mother—whomever she was. Miles ran his strong fingers through his raven-black hair and wondered if he was honored or cursed by this match.

2

King Henry ponderously climbed the stairs to the floor where Lord Edward Garrett was chambered. All about him the bustle of Hampton Court hummed like a great beehive. As always when the court was in residence, people were everywhere and the constant, if hushed sounds, of conversations, footsteps, and busy activity filled the hall. He took the familiar turns to the apartment, ignoring the pain in his leg and trying not to appear as out of breath as he was. Since his fall in a tourney four years before, he had suffered from an ulcer that defied all his physicians' healing efforts.

With a scowl Henry caught a reflection of himself in one of the long windows. At forty-nine years of age he was broadening to an impressive girth. His unusual height alone had made him a singular figure and his imposing weight made him even more remarkable. He was easily twice the size of his young bride. Unfortunately his excessive weight made him unable to joust or wrestle, or indulge in any of the other athletic pursuits he had enjoyed as a youth. Old age was approaching and Henry hated it.

Without bothering to knock, he opened the door to Edward's apartments and scarcely glanced at the flustered maids and courtiers who bobbed and bowed at his approach. He entered the bedchamber and motioned for the elderly man lying on the bed to be at ease. Indeed, on looking at him, Henry felt a stab of dismay. "Ho! Edward! Are you improved?"

The man quit trying to rise and lay back on the mounded pillows. "Not greatly, your majesty."

Henry frowned and peered down at the man. Edward's skin stretched like parchment over his bones and his once fine head of hair had thinned from his lingering disease. His long, narrow hands were curved from arthritis and trembled on the covers as if he were in his dotage. The man was in his mid-fifties, but looked much older. Why, Henry thought, Edward was only six years older than himself. His expression turned petulant. "Are you taking the potions Dr. Butts gave you?"

"Aye, your majesty, though they do little to ease me."

Henry cocked his head to one side and peered questioningly at his friend as though he might have thought Edward was being perverse in clinging needlessly to his illness. "Then I will prepare a decoction for you myself."

"One of your own making?" Edward asked faintly.

"Aye. I've doctored myself for years." He struck at his sore leg with the flat of his hand and refrained from flinching, though the pain he inflicted was great. "This old enemy of mine I treat with a poultice of my own. Marshmallows, linseed, lead and silver oxides, red coral, and dragon's blood. I mix it in oil of roses, rosewater, and a bit of white wine, just enough to boil. It works wonders, I can tell you. Better than anything Dr. Butts can invent. When I make your potion, I'll send it up by a page."

"Thank you, your majesty. You're too kind." Edward's voice held a note of anxiety. The king thought himself an expert at whatever he did, and though no one dared question his skills as an apothecary, few trusted the validity of his treatments.

"You fret too much. There lies your trouble. It's well known that a feeble spirit weakens the body."

Edward smiled and his face reclaimed a hint of his former handsomeness. "In that case, you must be immortal."

Henry's bellowing laugh made the maids jump. "Immortal! Ha! I like that. Ah, Edward, I've missed your companionship."

"As I have missed being there," Edward replied. He felt tired and feverish, and wished his sovereign would leave so he could get on with the business of dying. He wouldn't dare do so in Henry's presence. "I find myself thinking much of Gwendolyn these days. She's been gone ten years this month."

"Pah! Wives are easily replaced. You should have remarried. A young wife would put new life into you. Perhaps that's what you need! A young, buxom wife!"

"Not I," Edward responded quickly. "I'm not long from Gwendolyn's side now."

"Don't talk of such! I'll not hear it!" The king paced to the window and looked out onto the Thames's silvery water beyond the garden. "I hate this talk of age and disease," he fretted.

"Then let us talk of brighter things," Edward suggested smoothly. "How fares the queen?"

"Catherine is a jewel," Henry answered with a doting expression. "I call her a blushing rose without a thorn. I've even had coins struck in her likeness. I should have found her sooner and been spared my marital difficulties."

Edward refrained from pointing out that much sooner than this, Catherine would not have been of a marriageable age. She was, in fact, born during the reign of Catherine of Aragon and had probably been named for Henry's first wife. "She's a rare beauty. And very vivacious, they say."

"You'll see that for yourself soon enough. When you're back on your feet, you will be presented to her."

"Thank you, your majesty."

Henry ran his bejeweled fingers along the windowsill. For a brief regret-filled moment he thought of his queen's cousin, Anne Boleyn. This palace had been her favorite residence, as it was now her cousin Catherine's. Anne's first initial, intertwined with his own, still remained, carved into each of the beams of the great hall. Henry had not been able to bring himself to change those carvings, though all the other A's had been changed to J's for his sweet Jane Seymour. Jane had been the best of wives: she had given him a son.

"Prince Edward was sick again," Henry said with concern. "His nurses were with him all night as well as all day."

"All children ail," Edward comforted. "He will grow strong and hearty."

"And the queen will give me other sons," Henry said with forced joviality. "She's young and healthy."

Edward closed his eyes to gather the strength to keep his wits about him. He had lost stronger children than the frail prince and he knew how tenuous a child's hold on life could be. Of his large brood, only Miles had reached adulthood.

"There is rumor of plague in London," Henry said almost to himself. "If any come down with it here, I must move the court. I cannot expose my family to the plague."

"No, sire."

Henry turned from the window and beamed at the invalid, his magnetic presence seeming to fill the dim room. "I saw your son but a moment ago and gave him the good news."

"What did he say?"

"He was overjoyed, naturally. By St. George, what else could he be?"

Again Edward smiled. What else indeed. Knowing his son, however, he wondered. Miles could be uncommonly stubborn. "You've told Lady Alison of the marriage?"

"That I have." With that reminder, the king frowned. Her reply could hardly be termed gracious. "She will be given to him in two weeks. There's no reason to put off such matters."

"Two weeks? So soon."

"You'll be hale and hearty by then." Henry strode toward the door. "I'll send up my decoction, and mind you take it as I've ordered. No shilly-shalling about. We must have you on your feet by the wedding."

"Yes, your majesty." Edward watched his sovereign stride out and drew a breath of relief. He had been in Henry's court most of his life and knew only too well how the royal temper could ebb and flow, especially of late. Since he divorced Catherine of Aragon seven years earlier, Henry had become increasingly unpredictable. Dangerously so, at times. Though Edward would miss Miles, he was glad his son would be leaving court and Henry's sometime overbearing attention. The safest course with the king was none at all. Since Lady Alison was rumored to be the king's daughter, Miles might not escape Henry's eye. But the king had never acknowledged her, and so the marriage might be quite tranquil for Miles.

Edward rubbed his tired eyes. If only he had his youthful vigor and mental quickness, he could plot Miles's safest path away from court. But he didn't, and Miles was a full-grown man. He could take care of himself. Wearily Edward closed his eyes and tried to will himself to join his Gwendolyn. After what seemed to be a long while, he saw her beside him, as radiant as she had been as his bride.

Miles sat beside his father's bed and listened to his harsh and labored breathing, interspersed with Welsh phrases such as he had often used in conversation with Miles's mother. When Edward first started rambling, Miles had hoped his father was regaining consciousness, but after two days he had to admit that the disjointed words were merely a part of the old man's unconscious dreams.

That morning Miles had written to Lady Alison, telling her of his father's pending death and postponing the marriage until autumn. He had no desire to go to his unknown bride until he finished his duties toward his father.

What would she be like, this Lady Alison? Her name sounded sweet and pliant, but this wasn't a noticeable trait in the king's other daughters. Undoubtedly her mother had been docile enough, and bastards generally resembled their mothers, he was told. What would she look like, this woman who was to bear his name and his children? He hoped she would be pretty, and even more he hoped her mind was quick, for dull women bored him to distraction. Far better to have one with wit than beauty, especially since Wyndfell Castle was situated quite a distance from any sizeable town. Traveling performers would be scarce, and if Lady Alison proved to be shallow-minded, he would have only his men for companionship. Still, the king said he had received a reply in her own hand, so she must not be illiterate. Miles wondered what she had written, but when Henry didn't volunteer it, he could hardly ask. Everyone thought it sufficient that she was young enough to bear sons and that Wyndfell and its estate were magnificent for a baron.

His eyes drifted back to his father. He would rather be a baron for life than become a viscount because of his father's death. Miles had been reared at court, so, unlike most sons, he had been with his parents throughout his life. He had been eighteen when his mother died in birthing yet another stillborn child. Since then he had become as much a friend as a son to his father. When Edward was gone, Miles knew he would miss him sorely.

Having rarely been away from court, Miles wondered if he would be happy at Wyndfell. Not that it mattered, for he had been told by the king that he must spend most of each year there, like it or not. Such orders disturbed him, for although Miles was inclined to be accommodating, he grew stubborn when commanded—except when by royal decree. He wondered if Lady Alison objected to the match. Probably not. Women rarely were that headstrong.

Alison crumpled her needlework and angrily threw it down on the oak floor. "I hate being given away like . . . like a parcel of no account!"

Leatrice looked up as she drew her thread through her embroidery. "It's not as if you are of no account, my lady. No doubt it's taken the king this long to find you a suitable husband."

"A baron! And a Welshman to boot! That couldn't have taken him so very long! No, it's to thwart me that he's done this. I should have married Lord Roger and told the king afterward."

"To do that could have meant forfeiting your freedom. I hear his majesty is not fond of surprises."

"Nor am I. At least not in the form of a bridegroom. Who is this Lord Miles Garrett? I've never heard his name. Is he old or young, handsome or ugly as sin?"

"Few women are fortunate enough to know and love their husbands-to-be. Your first marriage was an exception."

Alison drew her stool closer to Leatrice's and spoke in a low voice. "What of our secret efforts? How can I ever hope to hear Mass again if I have a Protestant husband watching my every move?"

Leatrice glanced at the door to be certain it was closed. "Surely he cannot watch you every minute of the day. The servants are loyal. They will never betray you."

"My servants are only servants. If another was to pay them more, many would change their allegiance. Among my ladies-in-waiting, I trust only you."

"I'm flattered you trust me, my lady."

"You're a cousin of my Charles and were one of his favorite kin. After all these years as my lady-in-waiting, how could I not trust you? Who else in this remote place do I have as a friend?"

Leatrice smiled, and her resemblance to Charles was even more evident. She had his brown hair and her eyes were his shade of green. Alison knew her to be a staunch Catholic as well.

"There's also the matter of the abbess," Alison continued. "I cannot hide her from him forever. What will he say when he discovers a holy woman has walled herself into the anchorage in the south wall?"

"Surely he wouldn't harm a holy woman," Leatrice said with no conviction.

"In these heretic days? No Catholic is safe, even if she is elderly and harmless. Eventually Lord Garrett is bound to see me handing food into her cell."

"I could help."

"Dear Leatrice, you are so very kind. Yet she is my responsibility as lady of the castle." There were times when Alison wished she had been spared the honor of having an abbess take up residence in her castle's wall. True, the holy woman heard confessions and offered prayers for her parishioners' needs, but her presence could mean trouble. "It's a miracle that Sir Edmund Campbell hasn't discovered her."

"Do you truly distrust him? He seems so likable. I think he may be a Catholic."

"Why would you think that?"

"Yesterday he slammed his finger in a door and cried out 'By Our Lady' before he thought; then he looked guilty for having said it."

"That scarcely means he's Catholic."

"But Protestants speak of the Virgin Mary as if she were no more than any other woman."

"Heretics!"

"All the same, I think we can trust Sir Edmund."

"No. Not yet. I must get to know him better. After all, he came from the king."

"That's true."

"Oh, Leatrice, there are times I wonder if we'll ever be ourselves again, or if this madness will kill the true religion forever."

"Will Lord Bainbridge be by today?" Leatrice asked in a lower voice. "Will we meet in the tower room?"

"Yes. I dislike the secrecy in which we must meet, but what else can we do, especially now that I'm to marry another, and we can no longer pass Roger's visits as courting calls?" Alison lovingly touched the brooch she wore that contained a lock of Charles's hair. "I swore to further Charles's cause upon his death but it seems I've been able to accomplish so little."

"How can you say that?" Leatrice exclaimed. "Wyndfell is a meeting place for those who follow the old way. Lord Bainbridge says a Mass of sorts, and while he isn't a monk or a priest, he is better than nothing at all. Why, you even have an abbess in the anchorage, and surely her prayers keep us safe."

"Still, at times—" She broke off abruptly as Sir Edmund entered the solar. "There's someone to see you, my lady."

"Another royal messenger?"

"No, my lady, but rather a yeoman, by the looks of him. Shall I send him away? He refused to tell me his business but said to tell you he has news of a lost sheep."

Alison's eyes widened at the code signal, and she glanced at Leatrice. "Bring him to the gallery." When Sir Edmund left, she whispered, "The secret words! Who can it be?"

"I know not! Shall I go with you to meet him?"

"No, no. Mayhap it's a trap of some sort. You stay here. If I call out, run and get Walt."

"Yes, my lady." Leatrice's eyes were round and her fingers clumsy on her handiwork. No one was supposed to know the secret code except the ones who came here for Mass or to talk to the abbess. By now Sir Edmund should recognize all these parishioners, though not their real reason for coming to Wyndfell.

The gallery, which was just outside the solar, spanned the distance between two of Wyndfell's turrets. A fireplace burned on each end of the long corridorlike room to combat the cold wind that crept around the heavy tapestries covering the windows. Although this was one of the least comfortable rooms in the castle, it served well as a place for one to exercise on days that were too inclement for outdoor walks.

Alison waited near the fireplace and watched as Sir Edmund escorted the man in. The stranger wore a russet cape typical of any yeoman, but his face was almost concealed within the hood. Sir Edmund glanced at him suspiciously from time to time, but the man remained covered. Alison felt a twinge of foreboding, but kept her concern from her face.

When they were near enough to speak, Sir Edmund said, "Here is the yeoman, my lady. He still refuses to tell me why he must see you."

Alison was about to dismiss Sir Edmund when from beneath the hood came a very familiar voice. "I have found a lost sheep, my lady."

"Then why bother the countess?" Sir Edmund objected. "Surely this matter is better—"

"Leave us," Alison said abruptly to her steward. "I will take care of this."

Sir Edmund frowned, but he left as he was told to do.

When they were alone, Alison stepped nearer and peered under the folds of the hood. "Can it really be you?"

The young man brushed the hood back and smiled at her. The candlelight illuminated the harsh planes of his thin face. A fringe of dark brown hair bordered his forehead and swept behind his ears, making his shaved pate look very bare. "Are you surprised?"

"Damion!" she exclaimed happily as she recognized her half-brother. "What are you doing here?"

"Have you not heard? St. Benedictine has been disbanded."

"No! Not the monastery!"

"I came here because I knew not where else to go. Can you hide me?"

"Of course, but why is it necessary to hide you? Once your hair grows out you'll look no different from any other man, and in the meantime, you could wear a hat."

He pulled the hood back up to hide his tonsure. "I'm under holy vows as a monk, regardless of whether I'm in a monastery. There is, however, a more pressing reason that I must hide. I'm wanted by the law."

"Wanted! What have you done?"

"I have done all I could to fight this heresy. I used my talents as an illuminator to protest the king and other heretics."

"You didn't!"

"I used both verse and illustration on some of the better ones. Unfortunately, that led the authorities to suspect the culprit must be one of the Cistercians in the monastery. When the abbot refused to hand me over or even to say which monk I was, the monastery was seized and ordered closed." A hard look came into Damion's dark eyes. "They took our property from us and turned us out, every one."

"How terrible!"

"Not wanting to compromise you, I came to the nearby village and hid out, hoping to find a way to see you, for I felt you would not turn me away. One day a villager who saw my tonsure told me the secret signal, and here I am."

"If only Mother were still alive," Alison said. "How proud she was of you."

"I had a calling," he said a bit too humbly.

Alison looked around, realizing they were much too visible here in the gallery. "Come with me." She went to the wall near the fireplace and, after glancing around again, touched a spring latch under the mantel. A narrow opening appeared in what had seemed to be solid paneling. Alison took a flaming rush from the wall sconce and said, "Follow me."

Once inside the narrow passageway, she pulled the panel shut and heard it click into place. "Feel here," she said, guiding his hand to a metal clasp in the wood. "This is how it opens."

Damion's eyes flashed in the firelight. "Very clever, sister."

"This is one of several secret corridors that Charles showed me. Another leads outside. This one branches. One way leads to the hall below and past it to the chapel. The other goes to the master bedchamber, and up to the chambers above."

As she passed each turn, she told him where the path led and how to open the door at the end. There were peepholes in the doors opening into the hall, chapel, and gallery so one could see if they were occupied before opening the secret door.

"Who went to so much trouble?" Damion whispered as he peered through to see servants cleaning the hall.

"Charles didn't know. They have been here longer than anyone can remember. His grandfather showed them to him. They are so well-concealed that even the servants don't know they are here."

"No one else knows?"

"Charles showed them to only his most trusted friend, Lord Roger Bainbridge. The man is a true believer and needed to know all the ways in and out of Wyndfell, as he conducts our secret Masses."

"A layman is saying Mass? That can't be allowed," Damion objected with a frown.

"It couldn't be helped. Without Lord Bainbridge there would be no religious observances at all except the one in the village, and it is now Protestant."

Damion made no answer, so Alison led him back up

the narrow stairway that circled and doubled back in the space behind the chimneys. They passed the solid doors of her bedchamber and arrived at the top of the castle.

She opened the door and they entered a small bedchamber. Crossing to the door on the opposite wall, Alison slid the bolt into place, securing the door. "There. No one can come in, so you'll be quite safe."

Damion looked around to find a tiny cot, a stool, and a small table, the top of which was scarred from long years of hard use. The only window was a small one covered by a faded tapestry.

"This was once a servant's chamber," Alison said. "You'll have to be quiet at night, as there are servants sleeping to either side of this room. However, the walls here are thick. Whoever built it must have known it would be used by someone who had to come and go unheard."

"This will be quite adequate. In fact it reminds me greatly of my cell in the monastery."

"I will leave food and drink for you on the landing in the passageway just below your entrance. I would prefer you didn't leave the castle, but if you must, please do so only at night. And take great care that you are not seen. The outer door is bolted on the inside and opens into the kitchen yard. From there you can go out the servants' gate to the green."

"You've pleased me well, sister. I knew you wouldn't forsake me."

"How could I ever do such a thing? You're the only real family I have left." She smiled at him fondly. "Give me your robe and hood. I'll have Walt wear it out. He's about your size and Sir Edmund will think it's you leaving."

"You always were quick," Damion said as he pulled the coarse garment over his head, revealing his homespun habit of undyed white wool. Knotted about his waist as a belt was a frayed scourge that appeared to have been often used by Damion to flog himself as penitence. From the scourge hung his rosary beads with a large crucifix at the end. Even though it was cold outside, Damion's feet were covered only by the straps of his rough sandals.

"I'll bring you a brazier of coals," Alison said as she started toward the stairs.

"No, don't. I'm not accustomed to such luxury and don't need it."

"But the nights have grown cold and there is no glass in the window."

"I prefer to be cold. I must constantly abuse my flesh to maintain control over it. Otherwise I would fall into the trap of sensuality."

"Oh. In that case, I'll bring you candles. You do use candles, I assume?"

"Yes, I use candles."

"Keep them away from the window. I doubt that anyone from the courtyard below could tell which chamber this window belongs to, but someone might wonder."

"I go to bed early and rise well before dawn," he assured her. "And I pray very quietly. This Sabbath we will have a proper Mass."

Alison's smile lit her face. "I'll look forward to it, Damion. I never thought I'd hear my own brother say Mass."

"Sister, you must forget our sibling relationship. Now all people are my family and I address all women as my sisters."

Feeling rebuffed, Alison drew back. "I meant nothing, Damion."

"*Brother* Damion," he corrected. "And tell this Lord Bainbridge that he must no longer desecrate the Mass. From now on I will say it."

"Yes. I understand," she said in surprise. When he said nothing else but merely stared at her, Alison realized she had been dismissed.

As she turned to go, he said, "In the future don't

come to my chamber. It is neither proper for you to be here, nor is it permissible for me to allow it."

"But I'm your sister!"

"You're also a woman. Once I entered St. Benedictine, you became to me as all the rest of the world. No more, no less."

Alison frowned as she nodded and let herself out. The light from her rush guttered and flared in the encroaching darkness as she heard Damion snap the door shut. Angrily she glared back at it. As the only surviving child of her mother's marriage to Sir Winston, Damion had always been pompous and overbearing, and he had not improved with age. She decided to leave the candles on the landing and let Damion grope for them in the dark. Perhaps that would give him the humility that he so obviously lacked. She still felt stung that he had disavowed his relationship as her half-brother. He may have chosen to be a monk, but she was his only living relative.

With a muffled snort she went back downstairs and quietly slipped into the gallery.

3

Alison gazed glumly out the window in her bedchamber, watching the sky change from silver to a dull leaden hue. This was her wedding day. The village vicar and Wyndfell's chaplain awaited her in the chapel within the castle's courtyard. In the kitchen and cook yard, a feast was being prepared. All the local nobility was gathered in the courtyard below, their servants and animals spilling out onto the green. The rushes covering the cold stone floors in the great hall had been replaced by new ones, scented with lavender, and the tapestries had been cleaned and aired. On the bridal bed was a spray of rosemary, a sprig of which she twirled between her restless fingers. As was customary, she would adorn the groom with the sprig as a symbol of his virility. Only one thing was lacking—the groom.

"God's bones!" she complained to Leatrice, who looked as worried as Alison. "Will he leave me waiting at the very altar? What sort of man would miss his own wedding with never so much as a by-your-leave?"

"An accident perhaps," Leatrice suggested. "His horse may have gone lame."

"And could he find no other animal to convey him here? No, he's not coming, I tell you."

"He must. Be patient, my lady. Mayhap he mistook the day."

"Forgot it, you mean. The date was of his own setting. If you recall, he has postponed our wedding day twice. First because his father was ill, then because he had to have time to put his father's affairs in order after he died. Mayhap he has changed his mind altogether this time."

"I'm certain he will come. 'Tis early yet."

"Early? If it weren't for the dreary clouds, you'd soon see the sun setting atop the lime trees yonder. He's not coming, I tell you." She paced with angry strides. "He means to insult me in front of all my friends and the entire parish." Stopping again by the window, she said, "Look down at the courtyard. There is little room left to walk for all the people who have crowded in."

"Many turned out for the event, 'tis true."

"If there is to be an event!"

Leatrice joined Alison to gaze down at the milling crowd. "You're certain this is the date he said?"

"Of course I am. How could I mistake such a thing?" Alison lifted the white-and-gold brocade of her heavy gown as she began to pace again. Beneath the bell-shaped sleeves the scarlet tissue of her kirtle rounded to her wrists. The white lawn chemise underneath was tufted through the slashings of the scarlet tissue. The skirt of the kirtle was embroidered with a lily and rose design that she and Leatrice had worked hard to finish by this day. About her slender waist she wore a loose gold chain from which was suspended an elaborately filigreed gold pomander filled with cloves and sandalwood.

The gown above the waist was cut high and square in the front but came down to a point in the back, as did the kirtle, showing a wedge of her ivory skin. About her neck Alison wore a gold chain, which supported a large ruby pendant adorned with dangling freshwater pearls. Her bright auburn hair was drawn back neatly into a gold-netted coif, topped by a stylish French hood that sloped back from her heart-shaped face. The back drape of the hood was shimmering cloth-of-gold, and the cap itself was scarlet velvet trimmed in pearls.

"If he is not here very soon, I'll change my dress and get about my usual business," Alison threatened as she nervously moved about the large room.

"You'll do no such thing," Leatrice replied. "He will come."

Alison sat back down on a stool on the far side of the chamber and braced her palms on her knees. "He may have been recently elevated to the title of viscount, but as far as I'm concerned he's a knave and no gentleman. What more could I expect from a Welshman?"

Leatrice tried to smile. "There have been rains of late. Mayhap that slowed his progress. London is a long way to the south."

"For all I care, he may go to the devil. And if he ever deigns to show his face here, I'll tell him so!"

As the sun crept ever lower in the sky, its rays pierced the thinner clouds on the horizon. In moments the immense red orb slipped behind the lime trees that bordered the park, and the lengthening shadows turned from dark green to shades of blue. The birds began to twitter in a flurry of activity as they sought their resting places for the night, and in the distance an early owl hooted soulfully. Alison sat with her chin cupped in one hand, the other dangling over her knees. Leatrice no longer offered encouragement but merely gazed out at the empty roadway, which could still be faintly seen in the thickening dusk.

"There, my lady! Coming over the hill. 'Tis them!"

Alison looked up abruptly, relief and fury battling within her. Not daring to speak, she leapt to her feet and ran to the window. As Leatrice had said, a party of men was riding down the sloping road toward the castle. "Damn his eyes!" she muttered. "It must be him!"

Angrily swishing her skirts out of her way, she grabbed the wilted sprig of rosemary and strode out of the chamber with Leatrice in pursuit. The crowd below was more anxious and amused at her plight than they had been four hours earlier. The musicians were still playing, but their efforts clearly lacked their former zeal. At the sight of the viscountess, they struck up a livelier tune, then dwindled again as she swept through the hall and out to the courtyard.

Her brown eyes burned with anger and her cheeks were pink from barely suppressed emotion. The entourage of men was riding up the castle green toward the drawbridge, but rather than waiting to greet them, Alison headed for the chapel, the crowd parting to let her through.

With obvious determination, she mounted the stone steps set into the outside wall of the chapel and shoved open the carved wooden door with such force that it banged against the inner wall. At the altar, the vicar and chaplain, who had been lounging on pews, and the altar boy, who had been drawing invisible circles on the oak floor with his gold candle snuffer, leapt to their feet.

As Alison stormed down the aisle, she didn't spare them so much as a glance, but instead kept her vision fixed on the round stained-glass window on the back wall that glowed dully in the waning light. The chapel's side windows were thick green glass that scarcely admitted any light at all. Candles along the wall and on the altar had burned low but still emitted a golden light. Behind her Alison heard the local gentry enter the chapel and seat themselves on the oak pews. She didn't turn her head. Beneath the noises of their settling in, Alison heard murmurs of whispered speculation. Tears of mortification stung her eyes, and she blinked furiously to keep them from pooling and running down her cheeks.

Then, by the change of expression on the chaplain's face, Alison knew her groom had entered the church. At once an expectant hush fell, and the only sound that resumed was that of riding boots clopping on the wooden floor. She lifted her chin defiantly, still glaring at the window above the altar.

When the man stopped beside her, she glanced at him disdainfully, then looked away. He was tall, much taller than herself, and she was no small woman. In an instant she had noticed that his eyes were the same dark blue as the sky at sunset, thinly rimmed with ebony. She could feel him staring directly at her, and all her instincts told her he would match fire with fire. Defiantly Alison turned back to survey the rest of this man who was to be her husband. His nose was straight and perfectly shaped, his lips sensuous and pleasant, as if he were more apt to smile than to frown. In fact he smiled now, showing even white teeth, but Alison refused to return it in kind.

His hair was the blackest she'd ever seen, and he was stylishly clean-shaven. His neck was a tanned column of strength against the snowy white of his laced linen shirt. His doublet was deep blue velvet striped in silver tissue and belted with a sash of cloth-of-silver. His jerkin was white damask with a stripe of blue ribbons, and his gown was claret-red lined in black sable. At his waist hung a blue velvet money pouch and a dress sword in a silver scabbard chased with gold. A heavy gold chain set with garnets and sapphires hung about his neck, and his velvet slouch hat was the same blue as his doublet. The white satin netherstocks which encased his legs were not padded in the customary manner because such enhancement was not necessary. He had not paused to remove his leather riding boots, so she couldn't see his shoes, but his boots were of fine leather trimmed in sable. She had never seen so magnificent a man in all her life. Alison snapped her eyes forward again and nodded briskly for the chaplain to begin.

Nervously the clergyman began, "Will you, Lord Miles Garrett, take this woman as your wife and promise to have none other?"

"I will," his deep voice boomed out, causing Alison to jump.

"Will you, Lady Alison Wakefield, have this man as your husband and promise to honor him and obey him in all matters?"

For a long moment Alison was silent as she struggled to control herself. Obey him indeed! Feeling she was betraying herself, but knowing she had no other choice, she at last answered, "I will."

With an audible sigh of relief the chaplain stepped back and the vicar came forward. "Have you come to this altar of your own will?" he asked them both.

"I have," Miles said. Alison finally agreed.

"Does any here present know of a reason why this man and this woman should not be married?" When only silence met him, he said, "Do you promise, Lord Miles Garrett, to care for this woman and protect her from all harm and want, so far as you are able?"

"I do."

"Do you, Lady Alison Wakefield, promise to abide with him for all your days and have none other but him for as long as he lives?"

"I do." Her voice sounded much firmer than she felt at that moment.

"Have you a token of this bond?" the vicar asked Miles.

He took a ring from the slit pocket of his jerkin and held out his hand to Alison. After a pause, she put her cool fingers in his warm palm and felt him close his hand over them. Because she was a widow she wore no glove and her skin was smooth against his. A spark seemed to leap through her at his touch, and her eyes lifted to meet his.

As if no one else were present, Miles smiled, sending a sensuous tingle along her spine. "I, Miles, take thee, Alison, as my wife, to have no other and to protect you and care for you for the rest of your life."

Her lips parted slightly, for this wasn't a necessary pledge. She felt something begin to waken deep within her. Not to be outdone, she replied, "I, Alison, do take thee, Miles, as my husband. I promise to have none other save you and to care for you for as long as I live." She intentionally omitted the reference to obeying him.

He slipped the ring on and off her thumb first, then in succession the next two fingers, saying, "In the name of the Father, the Son, and the Holy Ghost." Then he placed the ring on her third finger. Alison looked down at it. It was fashioned in the shape of two hands clasping a large heart-shaped ruby. Carefully she threaded the wilted sprig of rosemary through one of the links of his gold chain.

Miles grinned and said, "With this ring I thee wed." Dramatically drawing his sword and holding it above his head, he said, "With this sword I thee honor." Then he handed the sword symbolically to the vicar, who blessed it and returned it to him. "With this gold I thee endow." He yanked loose the pouch of gold and dropped it heavily on the vicar's palm. Both the vicar's and Alison's eyes widened. A few gold coins was customary, but this was a small fortune. The vicar gave the pouch to Alison. Her dark eyes found Miles's and she studied them, trying to determine what sort of man this was.

The vicar looked past them to the witnesses and said, "Therefore shall a man leave his father and mother and shall cleave unto his wife and they shall be one flesh. What therefore God has joined together, let no man put asunder."

Before Alison could react, Miles pulled her to him and kissed her, his lips soft, yet firm, upon hers. She drew away and touched her traitorous mouth, for she had found herself returning his kiss. He threw back his head and laughed wholeheartedly as if she had well-pleased him.

Anger again flickered in Alison's eyes. Her body might respond, but her will was her own. She turned to leave him at the altar, but he caught her wrist. Fishing three coins from the pocket where he had kept her ring, Miles paid the vicar and the chaplain and tossed a smaller coin to the altar boy. Alison jerked to free herself but his arm around her slender waist held her fast.

Taking his new bride by the arm, Miles led her back down the aisle, the crowd stepping aside to stare at him. At the head of the steps outside the chapel, Miles lifted the arm he still held securely and bellowed out over the rush-lit courtyard, "I give you my wife, Lady Alison Garrett!" A roar of approval sprang from the crowd below.

Miles turned to Alison. "Have you no word of greeting for me?"

"Aye, I'll greet you! Where have you been these past four hours?"

His grin widened. "Do you long for me so quickly? I meant to arrive on time, but the roads are scarcely passable with all the recent rain."

"Have you never seen mud before? Why didn't you leave earlier?"

"Your voice is like warm honey. Yet I long to hear it sweeter. I made the most haste I could."

"Had I my way, you would never have left London at all!"

His smile remained, but his eyes grew more thoughtful. "You shed your promises with remarkable ease."

"I promised to take care of you and be faithful to you. Naught else."

"And to obey me," he added.

"That promise I wouldn't count upon," she retorted.

He chuckled again, though his eyes took her measure. "We'll see." To the crowd below he shouted, "To the feast! Strike up the music!"

He led her down the steep steps and onto the cobbled courtyard. "Wyndfell is beautiful," he said as he looked up at the massive castle, lit by the fitful brilliance of the rush torches the revelers were waving about.

"I'm glad you are proud in your ownership. I assume the king gave it to you?"

"Along with your hand, yes." He strode up the steps to the door as cheering yeomen and their wives let him pass. At the top of the steps he turned to one of his men. "Sir Trahern, hand out the bridal gifts."

The man nodded and opened a bag he carried and began handing out scarves, gloves, and garters in the green-and-gold colors of the Garrett family. Again the people cheered as if Miles were the king himself.

"Already they approve of me," he said to Alison. "I am welcomed to Wyndfell."

"Not by me," she ground out as he led her into the noisy hall. "You will not win my heart for a bag of gold." She thrust the velvet bag toward him. He took it and tossed it to her steward. Sir Edmund caught it and took it away to his closet for safekeeping.

"I hadn't thought I would win true love so easily. Such finer emotions require more potent coin."

"Nor will you win me by pulling me along as if I were a toy on a string!" She yanked free and rubbed her wrist.

"There you're mistaken," he replied with an infuriating grin. "I have already won you. There is only your heart left to conquer."

"And that you'll never have. I swear it!"

"Then you'll be forsworn." He looked past her and signaled the musicians to begin playing a galliard. When he held out his hands to her, she tossed her head and turned her back. "Surely you're not so provincial you know not how to dance," he teased.

She rose to the bait by whirling around and slapping her hand firmly in his. With challenging eyes she dared him to keep up with her. The music flowed from the smooth procession-type march to the quicker beat of five steps forward and five back. Despite the restrictive binding of her lacings, Alison was a tireless dancer and had often outlasted Charles. Confidently she leapt into the first lavolta, but Miles matched her steps exactly.

Faster they danced, and one by one the other couples switched to the relatively less exhausting twirl of the cushion dance. Alison refused to be the first to quit and her eyes stubbornly met his.

Miles appeared to be under no stress at all as he leapt higher and longer, moving faster and faster. At last Alison felt the room spin and realized the others were tiring even of the cushion dance. Telling herself she was doing so for her friends, who must politely dance as long as she did, she gave the traditional, "This dance it can go no farther." After a brief, final twirl, the musicians brought the music to an end.

Miles kept a smile on his face and forced himself not to pant. How this woman had managed to keep up with him he would never know. If his own muscles felt strained, hers must feel as if they were on fire, yet she smiled calmly in spite of the pink of her cheeks, and her breathing seemed scarcely labored. Not wanting to let her have the upper hand, he again held out his hand toward her as the strains of a pavane drifted over the hall.

Surprised, Alison looked at his outstretched hand and met the daring in his eyes. He still wanted to dance? The man was unbearable. Resolutely she grabbed his hand and let him lead her into the measured steps. At least this one wasn't performed at a heart-stopping speed.

As they circled the room, Alison noticed that Leatrice was led onto the floor by the man Miles had spoken to on the steps. "Who is that man dancing with the woman in the Judas-colored dress?"

"That's Sir Trahern Wallace. One of my closest and most trusted friends."

"Wallace? Another Welshman?" Instinctively she blushed at the insulting implication that had slipped from her tongue, then remembered that she didn't care whether he might be sensitive.

"That's right," he answered as if he weren't at all reluctant to admit to his heritage.

"Then you really are Welsh?"

"My mother was. I have castles at Llanduff and on the River Clwd." The foreign names rolled smoothly off his tongue. "You'll like them. Especially Llanduff. It was my parents' favorite. I also own Penshire Castle now that my father is dead."

"I never heard of it."

"It lies near Bath."

"That explains why," she said coolly.

He studied her curiously. She was angelically beautiful in spite of her quick tongue. Once he cured her of that fault, and he had no doubt he would, she would be perfect. She was a lady born and bred, and they were all naturally pliant. He knew this from observing his own mother. Willful behavior came only from living unprotected for too long. "How long have you been a widow?"

"Three years."

Alison glanced at Miles. Why had he asked her that? Did he think himself in danger of dropping from exhaustion and leaving her a widow again? She quickened her steps. Once she danced him into the floor, she could rest.

On and on they whirled, neither giving the other chance to catch his breath. Alison's lungs ached, and she was developing a painful stitch in her side.

Between dances, Leatrice came to her mistress. "It grows late, my lady. Shall I see you upstairs?"

"Yes," Alison said, disguising her thankfulness. No one else could retire for the night before she did, and she couldn't beg this wild man for quarter. In Wales were the women amazons that they could dance unceasingly for hours? To Miles she nodded a cool farewell, as if they wouldn't see each other in a matter of minutes.

"Leatrice, he's half-insane. I swear it," she muttered as she forced her aching legs up the turret stairs.

"He's mad!"

"Have you ever seen a civilized man dance so long, and with the same partner? I'm ready to drop!"

"Did you not tell him as much?"

"Of course not! I'll never let him best me."

Leatrice hid her smile of relief. "Then mayhap he didn't realize how long you had danced. Love blinds, you know."

"He doesn't love me. He never even gave me a compliment. Instead he boasted of his newest castle and told me my tongue is sharp."

"At times it is," Leatrice observed with the familiarity of a longtime friend and companion. "You know your temper."

"My temper is well-justified. How would you like to be left waiting on the very altar?"

At once she could have bitten her tongue, because Leatrice responded, "At least I would have been asked." As a poor younger daughter of a large family, she had never been betrothed.

"I'm sorry, dear Leatrice. That was thoughtless of me."

Leatrice smiled and said conspiratorially, "Did you see that tall blond man? His name is Sir Trahern, and I think he's ever so handsome. He's neither married nor promised."

"You learned this in the measure of a dance? 'Tis a wonder you're not breathless yourself."

"We walked a bit in the courtyard," Leatrice admitted with a blush.

"Careful where your heart leads. He is also a Welshman."

"I care not. He's devilishly handsome and quick of wit."

"Leatrice, Leatrice. Whatever will I do with you?"

When they reached her room, Alison froze, staring at the door to her bedchamber. This was the part she had refused to think about.

Leatrice walked in and Alison had no recourse but to follow. She was glad Leatrice hadn't noticed her moment of panic, for she didn't want anyone to know of her lack of courage. She would go through with this because she must, and for no other reason. As Leatrice chatted about who had said what that evening, she loosened the back lacings of Alison's gown and kirtle. Alison stepped out of the pile of clothes, and Leatrice hung them on a peg as Alison untied her light woolen petticoat. Bending, she unbuckled the small gold garters that held up her embroidered stockings.

"Look at this," Leatrice exclaimed. "You've danced holes in both your shoes."

"And in my feet as well, from the feel of them." Alison sank down onto a stool and rubbed the bottoms of her pink feet.

"Stand up and give me your chemise," Leatrice ordered as she held out her hand. "Hurry before they all come up and catch you naked."

That suggestion spurred Alison to action, and she shimmied out of her garment and hurried to the bed, being careful not to show her apprehension. From the hallway she heard raucous shouts that meant the wedding party was on its way up to the chamber. Leatrice pulled down the covers and laid the bouquet of rosemary on one pillow. Alison yanked out the cushioned footstool and climbed onto the high bed, pulling the covers to her chin as the revelers burst into the chamber, bearing Miles atop their shoulders.

With ribald songs and jokes, they ceremoniously

deposited him at the foot of the bed. Alison's eyes were wide and frightened despite herself as they divested him of his cloak and jerkin, leaving him there in his long shirt and netherstocks. Leatrice chased the revelers from the room, and with a respectful nod to her mistress, she exited the chamber.

In the sudden silence Alison and Miles stared at one another. Her abundant hair flowed about her shoulders, pooling like dark fire upon the pillows and around her hips. Without her hood and other garments, she looked younger and much more vulnerable. Frightened, even.

Miles moved slowly so as not to alarm her as he came to the side of the bed. "You look at me as if you were the hare and I the hound," he observed.

"Nonsense. I'm not so untried a girl as to come undone at the sight of a man in his shirtsleeves."

He sat on the side of the bed and touched the smooth fall of her hair. "It's beautiful," he said softly. "I've never seen such hair."

"You flatter me." In spite of herself, she flinched from his touch. She might not be a virgin, but she wasn't greatly experienced, either. Because of Charles's distaste for physical contact, he had rarely indulged in foreplay. For Alison the act of lovemaking had always been uncomfortable and frequently painful.

"I never speak idle words," Miles said. "Whatever I say, I always mean. I take chivalry very seriously, though some feel it is outdated."

Gently he stroked his finger down the warm flesh of her neck and chest and tugged the covers lower. Alison reluctantly lowered her clenched fingers and let the covers drop to her lap, exposing her breasts.

She forced herself to sit still while he surveyed her charms. "You're truly beautiful." A seductive smile lifted his lips as his long fingers traveled lazily down toward her breasts. Even before he began to stroke her nipples, they had swelled to fullness in anticipation. Silently Alison cursed her body's betrayal of her mind.

Not taking his eyes from hers, Miles removed the rest of his clothes and climbed onto the bed. Alison automatically moved away but he drew her back. Placing her hands about his shoulders, he circled her with his arms and eased her down into the billowy softness. Her nipples left beads of fire where they touched his chest, but he forced himself to restraint, for much depended on this first night. If he was rough or if he frightened her, it might take months to regain her trust, if indeed he had it now. She still watched him as if she were in mortal danger.

He arched her body to meet his and brushed aside the covers so that she lay naked before him. Bending over her, he claimed her lips for their first real kiss. Alison's body tensed as she tried to remain detached, but he was not deterred. She tasted the sweetness of his breath and the firm softness of his lips. When her lips parted beneath his gentle persuasion, Miles rewarded her by stroking his palm over the swell of her breast. She responded with a movement of surprise, for she wasn't accustomed to being caressed.

He tightened his arms more securely about her, and lowered his head to leave a trail of kisses over the warm curve of her throat, where her pulse beat wildly, like a caged butterfly. Gently he moved lower, licking her soft skin between kisses and murmuring at how sweet she smelled, like lemons and roses. His lips moved to her turgid bud, and he loved it with his lips and tongue before drawing it into his mouth.

Alison made a startled sound and moved beneath him, but she wasn't sure if she sought to escape or to surrender further. After a languorous moment she arched toward him, offering him all her luscious temptations. All this was so new to her, and she marveled that such pleasure had not been given to her before. She felt seductive and seduced at the same time, and she discovered she enjoyed the sensation.

His hand caressed the valley of her waist and the graceful swell of her hip before he rolled her onto her back to lie flat on the bed. Ever so slowly he parted her legs and sought out the seat of pleasure that resided there. At first she resisted, her last vestige of shyness at becoming one with this stranger. Instead of forcing his way into her, he took care to make her want him even more. With a knowing touch and loving words he drew out her longing until she murmured his name.

He had never heard it on her lips before and it pleased him the way she said it. "Alison," he whispered, as if her name were lyrical, "I'm going to make you love me." She tried to answer, but her body was in control and not her reasoning. Her only response was to sigh his name.

Miles knelt over her, reading the desire in her eyes to be sure she was ready, and then they became one. Fighting hard to contain himself, he moved slowly, stroking her to greater passion and more urgent desire. When her want became a need, he increased his movements and felt the answering ripple of her inner flesh as she cried out in ecstasy. Her completion triggered his own, even though he wanted to hold back and please her again. He moaned as satisfaction raced through him, turning his thoughts to dreams and his muscles to jelly.

Rolling from her, he drew her head onto his shoulder. Gently he smoothed her tumbled hair back from her dewy face. Marveling at her perfection, he matched her hand to his, palm to palm. The tip of her fingers scarcely reached his second knuckle. Gently enfolding her hand, he brought it to his lips and tenderly kissed the palm. Alison shivered with the delight of his caress. It seemed as though she had never experienced such pleasure as this before, and he was amazed.

She gazed at him in awe. She had never guessed she could feel this way. Whatever had just happened to her was nothing short of miraculous. Not only had he not hurt her, but she still seemed to glow from the inside out, and her nerves still seemed concentrated in that unsuspected point of pleasure deep within her.

His eyes met hers and she saw the depth of his soul. This was a man such as she had never met before. If she weren't very, very careful, she would surely grow to love him. Alison tried in vain to harden her heart against him as she fell asleep in his embrace.

4

Alison awoke shortly before dawn. The comforting illumination from the night-watch candle that was always lit against the darkness in the master chamber was being rivaled by the light of the pearl-gray sky outside the window. Alison turned her head and studied the man who slept beside her. His features were composed and looked younger than she had recalled, yet every bit as handsome. His coarse black hair, tousled from their dalliance and the night's sleep, contrasted sharply against the white cover on his chaff-filled pillow. One arm lay upon the covers, and even in repose it looked hard and powerful. A large vein corded the tanned skin, curving around his forearm to his wrist. His palm was square, his fingers long and blunt. From the obvious strength in his hands, one would never guess their gentleness.

Gazing up at the shadowy ceiling beyond the bed where the candle tossed restless shadows of the bed hangings, Alison began to reflect, with greater objectivity than before, on the events of the previous evening. The more she thought, the more irritated she became. How had she allowed herself to love him last night? She should have struggled and fought back. This was a man who was in league with the king who had been responsible for Charles's execution. Instead of refusing Miles, she had allowed herself to be taken, and had even enjoyed it! How shameless could she be! Not only had she returned his loving, she had slept in his arms most of the night and felt safer than she ever had in her life.

Disgusted with herself, Alison rolled out of bed, her feet finding the familiar footstool. As if he already missed her, Miles reached across the flock bed and drew her warm pillow toward him without ever waking. Alison detested the surge of longing she felt for him. He was her enemy! A heretic!

Hardening her heart, she tiptoed about the room, collecting her clothing for the day. Mayhap he could lie abed all morning, but she had chores to attend to. Pulling on her chemise, she crept barefoot into the antechamber where Leatrice slept and shook her awake.

Leatrice sat up and rubbed her eyes as she peered at the gray light rimming the tapestry-covered window. "Have I overslept? Pardon, my lady."

"You haven't overslept. I awoke early." Alison shivered from the chill in the room. Winter was coming quickly, and except for the harshest nights, Leatrice preferred to sleep without a brazier of coals. As quickly as she could, Alison dressed in a kirtle of russet damask embroidered with golden roses. Leatrice helped her lace the back tightly to narrow her already slim waist. Over this she put on her older yellow gown with a swirling design about the wide sleeves. As Leatrice began brushing her mistress's hair, Alison fastened the tiny hooks and eyes concealed in the satin cordwork of the front of her gown.

Alison's hair was thick and as straight as a sheer fall of water, except for a slight curl at the very end. Never having been cut, it hung well below her hips, and when wet, the weight of it on her slender neck was formidable. Leatrice brushed until her mistress's hair glowed in her fingers, then braided it into a rope as thick as her wrist. Coiling the mass into a coronet, she pinned it to Alison's head with ivory bodkins, then crowned it with a narrow French hood that clung closely to her head. The hood's bongrace was sheer yellow lawn that draped behind just below the top of her shoulders.

Alison had pulled on her white hose and buckled them securely. Stepping into the cloth shoes she wore about the castle, she fastened the brass buckles that gathered the shoes to fit her feet. "Dress quickly, Leatrice. We have candles to do this morning."

"Today? But the wedding guests are still downstairs."

"They came to see the bridegroom and have seen him. As soon as they are sober enough to leave, I will bid them farewell. In the meantime, we have chores." Her voice was determined and brusque.

"This isn't like you."

"On the contrary. This is exactly like me. You see, Leatrice, I've tried all my life to be biddable and docile, and what has it gotten me?"

"A title of viscountess?"

"A husband who was executed, my lands and castle confiscated, and a new husband who is half-barbarian."

Leatrice glanced toward the closed chamber door with interest. "A barbarian? In what way?" she whispered.

"Never mind. The point is, my meekness has earned me naught but frustration, and I'll have no more of it."

"What will you do?"

"Exactly as I please. If that doesn't suit my fine Welshman, he may leave for London." Her honey-brown eyes veiled thoughtfully. "That may be an inspiration! Leatrice, if I make him miserable enough, would he not leave? Of course he would!" She paced the antechamber, her fingers to her lips as she formed a plan.

"My lady, take care. If he is indeed barbaric . . ."

"I fear him not. So long as he is here, our work for our holy cause is at a standstill. How else may I be rid of him?"

"Lady Alison, I don't think—"

"Nonsense, Leatrice," Alison interrupted. " 'Tis a perfect plan! No doubt he is accustomed to a castle run like a well-greased wheel—no wobbles, no halts. I plan to toss a stick in his spokes."

"I don't . . ."

"Look at it from his view," Alison went on as she sat on Leatrice's bed and took both her friend's hands to sit her down beside her. "All he has to do is show up and he's married. To be fed, he must merely open his mouth and demand food. I have no doubt that the king's household runs smoothly, and thus must be my lord's custom." She smiled devilishly. "By St. George, Leatrice! This will do it! I wager that within a fortnight we'll be rid of this Welshman."

Leatrice stared at her mistress. As her lady-in-waiting, she had little say in the running of the castle, but she was also Alison's friend, so she again said, "I don't think this is a good idea."

"Nonsense, Leatrice." Alison stood and slapped her palm against her thigh. "I feel better already. Dress quickly," she added, tugging Leatrice's tumbled braid teasingly. "Otherwise, you may miss the fun."

Alison's mood was brighter indeed as she went into the next antechamber and cheerfully awoke the maidservants who attended Leatrice and herself. Sailing out into the corridor, she hummed a strain from "Fair, If You Expect Admiring." She hadn't felt so lighthearted and unrestrained since her childhood, when her hoyden nature was yet unchecked. If Charles was appalled when he once caught her whistling a tune, Miles would be put to his heels by the time she finished. She might still be wed to him—naught could change that—but she need not abide with him.

The hall was uncommonly full of sleeping bodies, not only her own men but also the servants of her guests. Alison threaded her way past the men and went out to the kitchens.

WYNDFELL

The cooks were up as usual, having started work at close to three o'clock so they would be well into cooking an hour later at dawn, when most of the others arose for the day. But as Alison rarely was up and about before sunrise, the servants gaped at her in surprise as she breezed past them and out to the kitchen yard.

In ancient days this open yard had been the place where all meals were prepared, rain, shine, or snow. Sometime during the fourteenth century, a thoughtful ancestor had built a small building in the yard to serve as a kitchen for use in bad weather, and a generation or so later, the bigger one was added. Now cooking was done in the yard only when great feasts necessitated more fires than the kitchens would accommodate. But on a regular basis the area was used for clothes-washing and candlemaking.

Following Alison's orders, one young page started a fire in one of the pits while another fetched a large vat of kitchen fat. Together the boys levered a large iron kettle into place on the rock stand above the fire.

Alison was stoking the fire when Leatrice arrived, still fastening the laces that held her sleeves closed at her wrists. "What are you doing, my lady?"

"Do you not remember? I said that today was the day for making candles."

"But you seem to be doing the work yourself!"

"You're very observant, Leatrice."

"A viscountess doesn't do menial chores! What are you thinking of? The entire parish will talk!"

"Good. That's what I have in mind. Let it be said far and wide that the viscountess of Wyndfell must prepare her own candles following her unfortunate marriage to a barbaric Welshman. His pride will send him packing."

Looking into the vat beside the kettle, Leatrice commented, "There has been some mistake, my lady. This is fat drippings, not beeswax!"

"Beeswax is so dear," Alison said with a smile. "I've decided to use the fat drippings. They're much more plentiful."

Leatrice wrinkled her nose. "They are also more odoriferous. Are you certain you want to go through with this?"

"Bring me that braid of rushes from the storeroom," Alison said in answer. Rolling her sleeves back, Alison took a ladle from a hook on the wall and began dipping the grayish-white grease into the black pot. As the fire heated the metal, the grease became a transparent liquid and a noisome odor wafted throughout the kitchen yard.

Tib, the maid in charge of menial household tasks, heard what was happening and ran from the cellars to find Alison calmly stirring the melting grease. "My lady!" she gasped. "Here. Let me do that!"

"No, no, Tib. You have other chores to see to. I'll do this. Tell the cook to come here. I have orders regarding breakfast."

Uncertainly Tib looked from Alison to Leatrice, then back again. Not knowing what else to do, she curtsied and retreated to the kitchen, where she conferred with the cook, who then hurried to the yard.

"You sent for me, my lady?" the cook asked.

"Yes. My lord husband, as you know, is not of these parts and therefore has a different taste in food. In the future, I want you to prepare the fare of the dais table in this fashion." As Alison stirred, she explained the changes she required. When she had finished, she said, "Do you understand my orders?"

"Perfectly, my lady, but—"

"Very well, you may go. And tell Grace that I must speak to her before she begins to prepare dinner."

The cook bobbed a curtsy and hurried back to the kitchen to repeat her mistress's instructions to the others.

"You, boy," Alison called to a passing page, "take

those rushes from Mistress Leatrice and cut them into lengths for wicks." The boy quickly obeyed.

Taking a rush by the middle, Alison dipped each end in the hot grease and then hung it on the dripping rack. She always oversaw the making of candles, but not since her training as a young girl had she dipped them herself. One of the most menial servants did that task.

Soot from the pot quickly smudged her beautiful gown, and when she wiped at the stain with her blackened fingers, it only worsened. Brushing her bongrace back from her face, Alison smeared her cheek, then winked at Leatrice with an angelic smile.

Miles slept later than was his custom. Usually he was up by dawn and onto the jousting field by clear sunlight. But this day he had a reason to sleep late. Even as he awoke, he recalled the night before. Had any man ever received so fair a bride? Not only was she beautiful, but she was keen for loving once she overcame her natural reticence. This was a woman he could love. In truth he loved her already.

He turned toward her side of the bed and was a bit disappointed to see she was already gone. He wanted her there so they could make love again. With a smile he stretched and sat up, the muscles rippling beneath his smooth skin. She wouldn't have had any way of knowing his desire for the morning, and no doubt she wished to be on hand to send their guests on their way.

Sitting on the edge of the bed, Miles pulled his shirt over his head, then slipped on his quilted petticote and after pulling on his netherstocks, he tied the points of the hose to the petticote. Next he donned a red doublet from his trunk at the foot of the bed, and over that he fastened a gold-and-white striped jerkin made of French brocade. At his waist he hung his dress sword and a gold pendant fashioned like the Garretts' griffin crest. He looped his kidskin riding gloves through his sash and buckled on his leather shoes before shrugging into a warm gold gown lined in red satin. After looping the gold chain about his neck and putting on a red velvet hat with a white ostrich plume, he was ready to meet the day.

The side door led to the chamber used by his men, but it was empty. Miles was a bit surprised. Even though he seldom asked for help in dressing, it was his menservants' duty to wait and see if he might.

As he left the suite of rooms, he noticed that the castle seemed unusually quiet for so late an hour. At the end of the corridor were a knot of servants with their heads together, but as he approached, they drifted away. Miles merely shrugged. He could find his way to the great hall. The corkscrew steps led down the inner wall of the turret just as he recalled, and at the bottom he stepped out into the hall, where more servants were bustling about. A man on a ladder was removing the old candle stubs from the iron coronas and replacing them with new candles for that evening's use. Two women were scrubbing the long tabletops with soapy brushes as another pair sluiced them clean.

Miles greeted the few remaining guests, who looked at him uncertainly. He grinned, trying to put them at ease. He had no idea why they were peering about like that. The men's wives were huddled together by the windows, and he heard their whispers, though not their words. One woman, on seeing him, signaled the others, and, hushing abruptly, they curtsied to him. To show his congeniality, Miles asked them to join him in the winter parlor for breakfast, but no one moved. They seemed transfixed.

Sir Trahern entered the hall and strode briskly to his friend and lord. Miles kept the grin on his face, but spoke in a low tone to ask, "Whatever ails these people? They act as if I've grown two heads." He smiled and nodded to the group of ladies as if he wasn't talking about them, and they dropped him another group curtsy.

"Come look out the window," Trahern suggested.

Nodding again to his guests, Miles followed Trahern to a window in the parlor, and looked down into the walled yard. He glanced back to Trahern as if he were confused by what he was seeing, then leaned out the window for a better look. Below him stood his new bride, clearly engaged in dipping candles. He straightened, a perplexed frown on his face.

A movement near the door caught his eye, and Miles summoned the small dark-haired woman who was trying to slip out unnoticed. "You. Mistress Leatrice, is it? Come here and tell me what you see."

Drawing a steadying breath, Leatrice crossed to the window and looked down. "I see Lady Alison, my lord." She leaned back and turned to leave.

"Wait. What do you see her doing?" Miles persisted, still not willing to believe his own eyes.

As if to humor him, Leatrice again peered down. "I believe my lady is making rush candles, my lord."

"Why is she doing that, do you suppose?" He fingered his lower lip as he frequently did when puzzled.

"I suppose in order that we might have light after sundown," Leatrice suggested.

Miles inquisitively studied her, but Leatrice's face was as guileless as a child's. "Thank you, Mistress Leatrice," he said at last. "You may go."

Leatrice curtsied and left the room, seemingly unconcerned. Trahern watched Leatrice until she was out of sight, then turned his attention back to the yard below. "I can think of nothing else she could be doing that would resemble that," he admitted.

"But the lady of a castle, a *viscountess*, doesn't make rush candles, especially when she has a hall full of guests."

"Is she . . . well, right in the head?" Trahern asked as tactfully as possible.

"Yes, yes. There's nothing the matter with her mind. What could she gain by doing this?"

"Your embarrassment, perhaps? I saw the fire in her eyes yesterday. I thought at the time she was more spirited than you were led to believe."

"Yes," Miles said slowly, "she could mean to embarrass me."

"For what purpose?"

"I know not. Mayhap she was against this marriage. I doubt the king knew or cared if she was content as a widow."

"No woman makes that choice," Trahern replied.

"Yet I've heard that some would prefer to decide for themselves. You recall how old Lord Bisbane was balked at every turn by that young bride of his. Women are fond of perplexing their husbands."

"I would hardly call Lady Bisbane perplexing. He finally had no choice but to banish her to his country estate as soon as she was with child."

"Lord Bisbane is aged and has no imagination left. I've always thought if a willful woman was given her own medicine, she would come about more quickly. Come, let us see." He strode to the steps that led down to the kitchens.

Alison was hot from leaning over the fire and steaming pot. Sweat glistened on her forehead and her cheeks were rosy beneath the smudges. As she hung yet another candle on the swaying rack, she wondered if Miles was awake yet.

"Greetings, my love," Miles's voice boomed behind her.

Startled, Alison jumped and knocked half a dozen candles off the rack. "Good morrow, my lord," she replied as evenly as she could.

Miles turned to Trahern and said with a proud smile, "See how fair is my wife? Tell me, Sir Trahern, is she not more beautiful, more genteel, more pleasing than you recall from the wedding and celebration feast last evening?"

"In truth, my eyes were liars, for I remembered not

such exquisiteness," Trahern said, following his master's lead.

Alison put her hands on her hips, still holding the waxy dipper.

"I'd not draw you from your pleasant task," Miles said, "but our guests are hungry and grow impatient to break their evening's fast."

"I have ordered that food be carried up to the winter parlor. You have but to tell a servant that you are ready," Alison answered with bare civility. "You and our guests may eat their fill."

"Without their viscountess at the table? I'd never be so churlish." Miles caught the hand holding the dipper and pulled her toward the door. "Come, my lady. We'll feast and send them on their way."

Alison protested and pulled back, but Miles never paused in leading her up the steps to the kitchen. Not looking to either side, he extolled to her the beauties of the day, and compared her favorably with the sweetest of seasons. Alison swatted at him with her free hand, but he remarked to Trahern that it seemed the midge flies were bad that year. He never slackened his pace. As they passed the door to the buttery, Alison grappled for a hold, but Miles hauled her onward.

At the door to the hall, her chin came up. So he thought to best her at her own game, did he? Unexpectedly, she pulled forward, freeing herself, then swept past him with her most beguiling smile as she addressed her guests. "Good morrow, my lords and ladies. I trust you all slept well and found everything to your satisfaction?"

Everyone stared at her disheveled appearance. A few, who were not too stunned to speak, managed to mumble a courteous greeting, but even their faces showed their shock. She was thankful to note that Roger Bainbridge had already left.

Waving the ladle as if it were a scepter, she said, "Come. Let us go into the parlor. Leatrice, have the servants bring in the food."

She led Miles to the head of the table and sat beside him in the smaller chair, plopping the grease-coated ladle beside her plate. When their guests were all seated, Miles and Alison were each served a bowl of cold porridge, a wedge of coarse bread, and a flagon of ale. As Miles stared at his plate, their guests were served a more usual fare. Seeing that Miles wasn't eating, Alison lifted a spoonful of lumpy porridge to her husband's lips.

Miles automatically opened his mouth, then grimaced as he tasted it. "Too salty," he muttered.

"More salt?" she asked innocently. "I'll order it changed for tomorrow that it may be more to your liking."

Miles bared his teeth in a mirthless grin, and he chuckled softly as he took measure of his opponent. "You're not eating, poppet," he observed. "Here. Take this spoonful from my own bowl."

Alison could scarcely refuse with all her guests watching, so she choked it down with a forced smile.

Miles reached for the bread and found that it was as stale as beggar's crust. He rapped it on the edge of his bowl and a few crumbs sprayed onto the table. Alison smiled sweetly and crunched into her own bread. Miles again made a chuckling sound as he bit into the hard crust. They were making such a spectacle of themselves that the guests could only stare. Amusement shone on the faces of some, but others were horrified. No one said a word.

Leaning past her, he peered suspiciously into her goblet. "Why, this ale is soured!" He tossed the perfectly good ale onto the rushes behind him and motioned for the server to bring more.

Alison's eyes flashed and she grabbed his goblet. She hadn't done anything at all to the ale. "Why, so it is," she exclaimed as she tossed the golden liquid over her shoulder and smiled as if nothing were odd about reacting in such a way.

After the server had scrambled to refill the two cups, Alison said, "I find I have no appetite. Please take my food away, Bayard." The man tugged nervously at his cap and did as she asked. "Eat up, my lord," she said triumphantly.

"Have another bite, my sweet," Miles retorted. "Just to please me."

"I care not whether I please you," she hissed under her breath while she smiled at him.

Miles threw back his head and laughed aloud. "What bawdy talk for a bridal breakfast! In faith, my gooseberry, you make a man proud to be wed!"

"Gooseberry?" she asked, a hint of real amusement showing in her eyes. Then, remembering that he was her enemy, she spoke through her clenched teeth. "How dare you imply I spoke a coarse word!"

"Ah, my dove," he boomed loud enough to be heard by all, "such discourse is better suited for privacy, but I'm well-pleased that you find me so able."

"Quit that, you rogue!" Everyone in the parlor was staring at them.

As if they were quite alone, Miles cupped Alison's begrimed face in his hands and said, "Your words fall like rose petals on my ear. Your beauty is greater than it was rumored, and yet when I heard tell of your magnificence I thought it to be grossly exaggerated."

"If you don't stop now, you'll be sorry," she murmured for his ears alone.

"Your skin is as flawless as the shell of an egg," he improvised. "Your scent"—he deeply inhaled the fumes of kitchen fat that clung to her hair—"your scent is indeed beyond compare."

"You wretch!" she exclaimed, forgetting her audience. "You spawn of . . . of . . ." Suddenly she looked down at the double row of faces that were fixed on her, and her jaw dropped. He had outwitted her! Without pausing, she grabbed her goblet of ale and dumped its contents over his head.

In one easy movement Miles was up and had thrown

her over his shoulder like a sack of grain. Addressing their guests over the curve of her rump, he said, "Enjoy your repast. My bride would have a word with me in private." He grinned at them and gave a growling chuckle before striding out.

Trahern quickly stood as Miles was carrying his struggling bride away. "A toast to the bride and groom. May good fortune bless so perfect a match!"

Alison groaned in frustration as Miles carried her up the winding steps. "Put me down, you blackguard!"

"Not yet," he ground out.

Hearing the anger in his voice, Alison ceased her double-fisted assault on his back. He sounded really furious.

When they entered Leatrice's room, he kicked the door shut behind them, then shouldered his way into the master chamber. He slammed the door unnecessarily hard and threw the bolt to lock it. Only then did he dump Alison onto her feet. Her face was flushed from the blood that had run to it, and hurt danced in her eyes. But she refused to show the slightest fear or hesitation. Courageously she said, "You made a fool of me!"

"Not I! You did it all yourself. I didn't start this!"

She had no answer for that.

"What made you do this?" he demanded, gesturing at her smoke-grimed gown. "Are you mad?"

"Not in the least! Nor am I a mare to be auctioned to the highest bidder! The king gave me to you without so much as a by-your-leave!"

"What woman is asked in her choice of mate?" Miles roared. "Women here in England have more freedom than any other women in Christendom. Would you now choose your own husbands as well? Next you'll want to sit in Parliament!"

"I wager there would be fewer wars if mothers were in charge of sending their sons into battle!"

Miles growled deeply. "It's not a woman's place to

rail at her husband!" He had had no more choice in this match than she had, but he was damned if he would admit it. "Be glad I don't lock you in the tower to cool you off!"

"You wouldn't!"

"I might! Who is to say me nay?"

"If you dislike Wyndfell and the way it's run, you can leave."

"Leave? Never!"

"What?" she asked incredulously as she stared at him.

"I can see my work is cut out for me here. Not only have I a rebellious parish to tame, but a wife as well."

"What?" she asked again.

"King Henry told me the folk of this area were rebellious. I never knew how much so until now."

"He told you we're rebels?" A flicker of fear raced up her spine, but she hid it.

"There's news of another popish uprising brewing." His eyes narrowed. "You wouldn't know anything about any such activity, would you?"

"Me?"

"Your late husband rode with Aske, as I recall. Now I see it! The king wanted me to marry you to prevent any plots from being hatched at Wyndfell itself! Of course!"

"I . . . I have no idea what you're talking about," she stammered.

"Of course! I thought he meant the rebels were tenants and yeomen, but he must suspect the gentry as well!"

"You're raving mad," she snapped. "There are no rebels here!"

"And there will not be! Not while I rule Wyndfell!"

Alison saw the iron determination on his face. Just past his shoulder, the hidden panel opened a crack, and as the distinct odor of the musty dampness of the secret passage wafted to her nostrils, her eyes met Damion's startled gaze.

"Lord Miles!" she burst out to draw his attention. "You amaze me. You suspect *me* of being a traitor?" Her voice was high and brittle. Thankfully, Damion had silently shut the paneling.

"You? I never said that."

"Well, you'd better not!" Was she really hearing Damion's steps as he ascended the stairs inside the wall, or was it her imagination?

"You're Catholic, aren't you?" Miles asked.

"How could I be? It's against the law."

Miles stared at her with an intensity that frightened her. Until then, he hadn't considered that she might not be Protestant. After all, a vicar had married them, not a priest. By all surface detail she might be a staunch follower of the king, yet when he peered into her eyes, he knew better. If she wasn't mixed up in some plan of rebellion, why did she look so frightened? He made a noncommittal grunt as he wondered what to do. She was rebellious by nature—this morning had shown him that. But a traitor? This he didn't believe. Strangely enough, he wasn't entirely sure he would tell the king even if she proved to be the leader of an uprising. Something about her tugged at his heart.

"Now that you're calmer, will you come back down with me?" he asked. He couldn't care less what these people thought, but it might be important to her.

"Not yet," she said hastily. "Give me time to freshen up; then I'll join you."

When Miles was gone, she ran to the panel and tripped the latch. It swung open, revealing the dark passage. "Damion?" she whispered.

A faint sound from above reached her ears and she looked up the steps. Gathering her skirts, she entered the passageway and closed the panel behind her. Feeling her way through the darkness, she went up to join him on the stairs. "He might have seen you!" she scolded. "It's a wonder that he didn't!"

"Who was that man in your chamber?" Damion accused.

"My husband! I told you the king had promised me to Lord Miles Garrett and that the wedding was to be yesterday."

"Pardon, sister. I had forgotten."

"Why were you coming into my room?"

"I became confused and thought it to be the chamber where the believers will meet on the Sabbath."

"Next time be more careful! The room you're seeking is there." She pointed to the shadows at the top of the flight of steps.

"Does he suspect us? I heard him shouting at you."

"No, no," Alison lied at the fanatical gleam in Damion's eyes. "It was but a quarrel."

"So soon? You've just wed."

In exasperation Alison said, "Are you monks such authorities on marriage? It was but a disagreement."

"Very well. You must take care that he doesn't become suspicious of you. Such curiosity could threaten my safety. I cannot let that happen."

She stared at him, not needing to ask what he meant. "He suspects nothing. I must go now or my absence will be missed."

Turning, she hurried back to her chamber, and after peering through a crack in the secret door, she entered quickly. What did she have on her hands? A brother she had loved who seemed to have changed so radically, and a husband who was in league with the very dangerous king. Alison leaned against the false panel and almost fainted when the door to her room suddenly opened.

"Leatrice!" she breathed in relief. "It's you."

"Of course it's me. What happened? Did he hurt you?"

"No, no. Nothing like that. We only argued."

"You have dust and cobwebs in your bongrace." Leatrice reached up to touch the silvery strand, but

Alison quickly pulled the hood off and shook it vigorously.

"Help me change and wash up," she said, not daring to trust Leatrice with so dangerous a secret as Damion's presence in the castle. The less she knew, the better. "I must bid my guests good-bye. By the way, Leatrice, did you know my Welshman is also a heretic?"

Leatrice's appalled look assured Alison that the unexplainable cobweb would be forgotten.

5

Alison sat in the cold alcove of the church, restlessly tapping her foot on the stone floor. "He's terrible, Mother! A barbarian! First he kept me waiting four hours for the wedding, then he danced with me until I was so exhausted I thought I would surely drop." She omitted mention of her own involvement in the contest of wills. Pensively she recalled the passionate night of loving spent in Miles's arms and then glanced at Charles's tomb with guilt.

"He's not the least like you, Charles. I wager he can read no more than his name, if he can indeed read that much. As yet, he has not discussed any learned topic with me." She tossed her head in disdain. "He is not a gentle man, nor a refined one. You have naught to worry about as to my ever loving him." Again she recalled her compliance with Miles's wishes and her pleasure in his arms, and she turned away from Charles's effigy to her mother's.

"Damion was displaced from his monastery and is in hiding here at Wyndfell, Mother. I wish you were here to talk to him for he has changed. Whereas before he was fervent in his piety, now he is near-fanatical." She stood and paced the small alcove, her hands clasped behind her back. "If Miles finds Damion, I know not what may happen. Already Damion has come close to giving himself away." She paused at the entrance to the church and said, "Bless me, Mother, for I now have much to bear." She smiled a bit as she added, "My patience is being greatly tried, but I am holding up admirably." It was a small lie, but she didn't want to worry her mother's spirit with such a matter.

Alison crossed the church and stepped out into the weak sunshine. The scent of autumn was in the air, a crispness that was almost palatable, like the taste of an apple. Next to spring, Alison liked autumn best because it was a season of change. The earth seemed to be rushing from one garb into the next, and Alison always felt a surge of excitement.

The church stood near the center of Wyndfell's village, not far from the wool merchant's building. As Alison rode past the blacksmith shop, on her way back to the castle's gates, she heard the familiar sounds of the smithy hammering away. The smithy was a huge man who always whistled while he worked, and as Alison rode by, he broke off the tune and respectfully bowed to her. She returned his gesture with a gracious nod of her head, and he resumed his work on a shoe for the apothecary's horse as a group of children ran by in a game of tag. The baker's apprentice in his worn blue jerkin crossed her path, carrying a bundle of bread he was delivering, and passed a quick greeting to the butcher's apprentice. The two boys were friends, even though their masters wouldn't speak to each other if their very lives were forfeit.

Here and there were cottages, most with no more than one floor, and all of them shaggy with thatched roofs above their mud-and-wattle walls. A few of the richer merchants had stone houses, and behind one of them Alison saw a wife upbraiding her scullery maid. At the edge of the village, where the tenants and hirelings lived, the accommodations were little more than one- or two-room huts, even smaller than those of the yeomen. Here the wives and daughters worked at spinning wool to feed the looms of the busy wool guild. Those women not fortunate enough to be hired as spinners were often hired out as menials or worked in the fields beside their men. The village was well run, and the few who audibly complained, objected to the abolition of their religion rather than to the rule of the castle.

Alison thought about this as she turned her horse toward Wyndfell's green. Roger Bainbridge wanted to foster an uprising of sorts, though he assured her there would be no bloodshed. He wanted the Catholics in the villages and castles nearby to complain to the king and refuse to attend the Protestant services. Since this was expressly illegal, Alison was concerned. Perhaps Roger and the others planned to kill no one, but what of the king's men? She wished Roger had not confided in her, but as mistress of Wyndfell he had expected her to be enthusiastically on his side. And she was, but not to the extent of taking part in a rebellion. Damion had been all for the idea. He and Roger had schemed together long after she had gone about her day's work. Now that Miles was in residence, what would become of Roger's plan?

She crossed the drawbridge and rode into the courtyard, where she dismounted and gave her horse's reins to one of the stableboys. All about her the castle hummed with well-organized industry. Her own smithy, a tall and wiry man, was hammering out nails for the repair of the hawks' mews as his apprentice pumped the bellows. An odorous breeze from the brewhouse told Alison that new ale was being prepared. From where she stood she could hear the clank of Wyndfell's busy looms. Many village women came here to spin and weave under her employ. Alison had her women work here rather than in their homes, so she knew if the wool was hers, or if she was losing yarn to the wood merchants on the side.

She strolled around to the kitchens and nodded when Tib called out in greeting. The woman kept all the scullery and kitchen maids working efficiently, and

Alison considered her worth more than her yearly pay. She decided to raise her salary to twenty shillings a year in addition to her clothing allowance.

Looking to see that no one else was in earshot, Alison asked Tib in a low voice, "Have you prepared the food?"

"Aye, my lady." The woman reached for a basket with her large red-knuckled hand. "Here 'tis."

"Thank you, Tib." Although everyone but Miles and Sir Edmund knew about the abbess, Alison considered it best not to make a show of what she was about to do.

She looped the basket over her arm and walked briskly toward the back gate. A quick glance told her Miles was nowhere in sight, so she let herself out. Wyndfell's curtain wall circled between the formal gardens and orchard on the inside and the less attractive vegetable garden on the green. As the moat didn't surround the entire castle, the green flowed right up to the impregnable wall here in back. Alison walked over the gold-green grasses, passed the vegetable garden, and went to the small door set in the wall behind some tall bushes.

No one knew why the small room had been built into the thickest part of the wall. It had been there longer than memory. Perhaps it had been designed for exactly the purpose it was now serving. At any rate, Alison was very thankful for its existence. When the nearby convent of St. Clare had been dissolved, the abbess had refused to reenter the secular world. One could scarcely blame her, for she had entered the convent before she was twelve and had never left its gates in the fifty-three years that followed. She had no known family save the church, and when Alison had suggested Wyndfell, the abbess had asked for the small cell in the curtain wall. Here she had entered the life of an anchoress, willingly locking herself away from the world to live out the rest of her days in prayer and solitude. Alison greatly admired her for taking such a drastic step, yet with Miles in residence, she wasn't sure this was the safest place for the old woman.

The anchorage door was weathered to a silvery hue, similar to that of the rest of the stone wall, and only a discerning eye could detect it behind the concealing hawthorn bushes which also covered the one tiny window.

Alison rapped on the door, and hearing the woman call out for her to enter, forced the door open and slipped through. Inside, the cell was dim and smelled faintly of candle wax and incense. The room appeared empty at first, there being only one stool and a curtain in evidence. Facing the curtain, Alison said, "I've brought your food, Mother Anne."

"Thank you, my child," an old, gentle voice replied from behind the curtain. "My blessing, Lady Alison."

"May I talk with you for a bit?" Alison asked.

"Of course, my child."

Alison sat on the stool and put the basket on the floor. "My lord husband arrived. We were married yesterday." She paused, but there was no word from behind the curtain. "I must confess to you, for I held uncharitable thoughts toward him. I still do," she added.

"You must confess to Brother Damion," Mother Anne chided her gently. "He is the proper one to hear confession now that he is in residence."

"But he's my brother. I can't bring myself to confess to him."

Alison waited in the silence, assuming that the unseen woman was thinking. After a long moment the abbess said, "It's more proper for him to hear your confession, but under the circumstances I suppose you may still come to me."

"Thank you, Mother Anne." Alison saw the curtain stir a bit, and wondered what the woman behind it did during the long hours. Could anyone pray so unceasingly? Since her withdrawal into the wall three years before, no one had seen so much as a glimpse of the woman.

"Is your lord husband of our faith?"

"No, Mother Anne. He's a heretic."

Again the silence grew long. Alison wondered if perhaps the holy woman was as charitable as she had assumed, for then she said, "Then must I assume you were married by the heretic vicar?"

"Yes, Mother. There was no other way."

"Then you are his wife only in the eyes of other heretics."

"I *had* to marry him. The king commanded it."

"I see, my child. We are not all cut out to be martyrs for our faith."

Alison frowned. She didn't see this as a religious issue so much as one of survival. Everyone but the anchoress accepted her marriage as valid. "If you met him, you would understand," she defended herself. "He's a hard man and nearly a barbarian. I couldn't have stood against him, even if the king had not ordered it."

"I understand."

"I am doing all I can to drive him away. Mayhap he'll soon tire of Wyndfell and return to London. Am I doing right to try to oust him?"

"Yes, child. Whereas I would counsel you to be obedient toward a true husband, this man is yours only in the eyes of the law. The sooner he leaves Wyndfell, the sooner you may return to grace."

Alison's frown deepened. She didn't consider marrying Miles a fall from grace, but rather an irritation. "I must return to the castle before Lord Miles notes my absence."

Kneeling for the abbess's benediction, Alison took the empty basket from her previous visit and let herself out. She closed the door securely and stepped out of the concealing bushes. That she might not be truly married came as a shock to her, and she resolved to ask Damion's opinion. In her heart she felt married to Miles. Not amiably matched, it was true, but still married.

As she went back to the servants' gate, she almost collided with Sir Edmund, who stared at her as if she had appeared from nowhere.

"My lady! Where were you? I thought I saw you step out this way, but when I came after you, I couldn't see you at all. Now here you are."

"Why were you looking for me?" she asked coolly. She still didn't trust this man sent by King Henry.

"There is a dispute between the farmers who till the back two rows of the common field."

"I settled their dispute at sowing time."

"I know, my lady. So they said. But now it is harvest and the dispute has arisen again."

She sighed. More pressing matters than this were weighing upon her. "Take the matter to Lord Garrett. Tell him of my decision in the dispute and have him enforce it."

Edmund paused and looked at her inquiringly. "Tell him what to do, my lady? He's lord and master here now. I know not how he would take being told what to do about this matter, him being a heretic and all." Edmund made his last few words seem like a slip of the tongue. He looked over his shoulder, feigning a worry that someone other than Alison might have overheard his comment.

Alison studied the man. She would have sworn he was Protestant too. "Nevertheless, the matter was already settled by me. Do as I've told you."

"Yes, my lady." Edmund felt it was better for her to conclude that he, too, was still Catholic, and in that way he could more easily gain her confidence.

Alison and Edmund walked back to the gate. Sir Edmund's words still surprised her. Was he Catholic? Certainly he made no slips of faith, such as swearing by the saints or referring to church services as Mass, but then, no one did lest his true feelings be found out. Sir Edmund might be a true believer. She decided to mention this to Damion as well.

"Sir Edmund," she said as he started to walk away.

"Be sure Lord Garrett understands that last spring I settled in favor of Ira Phelps over Arthur Lyman."

"Yes, my lady."

Alison watched the man walk away. Could she trust him? He had carried out his duties with faultless precision in the month since his arrival, and in all matters he was subservient to her. He had a better head for numbers than had old Walter Landon before him. Yet there was something about Sir Edmund that keened her senses whenever he was near. Shaking her head at the perplexity, she went about her duties.

As she circled the castle, she noted the kitchen maids were harvesting the last of the herbs to dry for winter. Four men were salting fish to make "Poor John" and a woman was raking the drying peas. Rings of pumpkins were strung on poles to dry in the sun, as were clusters of beans that had been strung into bunches of leather-breeches. Alison walked among the racks and salt bins and tested the various peas and pumpkins to assure they were drying evenly. Since the harvest had been plentiful, there would be no need to purchase food this winter.

Crossing through the low gate that separated the kitchen yard from the courtyard, she went to the wool house. All four looms were being worked, and one of the weavers, a lass from the village who was known for her sweet voice, was singing a ballad to the rhythm of her shuttle. The slip-bang of wood against wood punctuated the song and kept the other weavers in a like tempo. Behind them sat a number of spinners of varying ages. As it took nine spinners to keep one weaver busy, Alison was always on the watch for a likely woman with nimble fingers.

She inspected the yarn of one of the younger spinners, a girl not quite twelve. In a few years she hoped to give the child the better-paid position of weaver, as she had a true talent for working with wool.

In the back of the long room were more women carding rank-smelling bags of wool from the shearing the previous spring. These were the lowest-paying jobs, and most of the women were either very young or very old. Alison nodded at the progress of changing matted clippings into flossy cream-white puffs.

Beside the door were racks where the finished cloth was stored until it was needed by the seamstresses for garments or wall hangings. Alison prided herself on running a very efficient wool room, which even the merchants of the wool guild could manage no better.

She stepped out into the sunlight and saw the steward on his way to his office in the gatehouse. "Sir Edmund," she called. "Tell me of the dispute."

He hesitated before saying, "Lord Garrett gave judgment for Arthur Lyman over Ira Phelps."

"What? Surely you mean that the other way around."

"No, my lady. I did your bidding, but Lord Garrett decided Phelps was at fault."

Alison's smile was replaced with a frown. "Where is Lord Garrett?"

"In his closet, my lady."

Turning on her heel, Alison went to the castle. How could Miles have overruled her judgment like this? Lyman was a widower with no one to support and Phelps had not only his wife and children but also a spinster sister to feed. Phelps was always given the longer row.

Miles was in his closet examining a map of Wyndfell's fields. As his eyes traced over the map, he absently fingered the letter seal that bore his family's emblem: a rearing griffin. Behind him was the wall of books and ledgers Charles and other departed Wakefield ancestors had kept regarding the castle's operations and profits. Having always lived at court, Miles had never supervised a castle, and had brought to Wyndfell a number of books on husbandry and farming methods. After he had learned all he could from these books, he planned to read his copy of *Utopia* for a third time. He never tired of the book.

He glanced up when Alison came in, but before he

could smile she snapped, "Lord Miles, I must speak to you."

His eyes became wary. He had not seen her since their argument that morning, and her mood still seemed harsh. "Welcome to my closet, Lady Alison. To what do I owe the pleasure?"

"What business had you to overthrow my decision regarding Lyman and Phelps?"

"Your decision was about the planting of crops. Their new dispute is over the harvesting of that crop."

"Do you not know Phelps has a family to feed and Lyman has none? I always assign the longer rows to the men with families. Lyman is a troublesome man and prone to fighting and drinking, and Phelps is as steady as the sunlight on a summer's day."

Miles regarded her for a moment. "I am master here and I have made the correct decision."

"That you have not!" Her anger sparked and her eyes flashed. "I will send word to them that you have reconsidered and are reversing your decision."

Miles's dark brows drew together as he leaned forward on the desk. "You will do no such thing. Perhaps you were accustomed to being in charge as a widow, but you are now a wife. My decision stands." His deep blue eyes met hers and he refused to give an inch.

"If such is to be your rule, then I pity our tenants and hirelings," she retorted bitterly, "for I see the days of justice at Wyndfell are at an end." She turned to go, but his voice stopped her.

"Are you so sure of your own judgement without having heard the complaint? It seems Phelps has been sending the eldest of his children to harvest Lyman's crop by moonlight. Lyman lay in wait last night and caught the young thief in the act."

Turning her head slightly, Alison said over her shoulder, "Stealing is a serious offense. What punishment did you order?"

"I told Phelps to have the boy aid Lyman in an honest harvest and to take no pay for the boy's work."

Alison nodded silently. Such a punishment was more than lenient. The boy could have been hanged or had his hand struck off. All the same, she wasn't ready or willing to commend Miles so she left without speaking.

He watched the door close behind her and sat in his chair. Was there no way to soften this proud lady? He would far rather have her smiles than her frowns, and he wanted to live in peace in his own castle. Leaning back, he rested his elbows on the chair arms and rubbed his chin thoughtfully. There must be some way into her heart. If not by her good graces, then by being her master.

A dozen ideas filtered through Miles's head and were discarded. He had heard many men at court tell how they had mastered their wives. Most of their suggestions were overbearing, if not outright cruel. Miles had no streak of cruelty at all.

He had once read an Italian story, *Notte Piacevoli*, by a man named Straparolo. The story had enjoyed some success at court and several poems using the story's theme had circulated as a result. The Italian story was based on an even older one from a book called *Arabian Nights*. For it to have survived and been retold must mean there was a truth in the method. In it a man named Petruchio was wed to a cursed and shrewish wife. Miles and his friends had laughed to see how Petruchio tamed his wife by disclaiming all she said. A slow smile lifted his lips. Could he not try the same tact? Since Alison was already willful to a fault, little was at risk.

Alison went to her chamber and waved away her ladies. She wanted to be alone with her thoughts. Miles had indeed done the proper thing toward the tenant farmers, but Alison had let her pity for Phelps's womenfolk blind her to the man's true character. She went to the window and looked down the green to the neat little village. How many other decisions had she made that were biased toward the wrong? Was she even wrong to dislike her husband? Her eyes strayed toward the big bed where he had taught her to enjoy loving the night before. Miles Garrett was the king's man, but aside from that, he might not be so awful. Evidently he even knew how to read, for he had been holding a book when she confronted him in his closet. Certainly he was very pleasing to gaze upon, and thus far he kept himself clean. Leatrice told her he had bathed that very morning.

Would it be possible, she wondered, to give in to Miles a bit, yet not knuckle under completely? She had known him less than a day and thus far she had done little but gainsay him. Perhaps, she decided with a smile, in view of his leniency toward young Phelps, she should show him more tolerance. Quickly she went down to the kitchen to tell the cook to forget her previous order and to prepare the meals as she had in the past.

At supper, which was served as usual in the winter parlor, Alison sat calmly beside her husband. She was determined to show her approval by being pleasant, so when the carver brought out a pheasant and deftly sliced it, she offered Miles the first piece. He took it and she daintily took the other slice of breast. "Is the pheasant to your liking?" she asked with her most demure voice.

"Pheasant, say you?" He smiled with equal grace, prepared to put his plan into action. "Nay, 'tis a coney."

Alison blinked and looked back at the meat and carver. "You're mistaken, my lord." She laughed politely. "This is a pheasant."

"Nay, 'tis not so. I prefer coney to pheasant and would know the difference."

With a motion of her fingers, Alison sent the servant to fetch the next dish. How could he possibly mistake a bird for a rabbit? The server next approached with a platter of pike en doucette, its pastry top still steaming from the oven.

When the man knelt to serve him, Miles wrinkled

his nose as if in surprise. "Salt fish so soon in the year?" he asked Alison. "I find this displeasing."

She stared at him a moment. "This fish is fresh. I saw it taken from the holding pond myself."

"Nay. I say it is salted and cold. Take it away."

"Stay! I say it is neither, my lord." Realizing she was losing control, Alison fought to regain her composure before she continued in dulcet tones. "Look at it well. Do you not see the steam from the crust?"

"I see no steam. I see ill-prepared salt fish. Take it away, man, and tell the cook I'll have no salt fish until the river is frozen solid."

Alison always enjoyed pike en doucette, so her brows drew together. "I tell you to stay. *I* see the steam and *I* know 'tis fresh. Serve me a portion. You may take his portion away and feed it to the pigs."

Miles's teeth flashed in a smile. "There, my sweet. I knew you'd see sense." To the server, who was trying to put a serving on Alison's platter, Miles turned with a frown. "Varlet! Will you ignore your mistress? From her own lips she has refused this fish. To the pigs with it!"

The server stared from one to the other, but shrugged. Kitchen servants rarely dined on pike en doucette, but he wasn't one to pass up the opportunity. Quickly he returned the dish to the kitchen.

When they were alone, Alison turned on Miles with a scowl. "Are you mad? How can you say that dish was ill-prepared?"

"Not the dish, my poppet, but only the food upon it," he corrected.

Alison glared at him as two more servers entered with a plate of burrabrede and a bowl of hanoney. Miles allowed the men to spoon up a generous square of the gingery shortbread and a dollop of the onion-and-parsley omelet. She was still smarting over the pike dish, but she was hungry. Dipping her smallest finger into the salt cellar, she sprinkled salt over the hanoney.

Miles returned her frown with a smile and tasted the omelet. "Burned!" he roared.

Alison jumped and stared at him.

"This food is burned to a crisp!" he accused the puzzled servers. "Dare you beleaguer my lady wife with such fare? A pox on you!"

"Pray restrain yourself," Alison ground out between clenched teeth. "The hononey is perfectly prepared!" She could scarcely believe he was finding fault with the first decent meal he had been served that day. Perhaps his taste really did run to oversalted and burned food!

"I say it is not! You, knave! Take it away!" He shoved the plates toward the man. "Away with it!"

"Nay!" Alison exclaimed, striking her palm on the tabletop. "I say it stays!"

Miles whistled shrilly and the two huge lurchers in the doorway pricked their ears. He grabbed the plate away from her and put them both on the floor, where the dogs fell over themselves to wolf down the feast. Alison made a strangled sound of pure anger.

"No need to thank me, my pet." His scowl sent the servers scrambling out.

"You have fed our meal to the hounds!" she cried out in rage. "Are you daft?"

"Such sweet words, my dove. I swear you must love me already." He tried to hide the laughter in his eyes. A few more days of this and she would be conquered. He sought not to break her fiery spirit, but only to soften it.

"I'm not your anything, and I demand you address me by my name if you must speak to me at all!"

"Of course, my duckling. As you wish. My lady's whisper is but my command."

Alison tossed her head and swept regally from the room. If he was going to behave in an insane manner, he could do so alone. Miles watched her stamp out of the room, then turned to the servers, who flinched under his gaze.

"Well done, my men. Here's a farthing for you both." The first server was entering cautiously with the next course, a bowl of fruit. Miles gave him a brass coin as well and took the bowl. Whistling "Thrice Toss These Oaken Ashes," he carried the bowl with him out of the parlor.

Alison had walked at a rapid pace all the way to their bedchamber, muttering dire imprecations against her lord husband. Had the king given her to a madman? Not having had access to many books other than religious ones, she had no knowledge of Petruchio's crosswise wooing technique that Miles had so skillfully employed.

Leatrice and the ladies who were already in the antechamber looked at Alison's angry expression in surprise. "Are you finished with supper so soon?" Leatrice asked. "I had thought I would have time to finish this collar lace before you came up."

"He's a madman!" Alison fumed. "He claimed a bird to be a rabbit, called a hot dish cold, and threw our food to the dogs!"

"He didn't!" Leatrice's eyes were round with awe. She had talked at length to Sir Trahern, who had had nothing but good to say about the master.

"He did! Help me undress. I'm going to bed. Mayhap if I'm asleep, he'll let me be."

Leatrice dropped her sewing and obediently followed Alison into the bedchamber. Behind them the ladies bent their heads together to whisper their speculating on the new lord of the castle.

Suddenly the outer door burst open and Miles came striding into the room. The ladies shrieked and scattered like a flock of birds. He grinned broadly. Word of his behavior had obviously spread.

He pushed open the door to his bedchamber and saw Alison clutch her kirtle to her body. Leatrice's mouth was agape. "Leave us, Leatrice," he ordered, tossing her an apple from the silver bowl. "I will unlace my lady wife." His grin broadened at the implied meaning of his words. Already she must be lessening in her anger toward him.

Leatrice caught the apple, curtsied, and after an apologetic glance at Alison, the woman hurried out.

Miles chose an apple and bit into it. Holding it out to Alison, he said, "Will you share a plum with me?" His eyes dared her to correct him.

"There are no plums so late in the year. I will share an apple, however." She reached for one of her own.

"Nay, my lady," he said smoothly, holding the bowl just past her fingers. "I have here a bowl of plums. Have I not?" Again he bit into the apple.

Alison's stomach answered with a growl. With little civility she said, "If it pleases you to call a bird a rabbit or an apple a plum, I care not. I will have a plum then."

Miles looked surprised. "A plum? So late in the year? I fear I have only apples." He frowned into the bowl and started toward the open widow. "If you would have plums . . ."

"No, no! I see now they are indeed apples!"

He turned back to her. "Apples?"

"Or plums. Be they what you will. May I have one?" She had been busy all day, and her hunger was stronger than her anger at the moment.

Miles grinned as if she had pleased him greatly. He held out the bowl for her to take her choice. She picked the largest apple, on the supposition that she might not get another. Watching him warily, she bit into it.

"There, love," he said in a gentler voice. "Is it so difficult to please me?"

Alison didn't trust herself to speak as she devoured the apple and took another.

"All I ask is that I be master in my own castle." As he spoke, he lowered his lips to the curve of her neck and kissed the pulse he found there.

The warmth from his lips quickly spread through her body much as it had the night before, calling forth a surge of response. As Alison's head rolled back, Miles kissed her shoulders and pulled her against his powerful body. She tried hard to hold on to her anger, but it was dissolving in this newly born passion that threatened to overwhelm her. What was this magic he wielded to make her weak and willing with a single kiss?

Before she gave herself up altogether, she murmured, "In faith you are right, my lord. 'Tis neither plum nor apple."

He chuckled against the curve of her flesh. So soon was she conquered.

"It was a pear." She smiled. Then gave her lips to him before he could gainsay her.

Miles started to correct her, but her lips were dewy and open, and he found he really didn't care one way or another about the name of the fruit. He drew back to look at her for a moment, then engulfing her hand in his, he guided the apple to his mouth and sank his strong white teeth into the tart fruit. When he offered her another bite, she took it, letting him feed her. The act awakened a sensual urging in her.

As she chewed, his hands loosened the bodice of her gown and pushed it aside. He ran the tip of this tongue over the curve of her neck and her bare shoulder, then asked, with his eyes teasing her, "Do you want more apple?"

"I find I have lost my appetite . . . for apples," she replied. Watching the delight in his face, she stepped from her heavy clothing and slowly untied the ribbon that fastened her gossamer chemise.

Miles also lost interest in the apple as he watched in fascination as his nymphet gradually divested herself of the last of her clothing. Glancing at the window, he tossed the apple away and put his hands on the slender columns of her arms. "Your odd behavior puzzles me," he said in a low voice. "At times you're a shrew and at others you're like a virgin, then again you turn temptress. How can you be all these at once?"

She smiled provocatively. "I'm a woman, my lord."

When Miles drew her to him, Alison felt the luxurious velvet of his doublet against her sensitive nipples, then the teasing roughness of his brocaded jerkin. He kissed her fervently, letting his tongue explore the mysteries of her mouth. She tasted apples on his lips and smelled the sweet fragrance on his breath. "In faith I can see why Eve gave Adam an apple and not a lemon."

He looked down to her smiling face and studied her for a while. "For a bride, you have smiled very seldom," he mused.

She started to pull away, vexed that he would remind her of that. "My bridal status was not of my making."

"Come back, my love. How easily you are dissuaded from gentleness. I have much to teach you."

"Do you think you can turn me into a puppet who will please you and be naught else but a mindless thing to adorn your castle? If so, you are wrong."

"Perhaps that was a lemon you ate after all." He drew her to him, despite her token protest. Gazing deeply into her troubled eyes, he said, "I think your heart and your mind are at grievous odds."

Alison tried to pull away, but Miles held her firmly in his embrace. Again he bent his dark head and kissed her, this time encouraging her response not only with the gentle pressure of his lips but with the sensuous strokes of his hands on the tender skin of her back, hips, and sides. She returned his ardor in kind.

Alison found she wanted him to touch her as he had the night before. To touch her in all the enflaming ways that Charles never had. As if divining her thoughts, Miles lifted her and laid her on the bed. Not taking his eyes from hers, he removed his clothing and lay with her. When their naked bodies touched, Alison murmured with pleasure and her lips tilted upward.

As he stroked the hard bead of her nipple and cupped the fullness of her breast in his palm, Alison sighed and cleared her mind of everything except the delicious things he was doing to her body. When he lowered his head to suckle gently at her breast, her breath caught in her throat and she arched her back to give herself to him. Slowly she wrapped her leg over his and slid her foot down the length of his hard calf.

His lips moved lower, tasting, licking, loving the soft hollow of her waist as his fingers rolled and tugged at her breasts. Alison moved restlessly beneath him.

"Miles?" she whispered.

"Yes?" He didn't stop his exploration of her luscious body.

"Last night. The thing that happened. Does it . . . does it happen often?"

He raised his head to look at her. "Making love, you mean?"

"No, no. That . . . that whatever . . . that happened between us. I felt as if I were exploding and being created, all at once!"

"You mean you had never . . ."

"Oh, I don't know how to say it." She blushed and ran her fingers through his thick black hair. "I don't know the words to explain."

His hand stroked lower and his expert fingers touched the turgid button of her womanhood. "Do you mean this?"

"Yes! Oh, yes," she sighed as tremors of expectant pleasure sang through her.

Miles was surprised, almost shocked, by her question. Had her husband been interested only in his own pleasure, to the exclusion of hers? "With us it will always be that way. I promise it."

He shifted his weight and deftly entered her, and Alison moaned with the delight of having him fill her. Slowly he began to move within her, drawing her to heights even greater than the night before. When she writhed with eagerness for even more pleasure, he slipped his hand between them, and at his intimate touch she cried out in fulfillment that seemed to pulse through her forever, before finally subsiding to a gentle warmth that enveloped her being.

Lazily Alison opened her eyes and looked at him. Miles touched the corners of her smiling lips and he, too, smiled. Again he started moving, drawing her back into the eddy of desire. Alison followed gladly, matching cadence with him. The tempo of their glistening bodies increased to bring forth the greatest delight. Suddenly the light within her blazed brighter, and she felt an answering response in Miles. Their movements became more intense, more urgent. All at once the incredible flowering blossomed within her, and she cried out in ecstasy. At her release Miles found his own, and together their souls merged and danced in love.

6

Alison waiting until she was sure all the servants had left the cavernous main kitchen before she slipped inside. Normally full of jostling, chattering servants at this early hour, the room was eerily silent. At the far end, two enormous fireplaces, separated by a double row of brick ovens, had recently been stoked for preparation of the morning's meal. Running down the center of the room were flour-dusted tables, scarred from years of work and the readying of thousands of culinary repasts. Alison walked briskly across to the pantry, because she knew the servants would soon return from chapel. At Miles's insistence, the household staff was required to attend chapel three mornings each week, where the chaplain conducted a brief but edifying Protestant service. Miles hoped that more exposure to the new religious order would help ensure the conversion of those who might still be reluctant. Sir Edmund had been put in charge of seeing to it that the order was obeyed.

Taking one of the baskets she normally used to carry food to the anchoress, Alison moved quickly about the pantry. She gathered a number of apples and pears, then cut a thick wedge of cheese and wrapped it in a white cloth. Next she chose a loaf of white bread, but after brief consideration exchanged it for a loaf of the heavier barley bread that Damion had said he preferred. To that she added a large slice of ham and a double handful of shelled walnuts. After topping it off with one of the cook's warden pies, she covered the basket with a large linen towel. In the month since her marriage, Alison had become proficient in slipping food to her brother, but nonetheless she worried that Miles might notice her absence, or worse yet, discover Damion's presence.

Her movements were hurried as she again crossed the kitchen and went down the short flight of steps to the buttery, which was half below ground. During the day, light from the large windows at the top of the walls illuminated the huge room, but at this hour the oil torch near the door was the only source of light. Alison removed the torch from the wall bracket and padded across the tightly wedged flagstone floor. Beneath the stones was dirt which soaked up the occasional spills that occurred as the enormous barrels were moved about. Rows of casks mounded in the flickering light.

Alison paused by the charneco casks, for she knew Damion's preference for the heavy wine, then recalled that the last time she had carried it to him, he had upbraided her for tempting him with luxury. Of late she had found Damion to be quite moody. Hoping to please him this time, Alison stepped to the other side of the room and drew a pitcher of sturdy ale from the servants' barrel.

She replaced the torch where she had found it, and hurried out of the buttery by way of the kitchen instead of taking the stairway that led directly to the solar and gallery. She had taken more time than usual and was afraid someone might see her. Although she would not have to explain why she was fetching such a repast, gossip ran rampant in the castle, and word of her peculiar activity would surely find its way back to Miles.

As she stepped into the walkway that led behind the

hall, she heard the servants returning from the chapel. Walking faster, she stepped into a shadowy alcove and put her ear to the door. Hearing no movement inside, she eased the heavy door open and peeped in. The chaplain's vestments were hanging on pegs set in the opposite wall and the prayer books were stacked neatly on their shelves. The chaplain and altar boys were nowhere in sight. Alison entered the small chamber and closed the door behind her. Through a crack in the door to the chapel, she could see the translucent green glass of Wyndfell's chapel lightening with the approach of dawn. It was later than she had thought.

Unhesitatingly she hurried through the deserted chapel to the paneled wall behind the pulpit and pressed the hidden latch. When the panel moved slightly, she pushed it open with a practiced hand. Since Damion's arrival, she had become quite adept at operating the hidden doors.

Putting the food and ale on the narrow steps inside the wall, she went back to the vestment room for a handful of candles from the pierced tin box. With sparing use Damion could make these last almost another month.

Alison grimaced as she scurried back to the hidden stairway, lit one of the candles, then secured the panel in place. This was all a great deal of trouble, and she wished that Damion had found some other place to hide. He showed no signs of leaving of his own accord, and although she had tried to think of a safer place for him, nothing had come to her. Yet she knew she couldn't hide him forever, for eventually she would be caught. He had even started meeting Roger in the woods after dark. Alison had no idea what transpired during these meetings, but she was afraid they were far more revolutionary than spiritual in nature.

Thrusting the other candles in her sleeve, Alison again lifted the basket of food and pitcher of ale. The hidden passageway had been cleared of most of the annoying spiderwebs by her earlier treks, but the centuries-old mustiness remained. She held her breath as she passed the panel to the hall and prayed she wouldn't sneeze.

When she reached the tiny landing where Damion had asked her to leave his food, Alison put down the load and took the candles from her sleeve as she gazed upward toward Damion's entrance. The changes in Damion were unsettling. Now, for instance, she had the uncanny sensation that he was very nearby, watching her in silence.

"Damion?" she whispered, thrusting her candle upward to light more of the stairway's recesses. The sound left her lips and died in the dust on the steps. She heard no reply, yet uneasiness assailed her as she hastily retreated down the steps to her chamber.

She looked back at the landing. The food, drink, and candles seemed eerily out of place, and she still had the sensation of being watched. "Damion? Are you there?" she whispered again. When only silence met her ears, she snuffed out the candle and cautiously let herself into her chamber.

When she noticed that Miles was not still in bed, a wave of fear washed over her. She had to get out of the bedchamber before he came back. No doubt he had gone down for breakfast and would wonder where she was. She shook the dust from the hem of her mulberry gown and spread the material carefully over the cream skirt of her kirtle before dusting her black velvet day shoes. Suddenly the door to the antechamber opened and Miles came in. Alison straightened guiltily.

"Where have you been? When I awoke, you were gone, and I became concerned."

"I had duties to attend to," she said vaguely.

"How did you come into the room? I just left here and didn't pass you in the corridor."

"Did you not know I have the magic of fairies and may appear at will?" she said lightly in hopes of diverting him from questioning her further. She rose on her toes and kissed him fully on the lips, fighting hard to still the nervousness she felt.

Miles pulled back and curiously eyed her for a moment before saying, "I have good news. Guess who is at our gate at this very moment!"

"The king?" she guessed teasingly. "St. George?" In the past month she had declared an uneasy truce with him, but one with odd rules. At times it seemed to please him to say things were the opposite of the way they were. When he did this, she found that if she argued for a while, and then pretended to agree with him, he was quite happy. This seemed strange to her, but as he showed no other signs of madness, she assumed this play with words to be some sort of pastime he had learned at court. She wasn't sure whether this was yet another game.

"A band of musicians. They were journeying from York to Manchester and lost their way. In return for a night's lodging, they will entertain us at supper."

From his tone she concluded that this time he was being serious. "How marvelous!" Excitement sparkled in her golden-brown eyes, and she clasped her hands together. "How many are there?"

"Five in all. An entire concert, in that they play the lute, cittern, shawm, treble viol, and viola da gamba. I doubt not that they are good, for they say they have played at court."

"Wonderful! I'll order Grace to serve our supper in the hall rather than the winter parlor."

When Miles saw how happy Alison looked at just the mention of this diversion, he felt a little guilty that he had not already offered to take her to court, where such events occurred daily. When Alison was pleased, she seemed to glow. Yet he seldom saw that glow except at night when they were loving the hours away. "No need to tell the cook. I already have." Miles smiled pleasantly at her.

"You did? But she is under my rule." As Alison

studied him, she wondered if his smile was covering a smirk.

"I couldn't find you, so I did it instead."

Alison's smile disappeared. Miles was taking over Wyndfell stone by stone. Giving orders to the household staff was the wife's prerogative, and she wasn't going to give that up. "You had no right to do that. Now she will be confused. She won't know whose orders to follow."

"It's a good thing I did go to the kitchens. I found her preparing lemonwhyt, and I had her change it to St. John's rice instead."

"Why did you do that?"

"Rice is rice. What does it matter if it be flavored with lemon or with carob?"

"If it matters not, why did you change it?"

"I detest lemonwhyt."

"Well, I care naught for carob!"

Miles stepped closer and scowled down at her. She was truly vexing, and he couldn't understand her at all. "Test me not, my lady, or I'll ban lemonwhyt from Wyndfell's kitchens forever!"

"Try it, my lord!"

He sighed. There was no way to understand a woman. "Will you listen to the musicians or not?"

"Of course," she replied haughtily. "Would you assume I have no sensibility at all?"

He made a rumbling sound in his chest and turned away. Alison wondered why he got so angry over so small a matter. Yet she couldn't hand him all her power or he would never respect her. From childhood she had been taught to run a castle, and her mother had been most adamant that she never let her husband find her rule lax or lacking in any respect. Charles would never have considered stepping one foot into the kitchen, but Miles not only went in, but also found the cook and gave orders for a meal! Men were most perplexing.

The evening meal was served on time and with both

lemonwhyt and St. John's rice as a compromising measure. The band of musicians, having eaten earlier, played throughout the meal. After the tables were cleared, Alison and Miles, along with their attendants, sat back to enjoy an evening's entertainment.

The man who played the lute also had an unusually mellow voice, and at Miles's request he sang one of Miles's favorites, "Thrice Toss These Oaken Ashes." As Miles listened to the words, he let his eyes seek out Alison. The song reminded him of his own situation with Alison, as it told of a man who tried to cast a love spell upon his lady fair, but she broke each charm with a glance from her eyes. Alison was passionate in his bed, but he had yet to suspect she loved him. She seemed to don heart's armor with her kirtle and gown.

In the next song, the line "Cold love is like to words written on sand" stuck in his mind. Was she so cool in her affections that he would never be more steady in her heart than this? His concern surprised him, for he had not realized that he was in truth beginning to love her.

As he watched, Alison sat in rapt attention, her heart-shaped face lovely in the candlelight. Her intelligent eyes followed the musicians' deft movements on the strings as her foot tapped along with the rhythm. Here, so far from London or even York, she had probably never heard these new songs. Did she see herself in the role of cold lover, or was she entranced by the haunting melodies? Miles had no idea. She was an eternal mystery to him. He had conquered her with perverseness, yet at times her temper still flared. Lately he was starting to wonder if he had taken the wrong tack all together in wooing and winning her.

Alison felt Miles's eyes upon her, and she glanced at him. Their eyes met and held and she felt the warm tugging sensation he so often triggered within her. Merely gazing into his blue eyes sent her senses reeling. Would he ever love her? she wondered. Would he ever feel as if he might die for her love as the song implied? She couldn't imagine him ever being so vulnerable. Sadly she turned back to the musicians.

When she looked away from him, Miles frowned. Was this his answer? Could he not hold her regard even for the length of a song? He recalled some of the ladies he had known at court who had been his for the taking. Had he married one of them, he would never have doubted her love. Yet even with the embellishment of time on his memories of them, those women paled by comparison with Alison. All of them were biddable; none had her fire.

When the musicians finished their concert, Miles rewarded them properly, then stood to dismiss them. They bowed Alison and Miles out of the hall as if Wyndfell were the court and they the sovereign rulers. Alison smiled as she preceded her husband through the door.

The nights were growing cold, as were the unheated corridors, and Miles told himself this was the only reason he put his arm around her and why she pressed her body lightly against his as they walked to their bedchamber. When Alison was ready for bed and had wrapped a loose-fitting chamber gown about her, he dismissed their attendants and closed the world outside their chamber door.

Alison crossed to the window and looked out on the silvered landscape. The full moon hung like a huge pearl in the blue-black sky and a dusting of diamond-like stars was sprinkled beyond the moon's beams. She sat on the broad window seat and drew her knees up beneath her voluminous gown. Behind her she heard Miles undressing. She reached out and touched the new glass pane that kept the cold out and the fire's warmth in. No longer would she almost freeze on winter mornings.

"What are you thinking?" Miles asked as he joined her on the window seat, clad loosely in his white shirt and clinging netherstocks. She rested her head on the stone casement and smiled. "I was being thankful for the glass windows. See how cold it feels? Had you not installed that glass, the entire room would be at least that cold, and I couldn't sit here and enjoy the moon."

Miles gazed at the silver globe. "They say staring at the full moon brings madness."

"I'm not afraid. If it were going to make me mad, it would have happened long before this." She drew a deep breath. "The musicians were indeed wonderful. I adored the tunes and have tried to sing them in my head so I don't forget them. Perhaps I can learn to play them on my lute."

"I know those tunes and I'll help you learn them."

"You have a memory for music? I had no idea."

"Did you think I spent all my time at the tilt yard? I have a few accomplishments, I wager."

Alison studied him curiously. She had never heard him speak of his life at court, and she knew almost nothing about it. "Have you spoken with the king himself?"

"Many times." He laughed. "The king is accessible to every lord and lady at court."

"I heard he surrounds himself with guardsmen armed with pikes."

"Only when he mixes with the common people. At court none would harm him."

"What is he like?" she asked with guarded curiosity.

"He is your father, I am told. Need you ask?"

"I have never been to London, and he has never traveled so far north as Yorkshire. I've yet to meet him."

Miles paused and said, "He's big. That's the first thing one notices. Not only is he tall, but he's broad of shoulder and wide of girth. He wears a beard in the European fashion, and like his hair, it's golden red." Miles smiled. "Of late the hair on his head has thinned, so he always wears a cap or hat."

"Is he very vain then?"

Miles laughed out loud. "He makes a peacock look like a humble wren. He dresses in the finest cloth-of-gold that shimmers like molten lava and weighs as much as armor, velvets and brocades from the East, and embroidery studded with jewels and bright with diamonds. I saw him once dressed in white from head to foot, in damask studded with rubies and diamonds to bedazzle the eye." He brushed Alison's thick auburn hair back from her face and said, "I have also seen his children."

"What are they like?" she asked hungrily.

"Prince Edward is a sickly child, given to quacks and poses year around."

"The princesses? Are they beautiful?"

"They are now merely royal children, having both been declared illegitimate, but no, they are not beautiful. Lady Mary is so religious she is ever starving in a fast and looking dolorous. Lady Elizabeth has plainer features, but appears more attractive because of her clear wit. She has a man's mind in a maid's body, 'tis said. You, however, are far more beautiful than either of them."

Alison glanced up at him as if she were afraid of being baited.

"Queen Catherine is small and plump and pretty in a vacant sort of a way. The courtiers say she is the loveliest of his brides, but I found Anne Boleyn more attractive."

"I had heard she was swarthy and plain."

"Such is the political way to describe her now. In truth she was lovely enough to ensnare the most comely king in the world and wise enough to make herself queen."

Alison pensively considered all of this. For years she had craved knowledge of her father and half-sisters, yet there was no one she could ask for information. Her mother had cried for hours at the mere mention of the subject. "And the ladies of the court? Are they all beauties?"

"Some are, indeed," he told her, "but none had my

heart. When the king told me I was to wed you, I had no woman grieve my loss."

"I never considered you were told you must marry as I was," she exclaimed.

"It was as much a surprise to me as it must have been to you."

This explains Miles's perverse temper, Alison decided. In spite of his words, he might regret his fate.

"My parents lived at court, of course. I grew to manhood at Hampton Court and Whitehall or wherever the king was in residence."

"Not in Wales?"

"No, my mother was a Welsh heiress, but I have seldom seen the castles I own there. They were far from court, and my father had hoped I would become a confidant of the king such as he was. I was surprised to find he was eager for my marriage and removal from court, but now I understand why he changed his mind."

The look in Alison's round eyes prompted him to continue.

"Just before I left, one of the ambassadors displeased the king. It was a little thing such as a foreigner might do. He speaks rough English and our names are difficult for him to recall. During one of the banquets he referred to the queen as 'Queen Anne' —there is a family resemblance between them and anyone might make such a slip. King Henry overheard the remark and became enraged. It was as if he went mad for a while. Never have I ever witnessed such fury! I still find it remarkable that the ambassador wasn't ordered to the Tower!"

"He's as bad as that?"

"He's unpredictable. Sometimes he's the perfect courtier. In his youth no one was a gentler man or so excellent a knight."

"You have given me much to think upon," Alison said, drawing a deep breath. She left the window seat for the comfort of the feather bed.

"Mistake me not, love," Miles went on to say. "I am the king's man, regardless of being able to view him objectively."

"I never thought otherwise," she replied, but for a moment she had dared to hope.

Miles turned back to the pewter-hued hills that mounded behind Wyndfell and flowed down to the darkened village. "This is a night for fairies and love, not for dwelling on somber thoughts."

"The musicians were talented, were they not?" she said with a smile. "Would that we might enjoy music of that degree more often. The musicians here at Wyndfell are poor at best."

"Do you love music so? Then I will hire better musicians to please you."

"You would do that? For me?"

"I'll do even better. Here is a song very popular at court." He sang:

> *Joy, dearest lover, thine shall be*
> *And I shall lead thee tenderly*
> *Where hope would have thee seek thy pleasure;*
> *Alive I shall not part from thee,*
> *And still when death has come to me*
> *My soul its memories shall treasure.*

"I never knew you could sing!" she exclaimed. "This is indeed an evening of discovery. In truth you have a more pleasing voice than the musician!"

"I thank you, my lady," he said with a bow. "But unlike the musician's lyrical repetition, my words were sincere."

Alison's eyes widened in surprise. He stood and held out his hand to her as if he had no need to explain himself. This husband of hers was so confusing, and yet so tantalizing. She knew now he was no barbarian, and yet he was no flattering courtier either. Most of the time she knew not what to make of him.

Joining her on the wide bed, Miles leaned on one

elbow to study her. "At court there is a new style of sleeping in a garment called a nightgown. It's considered very fashionable."

"How could anyone be comfortable sleeping in clothing?"

"The gown fits loosely, rather like your chamber robe."

"I can't imagine sleeping in a sack. I'd feel like a trussed chicken," Alison said as she shrugged out of the chamber wrap and snuggled her naked body under the sheets.

Miles chuckled. "Your lack of interest in nightgowns is very commendable. In truth, if you were to want one, I'd try to dissuade you."

"On the other hand," she said with teasing smile, "it would keep me warm. This may be the very thing I need."

"I should never have told you. Put the nightgown out of your mind."

"I'll get cold!" she pretended to protest.

"Not in my bed, you won't."

"You seem overly sure of yourself," she teased.

He bent and covered her lips with his, drawing her soul to meet and entwine with his. Alison's kisses went to his head like strong wine and her luscious body delighted him. Miles let his hand stray over the valley of her waist and ran his thumb across the swelling mound of her breast. When he touched her taut nipple she murmured with pleasure and he rubbed it provocatively between his thumb and forefinger. Alison shifted to offer him easier access to her delights, and he warmed to her. She was so responsive to his loving, surely she must care for him! But she never professed to love him, so he dared not tell her of his own growing love. She was a strong woman and hard enough to rule as it was. If she knew of his love for her, she might feel she had power over him and would become impossible.

Slipping out of his clothes, Miles joined her beneath

the bedcovers, and his hands resumed their tantalizing roving over her willing flesh. Alison felt the sensuous surge that his touch always triggered, and as he nuzzled the hollow of her throat, making the tiny hairs on the back of her neck stand on end, she struggled to prevent herself from blurting vows of love. Miles was too powerful as it was! If he knew how much she loved him, he might become overbearing. She dared not show him any degree of weakness. Yet when he caressed her like this and murmured those endearing words in her ear, her heart was all his, as were her mind and body.

She breathed deeply, trying to steady herself, but as her nostrils filled with his uniquely masculine scent, she lost more ground. Instinctively, she ran her hand over the stout muscles of his shoulders and back and rested them on the firm flesh of his buttocks. He was a powerful man, every inch a warrior. His muscles had the solidity of a skilled athlete's which she preferred over the aesthetic lines of a scholar. This thought didn't bring so much as a twinge of guilt or regret for Charles. Every day more of her love was for Miles and for Miles alone. Aching from her need for him, she pulled him closer and felt the urgency of his body against her leg.

His hand caressed lower, beneath the nest of curls between her thighs, and when he began to stroke her bud of femininity, fires of passion burst into flame throughout her. His lips brushed her nipple again, then returned to sear her lips with kisses that stirred her very soul. She wanted him and loved him, and when he caressed her like this, her need for him was undeniable.

When he finally joined with her, Alison's love expanded into a brilliance that encompassed her, and her physical pleasure was intense. She kneaded the firm flesh of his buttocks and matched her movements to his, as she felt his desire sear her like a white-hot flame. Although she tried to hold back to savor the growing pleasure, her soul whirled in ecstasy and her passion found its peak in waves of fulfillment.

As Alison's awareness of the world about her slowly returned, Miles began to move within her again. Once more the fires ignited, blazing more brightly than before. Alison cried out as passion again overtook her and together they reached their completion. Tightly they held each other, washed in the climax of their loving. Love words hovered on her lips and burned to be spoken, but she was too afraid. She didn't know the repressed love was mirrored as clearly in her eyes as it was in his.

7

After a night in Miles's arms, Alison felt as if she owned the world. She recalled how he had sung her the love song and had promised to hire more competent minstrels for Wyndfell. She was fairly certain he was beginning to care for her. As her needle plied the silken thread into the tapestry in her lap, her mind was busy with ways to please him. For a start, she decided, she could play the perplexing word game he learned in London and seemed to enjoy so.

When he entered the chamber and again bade her good morning, she smiled and said, "Morning? Nay, 'tis evening, my lord."

He looked at her as if he had not heard her plainly and said, "Why, 'tis full morning, and a beautiful one at that."

"In spite of the rain? I swear I hear the rumble of thunder."

"Then there must be a storm in your head," he laughed, "for the day is fair."

"Hark, is that an owl?"

"I heard nothing."

"Mayhap 'twas a nightingale," she said placidly. This game wasn't so very difficult, although she still failed to see its purpose. But if it pleased him, she would be willing to continue it awhile longer.

"A nightingale? In winter? Are you feeling well?" He came to her and touched her cheek. "You're not feverish."

"A fever? Of course not, my lord."

"At times the sweating sickness begins with delusion. Are you certain you feel well? I've heard no rumors of plague about."

"As I say, I feel as healthy as always." She held up the end of the tapestry. "What think you of my new headgear? Will it not make a fetching bongrace?"

His head tilted to one side as he skeptically watched her. That cloth was surely for a tapestry, and a large one at that. "Where are your ladies and Mistress Leatrice?"

"I sent the ladies away so I could be alone with my thoughts," she said, dropping the game. "Last night was so lovely I wanted to relive it in my mind."

Disappointment swept over Miles. He had concluded that she was speaking in opposites, and thus she had just indicated that she hadn't enjoyed the night before. He certainly had. "What was wrong with last night?" he asked defensively.

"Why, nothing at all. It was a perfect night. Especially the ending of it."

What was that supposed to mean? No woman had ever complained of his loving before! "I suppose you have had better with which to compare it?" he said in a jealous voice.

"Indeed I have not."

He was keenly aware that her marriage to Lord Charles Wakefield had been a love match, although he tried not to think about it. How dare she taunt him like this! He had rarely been so confused in all his life. "That cloth you're sewing—is it a bongrace?"

She laughed and said, "Certainly not. It is a tapestry for your closet. Do you like the design?"

He picked it up by one corner. She had sketched the Wakefield unicorn and the Garrett griffin in mock battle. " 'Tis appropriate."

"I hope you don't mind my use of the unicorn. I've spent so much of my life here at Wyndfell. Charles's parents nurtured me from my betrothal at twelve years, and I have associated myself with the Wakefields for so long. Do you object? I patterned it after the two unicorns painted on the solar wall."

"It's well done." She was no longer speaking in opposites, but when had she stopped? Which of her words had she truly meant? Hoping to guide their conversation to safer ground, Miles said, "Speaking of the solar, I wish to add to Wyndfell. The solar and gallery are on the north side of the castle, and in winter they are difficult to heat. Already I can tell that, and we have yet to see the first snow."

"That is true. Winters are hard here, and there is no glass in the windows of either room. Perhaps we could order some from London?"

"I have a more ambitious project in mind." He led her to the window and pointed toward the formal gardens. "I have thought to enlarge the castle. See how the back wall ends so abruptly? If we add a turret there and another over there behind the chapel wall, we can fill in the span with a new gallery and a new ladies' parlor, with more storage chambers below and bedchambers above. What do you think?"

"Why, Miles, it would be perfect! I never considered adding onto the castle. I have always accepted it just as it is."

"We will have glass in all the new windows, clear glass, or colored, but not those dark, thick panes that scarcely let in the light. And there will be fireplaces in the main rooms. Will that please you?"

"Yes, that pleases me very well," she said, beaming up at him.

As he was making progress, he continued, "I have always yearned to build, but never had the opportunity while living at court. And there was no reason to expand my castles in Wales, as I rarely was in residence there."

"Then you expect to remain here at Wyndfell?" She wasn't sure when it had happened, but she had changed her mind about wanting him to leave.

"Most of the year, I suspect. Part of the time I will likely spend in London." He turned to look out the window again as the activity below drew his attention.

"Oh," she said, trying not to let her disappointment show.

"Naturally you will go with me. King Henry told me I should bring you along." In the yard below, a stable-boy seemed to be arguing with Sir Edmund, and Miles made a mental note to inquire about the incident.

Under different circumstances, she would have been excited at the prospect of going to the royal court, and honored by the ruling monarch's insistence that she come, but trepidation was the only emotion she felt. For her father to ignore her in Yorkshire was one matter, but if he did so at court, she would be mortified. And if he didn't continue to deny her parentage, what would she say to him after all these years: "Good day, your grace—'tis lovely to be your daughter . . . at last?"

As Miles turned his attention back into the room, he added, "That will be a perfect time for you to give the king your pledge."

"What pledge?" she exclaimed.

"The pledge of fealty, of course. Surely you must know he is asking it of all his subjects, especially the ones here in the northlands, and of those who were Catholics in particular."

"Will he ask this pledge of a woman? What is in it?"

"All the king's subjects must pledge loyalty to the king and acknowledge him as head of the church."

Alison paled. "I cannot do that!"

"You must. Everyone must."

"Not I!"

"Especially you, since your first husband was not only a staunch Catholic but also a convicted rebel."

"Charles was a scholar who knew not what he did.

He saw his activity as heroic and his death as martyrdom, not an execution for treason."

"Nevertheless, the king saw it as treason. Of late he has been adamant that all his subjects pledge their loyalty to the crown, even on pain of death, if necessary."

Death, Alison thought as she recalled the secret Mass she and a few others had heard in the predawn hours several mornings before. How could she acknowledge the king as head of the church when she knew that title was indisputably the pope's?

"Behind the new wing, we could plant roses," Miles said as if the matter of the oath were settled. "I have a white rose at Llanduff Castle and an unusual double one at Penshire. Wait until you see it. The petals are almost as numerous as those of a gillyflower. In summer their blooms will sweeten the air."

Alison was only half-listening. If Damion's presence at Wyndfell were to become known to the king, she would be considered a traitor for harboring him. So would Miles! She knew she could never convince Damion to swap his clerical robe for secular clothing and pretend, if he were discovered, that he had denounced his Cistercian vows. But she must somehow convince Damion and Roger to cease their treacherous activities. Her face was ashen with worry. She had to find Roger and see if he knew of this pledge and to confide her fears in him. She looked at the strong man by her side and wished she could tell him her concerns, but Miles was the king's man, by his own statement, and to confide in him would be foolhardy.

As soon as she could, Alison sent word for Roger to meet her in the oak woods that separated their lands. At the appointed time, she rode out and dismounted at the gnarled tree where they had met during their days of courtship, but Roger was not yet there. Alison immediately began to pace. If she didn't return to Wyndfell soon, her absence would be noted and she had no excuse for being away.

When Roger rode into sight, Alison viewed him with dispassionate eyes. Had she really considered marrying him? By comparison with Miles, he was lacking in every quarter. "I was afraid you weren't coming, my lord."

"Forgive me, Lady Alison. A matter came up that required my immediate attention. Why have you sent for me?"

"Have you heard of the oath of fealty the king is demanding?"

"Yes, but I thought little of it. I gave my pledge to the mayor of York when I was there last. What of it?"

"How could you give your word to acknowledge the king in the pope's stead!"

"They are but words," he replied with a shrug. "They don't affect the feeling in my heart or what I know to be true."

"I couldn't forswear myself," she objected, "not over so grave an issue. And I confess that I'm amazed at you."

"You will likely never be faced with the decision. Now that you're married to one of the king's men you are likely exempt and certainly less suspect of any wrongdoing. That's why it's a good idea for Brother Damion to hide at Wyndfell."

"But he can't stay there forever! I marvel that he has not yet been discovered. That's why I asked you to meet me here. You must help me convince Damion that he must leave."

"Nonsense. Where else would he be safer? I'm known to have been Catholic, and my castle has no maze of secret passageways. He would have to leave the area entirely."

"I also think you should quit meeting Damion here in the forest for Mass. 'Tis too dangerous. Every moment he is out of hiding increases the risk he'll be seen by someone loyal to the king."

"Where else could we meet? You say Wyndfell is unsafe now that Lord Garrett is there."

"Mayhap Damion should come to your castle in secret and live in the unused portion. He would be no more likely to be found there than he would be in mine."

"No, it's not safe," Roger insisted stubbornly. "Besides, he is your brother and you owe him sanctuary."

"But with Miles and all his men and Sir Edmund, Damion is certain to be discovered eventually! Your staff are all Catholic and you can trust them to keep his presence a secret."

"I think you overestimate the risk of discovery. I've talked to Sir Edmund and find him a pleasant sort of fellow."

"That has nothing to do with his loyalty, or lack of it. I say we mustn't trust him."

"As for your lord husband, he's easy enough to dupe. I doubt he has even a suspicion of the secret passageway."

"Lord Miles has a quick mind. He could become suspicious without having stumbled upon the passage."

"Perhaps if I speak to him, see how his mind—"

"No! You keep away from him. Miles is much too clever to be fooled by your probing and testing."

"How quickly you defend him. I see you've already begun to love this Welshman."

"His mother was Welsh. Miles is as English as we are," she said defensively. She didn't want anyone to know of the traitorous love she felt for Miles, since she had sworn to so many that she would never care for him. For that matter, she was not certain of her own feelings. Surely this emotional gamut wasn't love, for it had none of the serenity of her feelings for Charles.

Roger smiled, his thin lips narrowly drawn. "I dare admit my jealousy. If matters were as we had planned, you would be my firm supporter instead of defending this man who is from the king."

"But things are not as we planned and I owe a degree of loyalty to my husband. Therefore, speak not of our former relationship, or I must leave you in anger." She went to her horse and prepared to mount. How strange, she thought, that once she had seen Miles she ceased to wish she was given to Roger. In truth her emotions were enough to perplex a sage.

"If I befriend Lord Garrett, I will have a reason to visit Wyndfell," Roger said as he held her horse while she swung onto its back. "That will make it easier for me to see Brother Damion without arousing suspicion."

"No, it will not. For if Miles comes upon you in the castle unannounced or if you linger about after you were assumed to have departed, he will ask the same questions whether you are his friend or not. No, it's best to stay away from Wyndfell." She turned her horse and waved before urging the animal into a canter.

Already the angle of the sun told her she had been gone too long. Leatrice would be searching for her because this was the day they always went to market and the goods were frequently sold out by noon. Alison let her horse run faster over the smooth green to Wyndfell. She should never have met Roger today, but she was fearful that he would inadvertently give away their secret.

Leatrice was waiting for her in the hall, talking in a low voice to Sir Trahern. At Alison's arrival, they stepped apart, but Alison was sure they had been holding hands. Was there a budding romance here? She decided to ask Leatrice, once they were alone.

"My lady, I've looked everywhere for you," Leatrice said quickly. "Today is market day, you know."

"Yes, I remember. Are you ready to go down to the village?"

"I'm ready. Sir Trahern will be accompanying us, by your leave."

As the handsome knight bowed to her, Alison frowned. More than just the purchasing of food occurred in the market square, and having Trahern along would complicate things. She would have to dissuade him. "That's not necessary. Walt always fetches our purchases."

"But my lord has ordered it," Trahern replied. "In London, ladies never venture out into the streets without protection."

"This isn't London, Sir Trahern. I assure you we are perfectly safe in our village."

When Trahern smiled at Leatrice, she blushed furiously. "I would consider it an honor to accompany you. Besides, I was ordered by Lord Garrett."

Alison hid her impatience. To refuse him would cause suspicion. Perhaps he would be so busy courting Leatrice that he would overlook what Alison might be doing, other than looking through the wares for sale. "Very well, Sir Trahern. Come along."

They rode down the slope to the village. As always on market day, there were more women out than usual. The market was held on the village green, where the May Day festivities, the twice-yearly fair, and the other village celebrations took place during the year. Although Wyndfell's village was small, it was the largest in the parish, so the market was well-stocked with vegetables, nuts, poultry of all kinds, white meats such as cheese rounds and butter, and even a cow its owner hoped to sell so he wouldn't have to feed it through the winter. The weekly bargaining had begun hours before with the customary sounding of the guild-hall bell, and already many of the booths were nearly empty of goods.

"I had not expected so large a market," Trahern said as Alison inspected a hen.

"Two women and a goose can make up a market, they say," Leatrice told him. "We certainly have more to offer than that." She looked up at him coquettishly and smiled. He returned her affectionate gaze with obvious pleasure.

Alison made no effort to join their banter, for her mind was on the other business that might transpire at any given moment. As she nodded for the woman to cage the hens she had chosen, her eyes nervously searched the throng. Because the king was now closing the Catholic retreats here in the northlands, the holy people were being driven out onto the roadways to starve or beg. Most chose to return to their families, but many needed food and shelter on what were sometimes long journeys in a quest for sanctuary. Because of the cover of the crowds, this had become a rendezvous point between Alison and those displaced nuns and priests who sought her help. Before her marriage to Miles, she had frequently offered them a night's stay at Wyndfell.

Alison held her red cape about her against the wind as she glanced at Trahern, and wished she had taken the time to exchange it for another. Word had been spread to the displaced Catholics to look for a highborn lady in a red cape. Even though she and Leatrice were obviously the only highborn women there, without the red cape for positive identification, no contact would be attempted. She hoped no one would be in search of a meal and lodging today. But to be a bit safer, she quickened her step to put more distance between her companions and herself.

Still wary, Alison continued to browse. Because this was a market and not a fair, all the goods were displayed in booths or on the backs of unhitched wagons. No one was allowed to peddle his wares from carts or baskets. By tradition the fish booth was between the river and the sweetmeat booth. Next came the poultry, and so on, to the boys who had gathered walnuts to sell and the girls who sold freshly baked buns.

As most of Wyndfell's food was grown or made within the castle grounds, Alison's trips to the market were primarily intended as gestures of goodwill. She frequently paid more than was asked for the goods by the sellers, and because of her generosity, the village folk called her "Alison the Good." Charles had never been particularly concerned whether the commoners liked him or not, but Alison genuinely cared for her people. Naturally she could never become intimate with one of a lower station, but she was interested in hearing the fishwife's tales of her new baby and learning that the baker's wife's injured arm was satisfactorily healing.

Just when Alison had concluded that no subversive contact would be made that day, she saw an unfamiliar woman coming toward her, with eyes lowered and hands concealed in the loose sleeves of her homespun garment. Alison's heart sank, for this woman was certainly a displaced nun. Though she had doffed her habit for ordinary peasant's clothing, her pious bearing was all too evident. Behind her stood two other women similarly garbed, whose heads were covered with an outdated style of hood and whose hands were likewise hidden from sight.

Alison turned away, for Trahern was within earshot. Exchanging a pleading look with Leatrice, Alison nodded toward the women. Leatrice followed the nod, then smoothly drew Trahern's attention to a cage of rabbits several yards away, as the nun wove her way toward Alison.

"My lady?" the stranger said, touching Alison's sleeve. "My . . . sisters . . . and I have found some lost sheep. Mayhap they belong to you?"

Alison gave an almost imperceptible shake of her head and glanced at Trahern's nearby back. "There is a wolf stalking the sheep at Wyndfell. We have no stray ones there. Perhaps you should inquire at Bainbridge Castle over yon rise. Lord Roger Bainbridge also keeps sheep."

The woman paled and nodded. "I understand. My sisters and I thank you."

Alison nodded and the woman moved silently away as Trahern turned back to her. "These are fine coneys. Should I pay her and have Walt pick them up?"

"Yes. I fancy a course of visorye." She watched Trahern count out some coins and give them to the woman. "When Walt comes down he will take them to the castle." The woman slipped the coins into a pocket of her kirtle and moved the cage of rabbits aside.

"I tire of marketing," Alison said. "Will you finish for me, Leatrice? I'm sure Sir Trahern will gladly escort you."

Trahern looked slightly perturbed. He had been told to stay with both women and had not expected them to separate.

"Yes, my lady," Leatrice agreed. "We will return shortly."

Alison went back to where the horses were tied and led her mare to the mounting block. No doubt Leatrice would welcome the opportunity to walk alone with the comely knight. The lack of privacy in a castle made courting very difficult.

Miles had finished the day's accounts presented to him by Edmund. Wyndfell castle was like a small village unto itself, with wages and income that had to be reckoned daily, as well as the accounting of produce and supplies. All his life Miles had had no greater duty than to train an occasional fledgling knight at jousting, yet he found he enjoyed the complex challenge of running the castle. For the first time he appreciated the enormous job of the royal stewards who had responsibility for command of the populous court. Wyndfell's books must be simple by comparison to those of Hampton Court or Whitehall.

As he closed the door to his closet, Miles saw Edmund approaching. "What now, Sir Edmund? I thought we had finished."

"We have, my lord. I have come to announce the arrival of Lord Roger Bainbridge. He's in the winter parlor."

"Very well, Sir Edmund. Thank you." Miles strode briskly through the wide corridor toward the hall and parlor, looking about appreciatively. Already he felt great pride of ownership, and hoped Alison was happy too. He was glad he was so fortunate to have been given her, and not for the first time he wondered if he would have settled in so quickly if his wife had been a woman he liked less well. Certainly he could have done much worse in every way. Mulling over what he might do that would please her, he decided on a joust. All ladies loved jousts and tourneys. Furthermore, he excelled at the sport, and he wanted to show her his prowess. The following spring would be the perfect time for a meet.

He was deciding whom to invite to the jousting as he entered the parlor where Lord Bainbridge stood gazing at the magnificent stained-glass depiction of St. George. Miles looked at the colored glass proudly. Now, *there* was a man, saint or not, who looked as if he knew his way around a tourney. "Greetings, Lord Bainbridge. What brings you to Wyndfell?"

"I came merely to visit, Lord Garrett. I trust I am not taking you from the day's business?"

"No, no. I just finished. Have a seat."

Roger sat on one of the two chairs. "A lovely window. I've considered installing a similar one at my own castle."

"Oh? I intend to alter Wyndfell as well. Yesterday I finished plans for a new wing with a gallery on the east side."

"Much more sensible, if you ask me. The gallery here has always been cold and drafty. You know that it was originally the great hall but was converted to a gallery some time ago."

"Old Cardinal Wolsey started quite a trend with the one he designed for Hampton Court. It was one of the first in England." Miles privately thought his guest was a bit too familiar in his knowledge of Wyndfell, but doubtless he had visited here many times over the years.

"I believe the change was made here at Wyndfell even before that," Roger said with feigned modesty in his superior knowledge of Wyndfell's history. As an afterthought he added, "The old cardinal was a wise and learned man, even though he was a Catholic."

"Oh? I see not how a man's religion affects his taste or the workings of his brain."

"No?" Again Roger laughed. Edmund had followed Miles into the room and was ostensibly tending the fire. Watching Edmund closely for his reaction, Roger offhandedly stated, "I was once a Catholic myself. You know, he who rules the church rules the man." Edmund didn't respond in the least.

"So I've heard." Miles curiously studied Roger as he wondered why the man was saying this. "No one admits openly to Catholicism these days."

"Nay, nay. You misunderstand me. I said I *was* one."

Edmund's face was thoughtful as he maneuvered a log to the back of the grate. Stalling for more time, he pretended clumsiness at his task.

Roger continued, "No, I have given the king my oath of fealty. I'm loyal to the crown."

"I see." Miles fingered his lower lip as he thought. He was still surprised that Roger had admitted that he was once of the old faith. Even though virtually everyone in England who had professed a religious belief had been Catholic, no one admitted it in London these days. Even to suggest such a thing was risky. "Are there many in this area who still claim to be Catholic?"

"I've heard there are a few, but in time I'm certain they will convert. Until recently, this area was a Catholic stronghold. You know the Pilgrimage of Grace arose near here."

"Yes, I know." Was the man implying that those who still wanted the old ways restored were planning another uprising? Maybe this man was an informant who was reluctant to speak up in front of Sir Edmund. "The fire is fine, Sir Edmund. You may go."

"Yes, my lord," the steward replied smoothly. He left and shut the door. Although he put his ear to the door, he couldn't hear through the thick wood, so he went on his way.

"Lord Bainbridge, do you have information regarding another move against the king?"

"Nay. I've heard nothing." Roger pretended to be offended; then he continued. "But if I do, you'll be the first to know. Such unrest would disrupt the work of our people, and we would suffer a loss." Roger casually strolled to the fire to warm his backside.

Miles detected no duplicity, though he wondered about the man's choice of words. Perhaps he had completely misunderstood the man's intent. He had no cause to suspect him of anything devious. He hardly knew the man. Changing the subject, Miles said, "I'm planning a jousting this spring. Would you like to ride in it?"

"I'd be honored. In all modesty I must admit that I have some talent in that area myself."

Miles's practiced glance took in the man's slender wrists, slouching posture, and languid movements. He had seen pages who showed more promise. Still, one never knew. "I would consider myself fortunate to side against you," Miles said politely.

"Done. Tell me more of your plans." How simple it was to befriend this man, Roger thought. One had only to agree with him. As for jousting with him, Roger had no fears. He had ridden in several local jousts and was considered the most skilled in all the parish.

As Sir Edmund made his way down the corridor, he kept thinking about the parlor. He hadn't expected Roger to announce he had once been Catholic, as no one but a fool pointed that out. If he had been able to stay just a few more minutes, who knew what secrets Roger might have disclosed. Did he think Miles was Catholic? Edmund's eyes narrowed. That would be a plum! King Henry especially liked to ferret out those close to the throne who were heretic, for their bonfires burned hottest and brightest. Perhaps when he made his next report to King Henry he would be able, at last, to enclose some incriminating news.

Edmund was crossing the courtyard when Lady Alison rode in and reined to a clattering stop. She dismounted as Edmund held her horse, and smiled up at him with cool reserve. Was she in this game as well? Lady Alison was a great beauty, and Edmund had been charmed by her since the day he arrived, but since he couldn't hope to so much as touch her cheek, he wanted to implicate her from sheer perverseness.

"My lady, one moment," he said as she started for the steps. "There is a visitor inside."

"Oh?"

"Lord Roger Bainbridge is within the parlor." In a low voice he added, "He and Lord Garrett are discussing religion. Lord Bainbridge has freely admitted to having practiced Catholicism." At her sharp intake of breath, Edmund added daringly, "You had best hurry in before he reveals too much."

Alison stared at him searchingly, but Edmund's face was impassive. Was he with them or against them? Alison just couldn't tell. If he was her enemy, why would he warn her of this; yet if he was to be trusted, why did she always feel this uneasiness about him? "Thank you," she said at length, and hurried up the steps.

"I enjoy riding," Roger said to Miles as they stood in the warm glow of the hearth. "Some of my fondest memories involve rides. When I was courting Lady Alison, we frequently rode the countryside or hunted together."

"What?" Miles asked in surprise. "You courted Lady Alison?" He glanced over to see his wife standing in the doorway, looking as if she'd been turned to stone.

"I thought you knew," Roger said with a twinge of apprehension. "I naturally assumed—"

"We were never betrothed," Alison put in quickly, "Lord Bainbridge was Charles's closest friend. Naturally after his death, Charles expected Lord Bainbridge to look after me."

"Did he indeed ask for your hand?" Miles demanded. "Why was I not told about this?"

"The king denied our request to wed. I thought surely he must have told you."

"My father was the king's confidant, not I," Miles informed her. "I'm amazed you never told me you had wanted to marry another man."

Alison saw the hurt in his eyes and stepped nearer him. "A woman needs a protector. I had no male kin willing to take that position."

"Ours was to be a marriage of convenience," Roger said to smooth over his mistake. "As you know, our estates join and Wyndfell is a much better castle than my own. I have no village at my feet, merely a few poor shops that have attached themselves to my wall." He made a depreciating gesture. "It was not a love match."

Alison frowned. This was news to her. At the time, Roger had sworn undying love. "Why are you here, Lord Bainbridge?" she demanded. "Surely you've not ridden over to tell my lord husband that we were once thinking to wed?"

"No, no. Of course not." Roger placed his fingertips together to make a steeple of his hands. It was one of the Catholics' secret signals. Alison paled at his daring. "I came to forge a friendship."

Alison's brows drew together. She had expressly forbidden this! "In that case I find your revelation in odd taste. What else are you telling my husband?"

Miles looked from one to the other. Alison seemed more angry than he would have expected. After all, he was the one who had reason to be outraged. She had been absent all morning, he recalled, and Roger had just admitted that he used to ride with her before her marriage. Had they been together this morning? Newborn jealousy flared in him, and he had to fight to control it. Surely she wouldn't play him false! Especially not with this popinjay!

"It was merely a slip of the tongue," Roger stammered in the face of her anger. "Naturally I thought he knew."

"Forgive him, Lord Miles," she said testily. "He has but spoken out of turn and will not do it again."

Miles nodded slowly. Alison was clearly saying much more than her words expressed. What was going on here? Jealousy was making him sick as he thought of Roger Bainbridge kissing Alison, and her responding. No! He couldn't believe that of her! Not with her so eager in their own bed. Rather than confront her, he decided, he would watch her. If there was true cause of jealousy, he would know soon enough.

"I must be going," Bainbridge said as he backed toward the door. "I can see my own way out."

Alison was too furious to trust herself to speak to him alone so she said, "As you will, Lord Bainbridge." Miles said nothing at all.

8

Alison let herself into the dim passageway through the panel in her bedchamber and held her candle high. Her skirt grazed the dust on the stairs as she made her way to the landing above. Her foray for food had almost led her to trouble again. Miles had come unexpectedly into the corridor and would have seen her had she not stepped into the shadows of a nearby doorway. Then, as she was crossing the hall, Edmund had stopped her to ask her a question, and she had been afraid he would surely see the bulge of food concealed in her wide sleeves. However, he said nothing and gave no indication that he noticed anything out of the ordinary. Nevertheless, Alison felt very uneasy. It had been her intention to take Damion his food before the castle awoke, as was her custom, but she had overslept, and Miles had awakened in an amorous mood as she was slipping out of bed. This daylight delivery was imperative, for she had been unable to bring him food for two days. She knew he was running low and might begin to forage for food on his own.

She quietly stacked the food on the landing and set the extra candles beside it. Above her she heard a door click as if a panel were opening. "Damion?" she whispered. When there was no answer, she felt a shiver pass through her. Had the door been closing rather than opening? Even though Damion was her brother, she disliked the idea of him silently watching her. Resolutely she lifted her chin. To be so fearful of her own brother was ridiculous.

Picking up the food again, she walked up the twisting stairs and paused outside his room before tapping lightly on the door. There were no peepholes in the panels leading to the bedrooms, so she jerked with a start when it opened suddenly.

"I have told you not to come to my cell," Damion said in an angry voice.

"You forget, brother, that this is still my castle." She moved past him into the room as she glanced around at the austere furnishings. "What do you do to pass the time away?" she wondered aloud.

"I pray," he answered. "Why have you come here?"

"I must talk to you."

"A confession?"

"No, not that." She didn't want to tell him the abbess heard her confessions. If Damion was upset over Roger saying Mass, he would be furious at the abbess. Damion seemed to have developed a general dislike for women that bordered on hatred. "I have a great concern that you will be found here."

"I'm very careful."

"I know you frequently slip out to meet Lord Roger in the oak woods."

"I'm tending my business and that of my church. At times he brings his servants there to hear Mass or for confession."

"Then others know you're here!"

"Nay. They know not from whence I come, only that I will always be there to meet their religious needs. At other times we make plans to restore the true faith to England."

"A revolution?" she exclaimed. "Now that the king heads the church, it will be no less than treason!"

"You are fainthearted because you are only a

woman," Damion pointed out disparagingly. "But you must gird yourself to strength like the martyrs to our faith."

"Nay, Damion," she objected. "I am not martyr material. I want to live in peace. If you and Lord Roger wish to breed insurrection, you must do so at Bainbridge Castle."

"Silence, woman! Would you turn heretic before my eyes?"

"I'm not a heretic! I am true to our faith. I want only to live in peace."

"You are the sister of a priest, and wife of a Protestant. You must choose one path or the other!"

"I cannot!" she cried out.

"Even to hesitate is to be false to God and our church," he said in condemnation. "You cannot serve two masters."

Alison turned away and stared at the plain wall. Which would she choose: her faith or her husband? She had thought the choice would be easy, but she recalled the gentle lights in Miles's deep blue eyes and the sensuous stirrings she felt when she heard his deeply resonant voice. She could not deny that she loved him.

As if Damion heard her thoughts, he asked, "Is lust with this heretic so compelling that you can set aside your faith?"

"What I feel for my lord husband is not lust. He's a good man and I care for him."

"So in your depravity you even forget the honor of Lord Charles, who was martyred for his convictions!"

"Stop it! You're twisting my words!"

"Leave me, sister, lest you bring my curses upon you!"

"Will you then move to Bainbridge Castle?"

"That I will not! Wyndfell is better for my purpose, as the master here is a heretic and known to be loyal to the king. Here I will stay."

Alison was exasperated. As she tried to decide what

to say, Damion pointedly turned his back to her. The discussion was closed. She had no option but to leave, and she did so in an angry flounce. She went back through her bedchamber and down the turret steps to the hall. After calling for her horse, she told Leatrice to oversee the washing, then rode into the village to the church.

She strode down the aisle, turned into the alcove, and flopped down onto the stone seat. "Damion is becoming quite impossible, Mother," she burst out. "Yet now his obstinacy has a far more sinister cast. He will not soften or even try to understand my pleadings. Never have I felt so torn and dismayed. I *cannot* choose between Miles and my faith!"

She turned her head to look at Charles's carved features. "Things were so very different while you lived. I never felt this wild soaring of emotion, nor this depth of despair. My greatest struggle was to remember to speak with gentleness and move gracefully. How simple life was then." And how dull, a voice whispered in her mind.

She looked back at her mother's tomb. "Counsel me, Mother. Put the right course in my heart. If I should turn away from Miles, give me a sign." She held her breath and waited, but the cold stones of the church were as silent as the graves within it. With a sigh she rose to go. There was nothing for her here.

"My lady," Leatrice called out. "There is a peddler at the gate. Come and see his wares."

Alison smiled as she put down her sewing. She had not expected to see a traveling merchant until spring. Wrapping her cloak snugly around her, she hurried after Leatrice. While Miles was fastened away in his closet with Edmund and the accounts, she could secretly buy the braid she needed to trim his New Year's gift.

As Leatrice had said, the man stood beside his pushcart in the shelter of the gatehouse. Leatrice had already joined the other ladies who were crowding about the cart, but they politely gave way as Alison approached. Wyndfell's village had few shops, and none that sold such notions as lace, caddises, or worsted ribbons, and inkles or tapes. To purchase these fineries meant a journey to a larger town or a wait until the next fair.

The peddler was a young man as dark as a Gypsy. He had a flashing smile and eyes as black as coal chips. At his heels sat a shaggy dog with a brown spot on his back. When the man saw Alison he bowed from the waist and swept his bedraggled cap across the cobblestones. "An honor, my lady. May I serve you?"

Alison smiled and fingered a spool of wide red satin ribbon. It would be elegant on Miles's new jerkin. "How much for the ribbon?"

"A farthing a length, my lady."

"So dear?" she asked as if the price were outrageous.

"You'll not find better goods in London itself," he returned.

"I'll give you a farthing for two lengths," she bargained.

"My lady, you wound me!"

Back and forth they bargained, each enjoying the challenge. At last they agreed on a farthing for a length and a half, and Alison bought the whole spool.

"Look here, my lady," he said in a tempting voice. "An ivory comb for your hair and perfumed gloves for your dainty hands."

Alison didn't need a comb, but she took a pair of jonquil-hued gloves and sniffed the perfume. "Gillyflower?" she asked.

"Clove, my lady. I find the scent more enduring."

She nodded. "I'll take three pairs," she said as Leatrice purchased the comb for herself. "Have you come from York or are you journeying that way?"

"I came from Manchester, my lady, and lately from Dewsbury." He lowered his voice to a tone suitable for the disclosure of bad news. "I stayed not one day there, however, for the sickness has broken out."

"The sweating sickness?" Alison asked with dread. "Why, we're well into autumn." This relatively new disease, which had begun near the start of old Henry VII's rule, was the most deadly scourge known, but thus far it had occurred only during the warmer months.

"Nay, my lady, God be praised, but 'tis near as bad. It's the plague."

"Plague! In Dewsbury?"

"Aye, there were five deaths that day if I may believe the innkeeper where I stayed."

"Merciful heaven," Alison murmured.

"I felt it my duty to warn everyone in the area," the man said. "I left town as soon as I heard, and I've told all I've seen traveling in that direction what to expect."

"Yes," she said absently. "It's good of you to pass on the warning."

Although her mind was on far darker thoughts, she continued examining his goods, selecting a filigreed pomander on a silken cord and a length of yellow inkle to trim her favorite French hood. It was unsettling to think that the plague was less than a hard day's ride away.

With all the sales completed, the peddler folded his goods back into his cart and latched the watertight lid. Whistling to his dog, the young man strode toward the village.

"Did you hear, Leatrice? There's plague in Dewsbury," Alison said as she watched the man swing down the hill.

"That's miles west of here. We have nothing to fear." Leatrice's tone belied her words.

"They say it travels on the wind, and there's been a strong westerly breeze all day."

"There's rain in the air. Surely it will wash the wind clean before the plague can travel this far."

"Does rain do that?"

"I know not, but it does seem as if it might."

"To be safe, tell Sir Edmund to admit no travelers from that direction to the castle. They may lodge in the village at the Bear and Bull."

"Yes, my lady."

Alison went to put away her purchases. She had always been afraid of sickness. It struck so suddenly and there was nothing to combat it. Even the best of physicians were powerless against the deadly plagues. Perhaps they were indeed curses from God, as her priest had once said. Alison realized her present dilemma put her in a very poor bargaining position if heavenly wrath was about to descend.

Her guilty conscience reminded her that this was her day to take food to the abbess. Telling herself she was doing it out of charity and not to fend off celestial punishment, Alison prepared a basket. She wondered if there were some good deeds she might do to put herself in a better spiritual position, but no one in the village was ailing or birthing. She would just have to avoid travelers and hope to elude the plague in this way.

She went to the secluded door of the anchorage and tapped on it. After a pause, Mother Anne's soft voice called out for her to enter. Alison let herself in and placed the basket on the floor.

"I've brought your food and candles, Mother Anne. Do you need more blankets or anything?"

"No, my child. What I have is sufficient."

"I saw a peddler today. He says there is plague in Dewsbury."

"That's many miles away. We are safe here."

Alison wasn't so sure. The distance might seem far to an anchoress in a cell, but not to Alison. "I wish to confess," she said hopefully.

"Are you still unable to confess to Brother Damion? He is the proper one to hear your confession, you know."

"Please. May I talk with you then? I have much upon my mind, and I'm not sure a monk will understand."

"He's a man of God," the voice said, gently chiding. "He will understand. However, you may speak with me if you wish."

"Brother Damion tells me I must choose between Miles and the church. I cannot make a decision like that."

"Surely you know where your loyalty lies."

"Yes, but my head tells me that Damion will not agree with my heart. He expects me to put away my husband." When Alison heard the words coming from her mouth, she realized that her struggle was not making a decision, but justifying the one she had already made.

"You have chosen him over the church?" The woman was deeply shocked, and Alison realized too late that an anchoress was as unlikely to understand physical love as was a monk.

"Surely I can have both," Alison asserted stubbornly. "He is my husband and I love him." The words were comfortable on her lips, and she wondered how long she had loved him so dearly. The emotion had come upon her stealthily, making her unaware of its depth and breadth.

"Remember, my child, he is not your husband in the eyes of the true church."

Alison sighed. Since his arrival at Wyndfell, Miles had seen to it that Alison attended services in their chapel every Sunday, and she honestly could see little differences in the bases of the Protestant beliefs and those of the Catholics. If anything, she preferred the closer liaison without the intervention of the priest. At once her guilt doubled. What was she thinking of? Certainly she was true to the church. She wondered if this subversive thought alone was enough to bring the plague to Wyndfell.

"Forgive me for disturbing you, Mother Anne. I must return to my duties."

The abbess gave her a benediction, and Alison slipped out. And she ran straight into Miles.

"Steady there," he cautioned, putting his hands on her arms to keep her from falling. He looked at the empty basket she was carrying. "What have we here?"

"Nothing at all," she answered, showing him the basket was empty.

"Do you always visit the village sick in this direction? The village is on the other side of the castle."

"I . . . I took food to a peasant woman who is ailing," she answered lamely. Lying had never been one of her talents. "May we go in? It's starting to rain."

Miles glanced at the leaden sky. A veil of mist softened the distant trees in the park and thunder rumbled from far away. "Where have you been to visit this shut-in? You've not had time to go far, because I saw you leave from my closed window. Surely no one is living in our park."

"No." She managed to laugh as if such a notion was ridiculous. "What an idea. Let's go into the castle, my lord. The rain is cold and I have no warm cape." She held up a fold of her light wool garment.

"Here, take mine," he said, swirling his heavier cloak about her.

"Now you'll be cold," she objected. "Come. Let us go inside to the fire."

"You go. I think I see something there in those bushes." He nodded toward the hawthorn bushes that concealed the anchorage door.

"Please come with me, Miles," she said earnestly. "There is nothing there." She put out her hand to detain him.

With a look of disbelief, he brushed her hand away. " 'Tis a door! Why is there a door in our curtain wall?"

"I know not who built it. It has been there for centuries, perhaps."

Miles studied her stricken face. What was she hiding? "I will look closer at this curiously ancient door. Get in out of the rain."

Alison stared after him as he walked to the door

and shoved it open. When she heard a startled cry from the abbess, she raised her clenched fists to her cold lips. Miles stepped into the anchorage and slammed the door behind him.

As Alison stood there, immobilized by terror, the mist became a bone-chilling rain that sluiced over her pale cheeks and plastered stray strands of hair to her forehead beneath Miles's hood. Pewterlike sheets of water raced the wind down Wyndfell's green, and the old stone wall darkened against the sky.

What was Miles doing in there? Alison shivered with cold as well as with fright. He could do anything to the old woman and be within his rights. Anything at all, for she was an outlaw by the king's decree. Surely he wouldn't kill her! Miles was too gentle. But he might turn her out! In truth he could do little else. And once word spread that Miles had turned her out, no one in the village would dare harbor her, for to do so would be treason. Alison felt ill, for the years of safety she had given Mother Anne had come to an end, and the thought of the sweet abbess on the road alone was heart-wrenching.

After what seemed an eternity, the door opened and Miles came out. For a moment he stood in the doorway, his eyes boring into Alison through the driving rain; then he shut the door behind him. Alison's eyes were large and filled with fear as she clutched the cape beneath her quivering chin.

With long, purposeful strides, Miles came to her and looked at her for a while without speaking. "She won't come out," he finally said.

Alison's worst fears had come to pass, and she thought she might gag on the revulsion she felt. Swallowing so she could speak, she gasped, "Out? You would throw her out in this storm?"

"I meant to take her into the castle where she could warm herself."

"Do you not understand? She is a holy woman. She was the mother superior at the nunnery."

"So she told me."

"Are you offering her sanctuary?" Alison asked incredulously.

Miles shrugged as if embarrassed to be caught in such an act of benevolence. "She's an old woman."

"Then you'll not turn her out?" Alison probed hopefully.

"In this storm? Only you and I are fools enough to stand out here talking as the very heavens pour upon us. No, I won't turn her out."

"Not now, or not at all?"

"What harm can she do? She asks only to remain in her cell," he said, as if Alison were suggesting he should send her packing. "As I said, she's an old woman."

"You actually saw her?"

"Yes."

"You know 'tis unlawful to harbor her?"

"Yes."

Alison smiled up at him, her face glowing with happiness. "I love you," she stated against the roar of the storm.

Miles gazed down at her. Rain beaded on his long lashes and dripped off his hair, but the intense blue of his eyes met hers as if the day were clear and clement. "I love you too," he said, raising his hand to touch her delicate cheek. "I love you."

The words rode the rain and were almost hidden by the thunder, but Alison heard them in her heart. With happiness brimming from her, she took his hand. "Come inside, Miles. You're drenched to the bones."

He grinned and put his arm lovingly around her shoulders. "I'll take you to the fire and warm you. Later I'll send a brazier of coals to Mother Anne." At her surprised expression he defensively said, "She has no hearth, you know."

"She won't use them."

"At least I'll know I tried to give them to her."

"By the way. Sir Edmund knows nothing of our secret."

"I gather the rest of the castle does?"

"Except for your men. Also the village folk, for the most part."

"And you thought me such a demon that you dared not tell me? Alison!"

"Not a demon, but a heretic."

He stopped under the protection of the kitchen-gate archway and turned to face her. "You forget, love, I was raised as Catholic as you were."

"Then you, too, are of the old faith?" she asked with hope rising.

"I was . . . but am no longer." On seeing her crestfallen expression, he said, "This must mean you are truly Catholic and your earlier refusal to pledge your fealty to the king was not just for the sake of arguing with me. You were serious. Weren't you?"

She nodded unhappily.

For a moment Miles's eyes searched the rain and the leaden sky as if his answer to all this would be there. Then he faced her again. "We love each other. If a miracle of such magnitude is possible, then surely we will find a way out of this coil."

Alison put her arm around his waist and matched her steps to his as they crossed the kitchen yard.

6

By the time they crossed the formal garden and entered the castle, Alison was chilled and shivering. Miles seemed not to notice that he was soaked as well. As Wyndfell's solid walls muffled the growling thunder, Alison reached up to wipe the beads of rain from her husband's face. He had told her he loved her. She could still scarcely believe her good fortune.

Leatrice hurried over and clucked at her mistress for getting so wet. "You'll catch your death," she scolded. "And you too, my lord." She turned to a lackey and said, "Run up to their chamber and put a log on the fire."

"Thank you, Leatrice. I confess I am cold."

Miles hugged her to his side as he guided her toward the stairs. "You'll soon warm in front of the fire."

Leatrice walked briskly behind them, muttering about the foolishness of walking in so cold a rain. By the time they reached the chamber, a fire was flickering in the hearth and already the chill was abating in the large room.

"Turn around, my lady, so I may undress you," Leatrice said in a motherly fashion. She quickly unfastened the wet laces and helped Alison peel away the soaked garments. She tossed each layer to a serving girl, who sagged under the weight of the soaked velvet and brocade. When Alison was stripped to her chemise, Leatrice whisked a fox wrap from the bed and held it up like a curtain as one of Miles's men arrived to aid him. "The chemise, too, my lady," Leatrice ordered.

Alison obeyed and tossed the garment to the maid. Leatrice folded her into the warmth of the double-sided fur, and Alison clutched it to her. "Thank you, Leatrice."

"Girl," Leatrice addressed the maid, "go to the kitchen and fetch two mugs of hot mulled wine. And tell Bess to lay those clothes out to dry by the fire." To Alison she said, "My lady, you should be switched! You're courting sickness."

Alison looked over at Miles, who was wrapped in a sable fur, and smiled at him as the recollection of his kiss in the rain began to warm her from the inside. "Nay, Leatrice. I've rarely felt better." In a whisper she added, "He knows about the abbess."

Leatrice's eyes widened. "You told him?"

"He found her cell. But all is well. He says she may stay." With a dismissing nod she said, "You may leave us now."

"Not until I see the wine in your hand and you drinking it. Fie, lady. You know plague is about!"

"Plague?" Miles asked as he waved his servant out of the room.

"At Dewsbury."

The door opened and the maid returned carrying two possets of mulled wine. Leatrice tested the warmth of the tankard and nodded. "Drink it down, both of you."

Alison obediently swallowed some of the spiced wine. "Thank you for seeing to us, Leatrice."

"If you need aught else, ring the bell."

"I'll need nothing. You may go about your duties."

Leatrice curtsied to them both and left, still shaking her head over their foolishness.

"Leatrice looks after you like a mother hen with an only chick," Miles observed. "Such devotion is rare."

"She is truly a jewel. I know not what I would have done without her."

Miles led her closer to the fire, and they sat like children on the bear rug. "You mean in the years after Charles's death?"

"And that of my mother. To lose both so close together was a blow."

Miles studied her face in the firelight as jealousy pricked him. "Did you truly love him?"

She nodded slowly and took another sip of wine. "I cared for him deeply. But I've since come to realize that I am capable of a much fuller love. What I felt for Charles pales in comparison with what I feel for you."

Taking an iron rod from its hook on the mantel, Miles held the tip of the rod in the hottest part of the fire. The flickering light bronzed his strong, firm muscles. "I confess I feel a certain jealousy."

"There is no need," Alison reassured him softly. "What I feel for you I have felt for no other." Her eyes met his, and she seemed to spiral into their hypnotic depths.

Miles took the heated rod and put it into her tankard to warm the cooling wine, then did the same for himself. "Drink up. I'll not have you ailing."

"I've been wet many times," she reminded him with a smile. "Until today no one other than Leatrice has ever thought much of it."

"It's possible that no one ever cared for you as much as I do. In court it's fashionable to say that one woman is just like any other in the dark, and that wives are easily replaced. 'Tis not so. If something were to happen to you, I'd never find a woman to take your place."

Alison's honey-hued eyes gazed into his as she said, "Nor could I replace you, Miles."

"I love the sound of my name on your lips. When I first saw you, I thought to myself: God's bones, what a woman! You were all fire and ice, and I wanted to curb you to my desire. Now I prefer you just as you are."

"Where you're concerned, I'm far more fire than I am ice," she teased. As she leaned forward to place her empty tankard on the hearth, her thick hair fell forward over her creamy shoulders.

He reached out to finger a silken strand. "Never have I seen such hair. It's as if there is a fire deep within it."

"And I have never seen eyes so blue as yours. I get lost in them and never want to find my way out."

"If I could have chosen a woman to love, it would have been you." He drew her to him and eased her down on the soft bearskin, her fox wrap beneath her. "You're like a pagan goddess, gold and russet and ivory. In your eyes I see familiar realms. It's as if you have always been mine and I have been yours. Forever."

"When I was a child," she said softly as she traced her fingers along the hard curve of his jaw, "I dreamed of a handsome knight with hair as black as a raven's wing. He would see me and love me and take me away to an impossibly beautiful castle. There we would live happily forever."

"And so we will."

Alison's lips parted slightly and she pulled his head down for a kiss. "I love you," she murmured with her lips grazing his.

As he crushed her to him, she ran her hands over the satiny muscles of his shoulders and back and reveled in the controlled strength beneath her palms. He had the might to break her in half, yet he was always gentle with her.

His lips traveled over her warm skin and into the pulsing curve of her neck, where she was most sensitive. "You smell so good," he murmured, "like roses and lemons, and your hair is so glossy from the rainwater. I should never have let you stand out in that cold rain."

"Miles, you're so good to me."

A gentle smile tilted his lips as he looked at her. "I love you."

The rich timbre of his voice sent a thrill through her. "I love to hear you, to see you, to touch you. When you are not around, I hunger for you, and when we are alone like this my hunger only grows."

"You shall have me, my love. I promise it." His hands brushed aside the fox fur so he could fondle her breast. "Are you still cold?"

"No, I burn," she whispered as his fingers moved sensuously over her nipple. "I burn for you."

Again his hot lips claimed hers, and she moaned as he urged her to greater desire. "Kiss me," she sighed. "Love me."

His lips found her sensitive bud and drew it into his mouth. "You taste so good," he murmured. "So sweet."

As he loved her breast, his hand stroked lower to caress her hip and buttocks; then he circled her thigh and gently urged her legs apart. When she eagerly complied, his fingers found the font of her pleasure.

Alison moved against his hand and murmured softly as her desire blazed brighter. She was aware only of Miles, herself, and their love. The rain beating in sprays against the glass and the fire dancing and crackling on the hearth added sensuous music to their loving.

She pulled the sable fur from about Miles and looked at the long, clean lines of his body. If she were a pagan goddess, then he was certainly a Greek god. There was no spare flesh on his powerful torso, and his legs were well-turned and strong. He looked as if he could best anyone in a contest of strength, yet his were not the bulky muscles of a smithy. She ran her fingers over the swelling strength of his hip and up to caress his hard ribs. He was like a sleek panther she had seen once at a fair—graceful and lithe, yet incredibly strong.

Miles knelt between her legs and she deftly guided his maleness into her. She sighed with pleasure as she felt him fill her. Slowly he moved, teasing and pleasing her until she matched his rhythm exactly. Suddenly she was spiraling upward and her soul merged with his. Their chamber seemed to whirl as she neared her completion. Then, just as she felt the explosion of pure pleasure, Miles cried out, and they soared together in love's bliss.

As he lovingly held her in his arms, he gradually became aware of the thunder rumbling over the hills. Then from far below came the sounds of Wyndfell's musicians playing a haunting tune and the muffled noises of the castle's staff. Miles snuggled Alison closer and rubbed his cheek on her soft hair. "Never have I spent a more enjoyable rainy afternoon."

"Never?" she asked, raising her head so she could look into his eyes.

"Never," he affirmed, meeting her gaze honestly. "I love you, Alison."

"I love you too. Will you never leave me?"

"I will always be your true knight." He drew her head back down onto his shoulder. "Besides, now I know your dark secret."

Startled, she looked up again.

"The anchoress, love. Have you forgotten so soon?"

"Yes. The anchoress." She again relaxed her head on his broad chest. He had been very understanding about Mother Anne. However, she doubted he would be quite so gracious about a rabble-rousing monk inside the castle itself. She opened her eyes and gazed at the hidden panel. The icy fingers of growing apprehension settled on the nape of her neck and she shuddered with a sudden chill.

When winter arrived with a cloak of snow the following week, the brown grasses and bare trees became sheathed in an icy white blanket. The sky laden with more snow, hung heavy over Wyndfell, but was not quite ready to fulfill its threat. As always during inclement weather, beggars, who would normally take what they wanted from garden or field, became more dependent on the surplus of food at the castle.

Alison knew the distance some of the beggars traveled and hesitated to venture near them. The men and women at her back gate might unwittingly exchange the plague for table scraps. At last word, the terrible affliction was still at large in Dewsbury and had also moved eastward to Leeds and Wakefield. Nonetheless, Alison took pity on the poor wretches and couldn't refuse them food and shelter in her barn.

"The beggars are plentiful today, my lady," Leatrice observed as she put down the basket of table leavings.

"More so than usual." Alison took the long-handled bread shovel she had commandeered to feed the vagabonds at a distance, and placed several trenchers of bread on its broad blade. After Leatrice opened the gate, Alison handed it through. Quickly the hungry horde crouching in the snow mumbled their thanks as they devoured the life-sustaining morsels.

Once the food was gone, Alison handed out pottles of beer. "What news of the plague?" she called out. "Is Dewsbury clear?"

"No new cases this week," a crone called back. "Leeds is hit hard, they say. I be avoiding it myself." Her companions nodded grimly. No one wanted to chance the plague.

"You may bed down in the barn yonder," Alison said. "Go in through the back door and tell the man named Jack that I gave you leave. You'll find bedding in the far tack room." Leatrice had warned her time and again that such liberty would trigger wholesale stealing, but so far only two coverlets had been pilfered.

"Thank God for the snow," Alison said as they walked carefully across the kitchen yard to the castle. "The plague always abates with a snowfall. Mayhap it will soon be over."

"Sir Trahern told me that last autumn three hundred Londoners died each day."

"London must be enormous! Why, there are not that many people in our entire village."

"He says it's the largest city in the country. Barges float up and down the Thames all day, and there are more shops that you could visit in a fortnight."

Alison hid her smile. "Sir Trahern seems to say a great deal."

Leatrice blushed and looked down at the muff that concealed her hands. "I pass the time with him now and again."

"He's very handsome. Do you not think so?"

"Yes, now that you mention it."

"What color are his eyes? With his hair so blond, I wager they are blue."

"I seem to recall they are hazel. Dark hazel with clear gold flecks."

"You must have been very close to see them so well, or has your eyesight improved of late?" Alison teased.

Leatrice laughed shyly and admitted, "Close it was."

Alison was thoughtful. Leatrice and Trahern always sought each other out, neither being betrothed to another. Leatrice was a poor relation of the Wakefield family, but she was of a good bloodline, her grandfather having been knighted by Edward IV and her mother being distantly related to the Brandons, one of whom was the king's own brother-in-law. Sir Trahern could do much worse. Alison decided to ask Miles if they could be betrothed. She wanted Leatrice to be as happy as she herself was, and as Trahern's wife, Leatrice would stay at Wyndfell.

"There's news from the village," Leatrice said as they went through the corridor to the hall. "Mistress Phelps is with child again."

"Mabel Phelps? Has she not enough children as it is?"

"This will make an even dozen, my lady."

"Betimes I wonder that a poor family seems to have

a child a year and they all live, whereas the king seems unable to beget a male child who survives."

"Hush, my lady! Prince Edward lives!"

Alison lowered her voice. "He may live, but 'tis said he is consumptive. And Princess Mary has never had a strong constitution. Elizabeth thrives like the weed she is, but she's a girl and will doubtless be last in line to succeed—especially now that she's been declared illegitimate."

"Hold your tongue, Lady Alison. Who knows who might hear you and take your words to London? Besides, the king is still young enough to father sons."

"Perhaps. So Mistress Mabel is to give birth again. When is the babe expected?"

"In the spring, I believe."

"I must send word that I will come to aide her. She nearly died with the last three. The village midwife is less use than the village drunkard. I have long considered attracting a more capable midwife to the area, since Goody Smith is so old. Will you speak to Sir Edmund about it? Mayhap he knows of one in London who could be lured to Yorkshire. Tell him I will give her a cottage and small pension if she has no man of her own."

"A midwife, Lady Alison?" Leatrice looked at Alison curiously. "Do you desire a better midwife for yourself as well?"

"Not yet, but I do not doubt the time will come when I will have need of a midwife's service. And when that time is here, I don't want Goody Smith by my bedside. Would you?"

"Not I."

"Then it's settled. Speak to Sir Edmund as soon as possible and tell him to act upon it at once."

Leatrice went to do Alison's bidding, and Alison crossed the hall and went out into the courtyard. The dairy barns were beside the horse barns near the back wall of the chapel. She walked briskly through the snow and let herself into the nearest byre. The day grew steadily colder, and she guessed that it would snow again before morning.

The barn was almost warm from the heat of the cattle and milk goats. Dairymaids were going about the business of milking and carrying pails to the creamery or to the kitchens. Two men had been assigned the job of mucking out the stalls, and as part of their wage, the men received the dried dung for use as fuel. As a result, the stalls were usually kept clean.

The creamery, in a room behind the barn, was heated by a brazier of coals. Alison greeted the woman in charge and asked, "Is the milk dividing yet?"

"Aye, my lady. I looked at it just this morning." She was churning butter from the cream and didn't miss a beat with the wooden plunger. Alison moved aside the wooden lid and looked into the vat in which milk had been poured along with a small amount of rennet from a calf's stomach. Already the mixture was separating, and the curds were floating on top like thick globs of butter in a sea of watery whey. Alison took a large strainer and skimmed off a layer of curds. "It's already turning to cheese. Very good, Liz."

"There's near enough to press already," the head dairymaid agreed. "We'll not want for white meat this winter. The cows seem to be doing theyselves proud."

Alison checked the cheese press where the last of the whey was squeezed out of the cheese. The stone press was clean, but she reminded Liz to scrub it well before using it. Alison didn't subscribe to Liz's assurance that a bit of dust wouldn't hurt the cheese. She knew her maids considered her overly fastidious, but Alison like to have things done her own way.

"See to it that the children get a generous supply of whey to drink with their bread and cheese at supper."

"Aye, my lady. I'll see to it."

"Have any of the milkmaids been feeling poorly? Young Ellie was looking a bit sickly when I came through the dairy."

"She's not mentioned it, my lady, but I'll ask her if she's ailing."

Alison nodded. Milkmaids were often prone to sudden high fevers accompanied by body aches, and a mild pox for several days, but such never happened to a maid more than once. It was said such maids were charmed, for they never caught the deadlier smallpox. She wondered if there was some connection between the two, but decided it was probably idle speculation. She went back through the dairy and into the granary by way of the side door. Near the double doors at the far end was the mule-driven mill and several of the flat millstones that were used for grinding the various grains. Bundles of wheat, barley, and rye were stacked along the far wall, and the air was pale yellow with dust. Several men were on the winnowing floor threshing the husks and stems from the grain. As they worked, their voices were raised in the tune "Song of Lady Bessie," an old melody which told how Elizabeth of York had escaped marriage to her uncle, King Richard. When the men saw Alison, they broke off the song, respectfully pulled at their caps, then resumed work.

Several women were working on the other end of the long platform, scooping the golden mixture and tossing it lightly on their winnowing fans. A steady breeze from the open doors on either side of the barn lifted away the husks, leaving the grain to be poured into sacks.

This chore really fell more under Miles's jurisdiction than hers, but Alison loved to watch the process. The men were singing again in rhythm to the beating of the threshing paddles, one taking the lead and the others joining in with the words they knew. The women worked more quietly, one occasionally offering a bit of gossip or a quick exchange of conversation. It wasn't that they didn't enjoy their work as much as the men, but too much talking was an invitation for the capricious breeze to blow the husks into their mouths.

A half-grown boy was stacking the sacks of grain in the back of the barn. As he tied each neck shut, he made a mark to indicate whether it contained wheat or rye or barley. Because he could neither read nor write, a mark had to suffice, but as none of the other servants could read or write either, the mark was clear enough. Later the grains would be used by the kitchen and the brewhouse. The harvest had been unusually good and the granary was well-stocked.

Alison made a cursory examination of the winnowing and asked after the women's families. She prided herself on knowing the names and marital status of all her servants, as well as most of the villagers. Not only was it natural for her to care about her people, but she found her notice cultivated better work from them. Maids who were known by their mistress were less likely to laze the day away in a hayloft.

When she went outside, she peered through Wyndfell's gatehouse and watched as a white haze masked the far hills. The snow would soon arrive at Wyndfell. She was about to go inside when she heard horse hooves in the straw that covered the frozen drawbridge. Looking back, she saw Miles ride into the courtyard, his huge charger cutting the cold with his steaming breath.

Miles dismounted and told the boy, "See that you walk him about in the barn until he's thoroughly dry. Don't put him away wet."

"Yes, my lord."

"Where have you been this day?" Alison asked Miles as the lad took the horse away.

"I was riding the fields to be sure all the livestock are bedded in. It looks like we're in for a heavy snow." With a grin, he put his arm across her shoulders to walk with her up the steps. "Now I'd like to see you bedded as well."

"I wouldn't object to that," she said, laughing. "Speaking of conjugal bliss, I have a proposition to put to you. Is Sir Trahern pledged to anyone?"

"No. Why do you ask?"

"I thought not. Mayhaps you've not noticed, but he and Leatrice are taken with each other. Has he mentioned her to you?"

"Constantly. Her name is ever on his lips."

"Why not betroth them? Leatrice has no money, but her line is a good one. What of Sir Trahern?"

"He has wealth but no lineage to speak of." Miles considered the matter. "Yes, it would be a good match."

"I thought so! You speak to Sir Trahern and I'll talk to Leatrice. Mayhaps there will be a wedding to liven the winter."

"Done! Now, where is my tankard of hippocras? I find matchmaking to be a thirsty work."

Alison linked her arm through his as they went into the great hall.

10

In the predawn light, Alison knelt beside Leatrice for Damion's benediction. Behind them the handful of trusted servants that filled the front few rows of the chapel shuffled quietly. Alison shifted restlessly on her cramped knees. Would Damion not hurry? The translucent windows of the chapel were becoming green, which meant the sun was rising. She realized now that chancing a Mass at Wyndfell was foolhardy, even though the parishioners had no idea that Damion was lodging at the castle. But Damion had been insistent once he learned that Miles's chaplain was trying to forcibly indoctrinate Wyndfell's people to Protestantism. Alison had done well to get Damion to wait until the chaplain had reduced the number of services from four a week to just one on Sunday mornings. What if someone heard or saw them? Not daring to whisper for him to hurry, she flashed him a frown that she hoped he would correctly interpret.

But Damion's pleasant tenor voice chanted on, seemingly forever. Finally she recognized the final Latin words and her heart lifted. Damion sang "Amen" and the small congregation got to their feet.

Leatrice and the others slipped from the chapel just as the sun was casting a rosy pink glow on the courtyard. Damion stopped Alison by catching her sleeve. "A moment, sister."

Alison paused and looked back at him. She was tall, whereas Damion was small for a man, and their eyes were almost level. "Yes?"

"You have been bringing me delicacies again," he complained. "I have repeatedly asked that you bring me plain fare."

"For goodness' sake, Damion," she objected as they went to the secret panel. "You must eat whatever we eat."

"Such fine food is a temptation to the sin of gluttony."

"Then don't eat it!" she retorted.

"All would be simpler if you would but do as I ask."

"What shall I do? Go tell the cook to prepare a plate's worth of plain fare for the monk who lives in the walls? Be reasonable."

"So many fine dishes is hardly good for your soul, either." They stepped into the passageway and he shut the panel.

"My soul is doing just fine, Damion."

"*Brother* Damion. I've told you also about addressing me so familiarly."

"You're my brother!"

"I am your priest."

"You certainly complain a great deal for a priest. I'm glad Mother can't hear you talk like this. She would have wept for days."

"She has a mortal sin on her conscience and doubtless will weep and wail longer than that."

"What!"

"She lay carnally with the king and never so much as repented."

"She loved him!"

"That matters not."

"Then I, too, have a grievous sin, for Miles and I were married in a Protestant service, and I don't repent lying with him!"

"I will pray for you," Damion said coldly as he

started up the steps. Somehow he made his offer sound like a threat.

Alison caught his arm. "I don't want your prayers! I want your understanding."

"You ask the impossible. I know you weaker vessels are more easily cracked, but I marvel at his obstinacy. Are you trying to convert him?"

"No."

"Will you please be so kind as to release my arm? I've told you to touch my sleeve if you must halt me or get my attention. And you should be trying to woo Lord Garrett to the true faith."

Alison nodded thoughtfully. Matters would be simpler if Miles was on their side, and he had already shown leanings that way by allowing the abbess to stay at Wyndfell. "I'll give it some thought."

"You're a woman—allow me to lead you."

"You're a priest! Be humble!" she snapped.

They glared at each other and Damion lowered his eyes first. "You have always had the sin of disobedience upon you," he said in the pious tone that angered Alison. "I pray you may learn humbleness someday, while there is yet time."

"Pah!" She released the panel and stepped out into the empty chapel. "I'll bring you custard lumbarde tomorrow!"

"And I'll throw it out the window!"

"Ha! I will accuse you of wastefulness! Think of that, *Damion*!" She slid the panel shut and fastened the latch. At times Damion could make her so furious! It was beyond her ken why her mother had always doted on him.

She had almost reached the outer door of the chapel when Miles came in. Her steps faltered as he asked, "Where have you come from? I looked for you in here but a moment ago."

"I . . . I suppose you overlooked me," she said, her heart pounding wildly. "I . . . was near the front pews, praying on my knees." She waited to see if he would believe that.

"That must explain it." His face brightened as he said, "We have visitors!"

"We do? I have invited no one."

"Nor have I. These are friends of mine from court. The king sent them here on an errand of sorts."

"What kind of errand?"

"They haven't had time to tell me yet. They will be in the hall by now. Come and meet them." He took her hand and led her forth.

When they entered the hall, Alison saw four richly attired knights. Miles led her to them as he made a sweeping gesture with his other hand. "This is Lord George Renault, one of my closest friends. His father and mine were placed out for nurturing at Kenilworth Castle together. I've known George most of my life." The tall red-haired man bowed to Alison, his brown eyes skimming appreciatively over her face.

"Charmed, my lady."

"This man here is Sir John Moore. I taught him all he knows of jousting." Miles grinned over at the man with broad shoulders, dark hair, and hazel eyes.

" 'Tis easy to see why Miles is content to stay in Yorkshire," the man said gallantly.

"These two are silver-tongued cousins and you're not to fall for their flattery. Sir Stephen Wesley is the taller, and the other is Sir Vance Dyer."

Alison nodded to the two blond men who looked like brothers. "Welcome to Wyndfell, my lords. Will you have a cup of wine to take away the chill?"

"Thank you, my lady," said Sir Stephen. "We could be tempted."

Miles motioned for a servant to fetch the wine and for another to draw chairs to the fireside. "What brings you so far from London? This is scarcely the best season for travel."

"How well we know that," Sir Vance grumbled good-naturedly. "We're sent to do the king's bidding, or I'd be at home with my new bride."

"You've married?" Miles said with a broad grin. "I never thought you would settle down to one woman. Who is she?"

"Lady Margot."

In a teasing fashion his cousin said, "It took many months to get Vance down the aisle, but not long for him to father a child."

Alison looked at the younger man to see if he was offended, but he merely grinned and said, "A slight exaggeration."

Miles seemed to be in no rush to hear of the men's errand, but Alison was impatient. "And what are you sent here to do?"

"We've had word that attendance at the Protestant services has been sparse throughout this area," George Renault said in his deep voice. "As you know, this is unlawful, for if they are not in the vicar's church, they may still be holding to the papist ways."

With a laugh Miles said, "Did the king think it would take all four of you to accompany laggards to church?"

"Stephen and I only came for the ride," Sir John replied. "That and to keep an eye on these two. If Vance gets into trouble with a Yorkshire lass, Lady Margot has ordered me to break his head."

As dread swept over her, Alison asked, "Who has told his majesty that this parish is not in full attendance?"

George shrugged. "I know not. King Henry knows many things that seem beyond the ken of mortals."

"He has his fingers to the pulse of all England, even here in the northlands," Stephen told her.

Alison looked over at Miles. He frequently sent letters to London. Was he the informant? She knew of no one else it could be. A coldness settled over her as she realized how misplaced her trust had been, for she had begun to relax her wariness as she had come to love him. "We require our servants to attend chapel services here. How will you enforce church attendance in the villages?"

"Usually it is but a matter of showing the king's force. We talk to a few of the local folk and let them know their laxness has not gone unobserved," George replied. "Rarely is more than that necessary."

"Will you do this in all the parish, or is our village the only target?"

"The entire parish is supposed to come to this village for the service. We'll talk to the owners of the other castles here, as well as the prosperous merchants who have men working, to see that the law is understood and enforced. I was told that there is only one other castle in this parish. Is that right?"

"Yes. The other castle belongs to a viscount named Lord Roger Bainbridge," Miles said. "It lies to the east of here."

George nodded. "We had better get started."

"Where are your belongings? Surely you'll stay here at Wyndfell and not at the inn," Miles protested.

"I'd prefer it," Vance said. "I have no love for inns. They tend to be cold in the winter, and you know not who may join your bed before daybreak."

"That can be a blessing," John said with a grin, "if that person is of the fairer sex."

"I've never had your luck," Vance retorted. "Those who join me are always old men who smell and snore."

"I'll tell Lady Margot you said so," John offered. "I doubt she will take the implication kindly."

"Thank you for your offer, but we must stay at the inn to show ourselves," George told Miles. "Much may be averted by a simple display of strength."

"This is true." Miles took a goblet of canary from a servant and sipped it as he looked from one familiar face to the other. "God's bones, it's good to see you men again. You must tell me all the news of court."

"Not much has changed," John said over the rim of his goblet. "There are the usual intrigues and midnight liaisons."

"The queen is very vivacious," Stephen put in. "The king fairly dotes upon her. Thus far she is not with child, however."

"The king has promised to coronate her when it's proven Queen Catherine is breeding," Vance added. "It's said that love or no love, he'll not have a barren wife."

Alison absently touched her own slender waist. Wives could be put aside if no heir was forthcoming. Would Miles declare their marriage null? In the three years of her marriage to Charles she had never conceived. Was she barren? She glanced over at her handsome husband and hoped his love proved strong if she never bore a child.

"The queen is a plump little woman," Vance said. "Her coloring is not remarkable, nor are her features overly pretty, but there is an irresistible liveliness about her. King Henry cannot take his eyes from her when she is in the room."

"But when he is not in the chamber," John added, "she is a remarkable flirt."

"She's young yet," Stephen said defensively. "Even a queen must learn decorum."

"Let's hope she goes soon to childbed and brings forth another prince," said George. "The king is short of patience."

"I thought he loved her," Alison said.

"He does, but the years march on. King Harry is not as young as he once was."

" 'Tis said an old man gets only daughters," Vance added. "He's had daughters enough."

Alison glanced at him, but realized the man didn't know of her relationship with King Henry.

"They say he can get only daughters in marriage and only sons out of it," Stephen laughed.

"Then they say wrong," Alison said testily, "for Prince Edward is proof." She added, "If you will excuse me, my lords, I have duties to attend to."

"I will ride with them to the village," Miles told her. He motioned to a servant. "Have my horse saddled."

Alison was aware that Miles had scarcely noticed her departure. Rather, he was leaning forward eagerly as Lord Renault began to relay a bit of scandal. Was he then so hungry for news of court? Perhaps he would rather be there than at Wyndfell. Perhaps there was a woman there that he longed to see. Suddenly she felt very vulnerable. Had she given her love too freely to a man she only thought she knew? Had she allowed her physical desire for this man to overrule her good judgment? Tossing her head to cast off the unreasonable doubt she felt, Alison quickened her step in search of a task to occupy her mind.

She was gone before Miles could tell her to stay and listen to stories of the marvels and intrigues of court, for before long he would take her there. He was very proud of her intelligence and beauty, and knew he would be the envy of everyone. He listened attentively to the gossip John was relating of the torrid affair between one of the queen's ladies and the ambassador from Spain. Whether such tales were true or not, they were told with relish. Knowing the lady in question, however, Miles assumed this tale had a basis in fact.

When the men were ready to leave, Miles rode with them to the village. They laughed and joked as they passed beneath the gatehouse, but, nearing the cottages, their faces became hard and stern. They were intent on showing the king's authority.

George dismounted and climbed the steps to the rarely used pillory outside the inn's wall. "Hear ye," he repeatedly bellowed until a crowd gathered. Because all illiterate men were awed by one who could read, he made a show of unrolling a parchment. "By order of his royal highness, King Henry VIII of England, I command the following." His voice rolled over the heads of the dumbfounded people. "Ye will set aside your papish ways and abide by the new religion in all matters. Ye will attend the king's church on all holy days and heed the words of the vicar. Ye will set aside any likenesses of saints not recognized by the new church and not hold them holy." A gasp went through the crowd, for St. Ruan was their patron saint, as he was Wyndfell Castle's, and as yet he hadn't been acknowledged by the new religion.

George continued in a stentorian voice, "To do other than I have commanded will be an affront to the king and an offense against him as sovereign lord of the church. Disobedience will be punished by flogging, imprisonment, or a fine. Remember my words, as they are the king's." He leaned down and thrust the parchment at Sir Vance. "Fix this to yon wall." All eyes were on him as he descended and remounted.

Vance hammered the proclamation on the wall and vaulted into his saddle as the crowd's murmurs and whispers rose in volume. The five horsemen reined their animals about and galloped out of town, their horses' hooves spraying snow into the air.

Bainbridge Castle lay on the narrow drift lane that eventually wound to York. As they approached the castle, Miles curiously studied its square tower houses. There was no moat, and the simple gatehouse had only one portcullis, the towers being the castle's strength. This was the castle where Alison had hoped to live as mistress. The idea did nothing to endear the castle or its owner to Miles.

They were shown into a long hall with a screens passage at the end nearest the kitchen where they were asked to wait. On the balcony above them, Roger Bainbridge stepped out to see who had come to call.

Recognizing Miles, he walked swiftly to the narrow stairs that connected the two floors and came down to meet them. "Greetings, Lord Garrett. What brings you to Bainbridge?" He looked pointedly at Miles's companions.

Miles introduced the four men, whose stoic faces indicated that this was no friendly call.

Again George read from a parchment and gave it to

Roger when he had finished. "As master of this castle it is your duty to see that your people are in the parish's church this Sunday."

Roger laughed and spread his hands as if the matter were beyond his control. "The village is nearly two miles away so we have our services here. I've sent my oath of allegiance to the king. I'm amazed that you question my loyalty."

"Did your people not attend the village church in popish times?" Stephen demanded.

"Well, yes, but . . ."

"The church has not moved further down the road."

"But the snow!"

"It snowed in popish times as well. You have heard the penalty for disobedience. Have your people there as you are ordered to do. Do you understand?" John's sharp voice brooked no nonsense.

"Perfectly," Roger said coldly. He looked hard at Miles. He had never liked him anyway, and this gave him more reason for animosity.

Seeing that Lord Bainbridge was affronted, Miles said, "As you have pledged fealty, this will be no hardship for you. I'll see you Sunday." He cuffed Roger on the arm in a friendly gesture and left with his friends.

Roger glared after them before rubbing his arm. Brother Damion would hear about this!

An hour after dark Roger let himself into the secret passage at Wyndfell. Since he and Damion often met here in inclement weather, he knew his way through the twisting corridors. At Damion's door he knocked and opened it to step in.

Alison jumped and nearly dropped her candle. "Roger!"

He paused, then said smoothly, "Brother Damion asked me to come."

"That's right," Damion was quick to agree. Although

he had not specifically invited him, he knew that Roger must have had a good reason for coming.

"At this hour?" she protested. "And without my leave?"

"I don't ask your permission to do my holy work," Damion pointed out. "Especially as you come to my cell without *my* leave."

"I came only to warn you that there are visitors in the village. This was my first opportunity."

"Thank you. I am warned. Now you may leave."

She turned to Roger and said, "Do you come here often without my knowledge? You haven't the right to come and go here as you please. Besides, what if Lord Miles sees you?"

"The countryside is dark, and I was careful to approach from the back. It's because of Lord Miles's guests that I'm here." To Damion he said, "They are here by order of the king to enforce compulsory attendance at the vicar's church."

"What!"

"They came into my hall with their demands and were rude in their manner," Roger added.

"Lord Miles wouldn't behave rudely," Alison objected.

"He was with them. Before they left, he even struck me."

"*Miles* did?" she exclaimed.

"He is a rough man. What more can I say?" Roger rubbed his arm as if it still hurt.

Damion scowled. "We must not stand for this!"

"Be sensible," Alison retorted. "They are here by the king's orders. What else can we do? They will be gone soon, and things will return to normal."

"It's an abomination! A sacrilege!" Damion objected.

"I have attended these services and find them not so offensive," Alison answered.

"Heretic! You dare compare the two?" Damion's eyes flickered dangerously in his fury. "Take care, sister!"

"Even when the king's men leave, Lord Miles will remain, and his loyalty to the king is unquestionable," Roger pointed out. "What will we do?"

"We must do something or our cause is lost," Damion agreed thoughtfully. "It may be necessary to silence him."

"Silence him!" Alison gasped. "What do you mean by that?"

"Now, now," Roger soothed with a warning glance at Damion. " 'Twas but a figure of speech."

"Even so . . ."

Damion bit his lip as he thought. "Sister, how soon are the king's men to leave?"

"I know not. I assume they will abide a week or so. They are Miles's friends."

"I wonder if they should be allowed to return to court."

"What do you—?"

Interrupting Alison, Roger asked Damion, "How could we gain by that?"

"You're talking about murder!" Alison stared wide-eyed from one to the other. "Tell me this is some crude jest!"

"I never jest," Damion said abruptly. "We may gain the king's realization that he cannot command Yorkshiremen to heresy. We will not stand for it."

"But murder! They are Miles's friends! One is scarcely more than a boy! Surely you can't mean to—"

"I see no way this will aid us," Roger said, ignoring Alison. "If it would end the matter, I would be for it, but this might bring down a larger force upon us."

"Yes. You could be right," Damion agreed.

Alison went to her brother and pulled him around to face her. "You could do this? You could kill four men in cold blood?"

"I would do more than that to further the cause one inch," he assured her.

"Then henceforth you may not count on me, for I'll be no party to murder!"

"You already are," her brother snapped. "You have heard a murder planned and are an accessory unless you alert the castle at once and have Roger and myself dragged out and hanged."

She looked miserably at both men. "Hanged! I couldn't do that."

"Then you are one of us."

"I'll not see murder done! I'll agree to work with you to see the true religion returned to England, but not by bloodshed."

"Alison is right," Roger said. "The more peaceful, the better."

Damion frowned but said nothing.

"The hour grows late," Roger observed. "We must part. If you have need of me, send a message of a wounded sheep and I'll meet you in the oak wood."

"Done." Damion quickly raised his hand in a blessing and held the passage door open for them to leave.

As soon as they were out of Damion's hearing, Alison turned to Roger. "You'd not kill these men, would you?"

"No, no," he said with a little laugh. "This is only the way men talk!"

"Damion even threatened Miles!"

"He wasn't serious. He couldn't have been. He's a monk, for goodness' sake."

"Has no monk ever done murder?" Alison asked doubtfully.

"He's your brother. Would a brother hurt his sister's husband and protector? No, he was but upset and speaking too harshly. I give you my word that naught will happen to your lord husband or to his guests. Do you not trust me?"

"Yes, but—"

"Then it's done. You're not to worry about it any longer."

She nodded doubtfully and opened the outer door for him. She paused, watching him mount and ride silently away before she went back to her chamber.

* * *

The Bear and Bull Inn was neither the best nor the worst that Miles had ever seen. In the two weeks that his friends stayed there, Miles had become familiar with its sack and ale and its board of cheese and bread. He had never cared for the syrupy sweetness of sack, but the alewife was good at her business and many a tale had been exchanged this fortnight over a pewter tankard.

"I'll miss your talk and gossip," Miles said, clapping his hand on George's shoulder as they walked to the horses. "Are you sure you'll not stay a bit at Wyndfell?"

"No, we must ride before the next storm blows in. We have other parishes to visit. We gave our leave to your lady wife last evening. Besides, there was a brawl here last night after we retired, and we wouldn't want to get caught in the middle of another one."

"I envy you, Miles," John said with easy camaraderie. "Seeing your wedded bliss makes me long for a hearth of my own."

"Aye," Vance agreed. "A fortnight is too long when you've a bride waiting for your return."

"Come back soon," Miles said. "Maybe we'll come to London in the spring and will have a chance to meet this fair Lady Margot."

"She will be large with child by then. By early summer my son will be born," Vance said proudly.

"Or daughter," Stephen teased. "Perhaps you'll fill your castle with girls."

Miles laughed at the men's taunting. Vance was often the butt of the joke, as he was several years younger than the others, but because of his good humor, he didn't seem to object.

The men mounted their horses in the inn's walled yard, and Miles waved them a farewell as they rode away. As much as he had enjoyed the companionship, he wasn't sorry to see them go. He, too, had a bride, and his friends' visit had taken him from Alison's side more often than he would have preferred. He swung effortlessly into his saddle and rode out the side gate of the whitewashed inn.

The wall of the inn backed the pillory platform, and notices were commonly posted there for those who could read. Miles glanced at the king's proclamation, then looked back at the one beside it.

The placard was finely written in ink on heavy foolscap. On it was a poem about the king, and as Miles read it, his anger grew. At the bottom of the sheet, for the benefit of the majority who could not read, was a graphic picture of the king in a compromising position with the devil. Miles sucked in his breath and looked about before ripping the foolscap off the wall. The streets were unusually empty, and he wondered if the placard might be the cause. For a moment he considered riding after his friends and showing it to them, but decided he was capable of dealing with this himself.

Thrusting the paper into his jerkin, he kicked his horse into a gallop toward Wyndfell. His anger mounted as he neared the castle, and he was glad now that his friends had not seen the placard. This village was his own responsibility, and Miles didn't want to appear to have lost control of it. More than once during their visit, Miles had wondered why the king hadn't simply authorized him to enforce the compulsory attendance. Maybe Henry hadn't felt him competent. He wondered who had reported to the king that attendance was not what it should be. Regardless, Miles was determined to solve this new, much more serious problem of the inflammatory placard and report its resolution to Henry.

At Wyndfell, Miles strode into the hall, shouting for his men. Alison heard him and ran to see what was wrong.

"Look at this," Miles fumed to Trahern. "This was nailed to the wall by the village pillory." He thrust the parchment at the knight, who scanned it quickly as others read over his shoulder.

"Who wrote this?" Trahern asked.

"I know not, but we must find him!" Miles took back the paper and read it again.

When Alison saw the perfection of printing, her heart missed a beat. No common man had done this! She read the verse likening the king and his church to a drunkard and a harlot, and when she saw the picture she blushed.

"Look at the way it's written," Miles said to his men. "That's a priest's hand!" To Alison he said, "What has become of the village priest!"

"He . . . he left years ago," she stammered. "He went back to his cousins near Manchester. He was an old man who could never have made the trip back in winter." Her thoughts, however, were on a much younger priest, one who might be an arm's length away, listening to all they said. "What will you do?"

"I'll search the village. If a priest is found, he will be punished and sent away. Trahern, see that no house is left unsearched. You, Robert, scour the woodlands. I'll see to the outlying farms." He looked back at his wife. Alison was very pale and seemed to be quaking. "You seem very upset. Mayhap I should ask my questions closer to home. Have you knowledge of this?" He asked, thrusting the paper under her nose.

"I? No!"

"You were quick to say where your priest went."

"I know who did *not* do this. Had you known the old priest, you would be certain too! He was bent double with arthritis three years ago and must be even more crippled by now. No. It wasn't he."

"Is there any other in the village who can write a priestly hand?"

"In Wyndfell's village? No." She was careful to phrase her answer so that she would sound convincing. Her ire was piqued when he stared at her as if he didn't believe her. "Why are you looking at me thus? Do you think I am perhaps a priest in disguise?"

"If you are, love, then you are better at mummery than any man in the land," Miles said with a smile.

"Of course I don't accuse you." To his men he said, "To your horses. When you catch this knave, put him in the pillory until we try him for treason. We must make an example of him lest this be repeated."

Alison watched them leave and tried to force herself to breathe evenly. Damion had told her that he had caused trouble before with his pamphlets. Because of him the monastery had been closed. Now she could better understand why, for the verse was crudely put, and the picture even worse. She felt soiled to have seen it.

From the corner of her eye she glanced toward the inner wall where the panel was hidden. He was her brother, and she couldn't turn him over to be pilloried and hanged. She could only let the situation ride its course and do all she could to keep the matter as peaceful as possible. Even the threat of plague, now past, had not been as frightening as this.

11

"The plague has missed Wyndfell, Mother," Alison informed the effigy on the tomb. Outside she heard a patter of rain against the leaded glass. Soon it would likely turn to sleet, so she spoke quickly. "There have been no doors marked with red crosses and none of the villagers have had even a mild case of it. I've been vigilant this past month, but I believe the danger is truly over now."

She reached out to touch the carved features of the older woman. "Damion is still at the castle, but I wish he would leave. I believe he is still slipping out at night, as Miles has twice found pamphlets on the wall of the inn. I must confront Damion, but I almost fear him these days. He is becoming a warrior of God rather than a servant to humanity, and I know not how to dissuade him from this course. He no longer observes the holy feasts, but insists on being served the plainest of fare. Mother, do you realize how difficult it is for me to find plain food for him on a feast day?" Alison frowned and tapped her foot in exasperation. " 'Tis all I can do to keep him fed and hidden. I wish you could speak to him and set him straight."

Alison sighed, resting her forearm on the back of the stone bench. "Damion always was spoiled, though you never seemed to see it. I was surprised to hear he wanted to enter the church and now I marvel he lasted so long. His is not a biddable temperament."

Alison was silent for a while; then her features smoothed and she smiled. "My lord husband is well. You'd have liked him, Mother. He's not at all what I thought him to be at first. He is gentle with me and has never raised his hand against me. Though he has been provoked. Occasionally."

Looking at the other tomb in the alcove, Alison sighed. "Charles, you would not be as proud of me, for I fear my tongue is as quick as my temper these days." She felt no responding echo in her mind, and she said sadly, "I can scarcely recall your face. In my mind you look just like this effigy these days, though I never knew you so young. And your voice has left me altogether. When I try to remember it, I can summon up only your words, but not how they sounded when you spoke them." In truth, she rarely thought of Charles. These days all her thoughts centered upon her tall and handsome husband.

To her mother she said, "I know I promised to come often to talk to you, and in those lonely years I did as I said. Now I find I forget to come, and when I do, I no longer feel your thoughts reaching out to me. In a way, I'm sad, for those times of communion with you were my solace, yet I no longer need consolation. My heart has mended and I love Miles. I hope you understand why I don't come nearly so often."

She stood and walked to the opening of the alcove. Turning back, she added, "But I do wish you would intercede with Damion before he gives himself away and gets us all in great trouble."

Alison went out to her horse and mounted. The rain was turning to sleet as she had expected, and clots of ice were forming in the horse's mane, though she had left him in a sheltered spot. She put her heels to his sides, and he trotted through the dirt lanes of the village. Alison knew she shouldn't have ridden out today. The heavy wind was blowing from the north—an almost sure sign of ice or snow at this time of the year. Today was the Feast of St. Sylvester, meaning the New Years's feast, and gifts would follow. There was much going on at the castle, but as this was also her mother's birthday, Alison had hoped to feel her presence. As usual, however, the alcove had seemed cold and empty. Alison paused as she passed the inn walk. There in plain sight was another of the inflammatory leaflets. Hastily she yanked it down and stuffed it into her sleeve.

Alison rode back to the castle and went into the kitchen, where the feast was in preparation. At one table a group of maids was mixing the coloring agents for the various foods: sandalwood and rose petals for red, saffron for yellow, parsley and mint for green. The artichokes were boiling, and a cook was adding blueberries to the pot of rice and spices to make fruits ryal rice. Lentil rapes and parsley bread were baking, as was the custard lumbarde. An elderly woman with much experience in making spectacle sculptures was molding a marchpane castle exactly like Wyndfell. A year ago the lacy castle would have been dyed with turnsoles to duplicate the Wakefield blue, but now the tiny drawbridge was dandelion yellow and the soaring turrets were mallow green to reflect the Garret colors. Alison nodded her approval. In spite of the novelty of eating blue food, she thought this castle looked more appetizing.

In all the two kitchens there was not a morsel of simple food. Much more brazen than before, now that she had so much practice gathering food for Damion, Alison skillfully filched a stale loaf of rye bread that had been set aside for the beggars and dropped it into the pocket she had sewn behind the open flap of her gown's skirt. In the hall she paused to examine a tapestry while she waited for a maid to pass by; then she entered the hidden passageway and went up to tap on Damion's door.

He opened the door and tried to prevent her from

coming in, but Alison brushed past him. She was afraid her voice might carry in the passage.

"Welcome, sister," he said sarcastically.

She handed him the bread. "Have you cheese left from yesterday? And ale? Good."

"You could have left the bread on the landing."

"I needed to talk to you." She pulled the pamphlet from her sleeve and waved it under his nose. "This must stop!"

"What would you have me do? Become a vicar? Perhaps I could hire out as a kingsman and spend my days tearing down monasteries."

"There is no need to talk thus to me. Can't you understand that no one but a priest would be able to write in such a hand? Every time you do this, you advertise your presence in the area. Who places them on the wall for you?"

"I put them there myself in the dead of night. No one sees me, and none of the villagers would tell if they did."

"Don't be so certain, Damion. The vicar is becoming more popular. Already some of the merchants are turning to the new faith."

"Who? I'll excommunicate them!"

Alison made a silencing motion. "Not so loud! Would you have us overheard?"

"Are your minions false to you?"

"No, but there are Miles's men and their servants to consider. And mine are probably not above bribery if it comes to that. No one must suspect you're here."

"Where do they think I come from to hold the services?"

"No one knows for certain, and that's the way I want it. Some say it's miraculous how you slip in and out of Wyndfell's gates without notice."

"Good. Let them think that. The people need a miracle at times."

Alison looked at his serious face and turned away. She wondered how she had managed to become so embroiled in this. In the beginning she had merely wanted to hear Charles read to her about the saints' lives, and now she was sheltering a criminal, and was married to a man who ought to be her enemy.

"Has Lord Miles any idea where the placards come from?" Damion asked derisively.

"No, thank goodness, but he assumes they must have been done by a cleric." By riding down to the village often, Alison had managed to take down most of them before anyone else could see them.

"Look here," he said, gesturing toward a small table. "I've almost finished another."

Alison scanned the doggerel written on the foolscap and frowned. "This one is even more incendiary. I wish Lord Roger would stop giving you paper and inks."

"He understands what I am doing, whereas a woman lacks the wit."

"I resent that! I have more wit than you have!" she retorted through clenched teeth.

Damion looked unconvinced. "If I give up my verse, I will have to be more open, less circumspect."

"You call this circumspect?" she demanded, pointing at the very lewd and graphic poem.

"At the moment, my war is on paper. In time I will have stirred the countryside to a fever heat, and then I will be done with mere words. I will lead a revolt upon London itself!"

"And be hanged in the street!" she exclaimed. "Forget this revolution and leave Wyndfell. Surely there is a monastery somewhere that will take you. I'll pay your passage to France."

"My mission is here." He calculated her show of temper. "I see that living with this Welsh barbarian has sharpened your tongue. You should work to curb your outbursts."

"What do you know of Lord Miles?"

"I've heard of him. Ofttimes I sit in the passageway with my ear to the crack in the panel. I know much of what goes on in this castle, and I have yet to be seen."

"You must be careful!"

"I'm guarded by angels that lend me their invisibility."

"Nonsense! You are as visible as any man! Are you mad?"

Damion took his quill from the inkstand and examined its point. "Lord Miles was sorely vexed at the loss of the rye crop, was he not?"

"Yes, oxen somehow got into the granary and . . ." Realization dawned on her and she stared at him accusingly.

"You'll also find the new batch of cheese sours before the curds can set up," he said smugly.

"You can't do that to us! Do you not realize that if we go hungry, you do too?"

"I know Lord Miles is my enemy—something you have apparently forgotten."

"I love him. He is not my enemy."

"He is a heretic and as such is damned. As his wife, you may be damned as well."

"I've given this some thought. I plan to convert him."

"I don't believe you."

"It shouldn't prove so very difficult. Already he is showing some tendencies in that direction." To Damion's disbelieving look she said, "He knows of the abbess in the curtain wall. He even sends her coals and meat!"

"He would tempt her! Gluttony is a deplorable sin."

"He would but sustain her. Mother Anne is aged and her health has been impaired of late. She has requested herbs and unguents, though of course *she* never complains." Alison gave her brother a pointed look.

"So you think to convert this heathen, do you? When may I expect this miracle?"

"Never, if I stay here talking." She turned to leave, but his voice gave her pause.

"See that you do your job well, sister, for it's dangerous to be an enemy of my church."

Damion's sinister tone sent a shiver down Alison's back. His threat was barely concealed, and she feared its full meaning.

In the hall she found Miles polishing his long sword; the icy blue blade shimmered in the firelight as he finished honing the edge and rubbing it clean with a soft cloth. At Alison's approach he greeted her with a smile. "See how Widow Maker gleams? It's been too long since it was in a tourney."

"I thought swords were dulled for those," she said with trepidation. Miles had planned this tournament for several weeks.

"Not for exhibition fighting." He held up a piece of kindling and shaved off a long curl of wood as if he were slicing warm butter.

"You might be hurt! Even killed!"

"That rarely happens to a knight, and never to a man who is alert."

Alison thought of the secret panel just beyond his elbow and paled. Was it open just the merest crack? Damion could be sitting there listening to every word. "Will you ride with me, Miles? I have errands to run in the village."

"In this weather? 'Tis still sleeting out."

"I know. We must wrap ourselves very warmly."

"Can it not wait?"

"No, I must carry food to two of the families in the village. It's a matter of faith."

"What do you mean?"

"They are poor and sick and cannot see to themselves. As a penance for my sins, I look after such people rather than have them venture out."

"Your sins must be uncommonly interesting if they require you to brave the harsh elements on such a miserable day. What have you been up to?"

"I've spoken to you shortly," she said with studied humbleness. "And yesterday when I was peeved at your unreasonableness, I ordered joutes cooked when I well know you care not for beets."

"*My* unreasonableness!"

"I have forgiven you," she said meekly. "But I must still absolve my conscience."

"You're right," he agreed gruffly. "It does seem in need of tending."

"Then you'll ride with me?"

"Yes, I'll not have you ride out alone in this weather, nor would I order a servant out on such a miserable day."

Alison cast a superior glance at the crack in the paneling. "You're a good man, my lord. As gentle and godly a knight as any I've ever seen."

"I don't know about that. Get baskets of food or whatever it is that you're taking, and let's see this done before the weather worsens."

Before half an hour had passed, they were cantering over the hoary green toward the village. The distant trees were still shrouded in an icy glaze, and although the sleet had lessened, the ice pellets, whipped by a gusty wind, stung their exposed skin. Alison pulled her fox fur cape snugly about her face so that only her eyes showed. Had she known how much colder the air had turned, she might not have been so eager to ride out and convert Miles with her good works.

As though Miles were reading her thoughts, he looked at her with an unspoken question.

"This is very good for our souls," she called over the biting wind. "I feel better already. Don't you?"

"Not yet. But then, the guilty conscience was all yours. I'm only here to keep you from freezing in a hedgerow."

Alison felt a bit exasperated, but reminded herself that he hadn't tried to talk her out of coming. Perhaps he was nearer conversion than she had thought.

The first family they visited lived on the windy edge of the village. The ice-coated thatched roof of their tiny hut hung low over mud-and-wattle walls, giving it the appearance of an ice cave. The entire home would have fit into one end of the great hall in the castle.

Miles and Alison left their horses in the fenced lean-to where the family's skinny cow was kept and went to the door.

After Miles knocked a second time, the door opened a cautious inch and a woman's thin face poked out.

"We've come to bring you food," Alison said.

"In this storm? Come in, my lady. Come in." She ushered them into the hut's single room.

People were everywhere. Eyes young, old, and in between stared at the visitors. An old woman, who strongly resembled the one who had let them in rose and offered her low stool to Alison, but Alison refused it with a nod. A small fire burned in the hearth, keeping the room more temperate than the outside air, but not warm by any means. In one corner a man on a cot struggled to raise himself on one elbow. His eyes had the glassy stare of fevered pain and his mouth was drawn into a tight line. No one spoke.

The room was sparsely furnished with only a cot, a few pallets, a couple of stools, and a rickety table. Because of the poorly drawing chimney, a miasma of rancid smoke hung in the bare rafters, and the house reeked of onions and the stale odor of unwashed bodies.

"Is he better today?" Alison asked the woman she knew to be the wife.

"Aye, a little. He can keep down broth now, but as ye can see, he can't rise."

The man nodded apologetically.

"What's the matter with him?" Miles asked with genuine concern.

"It were a brain fever, my lord. At least that's what Goody Smith called it. She came over when he first took sick and looked at him."

"When was that?"

"About a fortnight back. He was doing right good in his work, was my Jamey. Worked over to the alehouse. That job is gone now. I don't reckon they'll take him back after all this time. Letty Rigson said her man was took on in Jamey's place."

"You mean you have no income at all?" Miles asked. His rough count tallied nearly a dozen people in the room, including the baby.

"No, my lord. If it wasn't for my lady's good charity, I reckon we'd have starved afore now."

Miles walked over to the cot and gazed down at the man. "What did you do at the alehouse?"

"Scrubbed out, mostly. Run errands."

Miles nodded. "When you're well, come to the castle. I'll find work for you."

Alison smiled as she placed the bundles of food on the table. The oldest child, a girl of seven years, timidly touched the bread with one finger as if she expected it might vanish. "This girl is old enough to be of help," Alison said to the woman. "When Jamey comes to the castle, he's to bring her along. I can use another bobbin winder in the weavers' room."

"Yes, my lady!" the girl's mother exclaimed. "I can bring her afore that if you please."

After surveying the girl's ragged clothing, Alison shook her head. "There's no rush to send her out in the cold. I'll see that you're fed in the meantime." Alison also decided she would send down a bolt of wool cloth. There wasn't a whole piece of clothing in the room.

The mother's eyes brimmed with thankful tears. "Bless you, my lady. Bless you."

Alison nodded and stepped out into the wintry storm with Miles. He made no comment, but his hands lingered on her waist in a caring gesture as he swung Alison up onto her horse.

The second house was a little larger than the first, and in contrast to the former's squalor, it was quite clean. There were two rooms to the cottage, a small bedroom and a tiny sitting room. A fire burned in an old hearth in the center of the house, the smoke finding its way eventually through a smoke hole in the roof. The sole inhabitant was an incredibly old woman who was bent with age.

"Good day, Goody Thorsen," Alison said loudly.

"Good day, my lady, my lord. Come in from the cold."

Alison put the basket on the nearby table and said to Miles, "She's almost completely deaf. If you talk clearly and loudly, she can sometimes hear you."

"Good day," he bellowed.

Goody Thorsen nodded happily and gestured for them to sit down. "You should not be out in this bad weather," she scolded in a reedy voice.

"I brought you food."

"Yes, yes, the day is good. But it's cold out. You'll catch your death."

"You have no man?" Miles asked, seeing the wood box was virtually empty.

"All right. I could use a hand. I need some wood, as ye can see," the old woman said amiably.

Alison explained to Miles in a lower voice, "Her only son died last fall. There's no one to look after her. That's why I bring her food and see that her wood is chopped. Will you bring some in? The woodpile is at the side of the cottage." To the old woman Alison called out, "I brought you some soup stock, cheese, and bread."

"Yes, my William is dead. Last fall, ye know. A pity."

Alison nodded as if she hadn't known. Goody Thorsen was also senile and repeated herself often. "He was a good man."

"Aye. He done me proud."

Miles came in with a huge armload of wood and a blustery gust of icy wind. "It's freezing out there!"

"What about his hair?" the old woman said. "I can't hear so good."

"He said it's cold," Alison shouted.

Goody Thorsen looked at Miles as if he were rather simple. "Aye, December usually is cold. Ye shouldn't have ridden down in this storm."

"We came to see about you," Alison said, patting the gnarled hand.

"Gramercy, my lady. I be quite all right, as ye can see."

"She shouldn't live here alone," Miles observed in a low voice. "She could fall into the fire, or any of a dozen other bad things might befall her."

"I know."

Raising his voice, Miles said, "I'm going to find a man to live in here."

"There's beer. Help yourself." Goody Thorsen looked pityingly at Miles. To Alison she confided in the loud whisper of the deaf, "He's a bit simple, ain't he? My old granny used to say such folk are touched by God." She nodded sagely and gave Miles a placating smile.

With an effort Alison kept a straight face. "We're going to find a man to live here with you. Would you like that? He could sleep on a cot in here, and keep you fed and the house in shape."

Goody Thorsen nodded and smiled eagerly. "I'd like that. A man about the place is good. Discourages robbers, too."

Miles glanced around at the woman's meager belongings. Nothing here would tempt a robber. "Why can she understand you and not me?"

The old woman nodded as if she had heard it all and said, "Come spring there'll be bees, my lord. You'll see."

Alison grinned at Miles. "Have you a man in mind?"

"The head carver at Wyndfell is aging, and has asked me for a pension. As he has no other place to go, I may offer to increase his allotment if he moves here. I believe he will take it."

"I know the man. He would be very trustworthy." In an evenly paced voice she explained the offer to Goody Thorsen, who nodded in agreement.

"He can bring the cot from my storage when he comes. It will be like having one of my son's friends about. Tell him to wrap himself warmly afore he ventures out."

"I will," Alison said. "I'll go tell him now."

Miles nodded and waved farewell.

The old woman pulled Alison to one side and said, "Don't fret none about him. Ye children may be as sound as a crock. Feeblemindedness ain't always passed on."

Alison was laughing as Miles helped her onto her horse. He pretended to glower at her. "You could have at least tried to tell her I'm not simple."

"No one can explain anything to her. Once she forms a belief, it's struck in granite."

"Saucy wench," Miles muttered as they cantered back to the castle. "I've a mind to take you to our bedchamber and teach you respect."

"Once around the beck?" she teased in Goody Thorsen's fashion. "It seems too cold for wading." She clapped her heels against the horse's barreled sides and raced Miles toward the gate.

With a grin he rode after her, keeping his plunging charger's nose to Alison's horse's flank. They rode all the way into the barn before reining in. The frigid wind whistled around the eaves, but inside the barn was warmer than the first hut they had visited.

A shivering stableboy ran out to aid them, but Miles waved him back to the castle's warmth. "I'll see to the horses." He skillfully unsaddled both, draped the saddles on the wooden forms, and laid the tasseled blankets on top, horse-side-up, to air. "Go inside, love. I'll do this."

"I can see to my own horse," she replied matter-of-factly. "I'm not helpless."

Miles thoughtfully glanced at her. "Do you think you can climb up into the loft and toss some hay down?"

"Certainly I can."

He watched her gather her long skirts over her arm and start up the steep steps to the loft. Although she faltered a time or two, she successfully completed her climb. After straightening her skirts, she tossed a large armful of loose straw through the hole in the floor above the horses's manger. When she turned back to the steps, she almost ran into Miles, who had come to join her.

"Shhh," he said, holding his finger to her lips. "Why go all the way to our chamber when there is a perfectly good haystack right here?"

"Here?" she exclaimed, then in a whisper repeated, "Here?"

"Why not? Everyone else is inside the castle."

"But . . ."

"Unless you're afraid to." His eyes dared her to make love with him in the cool barn.

Alison fell back in the hay and spread out her arms, her expression challenging him to make good his dare. Miles knelt beside her, his lips quickly finding hers and warming them with his kisses. Holding her close, he rolled her over in the mounds of dry grass until she was on top. They rolled again so that they were in the hollow between the haystack and the barn wall, shielded from the view of anyone who might come up the steps.

"A pretty crafty maneuver! Where did you learn this?" she asked with pretended anger.

He only grinned and kissed her again. She felt the swimming, dissolving sensation that his kisses always brought. "Did you think I came to you as a virgin?" he whispered teasingly in her ear.

She swatted at the thick quilting of his jerkin. "No, but you need not revel in your past conquests!"

"Peace, my love. I can honestly say there are few haystacks at court, and I have never had a taste for dairy wenches."

That soothed her only a bit, but she let it go. To be here with him and feel his hand passing over her body and caressing her legs beneath her skirt was enough. She longed to lie naked with him, but the chill in the air and prickle of the hay, as well as the threat of embarrassment should they be discovered, made her refrain. She threaded her fingers in his thick hair and guided his lips to hers as she moved sensuously against him.

Miles lovingly spoke Alison's name as he drew his thigh up to part her legs. She lay in a billow of hay, her face framed by the dark russet of her cloak's velvet lining. The fox fur, almost the shade of the highlights in her hair, further enhanced her beauty. Her voluminous skirts gave her the appearance of a flower in full bloom, and though they were very much in the way, Miles saw them as a challenge to be overcome. And nothing would stand in the way of the desire he felt for her.

Deftly threading his hands beneath her petticoats, he caressed her smooth thigh and let his hand drift upward to cup her rounded buttock. "You're a pleasing handful, love. Just the right size."

"I'm glad you think so. I'm also pleased that you are so tall," she said as she compared her length to his. "It's refreshing to me that when I stand beside you, I must look up to see into your eyes." Alison had always been sensitive about being taller than most women.

Her choice of words struck him as odd. Refreshing, as compared with whom? Instantly Miles thought of Lord Roger Bainbridge, a man scarcely taller than Alison. "Do you ever wish I were another?"

Thinking Miles was referring to Charles, she replied, "No, not anymore."

Miles pulled her close as his mind raced. Didn't that mean she had first come to him while loving another, and that she had at one time pretended his arms were Roger's? Unable to bear such an idea, Miles began to kiss her almost fiercely, trying to drive those thoughts from his head—and hers. Willingly Alison gave herself to his torrid loving, and soon cried out in her completion, bringing Miles to his own fulfillment. Love's oblivion erased all of Miles's pain. Alison was his, and his alone. Now he had no doubt.

Much later, when the cold kept them from lingering any longer, they got to their feet and took turns dusting each other's clothes. Alison pulled a sprig of straw from Miles's hair and used it to tickle his nose. Miles caught her to him and kissed her as hungrily as if he had not already sated his longings for her.

From the satisfied look on Miles's face, Alison concluded that he would never be more receptive to her suggestions than now. As they made their way back to the narrow steps she asked, "Miles? What would you say if I asked you to marry me again?"

"What?" He bent his head toward her and pulled her to his side, where her body melded against his in a perfect match.

"I would like a Catholic ceremony. If I could find a priest—"

"No, don't even ask it, for truly I find it near-impossible to say no to you at this moment, yet I must. What you ask is improper and illegal. Besides, 'tis unnecessary. We are husband and wife as surely as the sun rises in the east."

"But—"

"Do you not feel joined to me in your heart and soul? I do to you."

"Yes, but—"

"Would anyone dare say we are less than husband and wife?"

"Well, actually, the abbess said just that."

"What else could you expect?" Miles blurted out. Following the unexpected visit of his friends under the king's orders, Miles had thought much about the advisability of allowing the abbess to stay at Wyndfell. But for all his consideration of the matter, he could find no solution. As a man, he had done the right thing by allowing the woman to stay, but as a loyal subject and family friend of the King of England, harboring a Catholic who would not denounce her faith as ordered by law was dishonorable, if not treasonable. Every thought he had of the abbess caused him great stress, and Alison's mention that the woman had said they were not truly married raised his ire. Hoping to end the discussion, Miles said, "The woman is aged and no doubt her mind has begun to wander. And she can hardly be considered an expert on marriage."

"But she's a very wise woman and—"

"She is—in her way. But she is not the one to advise you in this matter. We were married in a proper church ceremony before all the parish. Besides, a Catholic service would not be binding. You must put aside these popish leanings before they get you crosswise with the law. Or worse, with the king." In his letters to Henry, Miles had always painted Alison as the obedient wife and a convert to the new faith. To have told Henry the truth would have not been fair. In time he knew he could correct Alison's behavior, just as he would manage to catch the culprit who kept posting those damnable placards that he had also not mentioned to the king. If word got back to Henry that all was not as Miles had said it was, Miles would be in serious trouble. He could offer the excuse that he didn't want to bother Henry with such trivial matters, but he was under a direct order to report the status of all things in the Wyndfell district that related to possible rebellion.

Alison wasn't sure why Miles's temper had flared so suddenly, but she knew that the discussion was closed. In silence they walked back to the castle and into the great hall.

Edmund Campbell needed to speak with Miles, so Alison moved away to the fire, hoping to dispel the chill in her bones that had been brought on by the weather and Miles's outburst. She loved her husband in spite of his stubborn ways and odd behavior, but it was evident that she had little hope of winning him back to the true faith when he wouldn't even consider repeating their vows before a priest. With a sigh, she concluded that she would have to lie to Damion. Her brother was far too excitable to handle the truth.

Leatrice came to her and unobtrusively handed her a note. As Alison read it, her breath seemed to stick in her throat. "What does this mean?" she whispered.

"A messenger came from Lord Bainbridge," Leatrice responded in a barely audible voice. "He says the man died after being beaten by the king's men who were recently here, and that Lord Miles was a part of it all."

"It cannot be true!" she said through clenched teeth. "Miles never mentioned such a thing! I don't believe it of him!"

"Nevertheless, the man is dead. I knew this man. He was quick-tempered and given to much quarreling. The messenger said the man spoke out against the king and the new religion. The beating was his punishment."

"He was one of Lord Bainbridge's men and a Catholic. I recall having seen him in church," Alison thought aloud. "He was known to be a troublemaker, you say? But wouldn't Miles have told me if something like this had happened?"

Leatrice shrugged. "The man could have been beaten in a fight at the Bear and Bull. But if this were so, why would Lord Bainbridge have said differently?"

Alison studied Miles intently, his tall body graceful in its leashed power, his large hands strong enough to crush whatever they encompassed. Physically he was more than capable, as were his four friends. But he couldn't be guilty of something like this. Or could he? Alison backed even closer to the fire, hoping to dispel the growing chill.

12

Miles crumpled yet another of the rebellion-inciting leaflets and shoved it at Trahern.

Trahern opened the foolscap and gave a low whistle as he read it. "At least the pamphleteer has a lively imagination."

"I wish I could see it in so humorous a light."

"In truth I find no humor here. Fortunately the king can't see these."

"We pray not. I've written to him that I have this area under control. And except for this pamphleteer, I have!" Miles took back the sordid poem. "Does he think to incite the village against us by profaning the king and the vicar?"

"I see not how it may, as most of the people are illiterate."

"That picture speaks plainly enough. Who could be doing this?" He rubbed his lower lip thoughtfully.

"The anchoress, perhaps?"

"You know of her?"

"Mistress Leatrice told me of her. She is scarcely a secret, however. As a former abbess she can likely read and write."

"I had not thought of her. But, no, it cannot be her, for I've seen her. She may be able to read, but she is much afflicted by arthritis and her hands are little more than claws. She could neither have made these letters nor have walked far enough to post them. This is the work of someone else." Though Miles was sure the anchoress was not to blame, learning that so many knew she was in residence at Wyndfell was unsettling.

Trahern looked around, as had Miles. "Who could it be?"

"I wish I knew." Miles motioned to several of his men who stood with their horses beside the town's well. "Have the men stay with you as a show of force. Call the people together and demand that they hand over the culprit."

"You know as well as I that they won't."

Handing Trahern a coin, Miles said, "Offer this as a reward for his arrest. There are several families here who are loyal to the king. Perhaps someone in need will turn informant." Miles mounted his horse and rode away toward Wyndfell.

Trahern put on his sternest face and mounted the pillory platform. Calling out loudly, he drew a crowd to stand below him. Gesturing with the foolscap, he said, "Look well at this. Do any of you know who has fixed this to yonder wall?"

A mass of blank faces gazed at him.

"Come now, I know you have some knowledge of this! Who among you can write a priestly hand?"

Still the townfolk stared at him as if he were ranting in a foreign tongue.

"Lord Miles Garrett, Viscount of Wyndfell, is offering a reward to anyone who knows of the man who did this," Trahern said. "He offers a gold angel for the criminal's arrest and conviction."

That loosened the people's tongues, and they mumbled among themselves, for no one there had ever seen, let alone touched, a gold angel. But no accusations came forth.

Trahern came down and swung up onto his horse. "Remember my words," he said. "If this criminal is found, you will receive the gold from Lord Garrett himself." He made it sound as if this personal touch was even grander than the large sum of money. Keeping their horses at an unhurried pace, the men rode toward the castle.

When a small rock struck Trahern on the arm, he jumped, more from surprise than pain. Suddenly he and his men were targets of numerous pebbles, sticks, and stones. Shielding his eyes with his forearm, Trahern wheeled his horse in pursuit of his attackers. A lean man leapt from behind a bush and ran for the close-packed houses. With an angry cry, Trahern thundered after him. Several other men ran from nearby bushes and scattered like a flock of quail.

Trahern's quarry dashed between two houses set so closely together that Trahern's horse couldn't pass through. He wheeled the rearing animal and galloped around the cottage, but by the time he reached the back, the man had disappeared. Trahern's men had no better luck.

"Spread out and search the village," Trahern ordered. "This must not go unpunished!"

Until sundown they unsuccessfully searched the village's winding paths and labyrinthine alleyways. Finally Trahern called off the search and again rode toward the castle.

When he told Miles what had happened, Miles was furious. "Pelted you! In my own village? And you captured none of them? Who did it? Surely you must have recognized at least one of them!"

"No, my lord. They were strangers to me, though clearly not to the village. They melted into it as if they had never been there. They knew the byways better than we did!"

Miles frowned. This was more than a matter of being pelted; it was the first act of open defiance. Rebellion had sprung from less than this.

Meanwhile, in the oak grove behind the castle, Roger and Damion were talking in growing darkness. "I saw it all from a distance," Roger said with a grin. "My men threw rocks and sticks at them and then escaped, every one of them."

"Were any of them injured?" Damion asked eagerly.

"No, but I wager there will be worry in the castle tonight. If nothing else Sir Trahern's pride was wounded."

"Pride heals quickly."

"Not for a knight like Sir Trahern, nor Lord Miles. They pride themselves on being bold warriors."

Damion smiled thinly. "Good. Then it's begun at last. What do you think will fan this spark into a true insurrection?"

Roger considered things for a minute before he spoke. "We could set fire to the vicar's house. By his own word, he is loyal to the crown, as are several other families."

"No," Damion said thoughtfully. "I have a better idea. Return with your men to Bainbridge Castle and see that you are in evidence there in case anyone questions your whereabouts. I will take the hand from here."

Reluctantly Roger nodded. He was eager to be included, but couldn't argue with a priest. The night swallowed him as he rode away.

Damion removed his off-white woolen cope, folded it neatly, and hid it beneath a bush, for he knew its distinctively embroidered cross would be telling should he be seen. Beneath the cope was his cassock, which, in the dark, he felt would pass for a peasant's garb. His eyes glittered dangerously as he walked toward the village. His plan would set the villagers firmly against Miles and his men, and from there, open rebellion would be a short step. The fat orange moon hung on the top of the distant trees, illuminating the field that bordered the village. Here and there the lingering pockets of snow gleamed like splotches of whitewash in the dips and rolls. Damion had walked this way so often to his meetings with Roger and his parishioners that he needed no moon to guide him. He could find the village on the blackest of nights, and indeed preferred to post his leaflets when visibility was the poorest.

The village had settled for the night. The Bear and Bull had lit its lantern at the gate, as had the wool merchant and the prosperous mayor. All the other paths and lanes were dark except for the light which filtered through the shuttered windows.

Unhurriedly Damion pulled a handful of dead weeds from beside the inn wall and twisted them tightly into a torch. Holding the end up to the inn's lantern he ignited it. Then as if he were merely out for a night's stroll, he walked over to the nearest house and tossed the torch onto the thatched roof. For a moment the fire guttered, then caught the dry grasses and spread quickly up and over the top.

Damion waited until the house, which belonged to one of his supporters, was covered with flames, then ran to the door and pounded upon it. "Fire! Fire!" he shouted as if he had just come upon the scene. "Fire! Save yourselves!"

Running to the neighboring houses, he aroused the sleeping inhabitants and waved frantically at the burning house.

Damion kept to the darker shadows, watching without expression as the alarmed owner tried desperately to organize a bucket brigade. Slipping near a group of men, Damion said, "I saw Sir Trahern riding toward the castle! He and his men set this fire!"

"Sir Trahern?" the man asked, trying to peer into the shadows to see who spoke.

"And I could swear I recognized Lord Garrett himself, though I hate to say it," Damion added. "He watched yonder from the shadows of the inn's wall."

"Lord Garrett! But why would he set fire to Ira Phelps's cottage?"

"Did you not hear of the pelting this afternoon? No doubt 'twas revenge on his part!"

"That makes sense!" one of the men exclaimed.

"Aye! It does at that!" cried another.

"Lord Garrett has set fire to the Phelpses' house!" The cry swept through the crowd and was repeated on every lip.

Damion hid his smirk as he faded away into the night. This was even more successful than the rumor he and Roger had concocted about the king's men beating Roger's man-at-arms to death. Although the man had died as a result of a drunken brawl, many accepted the story as fact, even disputing the accounts of the eyewitnesses. But no one could dispute Damion's assertion that Miles had set the fire to avenge the embarrassment to his men.

In Wyndfell castle, Sir Edmund Campbell was working late over his books in his room atop the gatehouse. Often he sat late over his accounts, making the columns tally to the last farthing. He prided himself on a job well done.

At least he was doing admirably as Wyndfell's steward. As King Henry's spy, however, he felt less successful. Something was underground here—he could sense it. However, he had few clues as to what it might be. Lady Alison was as close-lipped as the stone angels in the chapel, and Leatrice was little better. No matter how he fawned and smiled, he had thus far failed to get into their confidences.

Tossing down his quill, he stood to stretch his muscles. The hour was growing late. Already the hall was dark and silent. Men's and women's voices called across the courtyard as Wyndfell gathered her people under her wings for a safe night's rest. A door slammed somewhere below and Edmund heard men's voices as the guard was changed for the night shift.

Through his glass-paned windows he noticed the western sky was ruddy, and, thinking it odd that sunset still colored the sky, he ambled to the window for a closer look. To his astonishment, the cause of the red glow was a fire in the village. Two, no, more likely three cottages were on fire! As he watched, the flames leapt to yet another thatched roof.

Edmund hurried from his room and down the stone steps to the emergency bell rope. As he clanged the bell, the guardsmen's horns began sounding as they too saw the flames. Shouts and muffled screams came from the castle as the people inside scrambled to dress and hasten outside, not knowing if the warning meant attack or a fire in the castle. With the great hall and many of the major rooms piled thick with rushes, fire was a constant threat.

Miles, followed closely by Trahern, ran into the courtyard. Their faces were tense and their eyes alert. Alison, Leatrice, and the other women gathered to one side of the keep, looking about themselves fearfully and curiously.

"Fire!" Edmund shouted. "In the village!"

Not stopping to saddle their horses, the castle's men ran down the green to aid in extinguishing the fire. Edmund ran with them, wondering if this was a trick to lure them out of the castle. He too had heard of the pelting done that afternoon.

He grabbed a tall youth who seemed to be running nowhere in particular and pulled him to a stop. "Whose cottages are on fire! What caused it?"

"It started on Ira Phelps's roof," the boy babbled excitedly. "I seen it burning meself when I come out of me hut there! All the Phelpses was running out—asleep, they were, when it happened. Folks was everywhere! Then it caught the roofs of each side and 'tis spread to the next! I'm rousing the rest of the village to aid!"

"Wait! The Phelpses were asleep, you say? How did it start?"

"Lord Garrett and Sir Trahern set it as revenge over the chunking Sir Trahern got today." The boy then recalled Edmund's allegiance to the castle and yanked loose to run away.

Edmund looked back at the raging fire. He knew neither Miles nor Trahern could have set the fire, because they had been in the castle. However, the seed of suspicion might work to his advantage.

Edmund returned to the castle and found Alison standing on one of the battlements watching the fire. The other women were milling about in the courtyard as if they were anxious or concerned, even though the fire couldn't possibly reach the castle. "My lady?" he said as he approached.

"Yes? Sir Edmund, I thought you went with the others to fight the fire."

"I went down, my lady, but I heard a rumor I thought you should hear."

"Oh?" She gazed at him with detachment. Though they were alone on the parapet, she gave no sign of nervousness, and he had to admire her. She had none of the shyness most women professed.

"It's said in the village that Lord Garrett and Sir Trahern are responsible for the fires, because of this afternoon's unpleasantness."

Alison's calm face suddenly hardened. "That's impossible. They were both at the castle. Lord Miles was with me in our bedchamber, and Sir Trahern was in the anteroom."

"I didn't mean to suggest they did it *personally*, my lady, but that they ordered it done."

"I don't believe it," she stated flatly. "That's an utter lie! A spark must have come up a chimney and landed on a roof."

"It started on the Phelpses' roof and has now spread to three other cottages."

"Ira Phelps? That poor family. I must send word to comfort them and the others as well. Our men will rebuild the houses for them. Was anyone injured or killed?"

"Not to my knowledge. However, I find it odd that all the houses involved are owned by those still privately professing to be Catholics."

Alison jerked to face him and he knew he had guessed right. "Nonsense!" she snapped.

"All the same, it does seem to be a coincidence. *If* the fire was deliberately set, and *if* it wasn't started by one of the king's men, it seems the vicar's house would be a more likely target. Doesn't it, my lady? And it must surely have been set, for the village has been dark and asleep for nearly an hour. People there always bed down at sunset, you know."

"Yes," she said reluctantly. "I know."

"Only a rich household would leave a fire burning bright if they were going to be sleeping."

"Yes, that is true also."

Edmund shrugged as if he had no concern one way or another in the matter. "I merely thought you should know the rumor."

"Let us pray no one was injured. Or worse."

"Aye, my lady." Edmund turned away, making the sign of the cross over his chest as if he were as Catholic as the pope himself.

Alison's eyes widened at Edmund's seemingly unconscious gesture. Then she turned silently back toward the village, her mind overflowing with doubts.

Once the snows melted from the hills, spring came quickly. The river turned from black to slate gray and blocks of ice dipped and drifted downstream. Behind Wyndfell the little beck also woke from its winter sleep and whispered loudly as it splashed over stones and around spongy tree trunks. The rocky crevasses in the hill above the stream held longest to their pale fingers of snow, but at last the thaw reached even the most shadowy recesses, making the last remnants of winter disappear.

As Alison had promised, the castle men had quickly rebuilt the burned cottages and she had sent the families some of Wyndfell's cast-off furnishings from the turret storage. In spite of this, there was a begrudging feeling in the once-peaceful village. Alison no longer rode there alone, not that she actually feared her own people, but there was no sense in taking chances. As for Miles, her feelings toward him were more watchful, less open. She didn't want to believe that either he or Trahern had ordered the cottages burned, but as Edmund had pointed out, those burned had belonged to the most loyal of the Catholics. Had Miles known that? She wasn't sure and couldn't ask. At times he was like two men in one—he was bluff and hearty with his men and at the table, yet in their bedchamber he was as gentle as a poet.

She had carefully watched the messengers that came and went from Wyndfell, and knew words had passed from there to court. She made no mention of her knowledge of this to Miles, nor did she let Edmund know that she watched him more carefully than ever. True, he had made the Catholic sign of the cross on the parapet the night of the fire, but in retrospect she recalled that the motion had appeared a little awkward and must not have been as unconscious as she first believed. In the core of her being she still didn't trust him.

One day a message arrived from the king, and Edmund gave it personally to Miles, who was sitting with Alison in the winter parlor. Miles thanked him and anxiously broke the heavy seal. As he read, he frowned slightly and said, "We are summoned to court! You are to be presented in a fortnight."

"Summoned!" A cold dread gripped her. In Alison's experience a summons had always been bad news.

Leatrice said excitedly, "Mayhap the king to going to officially recognize you!"

"If that were true, why did he not write to me rather than to my husband?" Alison countered. "What does it mean, my lord?"

"It means you are to be presented as my wife, the Viscountess of Wyndfell." Miles smiled, but he was worried. This was no invitation, but a direct order to appear. Had the king gotten further word of the unrest in the area?

"I would rather not go," Alison said.

"The letter specifically says that you must."

"I have been the Viscountess of Wyndfell for a number of years," she pointed out, "and the king saw no need to have me presented to him."

"Now he does," Miles said as he looked about the room. "Trahern, you and your men will accompany us. As will you, Leatrice. I will leave the knights of Wyndfell behind to guard the castle. Edmund can oversee Wyndfell in our absence."

"We must tell the cook to care for the anchoress while we are gone," Leatrice offered as she began to plan for the trip.

"I care not for a journey to court. I would rather stay here," Alison said with trepidation. Now that she finally had an opportunity to meet her illustrious father, she found she was terrified.

"Are you turning shy, love?" Miles teased. "I'd have said you wouldn't fear a dragon."

"And you would be right. But the king is more dangerous." She sat up even straighter and paled. "The oath of fealty! He must mean for me to give my pledge!"

"Most likely," Miles agreed. He was more concerned over explaining why he had not reported those damnable placards than the oath, but he didn't want to worry Alison. "We will be there when the first flowers bloom. Wait until you see London in the spring! The streets are filled with flower girls pushing great carts of posies, and the air is as fresh as a bluebell!"

"The air is fresh here year-round and I have a surplus of my own flowers."

"You must go. This is a royal summons. See? This is the king's own imprint."

Curiosity overcame her and Alison glanced over to see the crest embedded in the sealing wax. "I shall not go."

Miles struggled to restrain the outburst he felt welling inside him. He would have difficulty enough maintaining his half-truths to the king without the added burden of confessing that his wife had come to court only under great protest, or worse yet, had refused the royal summons altogether. "Will you, nill you, you're going to London. We will start our journey shortly."

Correctly reading his barely restrained anger, Alison kept quiet, but her fingers jerked the needle and thread through her embroidery work.

"I know that look," Miles added, "and you're going if I have to tie you to your horse."

"It will be so exciting to see London!" Leatrice said, her eyes sparkling.

"Pah!" replied Alison.

13

The journey to court was slow. Although the snow was gone from the lanes, it had left behind a thick mud that caught at their horses' hooves and mired the carts that followed them. By the end of the first day the carts were far back, so most of their belongings would not arrive at Hampton Court until days after those on horseback. Everything they would immediately need was carried on pack mules just ahead of their rear guard.

The moorlands and heaths were bright with the ever-flowering yellow gorse, and the woodlands were already sporting drifts of colorful primroses. Everyone but Alison was in a good mood and eagerly anticipated their visit to the royal court. However, she could think only of her first meeting with her dread father, who refused to acknowledge her and had beheaded not only her first husband but also his own wife, and had allowed another wife to die in childbed for lack of proper care. What sort of person was he, and would he now greet her as his bastard daughter? Certainly he would demand her oath of fealty, and Alison would be forced to perjure herself or possibly die. She wondered if she had the moral fiber of a martyr. When she looked at Miles's loving face, she didn't think so. He gave her so much to live for.

Miles and his men rode with an alert watchfulness. Robbers were unlikely to attack a group with so many armed men, but it was not unheard-of. Because highway robbery was punishable by death, robbers seldom left witnesses who could describe them. Rather than making the roads safer, the law had turned robbers into murderers.

Often the roadways between towns were scarcely wider than a drift lane with high brush and trees that touched the horses' sides. In the hedgerows, hazel catkins bloomed profusely, with long tassels drooping over minute red flowers. In the fields, dry grasses lay matted and tangled; spring's growth was still a promise in waiting. The snow-flattened weeds gave less cover for robbers, and Miles was glad for the stretches where no brush grew close to the road.

By the time they reached the outskirts of London, inns were no longer a novelty for Alison, who had rarely traveled before and was tired of the tedious trek. Yet when they first sighted London, she began to feel excited and grew anxious with anticipation. The city, old beyond belief, was almost mythical in its legends.

Alison leaned forward to catch sight of St. Paul's Cathedral towering over the town on her right. To her left, the Tower of London sprawled on Tower Hill. Five centuries before, William the Conquerer had begun the construction of the tower, which, like most of the important structures, had been whitewashed and seemed to gleam in the sunlight.

The illusion of cleanliness faded, however, as the band of men and women rode into the city itself. The roads were narrow and as muddy as the country lanes had been. Deep ruts from heavy wagons and potholes large enough to swallow a small pig pocked the way. The upper floors of tall, narrow buildings jutted out over the street, almost touching one another. Everywhere Alison looked there were people—men and women and children of all ages whose voices joined the cacophony of city noises. In the area near some food stalls, the road was littered with wilted cabbage leaves, withered leeks, and other produce of too poor a quality to sell. Pigs, chickens, and even a stray donkey browsed on the litter. As they left the market area, they neared the Thames, and Alison had her first view of the great river.

The Thames was much wider than the river that flowed past Wyndfell or any of the others they had crossed on their journey. It was a dark blue-gray, and when the rays of brilliant sunlight caught the wind-driven ripples just right, the surface spangled like a thousand diamonds. Leaves, scraps of paper, and refuse floated near the banks, and barges and more mobile boats shared the wide passageway with several tall-masted ships. Alison stared as if she could scarcely comprehended it all.

They passed London Bridge and followed the Thames westward, away from town. The buildings here were spaced farther apart than those in the center of town. Ahead lay the city of Westminster, which, though smaller, was considered London's twin city. To either side of the heavily traveled road, magnificent houses of landed gentry and rich noblemen connected the two cities.

Miles stopped the party outside an inn and had one of his men trumpet their arrival. Shortly the innkeeper came out to greet them. He was a portly man with round cheeks, a product of a generous table. Miles acknowledged the man and bargained for rooms for his people.

"Are we staying here? I thought we would reach Hampton Court today."

"We could, love, but it's best that we stay here the night so we'll be rested and have fresh clothes when we arrive there tomorrow." As he helped her off her horse, he assured her the Pelican Inn was known to be clean and hospitable.

The innkeeper welcomed them warmly and ushered

them into the common room. The rushes were freshly turned and hardly smelled at all. A long bar stretched along one wall, where two men were setting up a new keg of ale and a maid was polishing the wooden bar top. A number of long trestle tables and benches arranged in two rows filled the center of the room, and at the far end was a large fireplace with a welcoming blaze. Near the hearth, several men were engaged in pleasant conversation.

As was proper, Alison acknowledged the innkeeper with a nod but ignored all the other men. The rotund little man showed them up a narrow stairway to the floor above. The upper hall was winding and set at an angle from the common room, for there had been many additions and alterations to the inn over the years. The hallway was dim, but they followed the innkeeper without concern. If the place had had a reputation for robbers, Miles would have avoided it. One of the better inns, the Pelican prided itself upon safety for its guests.

At the end of the corridor they were shown their chamber, a spacious one by comparison with the other inns, and much brighter because of its several windows. Miles looked out each one to be sure there was no access to the chamber from trees or ledges. He nodded his approval and gave the innkeeper six shillings for their room and an appropriate fee for the lodging of his retinue and horses.

With several hours remaining before dark, Miles and Alison, flanked by Leatrice, Trahern, and several of the guardsmen, went out to see the city. Not far from the inn was a row of tiny shops, the owners of which lived above them in the outward-jutting second stories. Very little sunlight reached the cobbled street of the fashionable area, and emerald moss grew along the noisome central gutter that carried away the street's liquid refuse.

At the first shop, a perfumery, Miles bought each of them an orange pomander studded with cloves. Even though the plague was most common in the warmer months, it was an ever-present threat, and cloves were known to prevent it. As they walked along the shady street, Alison was glad for the pungent scent of the pomander, which overpowered the more odious one of the filth all about them.

Across the street they entered the milliner's, where the women delighted in the vast assortment of caddises, inkles, and various ribbons of velvet, satin, and embroidery. After debating the merits of the different trimmings, Alison and Leatrice each bought a handful of the colors and types that were seldom available at Wyndfell's fairs.

Leatrice, Trahern, and the guardsmen lingered in the shop that sold leather and suede goods, while Alison and Miles wandered down the street. "I've never seen so many things!" she marveled as they stepped into a shop which sold only fabrics. Every spare inch of the walls was covered by bolts of rich cloth.

"Choose something," Miles encouraged her. "Enough to sew for the coming year. We'll likely not see London very often." He fingered a length of cloth of gold that shimmered like molten metal. "The ware is of a fine quality."

The shopkeeper had come to them and bobbed his head and upper body gratefully. "Welcome, my lord and lady. You honor my humble shop."

Alison acknowledged the man's politeness with a smile. "In faith, you have many lengths of beautiful material here. How much for the cloth of gold?"

When he quoted his price, her eyes widened, but Miles said, "Done! We will take the entire bolt." He gave instructions to have the cloth delivered to the inn and turned to another bolt in hues of peacock blue, emerald, and purple. "We will have this as well."

Alison was not accustomed to such extravagance, and though she knew they could well afford it, felt mildly apprehensive. After the years of her mother's and Charles's parsimony, she was reluctant to spend so freely. But a spool of wide lace imported from Flanders caught her eye and she sighed in appreciation of its intricate design. Almost shyly she placed it with the other purchases, and Miles smiled his approval.

By the time they finished in the fabric shop and ate the supper Miles bought from a pastry cart, the narrow strip of sky was darkening. Dusk was quick and short in the cavernous streets, and already a lamplighter was touching his torch to the few lamps and ringing his bell to let people know he was on duty.

Alison was glad for the guardsmen's presence as they started back to the inn. The side streets were already black pits and near one stood a group of rough-looking men. When Alison put her hand in the curve of Miles's arm, he patted it comfortingly, making her feel safe and protected. She noticed, however, that the guardsmen walked silently, their hands on the pommels of their swords until they were safely inside the inn's small courtyard.

Yellow light splashed from the square mullioned windows onto the cobblestones, and one could hear muffled singing. When the door was opened, music poured out. Several musicians had taken their places by the fire, and they were leading the inn's guests in singing familiar songs. Two barmaids were carrying beer, ale, and a stronger brew called hull cheese to the revelers. Miles put his arm around Alison and led her briskly to the stairs. This was an excellent inn, but Alison was a beautiful woman, and there was no point in advertising her presence. Nonetheless, most of the men had already cast admiring glances at her.

When Alison and Miles were safely in their bedchamber, the innkeeper and two of his sons brought in their purchases, as well as a repast of wine, cheese, and bread. The innkeeper left, but the boys stayed to entertain Miles and Alison while they ate, one playing a lute and the other a cittern. Alison felt as if she had stepped into a fantasy-filled world where anything and everything might happen.

"After seeing London, I swear I could believe in dragons," she whispered to Miles in an awe-filled voice.

He smiled and winked at her. "Wait until you see court," he promised. "Even London cannot equal it."

Alison's smile quickly faded as she felt a cold wash of fear. Tomorrow she would be face-to-face with the king, and until now she had deluded herself that some miracle might intervene and it would never happen.

Although the brightly painted red-yellow-and-white barge that transported them to Hampton Court was not an uncommon sight, as it was often hired by those who preferred the open waterway to winding through the dense forests surrounding the palace, it drew much attention from the people who dotted the banks of the Thames. Alison leaned on the rail, careful not to disturb the flowers and boughs of fragrant greenery laced along it, and marveled at the gray-brown swell of water, topped by the foamy white wavelets that curled back in the barge's wake. She had never seen a barge, let alone ridden on the water. Leatrice was almost as astounded as her mistress, but Miles and Trahern, who were both accustomed to riding on far grander barges than this, merely smiled indulgently.

London and the numerous parks and mansions that lined the Thames were behind them. Ahead was the magnificent palace of Whitehall, gleaming in the spring sunlight. Spectacular gardens rolled down to the water's edge, and a flock of snowy swans preened themselves on the grassy bank and swam lazily in the water. Two cygnets, still awkward and not yet beautiful, waddled after their mother in search of food.

"How lovely!" Alison said, almost breathless. "Do you think we might get some swans for Wyndfell?" The sights were grand, and Alison had allowed herself to become totally absorbed with them in order to keep her thoughts from racing ahead to their destination.

"Of course, love, but you must tell Cook not to bake them."

"She can purchase others for baking. I would have some for pets."

"Their temperament is unlikely for a pet, I fear," Trahern put in.

"Nevertheless, I shall try. They will look very pretty on our moat."

"If anyone can tame a swan, my lady can," Leatrice said loyally.

As they passed the fortresslike Houses of Parliament, the tower of the Palace of Westminster, and the magnificent peaks of Westminster Abbey, Alison grew more uncomfortable, craning her neck to keep them in sight as long as she could.

Mistaking Alison's nervousness for excitement, Miles patted her hand and said, "Don't fret, love. We'll ride back and see all of it once we're rested from the journey."

"Yes," she said distractedly. "I would like that very much."

"We will come to court every year, if it pleases you."

Her breath caught in her throat, and she couldn't answer. Meeting the king might be an ordeal she wouldn't want to repeat even for the lure of London.

Only moments later, a great parkland far more extensive than any they had seen before came into view. As their barge approached the landing, prominently marked with the royal coat-of-arms, Alison noticed the guards stiffen in readiness to defend the impressive royal barges that were anchored there for the king's use. The privy gardens were up the sloping green, and behind them was the imposing red brick palace. Alison felt her mouth go dry as she faced the moment she had alternately anticipated and dreaded all her life. She was about to meet her father—the most powerful king in the world.

The horses were led onto the grass, and Miles put

his cupped hands down to receive her foot. Although her knees felt too weak to swing onto the saddle, she had no choice but to try. With little effort, Miles lifted her onto her mount. She was wearing a new gown in the fashionable shade called lady's blush, over a marigold-hued kirtle, and as she settled into the saddle, she automatically spread the yards of satin and velvet over the horse's rump. Did she look presentable? Was the cut of her sleeves still the current fashion? Perhaps she should have worn the pearl-and-topaz pendant rather than the garnet one. Or a pale pink bongrace on her golden hood rather than the lemon-yellow one with silver embroidery. Was her hair still demurely hidden?—for the wind on the water had been rather blustery. And her rings—were there enough to show the status and importance of Wyndfell and the Garretts? Was she wearing too many? Could one wear too many jewels?

Miles covered her hand with his and smiled up at her. "You're beautiful," he said for her ears alone. "You'll outshine all the court beauties and earn all the ladies' jealousy."

"Are you certain I'm properly dressed?" she asked nervously.

"I shall have to fight off every gallant in Hampton Court," he assured her.

They rode up the broad tree-lined drive, and as they neared the great gateway with its arched entrance and hexagonal towers, Alison lifted her head. She was Lady Alison Garrett of Wyndfell and knew she was of better lineage than anyone at court save the royal family. She could brave her way through this.

They entered the deep shade of the cool gatehouse and emerged into Base Court. Ahead lay Anne Boleyn's Gateway, identical to the outer one but two stories shorter in height. The rounded gateway led to the inner court, and at Miles's urging, Alison looked back over the gateway to see the huge astronomical clock which gave the court its name. The marvelous clock, commissioned when the king married Catherine Howard, indicated not only the hour but also the month and day, how many days had passed in the year, the phase of the moon, and even the time of high tide at London Bridge.

Alison's eyes were large with wonder as she walked up the steps of the great hall on the north side of the court. Liveried servants were bustling about everywhere, and the massive doors opened for them as if by magic. The magnificence of the great hall left Alison breathless. Tapestries of the finest quality depicting the history of Abraham lined the walls. Above the tapestries, in the whitewashed walls, elaborate stained-glass windows depicted the heraldry of the great houses of England. Above it all a spectacular hammerbeam ceiling of dark wood boasted intricately gilded carving.

"I never saw such a chamber," Alison gasped. "I had thought Wyndfell was grand!"

"Wyndfell is not a royal residence. Here you will see the best artistry England has to offer. Old Cardinal Wolsey made it a great showplace. King Henry transformed it into a jewel. Plays are performed here because this room is large enough to seat most of the nobility who live at court. I doubt not that we will see some performance while we are here. The king is fond of all manner of entertainments."

Alison had expected grandeur, but this was much more opulent than she had ever imagined. As she looked about, she noted that everything in the great room was spectacular, including the people. She was glad now she had worn her best rings and that her garnet pendant was a large blood-red one encircled by teardrops of diamonds in filigreed gold. In a place like this, extravagance was the ordinary.

A servant escorted them through the watching chamber and down a long gallery that passed the chapel and opened onto a sunny gallery full of people. Rows of tall windows overlooked the Cloister Green Court with its miniature-scaled yew maze and statuary. The doors to the garden were open to admit the scents and freshness of spring, but the room was still close with its crowd of laughing and talking people. When the servant who had shown them in announced them, several turned to greet Miles and Trahern as if they were congenial friends.

Everywhere Alison looked were people, and brilliant colors, and tapestries and gilded carvings. The sound was as cacophonous as a fair day on Wyndfell's green, yet everyone seemed to have an air of belonging. Faced with so many grand strangers, Alison felt a rare shyness. Nothing in her secluded life had prepared her for this. If Miles was accustomed to such a display, he must find Wyndfell too rustic for comfort! She had never considered that anything could so outshine Wyndfell, by far the grandest of any of the castles in its neighboring parishes.

Miles introduced her to countless smiling faces, and soon she could recall only a blur of titles, features, and accents. His eyes roamed the room in search of someone—possibly the king. She felt her steps falter and lag as her eyes also darted about.

A tight knot of nobles was clustered near one of the open doors, and Miles led her to them. These men and women were even more sumptuously attired than the majority of the crowd, and they were laughing uproariously at a jest from a petite woman. At first Alison stared; then she remembered to lower her eyes respectfully. One didn't gape at a queen.

Queen Catherine was small and plump and had the quick movements of a bird. Her nose was rather long and her chin a bit too small, but somehow her plain features conveyed the illusion of beauty. In pitch, her voice was high and musical with laughter, and to Alison she looked more like a heady girl than a queen. Her thick hair was auburn, but not nearly as bright as Alison's, nor were her hands as delicately shaped. Her heavily lidded eyes took Alison in at a glance, and Alison felt as if a royal decision had been made.

Giving no show of disapproval over being presented with a more beautiful woman, Catherine acknowledged Miles's kneeling greeting and Alison's deep curtsy. "Arise, Lord and Lady Garrett. I vow, Lord Garrett, that court has been dull since your departure. Many of our ladies went into mourning at word of your marriage." Her retinue laughed at her witty thrust. "You mustn't mind, Lady Alison. He was a great favorite here, and after all, we saw him first." The look in Catherine's eyes lent an element of seductiveness to her words as she met Miles's gaze.

Alison didn't know what to say. Was she supposed to laugh with this woman over Miles's previous conquests? And how did the queen know so much about them? She shifted uncomfortably.

"You have never been to court," a decidedly masculine voice said at her elbow.

She turned to see a tall man with light brown hair and pale blue eyes. He bowed and swept his plumed hat in a courtly fashion. "Allow me to present myself. I am Lord Jarvis Hyde of Hyde Castle in the Midlands, at your service, Lady Alison."

"Honored, Lord Jarvis," she said automatically. She glanced back at Miles. The queen still claimed his attention.

"You mustn't hang upon your lord husband like a peasant wife on fair day. This is Hampton Court, where all mingle freely."

Alison was affronted by the man's audacity, and before her better judgment could prevail, she heard herself snapping back, "I was not hanging upon him in any fashion, my lord, and if I were you, I would mind my tongue. It is in danger of flailing you to death."

"Ah, so you have a temper as well as beauty," he exclaimed delightedly. "I can see you will be an asset to the gathering."

Curbing her tongue as she weighed his words against

his mien, Alison concluded that he was merely teasing her, and warily redirected the conversation by asking, "Are there always so many here?"

Jarvis looked about as if he hadn't noticed the crush of people. "I suppose. Some live here, others are here to be presented to his majesty or to beg a royal favor, or whatnot. Court is never dull."

"No, I should say it is not."

"See those men over there? Three are foreign ambassadors and can scarcely speak the king's English at all, though fortunately King Henry speaks their language fluently. The other two are barons. One is enamored of his twelve-year-old cousin and is striving to wed her by special dispensation; the other gentleman prefers young boys. That page yonder with the flaxen hair is one of his favorites."

Miles had managed to excuse himself from the queen, and returned to overhear Lord Jarvis' last statement.

Alison stared openly. "That's shameful!"

"That's court," Jarvis corrected.

Noticing Alison's blush, Miles moved closer to stand possessively by her side, forcing Jarvis to step back for propriety's sake. "I see you are telling my lady wife the newest gossip."

" 'Tis scarcely new. That page is merely the most recent in a series of boys for Lord Hayes."

"Yet I doubt such is entirely proper discourse for Lady Garrett's sensibilities. You forget that we have come recently from the country, where such ribald behavior is never mentioned."

Jarvis gave Alison a dazzling smile. "Pardon, my lady, if I have offended you. I forget there are some who still cling to the virtue of innocence." His words were polite, but his implication was that such practice was an anachronism.

Hoping to distract Alison from Lord Jarvis' insidious gibes, Miles said, "Look over there. See the man with the monkey?" Alison followed his gaze to a rather ordinary-looking man dressed in a green doublet and a cap with multicolored fringes. "That's Will Somers, the king's favorite fool. He is the king's confidant as well, and is famous for his mocking wit. I am surprised to see him here in the king's absence. The boy standing near Will is the replacement for old Sexton, who is now feeble with age."

"The king is not here?"

"He is in the palace, of course, but he is confined to his closet with an ailment," Jarvis explained in sympathetic tones.

"He's not seriously ill, I hope?" While she wouldn't wish him ill health, she wouldn't object to the king's remaining in his closet for their entire visit.

" 'Tis his legs again. The ulcer has spread from his affected leg to the other and is causing him much pain and fever," Jarvis said.

"I had not realized his condition had worsened," Miles replied with concern.

"The news is not bandied about freely, but all here at court know. He frequently keeps to his closet and will see only those gentlemen who have urgent business."

"I am amazed his queen comports herself so freely," Alison observed. "One would never guess her lord husband lies ailing."

The men exchanged a quick look, and Jarvis discreetly put a finger to his lips as he whispered with gravity, "You have touched on a subject that no one discusses aloud."

Alison looked surprised at the import of his words. Was there already trouble between Henry and his new queen? She longed to ask but dared not.

" 'Tis not as it sounds," Jarvis said quickly, reading Alison's consternation. "His majesty dotes upon Queen Catherine and desires her to be merry whether he may join her or not. She goes to his closet each night to amuse him and game with him and tell him all the new gossip. I doubt not your name will reach his ears very soon. Our queen is ever hasty to notice beauty of all sorts." Again he exchanged a furtive looked with Miles, and his eyes seemed to be signaling a warning.

Alison tried to shrug off the uneasiness she felt. What difference would it make when the king was told of her arrival? He was ill, and possibly the confrontation she dreaded would be avoided on this visit to court. She gazed up at Miles's face and found him looking back at the direction of the queen. Worry puckered her brow, for Queen Catherine had been very glad to see him. Could it be she had a flirtation in mind? Nonsense, she chided herself. Catherine was a queen and Miles a mere viscount. Besides, Catherine was married to a man no one would dare cuckold. No, she was imagining the entire thing.

But when she looked back at the group by the door, Catherine was watching Miles in a distinctly predatory manner. As Alison watched, an older woman with whom Queen Catherine was speaking turned from the queen to Miles and seemed to be appraising him. When the woman looked away again, Alison asked Miles, "Who is the older woman talking to the queen?"

"Her name is Lady Rochford. She's been with the queen since her majesty was quite young. In time you will meet her, as well." For reasons that Alison couldn't pinpoint, she felt deeply disturbed, and she put her hand possessively on Miles's arm.

14

In the parks at Hampton Court yellow blossoms of wild celandine and the royal purple of violets colorfully intermingled while the pale green flowers called lords-and-ladies nodded over the grasses. Wild strawberry lured a profusion of butterflies that skipped and flitted in the warming air, inspiring numerous designs under the quick needles of the ladies of the court. During her first week at Hampton Court Alison had melded into daily activities and was graciously accepted. No further mention had been made of her meeting with the king, and she had no intention of asking.

Always proficient at designing cartoons for embroidery, Alison was fashioning a length of primrose-yellow satin to resemble a strip of sun-washed meadow, while the other ladies were sewing their own devices. A pleasant hum of conversation filled the room, accompanied by the melodies of the ever-present musicians.

The queen was attending other matters in another part of the palace, and with the men away at a hunt, the woman were able to talk more freely. Leatrice sat near Alison and worked diligently on a length of velvet that would be part of her wedding chest.

A tall woman who was with child sighed and placed her hand on the small of her back to ease her muscles.

"The babe grows heavy early," she commented to no one in particular. "I wager 'twill be twins."

"Pray not," another woman said. "They are twice the burden, longer to birth, and much more bothersome than a single babe. I know, for I have twin daughters. Nor will giving your husband two at one blow give you longer reprieve. Come next year you'll be quickening again."

Alison tried to cover the disappointment such talk brought to mind. Pregnancy was a married woman's common state. Most spent at least half their lives carrying a child or recovering from childbed. Many had only a brief respite before the cycle started again. Yet Alison had no reason to believe she was with child. She had been married for months now, and she was becoming rather concerned. Sons were necessary for the continuation of the family name, and daughters would grow to become companions for their mothers as they matured. To be barren was not only deplorable but also a justifiable reason for having a marriage annulled.

Lady Amy Billingsgate, a woman who gossiped almost continuously, patted her tightly laced middle. "I, too, have suspicions that I've been caught again. Not that I can ever hope to take your title at proficiency, Lady Halston. Why, you've had a babe every year I've known you. Twins more than once. And few have died. Many would envy your breeding ability."

The thin woman smiled back but said, "It has not been easy. I suppose the angels know I will welcome all the babes I'm allotted. But in faith I hope to stay fallow awhile. The last lying-in nearly put me under."

"I had heard that babes are birthed more easily each time," Alison said.

"Aye, to some extent, but a body needs time to rest, methinks."

Lady Amy leaned forward, her bright eyes glittering. "Our lady queen could use a portion of your travail, Lady Halston. No doubt she prays for the visit of one of your angels."

Alison stared at the woman in surprise. Were there already whispers of this new queen's barrenness?

"Perhaps the problem lies in their great physical disparity," another woman said. "She is young and small, while the king is so large and is aging."

"Lower your voices," an elderly woman chided. "What if you should be overheard? Besides, 'tis well known an aging man may father children, and the king is up and about these past few days. He will sire several more children."

"Aye, girls or weaklings," Amy snorted. "The king needs a son like Henry Fitzroy, but born on the right side of the blanket."

"God rest him," a woman said automatically. "Lord Henry was a son to be proud of."

Alison looked down at her stitching. Henry Fitzroy had been a bastard like herself, but he had been groomed as a possible heir to the crown before his untimely death. How unfair it was that sons were so prized, while daughters were considered mere pawns to unite families or riches.

"Methinks the queen may not have to rely upon an old king's seed to get her babes. Thomas Culpepper buzzes around her like a bee to a flower."

"Hush!" the aging woman said angrily. "Are you daft?" She glanced about uneasily, as did several other women.

Alison's head came up, and she opened her mouth in surprise. "The queen has taken a lover?" she gasped. Alison knew nothing could be so foolhardy!

"Nonsense," the older woman scolded with a warning glance. "Nothing could be further from the truth. Lady Amy is telling lies."

Amy pouted as she jabbed her needle in and out of her cloth, but was smart enough not to defend her rash words. "I notice Lady Rochford is also absent," she said sullenly.

The old woman retorted, "Hold your tongue! I hear the view is fine from the pikes on London Bridge!"

"London Bridge?" Alison asked Lady Halston, not understanding the older woman's reference.

"When traitors are beheaded, their heads are left on those bridge pikes for the crows."

"Oh." Alison drew back and glanced at Leatrice, who also looked aghast. Court was a dangerous place despite its glittering patina. Alison longed more than ever for the peace of Wyndfell.

Miles rode near the king as the dogs searched for their quarry. These were the large boar hounds chosen as a pack for their hunting skills and the tune of their voices. At full bay the hounds' voices blended into a true note, as if they were singing.

The best riding horses came from the Continent, as had Miles's prized Barbaristo from Arabia. English horses were generally trained too young and worked beyond their endurance in their early years. No gift was more prized by the king than a good horse. Thus Miles had brought with him a huge Mantuan barb as a present, and the king was riding it for the first time.

"Does the barb's gait please your grace?" Miles asked. Since their arrival the king had been coolly civil and warmly affectionate by turns, leading Miles to believe that news of the incendiary placards had indeed reached Henry's ears.

"He travels well, though not so fine as old Govenatore. There will never be another to match him." He leaned forward to pat the bright bay neck that arched so proudly. Henry gave an unexpected but typical burst of laughter and added, "They don't make horses large enough these days, hey? I wager they are shrinking!" He struck his mighty girth with the flat of his palm.

"Perhaps so, your majesty." Miles smiled. He had looked long for a horse big enough to carry the king, and had finally sent his head stableman to Italy to buy

WYNDFELL

one. The animal had cost all of forty pounds sterling. It was a considerable sum, but Miles deemed it a small price to pay for royal favor, especially when he wasn't certain that Yorkshire wasn't on the verge of another uprising.

The king, like Miles, rode in the Italian manner, controlling his mount with the pressure of his legs and with verbal commands, and occasionally touching his horse's flank or shoulder with a wand. Both wore spurs as a symbol of their knighthood, but neither would use them on their prized horses.

Miles rode a powerful gray with a coat the hue of steel. The animal had been trained by Miles himself and could leap to a full run from a standing position, turn in full stride, and stop as quickly as if he had run into a wall. Miles had even taught him the difficult capriole, or goat leap, where the horse leapt into the air, kicked out, and landed in almost the same space in imitation of the dance step. It was an impressive maneuver. He had named the horse Excalibur after the fabled sword of King Arthur. Excalibur could soar over the highest hedge or brave the deepest thicket. Miles believed the horse enjoyed the chase as well as did the hounds.

"How goes it in Yorkshire?" Henry asked.

Miles was careful to keep his features calm and measure his words. "Quite well, your majesty. When I left Wyndfell the crops were in the field and the sheep were fattening."

"I didn't mean the welfare of your castle," the king said testily. "I meant the people of your district."

"They are going about their business as usual. There have been no incidents of open rebellion. They show me due deference as one of your men, and church is well-attended."

"Hmmm," Henry said noncommittally. He had just received a message from Sir Edmund Campbell that mentioned a sense of unrest among the servants. "Are there no heretic priests in the area?"

"Sire, I've not seen any priest at all." He omitted mention of the anchoress, whom he considered harmless. "Why do you ask?"

"By Jove! How like your father you are! I tell you, Lord Miles, I miss him sorely. All the men about me these days toady and nod and will not speak to me straight." He nudged his horse to a canter and rode ahead of Miles.

Miles hung back as he considered the entire interchange. In spite of the king's bluff manner, Miles had the sensation he had been baited. Yet who would have written to the king about the placards? And if someone had, did he also mention the anchoress?

As the hounds ahead of them raised their voices in a melodious cry, the hunters caught their first sight of the boar. Miles signaled Excalibur to a full run and tried to put the worry from his mind.

The boar was a huge beast with cruel eyes and curving tusks. After a short run he backed into a thicket of thorn bushes to protect his flank and lowered his head to lunge at the dogs. One hound, an animal new to the kennels, rushed the boar and was flung lifeless into the air. The more seasoned dogs harried the ferocious beast, leaping and dodging just out of his reach.

By design the king threw the first javelin, and the shaft struck deep into the beast's shoulder. Henry grabbed another javelin from his page and threw it, too, with keen precision. Then the rest of the men shot the animal with arrows and the boar fell to his side with a grunt of pain.

Henry swung to the ground and drew his sword to make the kill. His men hastened to his side to protect him, yet pretended to be competing with him. Using his considerable skill, Henry dealt the death blow. The boar went rigid, then collapsed. With a triumphant shout, Henry drew back again and struck the boar's head, almost severing it from its body. The men cheered and clapped the king on his massive shoulders. For a fleeting moment Henry was again the golden king and most able athlete of the land. Then his years and ill health settled on him again, and with great difficulty he pulled himself up onto his horse.

Miles motioned for the huntsmen to come forward as the nobles mounted, and gave them orders to transport the boar back to the palace. Already the kennel master had his dogs in check and was rewarding them with chunks of raw meat from his pack. When the boar was gutted, the dogs would also be given the parts considered waste.

Henry looked down at the stilled beast. "Look ye well, Lord Miles," he said in a tone that wasn't quite jovial. "Thus must we deal with our adversaries. Nature teaches us lessons of life if we will but take note."

"But surely there are no adversaries on this side of the channel," Miles replied carefully. "Not in these days."

The king lifted his large head and pointed toward the sky. "We are like that hawk," he said, using the royal plurality. "We are ever on guard, and when we strike, we do so like a bolt of lightning. No warning. No reprieve. And no escape." He grinned, and again there was the charismatic hint of the young god he had once been. "We are all animals, Lord Miles. The only question is, which animal are we?"

"Like my father, I would be the fox," Miles said with a smile.

Henry gauged him as he responded with a laugh. "A good answer, lad. Like unto your father. You could do no better than that." He waved his thick arm and shouted, "To the palace! I thirst for wine."

Miles followed at a quick lope, but he pondered the king's words. The king, who spoke in riddles to confound his companions, might have meant no more than a poetic allegory. Then again, he might have been issuing a warning. Miles looked forward to his return to Wyndfell's simpler life.

On hearing of the hunters' arrival, Alison went with

the other women to meet the men in the great hall, not realizing that the king would still be among them. When she saw Henry enter at the far side of the room, she felt a tremor of awe. Everything about him was oversized—his height, his breadth, his booming laugh, his expansive gestures. Even though he was stained from the hunt, his regal bearing was clearly evident as he dominated the room in a magnificent way.

Miles entered close on the king's heels, and as the king stopped to catch his breath, Miles sought out Alison. "There will be boar meat for supper. We took down a huge creature."

"You weren't hurt, were you?" she asked as she saw the red-brown flecks on his jerkin.

"No, not a scratch. We only lost one dog. The king himself made the kill."

Alison chanced a nervous look toward the king, and was surprised to see Queen Catherine adoringly by his side. The queen's kinswoman, Lady Rochford, the widow of Anne Boleyn's brother—her accused lover—stood by Queen Catherine. Her gaunt cheeks and dull-hued garments made her an unlikely choice for the young queen's companion, but the two were almost inseparable. Alison wondered how Lady Rochford must feel toward the king for not only executing her young husband but also linking him with his sister in incest. Whatever her feelings, Lady Rochford habitually dressed in somber colors as befitted a widow, and this suggested she had not entirely forgiven or forgotten.

The king was describing the hunt in heroic terms to those about him, but his disquieting gaze fell primarily on the ladies. His eyes met Alison's across the crowd and for a moment held. Her heart skipped and she felt herself pale. She knew not how to conquer her fear of the enormous man. On one hand, she desperately wanted a word, even a sign from him that would indicate he knew her to be his daughter. On the other, she dreaded being noticed at all, for the oath of fealty hung unspoken, and she knew she couldn't voice the words he would demand to hear. She couldn't place her soul in eternal peril to placate this tyrant, and the oath was worded such that no evasion was possible.

Henry began edging toward her, but Alison pretended not to notice. She smiled up at Miles and said, "Shall I fetch you a tankard of ale?"

"There are servants to do that."

"Of course, love. That's what I meant. I will go find one at once." She hurried away seconds before Henry drew close enough to speak. Avoiding him was not always going to be so easy.

Miles again congratulated the king on his kill. Henry left the room to speak to one of the members of the Privy Council that sought his attention on a matter of some importance. Across the room, Miles saw his friends Sir John and Sir Stephen and quickly went to them. They, along with Lord George, had been absent since his arrival at court, and Miles was pleased to see them at last. After the men warmly greeted each other, Miles learned that Sir Vance was in Stratford with his bride.

With a grin Miles said, "He seems reluctant to leave her, for all his complaints."

"You'd think no woman ever gave birth before. The babe's not due for a while, yet Vance will not leave her parents' castle until she is safely delivered," Stephen said with a laugh. "If she proves as fertile as Lady Halston, we may never see him again."

"He will weary of the lyings-in before that long." John grinned. "For the last month he has been unable to see her alone, for she has been ill, but not seriously. I hope for his sake the child is a healthy lad. Vance is the last in that branch of his family and needs a son."

Stephen nodded. "I would hate to see the name and lands come to an end. So many of the ancient names are dwindling these days."

"What of you?" John asked. "Is the Garrett name promised continuity?"

"Not yet." He smiled. "But I've time left before old age strikes me."

John made a ribald comment that made both men laugh. Miles looked from one open face to the other. There wasn't the slightest hint that they had given the king anything but the most glowing report of affairs at Wyndfell. Both were the sort who found duplicity impossible, especially John, who preferred an open battle to a game of words. He was a pure soldier and hadn't a subtle bone in his body. Stephen was more glib of tongue, but he was still forthright. If either had seen anything amiss, he would have told Miles as well as the king. Miles had fought beside all four of the friends and trusted them completely. But he couldn't ask if they had given the king a report of unrest, for they would certainly inquire as to why he thought they might have.

Seeing Alison reenter the hall, he made his way to her. As often when he saw her unexpectedly, he was amazed at her beauty. She used no paint nor artifice, but her cheeks had the bloom of country air and her eyes sparkled without the aid of eye-bright. In this company of bored eyes and too-brittle laughter, Alison was as fresh as a meadow-sweet breeze.

She smiled at his approach. "Your ale is forthcoming. Ah, here it is now."

Miles took the tankard from the servant and offered Alison the first sip. "I missed you today," he said in a voice that reached only her ears. "I would rather have ridden out with you alone. Mayhap we could have found a private hedge or an unbeaten path."

"I too would have preferred that. I confess I am confused by so many people," she said with a laugh. "And we thought Wyndfell lacked privacy!"

Before Miles could answer, the queen walked up and put her small hand on Miles's arm. "I have heard such tales of this great boar—surely they are exaggerated!" Her gaze was for Miles alone.

"He was indeed a monster, your grace. One of the largest I've ever seen."

"Goodness," Catherine sighed. "How brave you must be to face such a creature. I'm certain I should faint dead away at the sight of one."

Alison felt very awkward beside the petite queen. Because she had not been addressed, she couldn't speak, yet she didn't have the permission to leave. Nor did she really want to, for she saw how Catherine's eyes were devouring not only Miles's face but also the rest of him. Once again Alison recalled the gossip about the queen and Culpepper. Queen or not, Catherine was a woman on a hunt of her own, and the prey at this moment was Lord Miles Garrett. Alison unobtrusively slipped her hand into Miles's, and he squeezed it gently to reassure her.

As Catherine prevailed on Miles to recount the hunt in detail, Alison looked past her to see the king come back into the room. How could anyone dare to cuckold such a man? Either the queen was mad or the gossips lied. However, Alison was skilled at reading hidden nuances, and she saw how Catherine stood, leaning toward Miles and gazing raptly up at him. Propriety would have placed a greater distance between them, and whenever Catherine spoke, she managed a casual touch of his hand or his arm. Alison felt very uncomfortable. Could Miles not see how the queen's gaze set them apart from the crowd? She didn't think he had ever been Catherine's lover, but anyone observing them would guess it to be a future possibility. Alison trusted Miles completely, but the king would not be so tolerant of mere appearance.

Just when she was at her wits' end to know how to break up this all-too-obvious conversation, the king started toward them and Lady Rochford pulled secretively at Catherine's sleeve. At once Catherine's face lost its rapt interest and became merely polite and her small hand withdrew into her own sphere. When she looked away, Alison drew Miles into the crowd.

"Did you see how she looked at you?" Alison whispered. "She was like a cat in the dovecote."

"Are you jealous, love? You have no reason."

"I may have no reason on your account, but I have upon hers." She tiptoed up to whisper in his ear. "Have you not heard the rumors about her?"

Miles gave her a silencing look. "Such gossip is never to be repeated!"

"Then you *have* heard it! Marry, I think 'tis true!"

"True or not, it will never touch me, for I am yours. Besides, I believe it not."

"How can you say that?"

"You are not accustomed to the prattle of court. Rumors feed upon rumors, and there are tales told about everyone. It means nothing."

"Then 'tis a dangerous sport!"

"Aye, that it is, and for that reason I'll not have you partake of it." He put his arm about her waist. "Promise me you'll not discuss it."

"I promise. But you must swear you'll not let yourself get cornered."

He grinned as if he thought she was being adorably foolish. "I give you my word."

She didn't feel reassured because she could tell Miles didn't believe the rumor about the queen's affairs, but there was nothing else she could say. If only Miles weren't so contented to be at court, they could leave and avoid all the potential conflict.

The next week the marsh marigolds turned the riverbanks to gold and brought the first blush to the crabapple trees. Bees hummed in the pale pink blossoms, fulfilling their obligation to nature, and in the formal gardens some of the early-blooming flowers were making a show.

The gardens were a constant lure to Alison. Long winding avenues of yew were flanked by jewellike gardens on either side, tiny reflecting ponds with their lotus-shaped water lilies, and an occasional fountain.

She learned her way through the acres of beauty, sometimes hiding herself and Miles in the almost maze-like yew paths or getting away from the bustle of court life by strolling beside the silver Thames. She memorized the layout of her favorite knot gardens so that she might reproduce them at Wyndfell, and learned the names of the various types of damask roses with their flat, bright petals and gold centers, the exotic orchids which surprisingly had no scent, and the columbines that glowed in vivid colors.

Some of the gardens were populated by strongly aromatic plants that were in current fashion, such as white double violets, gillyflowers, and honeysuckle. Also some were bordered with mint, rosemary, and marjoram, which would give off their pleasing scents when stroked. Carpets of creeping thyme covered many of the winding paths.

Alison often lost herself for hours in the gardens, where there were fewer people to intrude on her thoughts. But in case she might see someone, she was prudent enough to carry a book of devotions and walk as if she were in devout meditation.

She was holding her small Protestant prayer book, but admiring a brilliant rose, when she rounded a corner of shrubbery to find herself face-to-face with the king. Her mouth fell open, and she clutched at her book to keep from dropping it. The king looked almost as startled as she did, and Alison had the awful thought that she might have interrupted one of his romantic rendezvous. Suddenly she recalled her manners, and at once swept down in a deep curtsy.

"Arise, arise," Henry commanded. "What brings you here, Lady Alison?"

"I . . . I was praying and meditating," she stammered, holding out her book as proof.

"So you read, do you?" He took the book and glanced at the open page. "I would not have suspected you of being susceptible to gluttony."

She blushed, for she had merely opened the book at

random, and had not noticed the text. "I believe in prevention, your majesty."

Henry gave a quick laugh and she jumped. "Prevention! Ha! I like that! Some men say learning makes ill company with a woman, but I think not. Prevention!" He bellowed out another burst of amusement, and Alison was very glad she hadn't inadvertently opened the book to a page impugning adultery or murder.

"I have seen little of you since your arrival at court," Henry said thoughtfully. "You always seem to be leaving a room as I am entering."

"The palace is so enormous," Alison forced herself to say. "I had not meant to be rude, but rather not to intrude. I know your time is spent on more important things."

She looked up to see Henry's silver-blue eyes studying her unabashedly. Although she quaked inside, she kept her chin high and met his eyes without flinching. The experience was unsettling, to say the least, for although she saw great intelligence, something sinister was there as well. A brittle coldness in his azure depths seemed to indicate he had been deserted or hurt by all he had ever held dear and that he no longer could summon the element of pure trust. Alison, feeling as if she had seen too much, looked away.

"You have been at court several weeks and have still not been formally presented," Henry said. "I am amiss." His voice was gentle and not at all what she had expected.

"I am not impatient, your majesty. I can wait."

"You intrigue me, Lady Alison. I think you may be the only undemanding person in my court," he said with a wry twinkle in his voice. "Have you no issue you wish resolved; no royal favor to beg?"

"None, sire." She could never admit to him that she did desire but one thing: she wanted him to call her "daughter" just once. Looking into his face, she could see no feature that resembled her own. His face might once have been angelic, as her mother had said, but it was now bloated from dissipation. His blue eyes were small, whereas her honey-brown ones were large and almond-shaped. His mouth was a pink cupid's bow and hers was softer, more femininely sensuous. His hair and beard were red-gold, though beginning to silver with the years, whereas her own hair was a deep reddish-brown. A dreadful thought dawned upon her. What if her mother had been mistaken about the identity of her father, or had even lied? Alison had never considered this.

"There is to be a banquet soon," Henry was saying. "You may be presented there, and I will hear your oath of fealty at that time."

"My oath?" she whispered. Her body suddenly turned cold, though her face was hot.

"Just a formality. Your lord husband is a man I know well. But your former husband was a traitor, and it would be remiss of me not to hear your oath."

"Yes, your majesty," she said helplessly, and curtsied.

He turned to go, but paused and looked back at her for a long moment before walking away.

Alison felt faint and pressed her palm to her middle. Why had he stared at her so? What if he didn't think of himself as kin to her, and he was considering her for a conquest! The very idea sent chills through her. Quickly she made her way back to the palace, resolving never again to walk alone in the gardens.

15

The great hall had been turned into a theater for the evening's performance, and rows of benches, stools, and chairs were arranged for the audience according to rank. Alison and Miles took their seats in the row of chairs, with Alison next to Lady Amy Billingsgate. Alison nodded to the woman's dour husband, who made a barely civil reply before turning his face stolidly toward the empty stage.

Amy leaned toward Alison as if they were the best of friends. "Isn't it exciting? I do love a play, and of course the ones here at court are much better than the ones done anywhere else. Don't you agree?"

"I hardly know, my lady, as this is my first play at court." Alison wasn't about to admit she had seen few plays at all. Wyndfell was so far into the countryside that it was rarely visited by actors.

"This one is called *Everyman* and is quite new. It's never before been seen at court." She leaned nearer. "No one knows for certain who wrote it, but there are rumors that his name is known in high places."

"Oh?" Alison was still amazed at the amount of conjecture, speculation, and outright gossip that went on at court. When Amy whispered the name of the alleged author into Alison's ear, Alison looked properly surprised, though she couldn't imagine why anyone would credit that particular nobleman with enough wit to write a play.

"Last month we saw *The Second Shepard's Play* again. It's as old as a rock and has been around more than a wheel! It was well done, however. You know the part where Mak and his wife have stolen a sheep and try to pass it off as their newborn babe, but the shepards bring it gifts and thus discover not a babe, but a sheep? Well, the sheep leapt out of the crib, passed the shepards, and ran right into the audience. I laughed until I felt faint! Then, later, the angel bids the shepards come to the manger at Bethlehem! Such a contrast between the holy birth and the sham one! Between the Virgin Mary and Mak's slatternly wife! I was moved to tears, and wept until my lord husband did command me to stop."

Alison looked at Lord Billingsgate's stony countenance and thought he wasn't far from requesting her silence again.

As if doing so to extract her from the likelihood of being bored to death, Miles took Alison's hand. She was glad for a reason to turn from Amy, who seemed about to detail yet another play. Miles's strong fingers laced in hers, and he rubbed the smooth skin of her fingers gently. His hypnotic blue eyes on hers warmed Alison's sense of belonging with him. His love for her was there so clearly, and she felt her face glow in response.

"You look very happy," he observed.

"By your side, I could never be otherwise," she responded softly. There was such a vast difference in the way Miles gazed lovingly at her and how Amy's husband ignored her with barely controlled patience.

"To have had so lame a start, our marriage now seems to have a firm course."

"Had I known you first and not been compelled to wed, I would have chosen you. In faith, I do hate to be forced to do anything. I fear I am most unwomanly."

"Never worry about that, love. You are more woman than I've ever known."

"My temper doesn't offend or appall you?"

"Your fiery nature intrigues me. You're not bad-tempered, just tempestuous."

Alison showed her appreciation for his tact with a loving smile, then settled comfortably in her chair. At last she was truly mated to a man who didn't require her to be anything except what she was. In spite of Miles's strength and his reputation for being a fierce knight in battle, he was gentle with her.

That thought brought to mind the unpleasant rumors she had heard at Wyndfell that Miles and his four friends had beaten one of the Catholics so badly that he later died. Miles was capable of striking men down in battle, but surely he wouldn't have turned five-to-one on that drunkard just because the man had a damning tongue. Alison looked down at Miles's strong, square hand corded with veins and muscles, and his long, sensitive fingers. Surely he had not done that. Had he? She wished she had never heard that rumor or that she had the courage to simply ask him. But if he didn't deny it . . . Alison stared at the stage as the first actor came on to deliver the prologue.

"God's" voice was heard booming from the timbers above the stage, deploring the sinfulness of mankind. Death, a dark actor in a cape of black stuff over a solid black jerkin, doublet, gown, and netherstocks, entered the stage at God's bidding and was dispatched to visit Everyman, who was making his cheerful appearance as if he were returning from a merrymaking.

Alison watched intently as Everyman, unable to avoid Death, made plans to take Cousin, Fellowship, and Kindred with him on his dread journey. As each refused, the audience murmured and nodded to one another. One by one Everyman asked his other companions, Beauty, Strength, Discretion, and Five Wits, to go with him. Each went as far as the edge of the tomb that yawned menacingly in the canvas backdrop, but then turned away.

The audience was intrigued. Would nothing accompany Everyman to Death? They argued among themselves as to who his companion, if any, would be. Knowledge stayed with Everyman almost to the end, but when he at last stepped into the tomb, only Good Deeds followed him.

Amy, her eyes glittering with tears, grabbed Alison's arm. "There! Have you ever seen so fine a performance? I knew all along that only Good Deeds would prove faithful. Such an actor! Did you see how Good Deeds made himself appear so frail and faint at first, but bolstered himself and became strong as he followed Everyman into the tomb? I do love plays! They are so like unto life!"

Alison nodded as she rose to go to the banquet with Miles. Would not evil deeds follow a man as surely? She wished she knew Miles had not been involved in that drunkard's death. To her mind the play had not been as enlightening as it was unsettling.

After the makeshift stage was whisked away by the actors, the castle servants set up the tables for the banquet. As the nobility and their lords and ladies waited to be seated, they were entertained by a group of musicians who played and sang songs written by the king.

Alison took her place beside Miles at one of the long tables which had first been covered with a white linen cloth, then overlaid with an intricately embroidered sanap as a runner. The salt cellar was a golden nef imported from Italy which was fashioned in the shape of a boat with elaborate rigging and jewels on its bow spelling out "Great Harry" after the king's flagship. Table fountains spouted canary and claret wines from silver-and-gilt fishes' mouths.

Silver goblets stood at each place for the nobility, but those seated below the salt drank from footed bowls called mazers. The royal surveyor stood at the tall ambry at the side of the room and handed ewers made of dinanderie, the fashionable bronze-hued alloy, and pitchers made of gold and silver to the table servitors for the wine service. Two gold spoons and a knife, the handles of which had been decorated with a fanciful intertwining of H and C, were laid between Alison's and Miles's plates. Alison carried her own knife, as was customary, in her kid leather chatelaine at her waist, but she had learned that at court, one used the knife that was placed on the table alongside each diner.

Rather than the bread trenchers used for daily meals at Wyndfell, shallow plates of chased silver were provided. Alison preferred the trenchers, which she ordered dyed and spiced with parsley or saffron, since a plate allowed the juices to pool under the food rather than soak into the bread to form a sopping for the beggars. But then, she had seen no beggars since arriving at Hampton Court.

Following the custom of centuries, the servers began bearing in the large platters laden with food. The first course consisted of whole-footed birds, in descending order of size from swan through goose and duck. Next came the finger-footed birds like peacocks, partridges, and pigeons.

After the courses of fowls came the baked meats, then the fish. Each had its own traditional sauce, such as garlic for the beef and goose, ginger for the fawn, cinnamon for the woodcock, yet the royal cook had his own carefully guarded recipes to make every dish his own specialty. Although the number of courses was limited by sumptuary law to seven, each course consisted of a dozen or more dishes.

As the fruit and illusion food was brought in, a loud noise erupted at the end of the hall. The diners looked at each other, and Alison saw Miles's hand automatically grip the handle of his short sword. At the high table, the queen was poised with a bite of haslet between her thumb and third finger. The king's chair beneath the great canopy had been vacant throughout the banquet, and Alison hoped it would remain so.

Suddenly a large group of men dressed as maskers came into the hall to the accompaniment of loud drums and fifes. Although the maskers' garments were cut in the fashion of shepherds' garbs, they were made of fine satins and cloth of gold. Masks covered the intruders' faces, wigs of silk tassels concealed their hair, and they wore artificial beards.

Alison looked fearfully at Miles, who was rigid in anticipation of battle. A tight muscle ridged his lean jaw and his eyes were flinty and intense. Inexplicably he relaxed, and glanced at Sir Stephen and Sir John, who sat across the table.

"What is it?" Alison whispered. "Who are these men?"

"Look more closely at the leader," he whispered back. "There is only one man who may claim that height and girth. 'Tis merely one of the king's jests. Pretend not to recognize him."

Alison swallowed nervously. There was something threatening about this procession of men that silently filed up the room toward the table on the dais.

One of the maskers stepped forward and explained to the queen that they were travelers from afar and wished to meet the magnificent ladies of the court. Catherine, who had naturally recognized her husband as well as some of the others, gave her consent.

Again the maskers circled the room in double file. At each lady they paused, pantomimed their appreciation of her beauty, and placed a cup of gold coins in front of her. Then they cast dice to see if the woman won or forfeited the gold, and moved on to the next.

When they stopped in front of Alison and silently placed the cup of coins before her, she could scarcely breathe. The huge man seemed uncomfortably close, even though he stood a yard away. Alison could hear his labored breathing, and knew his legs must be giving him considerable pain. She felt his intense eyes on her, but she dared not look up. The dice rattled onto a tray held by a servant, and the big man poured the gold into Alison's cold hands. As the servant refilled the cup, the leader continued to stare at Alison. A cold bead of sweat trickled down her back, and she hoped she wouldn't faint. After a tediously long time, the man moved on to the next lady. Alison slowly let out her pent-up breath and swayed toward Miles.

When the leader reached the queen, he cast the rest of the gold before her and threw the dice. As might be expected, she won and he motioned for her to unmask him. With what seemed to be real trepidation, Catherine pulled off the mask to reveal her husband, who threw back his massive head and boomed with laughter. Behind him the other maskers laughed and a nervous merriment spread throughout the hall.

"I don't understand," Alison whispered to Miles, the gold still clutched in her hand.

"He did this once before for Cardinal Wolsey's benefit, back when he was young and in his prime. He was married to Catherine of Aragon at the time. Then it was a marvelous jest, I've been told, and Wolsey unmasked Sir Edward Neville by 'mistake.' They looked remarkably alike. But now Wolsey is dead and that queen long since deposed. Several years back, the king executed Neville on grounds of treason." Miles's voice was tight and his words clipped. "What you have just seen is a desperate attempt by his highness to regain his youth and popularity."

"How sad!" she murmured.

"Look not stricken, my love. The king's jests are to be enjoyed, especially one so elaborate as this."

Henry swung about to face his court, his arms extended as if to embrace them all. "A feast!" he roared. "Bring forth the feast!"

To Alison's astounded eyes, the doors to the servants' hall burst open and a new banquet began. She made a show of eating, though the sight of so much additional food made her queasy.

Hours later, the dishes were carried away and the tables were cleared from the hall. Alison wanted badly to retire to her bedchamber but couldn't leave, since the king and queen remained. She was exhausted from the strain of forced joviality and her worry that the king would fulfill his promise to ask her oath of fealty. She had tried to say in private what he wanted her to publicly admit, but even then the words wouldn't pass her lips. She could not renounce her faith in the true religion, regardless of the danger. Her only hope was to avoid the issue. From her vantage point, Alison could see King Henry seated on his canopy-shrouded chair. As he spoke with the Venetian ambassador, he looked very tired and occasionally winced with pain. Silently she prayed for a reprieve, and almost made the sign of the cross out of ingrained habit. She was thankful she hadn't because just then Queen Catherine was walking directly toward Miles, who was between her and the king. As she watched, Catherine cornered Miles, and had him laughing at one of her sallies. The smile Alison had forced all evening was gone.

Before she could join them, Jarvis Hyde stopped her. "Did you enjoy the masking, my lady?"

"I found it . . . interesting," she said as evasively as she could.

"Such is common fare here at court. I hope you will abide with us long enough to see many such pleasantries."

Alison was barely listening to the man, for her attention was fixed on her husband and the queen. When Catherine touched Miles's arm and his dark head bent toward her, jealousy shot through Alison, overshadowing all her anxiety about the king. Danger aside, she had no desire to see a woman flirt with her husband.

Oblivious of the scene across the room, Jarvis said, "In truth, I hope you stay at court for other reasons."

Alison turned back to him with revenge in her heart. If Miles could so expose himself, she could do the same. He had told her on several occasions to avoid Lord Hyde, but he was ignoring her request that he not linger in the queen's presence. Putting on her most brilliant smile, Alison said, "Oh? And what reasons are these?"

Thoroughly captivated, Jarvis said, "Walk with me in the gardens in the moonlight and I'll show you."

Alison's bubbling laughter rang out, gauged to reach her husband's ears. Recalling the clever word game Miles had played when he first came to Wyndfell, she said rather loudly. "Moonlight? Nay, 'tis fair sunbeams, my lord!" She would show Miles she was as fashionable as any lady at court.

"Sunbeams?" Jarvis said doubtfully. " 'Tis full night."

"Nonsense. I hear a lark, though 'tis incredible one would be out in such wintry weather."

"Winter? Forsooth, there are flowers everywhere. Are you fevered?"

Alison saw that Miles was glancing her way, and she tapped Jarvis's arm flirtatiously. "Flowers in the dead of winter? Next you'll be telling me that pigs may fly." She waited for him to take up the game. Miles was not only watching; he was scowling.

"Lady Alison, I know not of what you speak. Winter? Pigs flying? What jest is this?"

Surprised, Alison said, "Do you not play this word game of opposites here at court?"

"I've never heard of such a game."

Alison frowned. This was odd. Why else had Miles driven her to distraction with saying opposites to her? With a shrug, she said, "A pity. It's played at Wyndfell all the time." Nodding good-bye to him, she intercepted Miles as the queen turned away.

"I told you to stay away from that fool," Miles growled.

"Jealous, my lord? I believe I gave you the same caution about the queen."

"I can hardly bolt and run when she signals to me. What was Hyde saying that was so amusing?"

"We were playing that word game that you taught me at Wyndfell."

"Word game?"

Alison warily scanned the room again to be sure she was keeping her distance from the king, but found he had left the room while she was distracted. With a deep sigh of relief she said, "The king is gone, and I ache from head to toe. May we go now?"

"Word game," Miles puzzled as he led her from the room. He could recall no word game at all.

They went up the great stairs and back along the corridor that led to their bedchamber. The hour was late, and he was as tired as Alison from the effort it had taken to appear amused at the pathetic mask. They were not the only ones to feel the strain, for Miles had noticed that the king had had to be carried away in his tram chair. The king's health seemed to have declined sharply since Miles had left court. Now Henry kept to the ground floor of the vast palace, and often asked to be carried from place to place.

After Leatrice and her assistants had helped Alison out of her gown and kirtle into a loose night rail, Alison dismissed them so she could be alone with Miles. Sitting at the table, she pulled a comb through her hair as she watched Miles remove the last of his clothing. Unaware she was watching him, Miles stretched as he yawned, muscles rippling throughout his naked body. It was no wonder he had been so popular at court, she reflected as he wrapped himself in his chamber cloak. As she pondered his sensuality and charm, it occurred to her for the first time that she might even have sat sewing with some of his previous lovers, though no one had hinted as such. She could understand why any woman would be captivated by that intense spark in his eyes that indicated that she alone filled his universe, at least for the moment. Though Alison didn't like this, Miles seemed to relish it. "I think you enjoy the queen's flirtations," she blurted out.

"Again you bring that up?"

"It still bothers me!"

"Well, it bothers me that you bestow attentions on Jarvis Hyde!" Blue lightning flashed in his eyes.

"Ha! You're jealous!" she exclaimed triumphantly.

"You play a dangerous game! Men are not accustomed to being led about at court and rejected."

"I marvel that you consider my flirtations dangerous when yours could easily be considered an act of treason!"

"What would you have me do?" he hissed as he crossed the room. "Chide the queen and send her away like the foolish child she is?"

"I would have you remember the end her cousin, Queen Anne, found along with her admirers!" Her eyes blazed up at him defiantly. "Even if there were no threat or danger involved, I would not sit meekly by while you play the gallant with a woman."

Miles grinned and lifted a tendril of her flaming hair. "I think I'm not the only one who is jealous," he commented.

She drew her hair from his fingers and said coolly, "Is it any wonder? The queen is not the only one whose eyes followed you tonight. I saw several other ladies looking as if they could devour you where you stood."

"Nor was Hyde the only man who watched you. This didn't escape my notice."

"He wasn't? Who else?" she asked in surprise, a smile threatening to break through.

"Now you will have me recount your conquests? For shame, Alison," he said with a laugh. "The king, for one, was much aware of you."

The teasing light left her eyes. "He never came near me but for the casting of the dice. Surely you're mistaken."

"Nevertheless, he watched you." Miles pulled her into his arms. "If I knew not his relationship to you, I would be as alarmed as you are over his queen."

Alison rested her head on his chest and put her arms around his waist. "Mayhap I'm not his daughter. I have studied his face and can see no resemblance."

"I would marvel if you could in such a bloated old man."

"Aside from the red in our hair, everything else is different. Could it be my mother was wrong?"

"I don't know, sweetheart."

"All my life I've longed to see him, to find some resemblance, or to hear him acknowledge me, and now I want only to flee as far from him as possible. He's a dangerous man, Miles."

"At the masking tonight I saw something I was never aware of before. He repeated his previous role exactly, according to descriptions I've heard. At times I wondered if he knew there was a difference and that another Catherine is now his queen."

"Is he mad?"

"To say so is treason." He rubbed his cheek against her hair. "Aye, he's mad."

"We must leave here! Tomorrow!"

"We haven't permission to go. Perhaps if you give him your oath of—"

"I cannot! You must see that!"

"I see he is dangerous and not a man to parry with!"

"All the more reason why I cannot forswear myself to him. I cannot acknowledge a madman as my spiritual ruler."

"Never admit that where another can hear you." Miles cupped her face in his palms and gazed down at her. "I would die if I were to lose you."

Alison stroked her fingers through the night of his hair. "You will never lose me. I love you so much I will do anything to remain with you."

"Even if it means saying the oath of fealty?"

"If it comes to giving my pledge or losing you, I will somehow give my pledge. But I pray it will never come to it."

Miles lowered his head and deeply kissed her, drowning their fears in the depths of their love. Alison uttered a loving moan, and he held her tighter, drinking of the sweetness of her lips until court and all its dangers were far away. Together they created a universe of their own.

Bending, he lifted her and carried her to the bed. She lay on the cool sheets, her night rail making a scarlet aura around her naked body. Miles tossed aside his cloak and lay next to her, their flesh touching and awakening to remembered passions. His hand glided around her slender waist and he drew her nearer.

"I long to have your children," she whispered. "I feel lacking to be so remiss in my duty."

"It will not be merely a duty with us, love, nor must you ever feel you are lacking in my eyes if children are not forthcoming. I too long for a child, but mainly because it will be a tangible proof of our love. And the babes will come. You'll see. Though I would not have you worn out from childbearing like Lady Halston."

"I love you, Miles."

His hand smoothed upward to rest beneath her breast and his thumb caressed the swell before reaching to tease her budding nipple. Alison sighed, and he smiled and nuzzled over the warm skin of her neck, past the quickening pulse in her throat, and lower to flick his tongue over her nipple.

Alison opened her eyes to gaze past Miles's dark hair to the ceiling, where bands of cupids cavorted with satin ribbons and garlands of painted flowers in the frescoes. Miles's tongue circled her nipple teasingly before drawing it gently into his mouth. Alison closed her eyes and gave herself over to the intense joy of his loving.

His hand took over the pleasuring of her breast as his lips moved lower, his tongue first exploring the indention of her navel, then going still lower. His other hand slipped between her thighs and parted them. "Beautiful," he said. "Beautiful."

His fingers explored the warmth of her moist recesses, and she murmured as he touched and teased the bud of her pleasure. Waves of urgent need washed over her as he continued his loving caresses. When she felt his lips and tongue upon her, she cried out as ecstasy exploded within her.

When the last of the flickering delight abated, Miles knelt between her legs and entered her. He moaned softly at the sensation of her warmth enclosing him. Slowly, ever so slowly, he moved within her, slipping his hand between their bodies to again stroke the essence of her femininity.

At once Alison felt the building of a physical urgency almost too great to bear and held to him tightly. As she reached her peak and tried to draw out the pleasure to the greatest possible degree, she felt Miles respond, and together they experienced the ultimate gratification of their loving.

Time had no meaning as she lay in the protection of his strong arms, snuggling close to him. Anticipating her unspoken need, he drew the warm covers over them both before he rose to blow out the last remaining candle.

16

For several days following his overzealous frivolity at the banquet, Henry remained shut away in his closet, while the queen occupied herself with long rides through the parks and barge trips up and down the Thames. Alison badly wanted to leave Hampton Court, but her efforts toward that end were much like the dreams she had had of running in mud that sucked at her feet and prevented her progress. One thing after another delayed their leaving, such as a young knight that needed instruction only Miles could give, and Lady Halston wanting Alison's help in designing a dress panel that employed Alison's special method of embroidering silk flowers. And over it all was the dreaded oath of fealty. Had the king forgotten, or was he playing an insidious game with her? She had no way of knowing.

Henry's health gradually improved and once again he was able to limp about the grand palace. Soon the royal court would be moving to Whitehall for the early summer before plague became too dire a threat. Court never remained long in any one place because the local supply of food was soon depleted by the multitude that made up the court, and with so many people living in such close quarters, basic cleanliness was a problem.

To celebrate the return of the king's health and the

preparations to leave Hampton Court, a masque was planned. Alison tried to convince Miles that they need not attend, as they had surely met their obligation to their host by joining in with every social event that had been arranged, but Miles disagreed. Henry's behavior toward him this entire stay gave cause for concern, and he couldn't risk offending him. After assuring her that they would soon leave for home, Miles overcame Alison's final objection that she had nothing suitable to wear by commissioning a seamstress to create a gown and a mask for her, and appropriate attire for him. After looking over bolts of material for her gown, Alison settled on one of cloth-of-gold shot with scarlet. The sleeves were to be trimmed in white fur and the kirtle beneath would be of crimson tissue embroidered with gold thread. Her mask was gold, edged with egret feathers and garnets that dangled enticingly at her temples and lower cheeks. Instead of wearing an artificial coif, she planned to use gold silk ribbon to intertwine feathers, pearls, and garnets in her own hair, and weave the remaining loose tresses into love locks.

Part of the mystery of a masque was not to know for certain who the other revelers were, or at least to pretend one didn't, so Alison dressed in Leatrice's chamber and kept her dress a secret from Miles's teasing questions.

Many of the guests were already there when Alison floated gracefully into the hall, a vision of gold and fire. She was well aware of heads turning toward her as she slowly descended the stairs. Below was a sea of apparent strangers bedecked in the most fanciful of masks and gowns.

One stood out from the crowd, and her lips tilted as she admired Miles's costume. He wore a cloth-of-silver gown over a sky-blue jerkin which was ribboned in silver satin and sewn with diamonds and sapphires. From a heavy chain about his neck hung a large dark amethyst pendant. Another chain of silver filigree, set with sapphires, crossed the broad expanse of his doublet, which was a blue so dark as to be nearly black. His mask was trimmed in sable and was supported by a slender silver wand.

Alison could feel his eyes undressing her as she stepped down to the crowd, but she pretended not to know him. Her eyes boldly sought his and her lips curved in sensuous invitation, but when he came toward her, she melted into the crowd to emerge again across the room. She kept her mask firmly in place, but continued to lure Miles and weave an enchantment with her smiles and inaccessibility.

When Miles almost maneuvered to her side, Alison stepped out the doors and into the garden. Shrubbery trimmed into dark avenues hid her from view, though she could see him through the leaves. He paused, his stance alert as if he were seeking her with his senses; then he glided into the dark green shadows.

Stifling her laughter, Alison stepped back into the dense foliage and crept silently away. Unexpectedly a voice drew her attention and she paused. Stumbling onto a romantic tête-à-tête was the last thing she wanted. When another voice sounded, Alison cocked her head to one side. Two women? Why would two women be alone out here in the night? Curiosity made her step closer.

"Has he any suspicions?" a rather familiar voice asked. "He didn't see me come out here?"

"No, he was intent on the charms of the Countess of Thornsbury."

"She may well have him," the first voice affirmed. "What of Thomas? Have you given him word where I will be?"

"Aye, your majesty. I grow amazed he is not yet here."

Alison's breath lodged in her throat. That was Queen Catherine on the other side of the privet hedge.

"Did I hear something, Lady Rochford? A sound over there?"

"No doubt 'tis Master Thomas."

"Leave us. We have such little time together. If his majesty seeks me, give some excuse so Thomas and I may tarry here. If he asks for me twice, come and fetch me."

"Aye, your majesty."

Alison froze in place as the somber-cloaked Lady Rochford passed by her. Another rustle of leaves brought an exclamation of delight from Catherine, and Alison tiptoed to see the plump queen embrace Thomas Culpepper's lanky frame. Alison felt a knot of fear burst and spread throughout her body. If she was caught here, she would be an apparent accomplice. Alison couldn't care less if the queen found happiness or solace in the arms of Thomas Culpepper, she only wanted to find Miles and get back to safety.

She crept silently along the bark-strewn path, which twisted and turned, narrowing, then widening again as she felt her way in the darkness. When she reached the outer hedge of yews, she heard a rustling. Pausing, she saw Miles about to turn toward the lovers' secluded nest. Frantically Alison grabbed a bush and shook it hard to get his attention.

Miles stopped and looked back. Alison let the moonlight catch her gold mask, then moved swiftly back toward the hall. With a grin, Miles pursued her. Alison stepped gladly into the candle-scented chamber and allowed Miles to catch up with her.

"You have led me a merry chase, strange lady," he said. " 'Tis a pity you didn't travel more slowly so I could have found you in the moonlight."

"Trust me, noble knight, the garden is too full for comfort this night." She took his hand. "Will you dance with me? A galliard is beginning."

"You're full of energy this night. First a run through the bushes, now a galliard." He took her hand in the formal stance, and they joined the circle of dancers in the slow steps of the pavane. Five steps forward, five back. Almost imperceptibly the music quickened into the galliard proper.

"So we danced on our wedding night," he said as he performed the intricate steps.

"I recall. You near danced me into the floor," she laughed.

"You had only to say you were tired. I had ridden hard, if you recall, to reach Wyndfell in time for our wedding."

"And at that you kept me waiting at the altar until I was a laughingstock. I would have broken my strength before I would have admitted I was tired. I was avoiding your bed, my fierce barbaric Welshman."

"I've never heard you complain."

"I've never had reason to."

"Let's step out into the garden. I feel a bout of barbarous behavior coming on."

"No! Not the garden. Let's dance now and be uncivilized later. In our chamber, for instance."

"What? Are you the same wench I tumbled in Wyndfell's hayloft or not? I fear I have mistaken you for another."

"Trust my word, fair knight. If you wander about in the garden, you'll wish you could mistake an identity."

Before he could reply, the dance ended and Alison was whisked away into a cassamezza by a man who could only be Sir Stephen. Alison let herself be led into the dance steps, but her thoughts were racing. She kept glancing over her shoulder to see that Miles was remaining safely inside the hall.

"Your attention wanders, my lady," Sir Stephen said. "Your knight will not go too far astray, for his eyes are full of you."

"Sir Stephen, I thought it was you." This was one of the king's men whom Roger had accused of beating his servingman.

"I wonder if anyone is ever really fooled by these masks. I know everyone in the room. Good news came today, my lady. Sir Vance is the father of a healthy boy. Though the babe came earlier than expected, he is doing fine. The mother is well and Sir Vance's family line is secure."

"That's good news." Was Miles moving toward the gardens or was it just her imagination?

The music ended and another piece began, but before Alison could step out of the circle, another pair of arms whirled her about the floor. She paid little attention to her partner, who was clad in green-and-yellow particolored garb. She had to get back to Miles and repeat her warning.

"Not so fast, my pretty, you'll be winded before the dance is over."

"Pardon, my lord. My mind was on other matters."

"A love meeting perhaps?" he asked suggestively. "The gardens are near. We could—"

"No! Not the gardens!" Was everyone determined to walk out there tonight?

"Then perhaps a more secluded spot. I'd prefer that myself. My chamber is on the next floor and is quite private."

"What?" She had been only half-listening to him.

"Come upstairs with me and I'll see to it that you return with a smile." He had her attention now, and he leaned down to whisper a graphic suggestion as to how they might spend their time in his chamber.

Alison's mouth dropped open, and she stopped stonestill. Grabbing his mask away, she said, "Lord Hyde! How dare you speak to me thus!"

"We aren't supposed to unmask until midnight," he objected.

"Don't you ever suggest such a thing to me again!" she snapped, striking him smartly with his mask. "You may consider our friendship ended!" She hurried off the dance floor, leaving the thwarted nobleman staring after her in amazement.

Miles met her at the side of the room. "I gather you believe me now about Hyde's intentions?"

"Oh, Miles, you were so right!"

"Should I call him out and cut off his ear or nose, or have you vented your own justice?"

"He won't ever dare speak to me again!" she fumed.

"That must have been some proposition. What did he say?"

Alison hesitated, then tiptoed up to whisper in Miles's ear. Miles looked surprised, then threw back his head with a hearty laugh. "I never knew he had so much imagination. Actually," he said with a teasing leer, "if we tried it, we might find it enjoyable."

"Court life has made you daft," she confirmed with a smile.

Not far away, she saw the king's unmistakable form. He was looking around the room in a most suspicious manner. Suddenly it occurred to Alison that it would be prudent for Henry to see Miles was with her and not in the garden. Drawing on her courage, she took Miles's hand and led him toward the king.

Henry's discarded mask hung at his corded belt, and he looked a bit disheveled, as though he might have had too much ale. Alison made a deep curtsy, and Miles bowed in greeting. "Ho! What have we here? The most illustrious jouster at court and his very elusive wife. I had begun to believe you were a fairy or had cast some enchantment, Lady Alison. Or that I had imagined you entirely."

"As you can see, your majesty, my husband and I are here."

"Have you at last come to beg a boon? I should have known you would eventually."

"A small one, if you please."

Henry sighed and his eyes grew weary. "Well, what is it? An earldom for your lord husband? An appointment for some relative? A judgment in your favor over some feud?"

"No, your majesty," Alison replied, keeping her voice modestly modulated, as her mother had taught her, but meeting the king's eyes squarely. "We wish to go home."

"You wish to go home," Henry rumbled, his face a blank. "To leave court, you mean?"

"Yes, your majesty. We wish to return to Wyndfell. I'm not accustomed to such a gay life."

"What about you, Lord Miles? Are you, too, jaded with court?"

"Never jaded, your majesty. But we are still newly wed, and I would be with my bride."

Henry nodded, a wry smile on his cupid's-bow lips. "I see. So it's become a love match after all. Very well, you have my permission to leave."

Alison's radiant smile lit her face, and she thanked the king profusely.

"There is only one matter left to attend to. I have not yet received your oath of fealty."

"Now?" she gasped, her face paling.

"No, no. Not now. This is a party, a time for merrymaking, not ceremony. Tomorrow. I will send for you and you may kneel before me in the presence chamber."

"Yes, your majesty," Miles answered for her. "She will be there."

"Good," the king said, "good." His eyes gauged her coldly, uncertain what to make of her. She might well be eager to return to Yorkshire to formulate some plot of insurrection. He found it hard to be sure anymore, even when his mind was clear of spirits. At one time Henry had prided himself on being able to read men's hearts, but since those days, he had sent so many to the gallows—his advisors, kinsmen, friends, Edward Neville, whom he would have trusted with his life, even Anne, for whom he had turned the world upside down. Henry shook his head and waved his fingers to dismiss Alison and Miles. "Tomorrow," he repeated. "In the presence chamber."

Miles and Alison made their obeisance and moved away before Henry's mercurial mood could swing again. Through the crowd, Alison saw Lady Rochford slip out into the night-filled garden and moments later return with the queen. Alison raised her brows toward Miles as if to say she had told him so. He made no answer, but his eyes followed Catherine, who made her way to the king as if she had been in the room all the time.

The Italian ambassador, reeling from the punch of the heady sack he had consumed, approached Henry in jovial humor and bent low in an unsteady bow. "Your majesty," he said grandly, "I have a plan."

"What sort of plan?" Henry was smoothing a tousled lock of Catherine's hair and rubbing his thick fingers over her flushed cheeks.

"I have reason to believe—the best authority, mind you—that if you will admit the pope's true power as head of the church, he will pardon you."

"What?" Henry roared, the cobwebs clearing from his brain in an instant, as all around him flinched back. "The pope dares pardon me!"

"You have only to admit an error in your perception," the drunken ambassador said hastily. "He wants only your word."

"A pox on the pope!" Henry bellowed as he strode a few paces in the now tensely silent room. Even the musicians stopped playing. "Pardon me, will he?" He went up to the now sobering ambassador and glowered over him. "I'll tell you what I say to that! I'll send an army of men to Rome and have them fetch the pope back here to London! Then I'll pardon him!"

A hushed murmur rippled around the room.

Again Henry took up his pacing and ranting. "Those Catholics are ever a thorn in my side," he growled, his small eyes sweeping the room as if in search of his enemies. "Perhaps 'tis time for another debate! You! Lord Miles! You recall the debate I had with that priest! 'Twas not so many years ago."

"Yes, your majesty! I remember." Miles's voice was calm and collected, but Alison felt the steel in it.

"Some of you don't, more's the pity," Henry continued, his voice ringing out in the large hall. "I challenged a priest—a renegade cleric named John Lambert, it was. At York Place. November 1538!" The king's bejeweled finger jabbed at the air. "Lambert refused to believe in the miracle of transubstantiation. He said the bread was bread and the wine was wine! Such radical teachings had to be set straight."

Alison's hand slipped into Miles's, and his strong fingers closed over it protectively.

"We had a debate!" Henry roared triumphantly. "I, the king, and my theologians, and this John Lambert. I can tell you his faith was weak. By the end of the day he threw himself on my mercy! A heretic! Pleading mercy!" The king turned back on the terrified ambassador. "And you want *me* to beg the pope's pardon? Never! If I had my way, he would burn as brightly as John Lambert did six days later at Smithfield. Does that answer your question?"

"Yes, yes, your majesty," the man stammered, falling to his knees. "Yes, yes. Forgive me. I didn't understand."

Henry's cherubic smile suddenly broke forth and his laugh rang out. "Forgive you? Of course I forgive you," he said in flawless Italian. "Are you not a guest in my court? Arise, arise. You cannot dance on your knees. Music! Let us have music!"

The stunned musicians hurried into a song, one Henry had written himself in happier days. Holding his massive arms out, Henry led the queen and the Countess of Thornsbury into a dance. The music played louder, and the king danced faster, his legs straining under his enormous weight and wild antics.

Alison and Miles looked at one another, perplexed by this exhibition. As Alison turned back to the king, she prayed her mother had indeed lied and that this madman was no kin of hers.

Another thought, one she had managed to suppress since coming to court, came to the surface. Roger and Damion had been right. The king was indeed mad and he must be removed. Otherwise there might be a bloodbath that would make the Pilgrimage of Grace look like a mere unpleasantness. She declared silently that as soon as she returned to Wyndfell she would do all she could to overthrow this tyrant.

Suddenly the king staggered, and the petite queen jumped aside as several of his men rushed forward, catching Henry before he toppled to the floor. While they steadied him, others ran for his portable chair. When he dropped into its velvet trappings, Henry's face was the color of oatmeal and his eyes were glassy with pain. Once again he was merely a pitiful old man who was beset by ill health he would never outlive. Four of the larger guardsmen carried him away toward his closet. The queen wavered, but followed after him.

"Tomorrow," Alison whispered to Miles. "Oath or no oath, we must get away from this place."

Miles nodded as he put his arm around her, his jaw clenched from his own apprehension.

Alison slept very little, tossing and turning as she silently prayed for divine protection. The next day, when word spread throughout the palace that the king was again indisposed and was keeping to his privy chamber, seeing no one, Alison felt her prayers had been answered. Immediately she and Miles began packing. But before they could take their leave, a summons came for Miles to go to the king.

Alison gripped Miles's hand as if doing so could prevent him from going. Reassuringly, Miles kissed her cold fingers before uncurling them from his hand. "Don't look so fearful," he said as he turned to go. "Doubtless he but wants to say farewell or give me some instruction. You forget my father was very close to him."

"Be careful," she whispered.

Miles kissed her forehead, then her lips, before saying, "Have Trahern load our belongings and see to the final details. I'll not be gone long."

As soon as their chamber door closed behind him, his smile disappeared. There had been a great change in the king during the last few months. Or maybe the change had occurred earlier, and Miles had been too close to see it. At any rate, the lusty geniality of the king had turned to a fine madness. Henry reminded Miles of a shark he had seen once while on a campaign. The shark had attacked everything that drew its attention, with no apparent discernment about what or who it might be. The kill was worth the loss to the state as far as Henry was concerned. Miles wasn't at all sure this was simply a farewell summons.

Passing the royal chapel, Miles went down the long gallery that opened onto Cloister Green Court, then through another gallery, to the king's presence chamber. Two guards barred Miles's way until he gave his name and stated his business; then they drew back and allowed him to enter the king's suite.

The modest-size privy chamber was decorated with ornately woven tapestries, and was carpeted with a woolen rug from Persia. One of three tables in the room was covered with black velvet that contrasted tastefully with the jewel tones on the walls. Another table had been laid out with the king's breakfast, now being cleared by a page. Behind it was an elaborate cupboard with whatever dishes and goblets the king might need during the course of the day. Several chairs stood about, one in front of a large black leather-topped desk beside which was a clock stand. The fireplace, on the wall opposite an inset alabaster fountain, crackled with a low fire. Several of the king's gentlemen, two barbers, and three physicians stood about the room. Henry sat in the intricately carved chair of estate.

Miles bowed and drew nearer when the king motioned to him. Henry flicked his fingers at the hovering physicians, sending them to group at the far side of the room. "So, Lord Miles. You're leaving us?" Henry's voice was rasping with his effort to conceal his pain.

"Yes, your majesty. I dare not stay gone too long from Wyndfell," he said with a pretense at joviality.

"Oh? Then there is unrest?" Henry's quicksilver eyes narrowed in cold speculation.

"No, your grace. I was referring to the overseeing of my crops."

"Have you come to this, then? The best jouster of my court has become a farmer?"

"I plan a joust later this spring, but the crops are very important to an isolated castle like Wyndfell. There is no city nearby where we may purchase our daily needs."

"Thus you run your small court as I run mine?"

"Only in that my people and my beasts must eat, your majesty. You have the only court in England."

Henry made a noncommittal grunt as if he had hoped to trap Miles into comparing himself with his king. He turned his massive head to gaze out the windows past the formal gardens to where the silver Thames rolled silently by.

"I'll soon see this castle of yours," Henry said thoughtfully.

"You will?" Miles looked at the king in surprise.

"I plan a progress to the north. King James of Scotland has promised to meet with me in York. On the way back I will pass near Wyndfell and will spend a night or so there."

"I'm honored, your majesty." Miles's thought leapt to the infamous placards in Wyndfell's village. He would have to capture the villain responsible for those before the king arrived. And there was the matter of food. Even in a couple of days, the court consumed a vast amount of food and drink.

"I've never seen York," Henry mused. "A king should see all the country he rules."

"Will the queen journey with you?" Miles asked to get some hint at the number of people he must host.

"Aye. She would grow lonely here." Henry's voice was clipped, and Miles was reminded of a few questioning, if not accusatory, looks he had seen Henry cast upon his queen. "We will have been married a year by then. If she is not with child, she will accompany me. As will my daughter Mary." Again he stared thoughtfully out the window. "Prince Edward will not come. He must see to his lessons."

Miles nodded. The prince was still in delicate health and Henry could not chance losing his only heir. Catherine's evident barrenness could well be the reason Miles had detected a coldness toward her from the king.

"I will also have my army with me as a show of force to those in the northlands, and as a protection for me should King James prove himself less than a man of his word. About four thousand men."

"Yes, your majesty. Wyndfell cannot hold so many, but there is another castle in the area, called Bainbridge. The rest may lodge there."

"Is it Lord Roger Bainbridge's castle?"

"Yes, your grace. I didn't realize you knew him."

"His name has come before me." Henry looked hard at Miles, as if he were probing the knight's thoughts. "I need not tell you that I am looking for traitors and will deal severely with them, as with anyone found to be harboring such."

"I know of no traitors in Wyndfell's area," Miles said firmly. "If I knew of any I would deal with them myself."

"Good." Henry beamed. "Well spoken, Lord Miles! Deal with them firmly. Godspeed on your journey, and I will see you in good time."

Miles bowed and took his leave. As he returned to Alison, he felt relieved that Henry hadn't asked for Alison's oath of allegiance. Whether it was forgotten or merely postponed, he didn't know, but he fervently hoped it was the former.

17

Drifts of crimson and Dutch clover had spread over the pastures in the time they had been gone from Wyndfell. Bees hummed from flower to flower and butterflies flitted like free-blown blossoms. Oxeye daisies turned their yellow eyes to the sun, swept by the fingers of May breezes. Along the muddy banks of Wyndfell's moat, the brooklime flourished.

Following her return from court, Alison saw Wyndfell with new eyes. Since she had come here as a child, she had rarely been farther than a few hours' ride from the massive gray walls, and this extended absence offered her a new perspective. After the grandeur of Hampton Court, the familiar castle seemed small, but at the same time more protective than it ever had before.

Although Sir Trahern reported that things at Wyndfell and in its village had been relatively uneventful during their absence, Miles seemed to be more wary than ever. Alison surmised that his apprehension must be due to the planned visit of the king and his concern that the troublemaker he had not captured might renew his rabble-rousing while the king was there. That thought distressed Alison as well. She had spent a great deal of time trying to determine a way to convince Damion to cease his activities until the king was gone from the area, but this resulted in more confusion. All she could do was to hope that when the right time came, she would know what to say to him.

On her second day home she went to see the abbess in the outer wall. When the woman's voice bade Alison enter, she stepped into the cool recesses of the cell. As always, the white linen curtain hid the woman from view, but Alison found herself intensely curious about the anchoress's true appearance because of a recent rumor among Alison's ladies that a miracle was causing the woman to become more youthful day by day. Her voice, they had said, was proof, for she no longer had the aged crackle of an old woman. Alison sat on the stool and asked after the woman's health, listening keenly so she could judge for herself.

"I'm well, child."

Unable to discern much from the three words, Alison impulsively asked, "Do you never long to go outside to see the fields in bloom or to hear children laughing? Even to seek out company?"

"Never," the voice said with surprise. "I am here by my own choosing. There is no lock on the door. I'm not a prisoner."

To Alison the voice sounded much the same as it always had, but the anchoress's words captivated Alison's full attention. The old woman's unswerving devotion to her religious order and the vows she had taken years before were inspiring, yet hard for Alison to comprehend fully. "I couldn't choose so much loneliness."

"I have my prayers. Not everyone is meant to live the life of an anchoress," the woman replied with what might have sounded like pride in a lesser woman.

"I've been at court, you know. It was far different from Wyndfell."

"You mustn't be lured by the ways of the world. Opulence is the devil's snare."

"You misunderstand me. I am glad to be home. I was able to avoid making my oath of fealty."

"Very good, my child. You must stand fast on this. Nothing is more important."

Alison recalled the king's unreasonable rages and suspicious eyes. Aside from the threat to her own life, her lack of obedience to him could result in Wyndfell's being razed and Miles's being accused of treason for not reporting her disloyalty. She rubbed her eyes as if she were suddenly tired. At least this danger was averted for a few months. "The king is coming to York in August, Miles says. He will come by Wyndfell for a short stay on his journey home."

"You must not allow it! You cannot harbor that vile man under this roof!" The abbess's voice was jolted out of its normally reverent serenity.

"He is the king! How can I forbid him?"

"You must think of something. Ask Lord Bainbridge to counsel you."

"Against the wishes of my husband? Nay, I cannot!"

"He is only your husband under the law. You must stand up for your faith, whatever it takes."

Alison stood up to leave. "I will not and cannot go against my lord husband. And Miles *is* my husband, no matter what anyone says."

Alison heard a startled gasp from behind the curtain as she swept out. Once she was in the bright sunshine, she leaned against the door and closed her eyes. Not only had she spoken against the church's rulings, but she had spoken sharply to the holy woman. If a bolt of lightning struck her down, she wouldn't be surprised. She fearfully glanced to the heavens, but the sky was clear and blue. Aghast at what she had done, yet feeling justified in defending Miles, Alison went back to the castle's gate.

After much deliberation during the afternoon, Alison sent a message to tell Roger of her return and that she wished to meet with him in Damion's chamber. At the appointed hour she stealthily slipped off to join them. In her absence, Damion had grown even thinner; his once-lean cheeks were gaunt and hollowed, and his brown eyes looked feverish and large. His movements were also quicker, reminding Alison of a bird's, or perhaps those of a caged fox.

"Have you eaten well while I was gone, Damion?" she asked with sisterly concern.

"I saw to him as I told you I would," Roger answered for the priest.

"As usual, you are too concerned with the temptations of the flesh," Damion reproved.

Alison sighed. If Damion was this scornful over her insistence that he eat properly, what would he say if he knew of her love for Miles? Briefly she recounted her experiences in court as both men listened eagerly. As she observed them, she noticed a bond between them that she had never seen before. Roger seemed to be mimicking some of Damion's mannerisms and was espousing all Damion's viewpoints as his own.

"He will be in York in August?" Roger mused. "That is bad news indeed."

"Damion, you must not distribute those placards while the king is in the area."

"Nonsense. We must show him our dislike of his heretic ways. We are free men, not serfs to bow before him no matter what he may do."

"But you have been given sanctuary here, and his wrath will fall on Miles and myself!" she objected.

"We must make a plan," Roger said as if she hadn't spoken. "There must be some way of rallying the people to us. Is the queen breeding yet?"

"No, and she seems unlikely to."

"You are holding something back," her brother said. "I can see it in your face."

"I have reason to believe the queen is unfaithful," Alison said with reluctance. "I overheard what had to have been a meeting with her lover."

"The king is again cuckolded?" Roger exclaimed cheerfully. "That's good news!"

Damion paced his cell. "This man—what is his name?"

"Culpepper. Thomas Culpepper. He's one of the king's intimates."

"Even better." There was a dark light in Damion's eyes.

"We must see to it that the king becomes aware of her falseness," Roger said eagerly.

"What will we gain by that?" Alison protested.

"He will put her aside."

"He will behead her!" Alison corrected.

Damion pointed at Roger to make his point. "That will leave him free to wed again."

"Again!" Alison gasped.

"Recall whom he considered before this Howard woman took his eye," Roger said to Damion. "At the time, all thought he was certain to choose Christina, Duchess of Milan. A Catholic!"

"She has been widowed nearly three years," Damion said thoughtfully. "That makes her sixteen years old and prime for bearing sons."

"And her beauty is legendary. She's said to be the most beautiful woman in Europe."

"It's said the king wanted the match. It's possible he still would."

"A Catholic queen will see to it that the true religion is returned to England," Roger concluded triumphantly.

"You assume much," Alison observed caustically. "The king is greatly taken with Queen Catherine, and she, too, is of a fertile age."

"But she is unproven. If she were going to bear, she would have already done so," Damion said.

"It's said Christina is both widow and maid," Roger pointed out. "Just as Catherine of Aragon was."

"No one knows that for certain, save Catherine of Aragon and her husband, Prince Arthur," Alison disputed. "There is evidence that she was his true wife. Besides, I hardly see how any parallel with the old queen is likely to endear a woman to the king. Even assuming he is ever free to remarry and that the duchess will have him."

"Of course she'll have him," Damion said curtly. "He's the King of England!"

Alison thought of the hulking man with the animal-sharp eyes and the unpredictable rages. She didn't see how any woman would dare become his consort. Not even for the throne of England. "I see a dozen ways for your plot to fail, and I entreat you to dismiss it from your minds."

"I believe it will work," Roger said, ignoring Alison. "I will put some thought to how we may best use this information."

"As will I," Damion agreed, taking Roger's hand in a fervent shake. "We will meet in the oak coppice in two days' time."

"Agreed!"

Alison looked from one excited face to the other. She had the sensation of being hurdled about with no control in the matter at all.

She and Roger made their way down the passageway to the hall. Alison put her eye to the peephole and swung open the panel. "I wish I had never told you," she said in a tight voice. "I never dreamed you and Damion would think of such a scheme!"

"You worry too much," Roger chided as he clicked the panel shut behind him.

Sir Edmund Campbell, on his usual round of business, had just stepped out of the hall when he heard the voices. He glanced about nervously, for he knew the room had been empty only seconds before. He stepped nearer to hear what was being said.

"It's a foolhardy scheme and you're a fool to consider it."

"Soft, Alison, soft," Roger counseled. "Your sojourn at court seems to have made a sword of your tongue."

"Would you have me simper and twitter as if I had

no mind at all?" she demanded. "Think what you're doing!"

Edmund heard the voices drawing nearer and assumed an innocent expression, as if he had just stepped into the hall.

On seeing him, Alison stopped abruptly. How much had he heard? Neither she nor Roger had been speaking quietly.

"Greetings my lady, Lord Bainbridge," Edmund said smoothly. He noticed Miles was nowhere about, and a smile crossed his swarthy features. He had wondered about Bainbridge's loyalty for some time, and during the lord and lady's absence, Edmund had thought he saw Bainbridge riding over Wyndfell's green in the moonlight.

"Good day, Sir Edmund," Alison said cautiously. Had she mentioned the king or queen's name? She couldn't remember. "Have you seen my lord husband? Lord Bainbridge wishes to speak with him."

"I believe he is away from the castle. Forgive me for not realizing you had arrived, Lord Bainbridge. I didn't see you ride up."

Roger nervously glanced at Alison and said, "I came through the orchard gate. It's closer that way, you know."

"Oh, yes. So it is." Edmund smiled. Perhaps this was only a tête-à-tête between Bainbridge and Lady Alison. He had thought she loved her husband, but one could never be certain with women. Perhaps she was Bainbridge's leman. Such a twist would be interesting but scarcely noteworthy to the king. On the other hand, Edmund sensed more to the matter than that. "I am glad to see you have safely returned from court, my lady. One can't be too careful these days."

"What do you mean?" Roger asked.

"Why, the king, of course. I have heard tell of his rages and all. I imagine all at court must walk on tiptoe to keep from upsetting him."

"These are strange words from a man the king appointed as steward here," Alison said suspiciously.

Edmund smiled. "I was glad to leave London. It's not safe there for those like us."

"Us?"

Edmund glanced around as if afraid of being overheard. "We Catholics, I mean."

"You're Catholic?" Roger exclaimed.

"I don't believe it," Alison said, and quickly asked, "Why are you telling us this?"

"I assumed . . . that is, I had hoped that you were too," Edmund said innocently. "I have heard of your late husband's martyrdom and I saw for myself that you rebelled against marrying a heretic. Tell me I'm not mistaken!"

"Calm yourself, man," Roger said in a quieting voice. "You're safe here."

"Roger!" Alison exclaimed.

As Roger stroked his pointed beard, he asked, "Does the king know you're a Catholic? No, of course not, or he'd never have sent you here. You haven't told anyone else, have you? Lord Garrett and his men are all heretics."

"I thought so!" Edmund's eyes were wide with apparent relief. "Then might I assume the rest of you are of the true religion?"

"For the most part. You must be careful, though."

"Roger! Hold your tongue!"

"Peace, my lady," Edmund said. "You may trust me with your life. Especially now that I know your faith. Are there any priests in the area? I've not been to confession since I left London."

"There is an abbess living here in the curtain wall just beyond the entrance to the kitchen garden, and there's—"

"Enough!" Alison hissed.

"An abbess? Here?" Edmund's surprise was unfeigned.

"If you follow the outer wall and look closely into the clump of bushes, you'll see her door. Her name is Mother Anne."

"Lord Bainbridge, you've said quite enough!" Alison said firmly. "Sir Edmund, leave us."

Edmund bowed and smiled again. "Yes, my lady. And thank you."

When he had gone, Alison whirled upon Roger. "Have you lost your senses? You just told him we're Catholic!"

"So is he, by his own words. I believe the man."

"I don't!"

"Why not?"

"I have no reason I can explain. I just don't."

"Nonsense. 'Tis merely a woman's natural fearfulness. We may trust him."

"What makes you so certain?"

"Why else would he admit to something that could deprive him of liberty if not of life itself?"

Alison frowned at the door through which Edmund had gone. Why indeed?

Leatrice and Trahern were married in Wyndfell's chapel. At their betrothal, Trahern had separated the three parts of the ring that his grandmother had worn, and had given her one of them to wear during the intervening weeks. Now he took that circle and interlocked it with the one he had retained and the one the vicar had been holding for them. Together the pieces made one ring that appeared to be woven of rosemary and thyme. Leatrice wore a poppy-red gown that glowed like a jewel in the dim chapel. Trahern looked bold and aristocratic in a doublet of Venetian brocade and a jerkin of popinjay blue.

Alison slipped her hand into Miles's, and he fondly smiled down at her. "Mistress Leatrice is lovely," he whispered, "but never so beautiful as you."

Alison turned her adoring eyes up to meet his gaze. "I was just thinking that there has been no more handsome a groom in all of England than you were." She pressed his hand and smiled.

The vicar gave the brief sermon uniting the new couple and ended with a prayer for their domestic bliss and a blessing on their union. At the vicar's signal, Trahern kissed his bride and everyone in the church rushed forward to express best wishes for a long and fruitful marriage.

Leatrice, all smiles and blushes, held tight to Trahern's arm as he handed out gifts of ribbons, brooches, and gloves. Miles signaled for the knitting cup full of canary wine and cheered his approval as first Trahern drank, then Leatrice. Miles took the double-handled cup and drank before passing it to Alison. Others crowded near for a sip that would make them official witnesses.

Above them the chapel bells rang out, and clouds of doves fluttered from the bell tower. The bridal cake was brought forward, and Leatrice cut it with her silver knife and gave her new husband the first piece.

As usual, a number of bawdy jests were bandied about, and Alison laughed with as much amusement as Miles. Leatrice blushed at first but then joined the laughter.

A banquet followed with Leatrice and Trahern in the seats of honor usually reserved for Alison and Miles. Jugglers and acrobats performed antics in the center of the hall as the new musicians they had brought back from London played in the balcony above.

Alison had prepared a chamber for the newlyweds not far from the master chamber. When they had danced to the pavane, galliard, and coranto, Alison motioned for Leatrice to slip away.

Arm in arm they climbed the steps to the bedchambers above. Leatrice's face was flushed with happiness and shyness, and Alison teased her about being so timid.

"He's a truly handsome knight, isn't he?" Leatrice

marveled as she removed the French hood from her hair.

"He is indeed, and he will make you a very good husband. Here, let me unlace you. I'll be your maid this night."

Leatrice turned to let Alison unlace the back of her kirtle. "I wouldn't care if Trahern were as poor as a shepherd and of no lineage at all. I'd still love him."

"Yes, I know. It's how I feel about Miles."

"Then you've truly come to love him? I thought so, but my own views have been so colored that I have been seeing love everywhere." She stepped out of her clothing as the maids entered with her bathwater. Leatrice sank into the luxury of the copper tub while Alison turned back the heavy white coverlet on the bed and plumped the pillows.

A maid arrived with two goblets of sack, which Alison heated with a rod from the fire until the sugary spiced wine was near boiling. Leatrice pulled on her new wrapper and sat by the fire so Alison could brush her hair. When it gleamed with rich highlights, Alison waved away the maids and put aside the brush. Awkwardly Leatrice went to the wide bed and Alison took her wrapper and laid it across the foot of the bed as Leatrice got under the covers.

"Alison?" Leatrice said. "I'm fearful. I'm no longer a fresh young maid. What if Trahern doesn't find me attractive or what if I don't please him?"

Alison smiled with the wisdom of a happily married woman. "Just love him, Leatrice. That's all the rule you need. Merely love him and let him love you."

Leatrice looked doubtful, but she nodded.

At the door Alison paused again and said softly, "Be happy, Leatrice." With a smile she went out into the corridor and started back to the hall. A great singing drew nearer, and soon a small band of Trahern's friends, escorting the nervous-looking groom to the bridal chamber, rounded the corner. Alison stopped the revelers with a smile. "Where are you off to?" she asked. "Surely you're not leaving the festivities so early in the night."

"We are seeing Trahern to his bride, lest he lose his way," one man informed her with intoxicated sincerity.

Alison laughed and took the man's arm firmly and turned him about. "Sir Trahern can find his own way, I wager. Love is a powerful lodestone. Come, men, I would have you taste the new cask of charneco that arrived last week."

She led the willing men away, giving Trahern a teasing smile. He grinned with relief and bowed to her before hurrying along the corridor to Leatrice.

Alison ordered the charneco brought up, then went to find Miles. He was standing near the outer doors, a pensive look on his face. "Why are you not reveling?" she asked. "I thought to find you on the dance floor showing all the newest steps from court."

"I have no heart for dancing with anyone except you," he said with a smile.

"I must be more tired than I thought after all these preparations. I feel rather light-headed."

He pulled open the doors. "Walk with me in the moonlight. That will clear away the faintness."

Hand in hand they crossed the moon-washed courtyard and climbed the steps set in the curtain wall behind the gatehouse tower. High above the ground a steady breeze brought scents of spring and growing grasses. As they strolled together on the broad wall walk, they gazed over the silvered countryside.

Pausing at one of the lower crenels in the battlement, Alison rested her palms on the cool stone and looked down toward the village. Not all of the villagers had gone to bed, as was attested by the many golden squares of lamp- and candlelight in the tiny windows. The lamplighter, a man too old to work in the fields, was slowly lighting the few streetlamps that would burn all night to mark the inn, the bridge across the river, and the tavern.

Miles put his hands on her shoulders and followed her gaze. "Those lights down there are like fireflies settled among the grasses, or stars fallen from the sky."

"You may be the king's most skillful jouster, but you also have the soul of a poet," she said with a contented sigh.

"I once worried that such thoughts would make me seem weak," he confessed. "Only with you have I dared share them."

"In my eyes they make you stronger," she whispered, leaning back against his chest and pulling his arms around her.

"You no longer consider me to be a barbaric Welshman?" he teased.

"That was long, long ago. Although there are times the barbarian still rises in the fore—in our bedchamber, for instance."

"You seem to relish those times."

"That I do. You're everything to me—poet, warrior, gentle knight. I love your complexity."

"No one would ever confuse you with a simple person either." He grinned.

"You would grow tired of a woman who thought no further than her stitchery and her management of the castle."

"You're right."

For a while Alison contented herself with the feel of his strong arms about her and his hard chest against her back. In the steward's apartment, a candle flickered to life. Thoughtfully she asked, "What do you think of Sir Edmund Campbell? Do you trust him?"

Miles paused, then said, "I have found no error with his bookkeeping, and he is always prompt in preparing his accounts."

"But do you trust him as a man?"

Again Miles was silent. "If I were gathering a troop to fight an enemy, Sir Edmund would not be one of my choices. I've seen his sort and they usually prove cowards on the battlefield. Why do you ask?"

"No reason." She watched Edmund pass between the window and the lamp. "No reason at all."

18

Miles slammed his open palm on the massive oak table near the foot of the bed. Alison was brushing her hair, but paused in mid-stroke for a moment when her eyes met his in the small oval hand mirror. The anger she saw there was disturbing, but, deciding it would be best for her to say nothing, she resumed her methodical brushing.

"The vicar has just reported to me that attendance at his service yesterday was even more sparse that the last one. It seems that most everyone claims to have been ill, but by this morning all were back to work. My guess is that the priest who is in hiding near here is responsible. How can he evade me so well?" Miles demanded.

"Are you so certain it is a priest who is doing all this?" she asked with careful unconcern. "Perhaps 'tis some disgruntled merchant or a bookkeeper."

"I feel sure the person who was behind the placards is also responsible for this too. No one but a priest would be taught to form letters that way, and then illuminate his work. The placards were very well done and might be considered works of art were the messages not so foul. His last called for the people to unite against the king, and referred to the queen as a whore."

"They were indeed obscene," she admitted.

"It's as if he printed them to prove that he's a priest and to taunt me!"

"What will you do with this man if you catch him?"

"I'll haul him to London in chains and have him stand trial for treason."

Alison slowly laid down her hairbrush and stood, her night rail flowing about her to the floor. "There will be no clemency for him?"

"Of course not! The man deserves none." Miles strode to the window, his robe billowing over the oak floor. "Rumor has it that this man is French or is in the hire of France, that this is a plot by King Francis to incite a civil war in England."

"I see no reason to assume that," Alison said without thinking. "At least I know of no strangers, let alone Frenchmen in the area."

"You also have said you have seen no priest in the village. Yet someone wrote those placards."

"They were only paper. Surely . . ."

"You know better than that. I've not mentioned them to the king in my letters as I should have. I was certain I could quickly apprehend the man, then report that I had done so. By now he has begun his progress north. Before he reaches Wyndfell, I must find this inciter!"

Alison went to him and ran her hand over the silky velvet of his robe. "Come to bed, Miles. You can do nothing about it tonight."

He sighed in frustration. "There must be something I've overlooked. Some person I've forgotten."

"The joust is tomorrow. You must be rested or you'll be too tired to perform. You know how you've looked forward to jousting again."

"At this moment I wish I could call it off. People are gathered here all the way from Wakefield and Leeds. If another of those placards shows up, someone else may find it and send word to the king."

"You've become obsessed with those ridiculous leaflets," Alison protested.

Miles turned to her and gazed down into her golden-brown eyes. "It's your safety I worry about. I swore to protect you, and if this issue becomes known, we may both be arrested for treason. I couldn't bear to have you imprisoned or perhaps either killed or left alone to fend for yourself. You might even be denied any revenue at all, or a place to live."

"I would be bereft without you, even if I had Wyndfell about me. You're my life."

"You were spared when your first husband was hanged as a traitor. It would be a miracle for you to survive unscathed again."

She put her fingers to his lips to stop his words, then tried to smooth his worried frown. "Charles was guilty. You are not."

"You've seen the king. Do you believe he is capable of making so fine a distinction?"

Alison didn't answer, but put her arm around his waist and led him to bed. What Miles said was true. Somehow she had to prevent Damion and Roger from causing more trouble.

"There now," Miles said gently. "I've caused you to worry. I shouldn't have spoken so freely."

"I'm your wife. I want to share your troubles. Don't ever shut me out with silence."

Miles drew her to him and cradled her securely against him. "I love you, Alison. I want nothing to come between us."

"It won't. Somehow we'll get through this."

He lowered his head and deeply kissed her, taking great pleasure in stroking the luxuriousness of her long hair and smelling the scent of lemons and roses of her sachet. Holding her close, he chuckled. "Your perfume haunts me. I can never smell a lemon or walk through a rose garden without longing for you. They are aphrodisiacs to me."

"I would have it no other way." She loosened the

satin ribbon that closed her night rail and tossed the filmy garment to the end of the bed. She then removed his robe. His skin was a pale topaz in the golden glow of the candlelight; his black hair was startlingly dark above the deep night-blue of his eyes.

"When you look at me like that, my heart turns and I grow warm all over," she whispered.

"You're a beautiful woman, but above all I love you." He lifted a shimmering handful of her auburn hair. "You're a treasure to me."

"I'll never want anyone else. I belong to you, body and soul."

"As I belong to you."

She moved nearer and the tips of her breasts grazed his chest. Running her hands over the satiny warmth of his skin, she said softly, "Be careful in the joust tomorrow."

"You'll be proud of me," he said confidently. "I look forward to showing you my skills."

"I'm already proud of you. I would rather have you in one piece."

"You worry needlessly."

"All the same," she whispered as she kissed the firm flesh of his chest and shoulder, "be careful."

"I will, love." He helped her up the stepping bench and onto the bed. Lying beside her, he smoothed her hair over her breasts and hips.

"Do you ever wish my hair was golden like the heroines in the romantic ballads?"

"Never."

"Or dark, perhaps, like that of a wild Gypsy?"

"Not for a moment. Your hair is much like you are—silken and beautiful to look upon, yet with a fire hidden within."

"My poet knight." She smiled. "I see chivalry is not dead."

"You inspire me to chivalrous discourse," he replied, rolling her on top of him.

"You should save your energy for the morrow," she teased as she moved against his length.

"Making love with you increases my strength tenfold."

"In that case," she said, running the tip of her tongue over the curve of his ear, "I will do my best to inspire you."

They kissed with growing passion, and Miles ran his hands over her back and sides, over her hips to cup her buttocks. Sensuously he moved against her, and Alison murmured as she responded.

She shifted so that he could enter her, and they both lay still, savoring the sensation of becoming one. Slowly she began to move, at first only rippling her body in a suggestion of passion, then increasing her tempo until he moaned with the delight she gave him.

Alison raised herself, putting her palms on his chest and arching her back to let him penetrate her more deeply. Miles covered her breasts with his hands, and she felt her nipples throb with quickened longing. Gently he rolled her nipples between his thumbs and forefingers, forcing her to close her eyes and let her head roll back on her slender neck as she savored the ecstasy of his touch.

He raised his head and guided first one tempting bud, then the other into his mouth. His hot tongue circled and licked, and his teeth grazed the tender flesh. Alison murmured his name as if it were a synonym for love, and he rolled her beneath him.

His powerful body covered hers, and she stroked the hard contours of his muscles, feeling delightfully overpowered by the strength beneath her palms. She matched his thrusts as her long legs entwined with his to seek even greater pleasure.

Subtly Alison sensed a change in his rhythm, an urgency in his kiss. Then in perfect tune with him, her body responded and together they reached love's pinnacle. Waves of pleasure pounded through her, and she knew Miles was experiencing the same fulfillment.

As always when they made love, their minds and bodies blended in perfect harmony.

Afterward they lay quietly, stroking each other with the endearing touch of lovers. Alison felt safe in Miles's arms, for when he held her tightly, lovingly, she knew nothing could harm her. Surely nothing could take this from her. So much love and happiness must give a safety of its own. Yet far back in the recesses of her mind she remembered her mother cautioning her against too much happiness for fear the angels would grow jealous and retaliate. Alison resolutely put the thought aside and gave herself over to loving Miles.

The next day dawned perfect for a joust. The sky was clear and the past week's rain appeared to be over at last. A city of tents had sprung up over Wyndfell's south green, and the other slopes were covered with a vivid array of scarlet poppies.

Lists for the jousts had been built behind the formal garden, and rows of benches stood to either side. Men rode their spirited horses to and fro to temper the beasts for their time to joust. Flags flew everywhere—above the tents, along the lists, and over the green-and-gold canopy erected to shade the ladies and their attendants from the bright sunlight.

Earlier in the day the men had drawn lots to determine who would be set against whom. Trahern was riding in the first group of sets, and Leatrice was as nervous as Alison. Neither had ever seen a tourney of such scale.

"Do you think Trahern will be safe?" Leatrice whispered to Alison. "His opponent is truly a giant."

"Of course he will be," Alison said with an attempt at confidence. "At court they did this all the time. Both Trahern and Miles are skilled."

"Are you afraid for Lord Miles?"

"Yes. But I refuse to let it show." Alison twisted her scarf of bright green silk, embroidered with the gold Garrett griffin, into a rope as she moved restlessly on the padded bench, her eyes searching for Miles.

"One would never guess," Leatrice said with a laugh as she rescued the scarf.

A young man stepped out into the center of the list and began crying the tourney. He called for all knights within the sound of his voice to gather and be judged according to their talents. When he finished, the sound of many brasses trumpeted the entry, and the knights rode by twos onto the field. Miles was in the lead, his large Barbaristo prancing and gleaming like silver beneath the green-and-gold trappings.

Alison had not seen Miles dress for the joust, and was surprised to find that this fierce warrior in shining mail and polished plates of steel was her husband. His helmet was raised but his face was intense, as if he were already immersed in battle. Alison could scarcely equate this warlike knight with the gentle lover who had held her all night. Her blood stirred at the idea of making love with this magnificent warrior.

The men circled the field and reined to a stop in the center. One by one they rode toward the audience to receive a scarf or sleeve or stocking from a lady as an indication of her affection for him.

When Miles pointed his lance toward Alison, she was seized by a shyness that was rare for her. She met his eyes to force herself to bravery. Within the blue depths, she saw her Miles and realized he was thoroughly enjoying himself. With a smile she thrust the green silk scarf forward and knotted it about the lance. Miles lifted the long lance in a salute and wheeled his horse, using only his heels and knees.

Alison's heart was racing with excitement. She had never expected a jousting to be a sensual experience! The smile usually reserved for Miles alone tilted her lips.

In their turn Leatrice and the other wives and sweethearts gave a token to their men as each knight was recognized and called forward. The last to be summoned was Lord Roger Bainbridge. Alison leaned forward to see where he would ride, for she knew he had no woman to give him a gage. To her surprise and embarrassment, he stopped in front of her and lowered his lance straight at her.

Alison looked at Leatrice and at the woman on her other side, but there could be no doubt whom he meant. A murmur ran through the crowd as she hesitated. She threw a quick look at Miles, but could see only his fierce helmet. Was it common for a lady to bestow a favor on two knights? She decided it must be proper, for Roger knew more about jousting than she did, but she was still uncomfortable.

Not knowing what else to do, Alison pulled the bongrace from her French hood and stabbed it onto the point of Roger's lance. He grinned, but she glared at him before he rode away.

"You gave him a favor!" Leatrice exclaimed under her breath. "What will Lord Miles say?"

"What else could I do?" Alison hissed back. "He seemed determined to stand there all day. I had to give him something." Her eyes followed Miles as he kneed his huge horse forward and led the procession off the field.

Miles was a mixture of anger, surprise, and confusion. Roger Bainbridge had actually requested a token from Alison, and she had given him one! What did that mean? Proper custom would have had her wave him away. Yet she had given him her bongrace, and in a way that seemed very resolute. Miles angrily snapped his visor shut and latched it for his first round.

His opponent was a man from Leeds who rode a large charger with saffron trappings. Miles guided Excalibur to the head of the list and appraised his competitor. The horse was ill-trained and skittish, but the man exuded confidence. The crier gave the readying command and Miles lowered his lance to a horizontal position along Excalibur's neck. The horse, flicking his ears back and tossing his mane in eagerness, didn't waste his energy in capering about. The crier waved his banner and Miles leaned forward, sending Excalibur into a hard run. He steadily aimed his lance at his opponent's shield, his mind focused on winning this set.

They met almost in the center of the list, and Miles felt the familiar bone-jarring jolt as his lance contacted its target squarely, and the other man's lance skittered off Miles's shield and across his breastplate. Even as he thundered past, Miles heard the thud of the man being unhorsed.

The crowd cheered loudly as Miles sat back and let Excalibur slack his speed before circling the list. The Leeds man's pages had run forward to catch his horse and help him to his feet. Miles was pleased to see that the man was not hurt, though his expression was anything but satisfied. He had ridden all the way from Leeds, and now, just five minutes into the joust, he was out of the contest.

Miles rode Excalibur around to calm him, but his mind was still on his rival. Although Miles was certain of Alison's love, he also knew she had chosen to marry Roger Bainbridge. He recalled the few times he had seen a man he thought was Bainbridge riding away from Wyndfell, but Alison had never mentioned their neighbor's visit. Jealousy seared him, and the gentleness left his eyes. When Roger also unseated his opponent, Miles was glad. He wanted Roger to last until he himself would meet him in the list.

One by one the little wars were fought, and the defeated retired to their tents and pavilions to remove their armor and have their minor wounds attended.

At midday, one of Miles's pages brought a bowl of meat and fruit for his master, but Miles waved the boy away, wanting no food to weigh him down and slake his battle lust.

Four more times Miles met men on the lists, and each time he rode away the winner. Alison's bongrace on Roger's lance taunted him and kept his mind alert.

Trahern fared well in the lists, but eventually he was felled by a man more lucky than skillful. Miles saw

Leatrice leap to her feet and press her hands against her mouth, but Trahern rose unaided and retired with grace, saluting his opponent.

There had been few serious injuries and no fatalities. A few men had been cut badly enough to require stitching by the barbers who waited in the first tent, and one man had fallen crookedly and broken his arm, but all in all the tourney was a good one. Miles stood or paced between bouts and spoke as little as possible. He kept his battle flame burning and gave no thought to exhaustion. The heavy bone-tiredness would come later.

The winners matched coins to determine opponents, and gradually the same faces appeared again and again. At last it was down to three men—Miles, Roger Bainbridge, and a knight from York who earned his living by attending tourneys.

They met in the circle beneath the oak tree at the side of the list. Their pages came forward to match coins. Miles's unsettling glare fixed Roger, willing him to back down and request the other man. Roger blinked uneasily, but nodded for his page to throw for the last match. The three tokens flashed in the air and landed on the grass. Miles was pitted against Roger. A slow smile spread over Miles's face, and his eyes didn't waver until Roger looked away and went to his horse.

Miles rode Excalibur into position, and on the signal he lowered his lance. The horse's gray neck was flecked with foamy sweat, but his movements were tireless and strong. Miles felt himself becoming one with the horse, and at the crier's signal he galloped forward with a single goal. Roger also pounded forward, his lance directed straight at Miles's shield, Alison's begrimed bongrace whipping from the cold metal.

Suddenly, just before they made contact, Roger's lance tip shifted slightly. Too late to parry the devious thrust, Miles felt the lance graze his shield and strike his shoulder. Pain coursed through him and his lance failed to meet dead center on Roger's shield. Excalibur stumbled as Miles reeled in the saddle, but Miles's knees clasped the horse tightly as he pulled himself erect.

Because of the limited movement of his helmet, Miles couldn't see how badly he was wounded, but he felt warm blood bathing his left arm and dripping down his side. He turned Excalibur to readiness, and at the signal again plunged forward. This time he was prepared for Roger's trickery, and he deflected the thrust with his shield as he struck Roger with all his force.

Roger gave a cry and fell backward. Miles let his horse slow down, then circled to see Roger sitting dazed in the trampled grass. His battle lust still high, Miles motioned angrily for the one remaining opponent to take the field.

Roger's pages quickly hauled their master out of the way as Miles and the knight hurtled toward each other. With a clash of steel against steel, the knight was down.

Drawing deep breaths into his burning lungs, Miles rode in an easy canter around the lists, his lance upended in victory. As he passed the canopy on his way back to his pages, he saw Alison's pale face and frightened eyes. Thinking she was sad because he had unhorsed Roger, he became even angrier. He wasn't aware of his pain until he reached the oak and tried to lift his arm to dismount.

After a page pulled off his helmet, Miles looked down to find his left arm bloodied and the mail ripped. The other page hurriedly unbuckled Miles's armor and helped him shuck off the metal casing that covered his body. The wool garment that was worn as padding under the armor was blood-soaked. When the first tearing pain coursed through him, Miles's knees buckled, and he grabbed the metal poitrel that protected Excalibur's chest. Exhaustion engulfed him.

Trahern was there beside him, his eyes worried, but with a strengthening smile. He easily slipped Miles's good arm around his neck and helped him toward the barbers' tent. "You and I are growing too old for this foolishness," he commented to Miles. "I feel as if my horse rolled over me."

"Jousting has its drawbacks," Miles replied through set teeth.

Alison fought her way to the tent and ran to Miles, her eyes brimming with tears. "You're hurt!"

"I won," he challenged quietly. "And how is Lord Bainbridge?"

"How should I know?" She pulled out her knife and started cutting away the bloodied sleeve. Though the sight weakened her, she kept on. A barber, his hands red from his work on other wounds, grabbed a basin and his sewing implements and headed toward Miles.

"Wash your hands first!" she commanded sharply. "And bring fresh water to cleanse his wound."

"But, my lady, blood is blood," the man argued.

"Do as I say!"

Miles frowned and tried not to flinch as Alison drew away the sleeve. She was here beside him and not with Bainbridge. Now that the battle lust was gone, he knew he must have judged her falsely.

"You promised you wouldn't get hurt," she scolded.

"Forgive me, my lady. If your other knight had not parried falsely, I wouldn't have."

"What do you mean?" Alison tried to mask the alarm she felt, but her words came out hurriedly, tinged with acrimony.

Thinking she was being defensive, he bluntly said, "Lord Bainbridge aimed at my arm, not my shield. Why did you give him a favor?"

"He demanded one and I knew not what else to do," Alison said.

Before Miles could respond, the barber returned with fresh water and began washing away the crimson stain. Alison blanched as the cut appeared and felt as if she might faint. Instead, she held Miles's other hand and met his eyes as the barber skillfully closed the wound. When it was done, she bound the arm with strips of white linen.

"Are you able to walk?" she asked anxiously, her concern for his welfare overshadowing her indignation.

A page handed Miles a goblet of red wine, and as he downed it in one draft, he could see the genuine concern Alison was feeling. "Of course, love. This is not my first wound." He stood and motioned toward the last man he had defeated. "Trahern, give that knight a purse of gold. He fought well."

When Miles's page had him dressed, he shouted out, "To the banquet!"

Musicians struck up a lively air and the horses were led away. Alison walked back to the castle beside her husband and marveled at his imperviousness to pain and exhaustion.

Miles matched his pace to hers and wished he could skip the banquet and sleep the rest of the day. He had proved himself, but he didn't care to joust again soon. After a man topped thirty years, he wasn't prime for the rigors of the tournament field, and Miles wanted to retire as champion of the day.

19

After several days of hunting and feasting, the tourney was over. The knights, their ladies, and their servants went back to their homes, leaving the south slope of Wyndfell a trampled field of dirt and litter. Alison dispatched several men with tow bags to clean up the mess. In time the grass would return and Wyndfell would again be surrounded by an apron of green.

She worried far more about the wound on Miles's arm, and she spent hours concocting salves and elixirs to speed his healing. Miles, however, was not a willing patient.

"Again?" he demanded when she entered his closet, a tankard in one hand and a bowl in the other.

"It seemed a bit red this morning."

"I have work to do. God's bones, Alison. I've been wounded worse than this and recovered—and with less medicine."

"All the more reason why I am trying so hard to find the correct cure. Drink this."

He peered distrustfully into the tankard. "What is it?"

"It's an infusion of prickly ash and wintergreen."

He tasted it and grimaced. "This is the worst yet!"

"Then perhaps it will be more effective," she countered. "Drink it while I loosen your sleeve."

"What have you got in that bowl?"

"It's a paste of myrrh and water betony. Be still. It must be applied while it's still warm."

Miles gave a mild protest, but allowed her to untie the ribbon that gathered his sleeve to his wrist. Alison carefully pulled the sleeve up and stuffed it into his jerkin to keep it out of the way. She untied the linen bandage and removed the cloth to inspect the long red wound.

"You see? It's healing nicely," he said triumphantly.

"And this will help it even more." She dipped her fingers into the white paste and smoothed it over the cut.

"By the saints, Alison, that burns like hell!"

"Why, Miles, you call upon the saints?" She smiled. "I'll have you turn Catholic yet."

He glared at her. "You didn't tell me it was near-boiling."

"Nonsense. 'Tis but warm. Don't carry on so or I'll quit doctoring you and then where will you be?"

She frowned in response to Miles's hopeful look. "Drink the infusion."

With a resigned sigh, he swallowed the bitter brew.

"That's much better," she said encouragingly as she took a clean bandage from her sleeve and rebound his arm. She bent over and kissed him on the forehead and smoothed her hand over his hair. "There now. I'll look in on you later."

As she left, Miles shook his head in mock exasperation. He had seen mortal wounds that had received less attention than this one. He pulled down his sleeve and reknotted the ribbon, using his right hand and his teeth.

Alison went back to the kitchen to dispose of the soiled bandage. Tib, the maid in charge of the kitchen workers, was moving restlessly about the large room. Alison nodded to her and Tib greeted her abruptly.

"Is aught wrong?" Alison said. "You seem upset."

"I know not what is bothering me. I was talking to

several of the maids and servers, and many of us have this dread fear."

"A fear? Of what?"

"I know not, my lady. It came on us suddenly this morning. Young Bess can't leave off talking of death, and Liz said several of the dairymaids are doing the same."

Alison looked at the normally stolid maid. Tib was not one to have unsettling vapors of the blood. "Have you been bled lately? Perhaps 'tis an overabundance of fluids."

"I saw the barber-surgeon just last week." Tib moved restlessly to the drying table and stirred the tray of herbs that were drying in the warm air.

"Have you taken food to the anchoress?" Alison asked in order to prolong the conversation and observe Tib. Something did seem to be wrong with her. Tib's eyes looked watery and her face was a bit flushed.

"I took it to her not five minutes ago, my lady."

"Is Mother Anne feeling this odd fear?"

"If she was, she didn't say."

"Very well, Tib. I'm certain this will pass. No doubt there is some miasma in the air. I'll have the gong-farmers clean out the jakes. Perhaps that's the problem." She went to the outside door and paused to look back at the maid. A concerned frown puckered Alison's brow.

She went out to the kitchen yard and looked closely at the servants working there. Across the yard she heard Bayard, the server, speak sharply to one of the lackeys, who responded in kind. Everyone seemed on edge, yet Alison felt well. Before going inside, she spent a few minutes supervising two young maids who were just learning how to cut the rosemary and thyme for drying. She was glad to see that they seemed as cheerful as ever.

Alison looked over at the wooden door that led to the wall where Mother Anne lived. Of late Alison had rarely gone to the cell. The anchoress always seemed to speak against Miles or to upbraid Alison for loving him. Alison hadn't confessed to the holy woman in over a month. She knew Mother Anne would assume she had at last started confessing to Damion, but she hadn't. Of late she had felt less peace after confession, and she wasn't about to admit that to either Mother Anne or Damion. Nor could she admit that the required Protestant services were not as offensive as they once had been.

Going back into the castle, she found Leatrice and the ladies sewing in the solar. Alison took up the Turkey work she was finishing and listened to the usual round of conversation and gossip. Leatrice, who sat beside her, was unusually quiet.

"Is something the matter, Leatrice? Surely you and Trahern have not quarreled."

"No, my lady." As Leatrice pulled the silk thread through the piece of embroidery, Alison noticed her hands were shaking. "I know not what is the matter. I find myself feeling uneasy over nothing. For some reason, thoughts of death are crowding about me."

"You too?" one of the ladies said in surprise. "Mistress Nan and I were saying the same thing earlier."

Alison's frown returned and she looked about the room thoughtfully. When the strange complaints had been centered only in the servants, she had wondered if some natural calamity was about to occur, but she knew that Leatrice, and certainly Mistress Nan had no talent for second sight. For so many to have this unnamed fear was more than remarkable. "Are you feeling ill?" she asked Leatrice.

"The room seems rather close, but it's a warm day."

Alison felt a sense of foreboding. There had been few warm days this summer and this wasn't one of them. She stood abruptly and left the room. When Leatrice halfheartedly offered to come with her, Alison waved her back. There was a warning going off in her brain. She could almost hear her mother telling of a like incident from Alison's childhood. Something linked with summer and unfounded fears and . . . The memory was elusive.

She had crossed the long gallery and was about to descend the curving steps when one of the young maids came running up to meet her.

"My lady! My lady! Come quickly. Tib!"

"Tib? What's wrong now?"

"She's . . . well, I don't rightly know what's wrong. I never seen anything like this!"

Hurrying after the frightened girl, Alison ran across the hall, down the corridor, and out to the kitchen. The change in Tib was remarkable. Her rather large eyes were glassy, and streams of sweat were running off her rotund body. Already her face and arms were turning bright red. Alison stopped and stared as the nagging memory became complete. She knew before she ever stepped close enough to catch the appalling stench from the woman's diseased body.

"Sweating sickness!" she gasped.

The other servants exclaimed at the thought, and several reflexively crossed themselves despite warnings to avoid such open display of their Catholic loyalty. They all knew the danger, for in a previous epidemic in London, forty thousand had died. A town was considered lucky if only a third of its population was lost. Sweating sickness was feared more greatly than the plague.

Alison knew she must take charge quickly. The men and women still on their feet showed every sign of bolting and running away. "Bayard, take the yeomen and bring bedding to the hall. It will be easier to care for everyone in one place. You, boy, I see you slipping out! You'll not leave the castle. Do you understand? Maybe the village is as yet unaffected."

She watched to see that they obeyed her, then turned to her chief cook. "Grace, fetch several casks of vinegar and have them carried to the hall. Rob, bring in braziers of coals so we may burn spices to purify the air. Walt, fetch blankets and comforters and furs and take them to the hall. Also get the pallets from the beds of all who are becoming sick. Hurry!"

Going to Tib's chair, she put her hand on the woman's shoulder. "Be brave, Tib. I've heard that the will to survive this is better than any medicine."

"My lady, I'm afraid," cried one of the younger maids.

"Don't be! Physicians say that fear of it will bring on the disease. Say an Our Father or count the linens or sing a song, but don't let your mind grow fearful."

"Yes, my lady," the girl said doubtfully.

Alison took the heavy ring of keys from its wall peg and began securing the doors in the curtain wall to prevent anyone from entering or leaving. When she locked the doors at the kitchen entrance, she paused. Tib had been to see the abbess that morning. Alison went along the wall and rapped on the almost hidden door. When there was no answer, she pushed it open and went in.

She heard a labored breathing behind the curtain and called out to Mother Anne, but still got no response. Without further hesitation, Alison pushed the fabric aside. The anchoress lay on a low pallet, fully dressed in her stark black-and-white habit. Despite the rumors of Mother Anne's returned youth, Alison saw a woman who was as wrinkled as the apple-faced dolls made for children. The stench about the woman and the bright redness of her face and hands proved the sickness had already reached the cell.

Alison pulled the old woman to her feet and looped her arm around her neck. "Try to walk, Mother Anne. I must get you into the hall."

"No, no. I must not leave my cell. I must uphold my vows of isolation."

"I cannot care for you properly out here."

"But I have withdrawn from the world. Leave me here to live or die as God wills."

"That I won't even consider," Alison said firmly.

"I'll not go!"

"Yes, you will. Remember your earlier vow of obedience."

The old woman murmured in protest, but Alison was already shoving open the door of the cell. Mother Anne gasped when the sunlight struck her eyes for the first time in years. Alison half-carried the frail old woman, who, beneath her voluminous gown, was as thin as a reed.

By the time they reached the gate, Miles had heard of the threat and had come to help her. Alison looked up at him and found strength in his eyes. "It's the sweating sickness."

He looked at the anchoress and nodded. There was no need to question Alison's diagnosis. He bent and lifted the vaguely protesting anchoress before saying, "Have you ever had this malady, Alison?"

"I don't know. My mother told me of an epidemic when I was a child in my stepfather's castle, but I don't know if I had it. Have you?"

"Yes, in the great epidemic of 1528."

Alison locked the gate and hurried beside him into the castle. The usual rhythm of Wyndfell's busy life was considerably altered. People were running about in all directions. Already the astringent smell of vinegar pervaded the rooms. Miles collared a yeoman running by and sent him after a pallet for the anchoress.

The appearance of the holy woman caused quite a stir as many in the hall whispered their conjectures. When Miles laid the woman down, she curled into a knot as if she could not tolerate so much contact with people.

Alison saw Walt enter the room and motioned for him to come near. "Draw the bridge," she commanded. "Let no one enter or leave. I've locked the wall gates."

"No one, my lady? 'Tis well known that the wise flee from illness lest they also be stricken."

"And 'tis also observed that the disease follows in their footsteps. You have a sweetheart in the village. Would you take this to her?"

Walt shook his head. "I'll raise the drawbridge, my lady."

Soon Alison heard the uncommon sound of the great chains straining after many years of rest. The heavy boards in the drawbridge sighed and popped as the end that had been the floor of the gatehouse pivoted down into its cellar. After a brief silence, Alison jumped as the lead-tipped portcullis dropped onto the bedrock on which Wyndfell was built.

Apprehension swept anew among the castle people. Most couldn't recall ever seeing the drawbridge raised or the portcullis lowered. These were measures for wartime, for siege.

Miles and Alison moved among the people, quietening them and explaining the reason for their enforced isolation. Few agreed with their decision, but no one dared speak against the lord and lady.

All the servants who still seemed well were sent to the isolation of the kitchen and dairy, from which they would tend to the needs of the others. However, they were instructed to bring themselves immediately to the hall at the first sign of an unexplainable sweating.

Leatrice, along with the other ladies and the unfortunate among Miles's men, was placed in the long gallery above and behind the hall. Both the hall and the gallery were forbidden to those who had so far escaped.

Everyone, sick or well, was commanded to drink copious quantities of vinegar and water. The sick were wrapped in blankets to keep air from their skin as their temperatures rose to alarming heights. Influenza soon set in, adding to the patients' misery. Wyndfell's physician, as well as the two barber-surgeons, moved from cot to cot, bleeding the people, all the while debating among themselves whether it was better to bleed a patient from the arm, or between his thumb and forefinger, or between his shoulders. Several people were bled twice in the confusion.

Then the deaths began. Heralded by a rash showing

signs of infection, the unfortunates next became dazed, then died. Bayard, the server, was the first, followed quickly by Mistress Nan and a dairymaid.

The sickness gave little warning and respected no one's rank or duty. An attendant would be well one minute and clutching a raging headache the next. In a few hours' time, he could be dead.

Miles supervised the servants in the hall, while Alison took control of the fever patients in the gallery. Aside from seeing that vinegar was added to all the sauces and drinks, the next-most-important step was to keep the patients awake—not an easy task when the fear sent the patients into a stupor.

Trahern sat beside Leatrice, forcing the unpleasant liquid down her throat as he alternately cajoled and commanded her to get well. Alison saw the heartbreak in his eyes, but nothing more could be done.

The physician mixed huge amounts of exotic medicines made palatable with cloyingly sweet treacle and herbs. Few fought against swallowing it. After the tankards of vinegar water, the medicine was a welcome respite.

The day slowly turned into night, and candles and rushlights were lit in the large rooms. Their smoky odor mixed with the vinegar, and the stench of the disease itself was almost suffocating. Alison longed to step out for a brief breath of fresh air, but she dared not, for while she was away, someone might fall asleep and die.

By midnight the death rate was at least one per hour and the small store of coffins in one of the cellar vaults was soon depleted. In the dark hours of the morning, carpenters could be heard sawing and hammering to stay abreast of the need.

At first light men were sent to the west green to dig graves. The dead were buried with a short sermon by Wyndfell's chaplain and a promise to give a more fitting memorial when all this was over.

Alison moved between the cots, often seeing a new

face in the place where one had just died. Trahern looked up as she approached, worry etched on his tired face. "She seems less feverish," Alison said, touching Leatrice's brow.

"I thought so, but I couldn't be sure."

Alison put her ear to Leatrice's chest. "Her heart seems strong." She smiled for the first time since the previous morning. "I believe she will live."

"Do you really think so?" Trahern was still afraid to hope.

"I've heard if the sick live an entire day, they usually recover. In three hours the day will have passed. Keep giving her vinegar water and don't let her sleep." She looked at Leatrice's drawn face. Though her eyes were open and she blinked occasionally, she showed no animation.

Alison stood and rested her hand on Trahern's shoulder. "We mustn't quit trying now." She moved away to see to the other patients.

By that night Alison was too exhausted to keep going, so she reluctantly turned over her duties to Sir Edmund. Going down to the hall, Alison watched Miles moving from cot to cot. One of the barbers had relieved him earlier from a brief rest, and now he was back at work, seeing to the needs of those in his charge. They had agreed that one of them should be awake at all times to supervise things until the disease had run its course, and when Miles saw Alison across the room, he nodded for her to go on upstairs.

Aching from head to toe, Alison climbed the spiraling steps to the bedchamber. At the head of the stairs she opened a seldom-used door that led into the battlements and stepped out to breathe the fresh air. A blue-gray gauze of night mist was falling through the still air. Below was the village, but from this distance she couldn't tell if all was well there or not. Many cottages had lights in their windows, but that didn't necessarily mean people were ill. Folks might be sitting about wondering why the drawbridge was raised, for instance, and why the castle had sealed itself off. Whatever their speculations, they could hardly be worse than the truth.

Alison rested her hands on the crenel notch and leaned her forehead against the damp coolness of the merlon that rose between the crenels. Had she done right in not allowing those who could to leave? Several of them were sick now. Perhaps if she had let them go, they might have avoided the illness. A sadness swept over her. So many had died. Hopefully, the village had been spared.

Turning back to the castle, she recalled her brother. Days had gone by since she had seen him. Somehow, while Miles was busy in the hall, she had to summon the strength to tell Damion what was happening.

She entered the passage through her bedroom and went up to the closed door to his chamber. "Damion? Don't open the door. There is sickness in the castle, and it might be lurking in my clothing."

Despite her warning, Damion threw open the door. "Don't be daft. A healthy person can't carry disease—I doubt if anyone can. Come in before we're overheard."

Alison noted the change in Damion right away. He had always been argumentative, but now he was like an avenging angel. He stood with his feet planted firmly apart. The expression on his face was not priestly. "Damion? Are you all right?" The sweating sickness usually started with fear, not agitation, but nevertheless she was concerned by this pronounced change in him.

When she tried to test his brow for fever, he shoved her hand away. "Dare not touch me, woman! What sickness is this? I looked through the peephole in the hall and found what looked like an infirmary."

"It is. Sweating sickness is at Wyndfell."

A bright smile broke upon Damion's face and his eyes glittered. "Hallelujah! Praise the saints!"

"I beg your pardon?"

"Don't you see, sister? This is divine retribution for

the sins of this castle." He paced the room quickly. "The sweating sickness first broke out to punish old Henry VII for his sins. Before then it was completely unknown. Every outbreak can be traced to the sinfulness of man!" Damion looked as if he were experiencing a divine revelation.

"Then I find this retribution rather puzzling," Alison snapped, "for most of those sick are known to be firm in the Catholic religion."

"They must be giving mere lip service," he said scornfully.

"Mother Anne died this morning."

Damion frowned. "She did? Then doubtless she chose to do so to intercede for the true Catholics' souls."

Alison sighed and turned to go. "Keep to your chambers until all this has passed. I know not if it has spread to the village. If you were to fall sick up here, I could never tend you. You might even die before I knew you were sick." In an inspiration she added, "Your prayers are much needed."

"Yes!" Damion exclaimed with great zeal as he dropped to his knees on the hard floor. "I will pray unceasingly until this is past."

"Good," Alison agreed in a tired voice. "I'll leave your food on the landing and not come up until the sickness is over."

Damion was already deep in prayer, his eyes closed and his lips moving in a quick whisper. Alison let herself out and went back to her bedchamber. She could no longer pretend Damion was merely overly devout. There had been madness in his eyes. She collapsed fully dressed on the bed and was trying to think of a way to get Damion out of her castle when a heavy sleep overtook her.

As Sir Edmund worked with Miles tending the sick, he noticed that Miles seemed remarkably unperturbed that the dying prayers on many lips were distinctly

Catholic. Then there was the matter of that nun. Edmund had never seen her before, but Miles had treated her as if she were familiar to him. Edmund decided she must have been the anchoress Lord Bainbridge had once mentioned, but that didn't explain how Miles knew about her. He considered sending a dispatch to the king, but reason stopped him. There was nothing so very untoward in a knight giving aid to an old woman in a black habit, except that the king had expressly forbidden anyone to harbor a Catholic who had not renounced that faith, and Edmund had no way of knowing whether the old woman had or had not. Besides, the king, queen, and Princess Mary were already on their progress to York. A letter might not find them at all. No, it would be better to report to the king at York in person. Somehow Edmund could contrive a reason to leave Wyndfell for a few days.

In the meantime he pretended to be Catholic when Alison was near, as if he trusted her with his secret. At other times he managed to work near Miles, waiting for him to make some slip that would connect him to the underground movement. He wanted a steadfast reason to cast doubt upon Miles. It was galling that Miles was rich and married to a woman Edmund desired. The king had promised he would reward Edmund handsomely for uncovering a revolutionary plot, but there were no rewards for reporting all was well at Wyndfell.

20

The sweating sickness finally abated, taking with it over a quarter of Wyndfell's population. Alison thought it nothing short of miraculous that so many survived and that neither she nor Miles succumbed to the disease. The survivors were weakened by their ordeal, and Alison wasn't sure Tib would ever again be her robust self. The blacksmith's apprentice was slow-witted after having such a high fever for so long, and the physician had grave doubts that he would ever regain his mental agility. The blacksmith relegated the unfortunate boy to a permanent position as his helper, and began looking for another lad to train in his place.

When the danger was past, the drawbridge was lowered, the portcullis raised, and the wall gates unlocked. The village folk who had been locked in under the quarantine headed for their homes to see if their families had been spared. Luckily the village had escaped contagion, and quickly the castle's staff was replenished.

Miles was in his closet going over the books presented to him by Sir Edmund when a messenger arrived. Walt showed him in, and Miles at once recognized the king's livery. So did Sir Edmund. The messenger bowed to Miles and gave him a letter sealed by the king's own ring.

Miles broke the seal and read the letter silently. "I've been summoned to York," he said thoughtfully.

"I thought the king planned to journey here on the way back to London," Sir Edmund said.

"So did I. Perhaps he has had a change of plans." He thanked the messenger and gave him a coin. To Walt he said, "Go to Lady Alison and ask her to come here. Sir Edmund, that will be all for today. I must make ready for the journey."

"Perhaps I should come with you, my lord."

"No, no. I need you here to look after Wyndfell. Harvest is beginning and someone must supervise the collection of rents."

Edmund had no choice but to acquiesce. He bowed stiffly and turned to leave as Alison entered the closet.

"You've had a message from the king?"

"Yes, I've been summoned to York. We must make ready for our journey."

"We? I thought you said he had summoned you."

"He did, but I'm certain you are invited."

"Surely he would have mentioned us both if he'd wanted me there too. Besides, I can't go. Mabel Phelps is due to give birth at any time, and I promised her I would be there."

"Send the midwife."

"Goody Smith loses half as many mothers and babes as she delivers. Mabel almost died last time, and she's frightened. No, I can't go." She went to Miles and put her hand on his arm. "Does this mean the king doesn't plan to come here after all?"

"You sound so hopeful. Do you expect to avoid that oath of fealty forever? I assume it means the king will return to London by another route. Otherwise, why would he summon me?"

"I hope that's what it means. Will you make my excuses to him?"

"Yes, but he may send for you anyway. I know not what is meant by this command."

Alison frowned. "He can't have learned of those placards, can he?"

"Possibly."

"Will you be safe?"

Miles smoothed his worried frown and said, "Of course, love. This is probably nothing. Don't worry so."

She reached up to kiss his cheek, and nodded her agreement as if she could control her thoughts so easily. "I know you'll be safe. When will you leave?"

"Tomorrow morning at dawn. I'll leave Sir Edmund in charge and take my knights to ensure a safe journey. I should be home in a week, a fortnight at the most."

"I'll miss you. We've never been apart before."

"And I'll miss you, love. You'll be in my thoughts day and night."

"I suppose you have no other course but to go?"

"You know I must."

She nodded. She had already known the answer. "I'll go see that your belongings are packed."

As Miles watched her leave, his dark mood returned. He could think of only one reason for his summons: the king must have learned of the placards and unrest in the area. What could he tell the king? Aside from the damnable placards and a few burned houses, Miles had nothing substantive to report. True, these problems were more noteworthy than the intentional slowdown of his field workers, but as yet none of the villagers had openly challenged his authority or that of the king. Miles had never been good at bending the truth, so he decided, if asked, to lay all this at the king's feet and hope the king's madness had not robbed him of all trust in a man who had always been loyal to the crown.

Alison packed Miles's clothing, some bed linens, towels, soap, and everything else he might need for the journey. In the next room she heard Leatrice doing the same for Trahern. She didn't worry about

Miles's safety on the road, for he would take those of his men who had not been weakened by the sweating sickness. But she was terribly worried about the king. She had witnessed the king fly into rages with little or not provocation. What if one of those rages was directed at Miles?

Alison sat on the chest and thought for a moment, then went to the door and called to Trahern. When he came in, Alison closed the door and said quickly, "I know you are Miles's closest and most trusted friend. I must ask you to do something, and you mustn't ask any questions or tell anyone what I bade you do. Will you agree?"

Trahern nodded. "I will, my lady."

"Miles may be in danger while at court. No, you promised not to ask any questions. Stay close to him. If anything . . . untoward befalls him, send me word immediately. Which of the men who are staying here is most loyal to Miles and myself?"

"All may be trusted completely, but I would say Sir Robert of St. Giles is the best of the knights."

"Will he do my bidding to save Miles, no matter what it might be?"

"Aye, my lady. Sir Robert would lay down his life for either of you."

"Good, Sir Trahern. You have answered me well. Now, remember! If anything happens to Miles, I must get word at once."

"I'll remember."

Alison saw him out, feeling much better. If Miles were arrested, the king would no doubt send him back to the Tower of London. She could lead a party of knights to intercept his captors and free him. Then they could ride straight to Kingston-upon-Hull and get passage to France. As soon as Trahern sent word, Alison could send Leatrice and the rest of their attendants on ahead to book passage and meet them in France.

To be certain her plan worked, Alison found several

canvas bags such as were used to store beans or shelled corn and went about packing their jewelry and as much of the gold plate as could be hidden away. She sewed the majority of their coins into little pockets at the bottom of her petticoat and her riding gown. Leatrice could be trusted to safeguard the rest.

She looked about the castle with regret for what might be. She had had every reason to believe she would spend the rest of her life here in these sheltering walls. She hoped desperately that her fears were for naught.

That evening Brother Damion slipped out of Wyndfell to meet Roger in the oak thicket. He had learned, while listening through the panels, as had become his habit, that Miles had been commanded to go to the king the next day, and this meeting was essential. Dusk was gathering and early autumn hung in the air, but Damion ignored the coolness.

Roger was late, and Damion was pacing nervously when he arrived. Without bothering to greet him, Damion said, "The time to strike is at hand. Lord Miles goes to York tomorrow. That means the king must be suspicious of him for not putting down our rebellion."

"You know this for a fact?"

"What else could it mean for the king to decide not to visit Wyndfell and instead command Lord Miles to appear before him?"

"You must be right. What is your plan?"

"We must somehow bring to light the queen's affair with Culpepper, and make it appear as if Lord Miles is involved."

"How can we do that?"

"You're to go to the court at York. Use your eyes and ears. Watch not only the queen but also this Thomas Culpepper. One of them is certain to slip up. You heard what Alison said—they are practically lying together under the king's very nose! When you learn where they are likely to meet, send a command to Lord Miles to go there at the appointed time as if it had come directly from the queen. Then go to the king and tell him the three are meeting French-style. He will think Queen Catherine has two lovers and will do away with them all. That will free him to marry the very Catholic Christina, Duchess of Milan, and rid us of a king's man at Wyndfell as well."

"Brilliant! It will also enable me to wed Alison, and at last unite our lands and riches!"

Damion made a deprecatory gesture. "I care not for increasing your purse. This is a holy cause."

"Of course. Of course. I'll leave at first light."

"Take care that you don't happen upon Lord Miles or his men on the way there or at court. He would be suspicious."

"Have no fear in that quarter. I have a grudge of my own with Lord Miles. He took too much pleasure in unseating me in the tourney."

Damion smiled, and in the fading light his face resembled a skeleton. "Go with the angels, Lord Roger. Godspeed."

Roger knelt for the priest's blessing and mounted before waving a final farewell. Damion nodded, his bony hands concealed in the folds of his sleeves. When Roger rode away, he turned and walked back to Wyndfell.

By habit he climbed the northeast slope of the green and made his way through the vegetable garden to the servants' gate. From this angle he couldn't be seen except by someone on the battlement, for all the windows faced the flower gardens and orchards.

He entered the kitchen garden and let himself into the chapel by the chaplain's door. The cool silence of the empty room washed over him. The long row of windows glowed dully green, as darkness had almost come, and the aroma of candles and incense hung in the air. He often came here while the castle slept, and prayed at the altar rail until dawn. But this night he had much to contemplate in his chamber above. Even with so little light, Damion had no difficulty finding the familiar catch that released the secret panel.

Inside, the corridor was black and very musty, but he didn't mind. The darkness greatly appealed to him. Resting his fingertips on the cold stone walls, he pulled the panel shut, then started up the stairs, his mind brimming with his plans to cause havoc in York.

Damion was unaware that the latch that secured the panel in place had not caught completely, and the panel had gaped open the barest crack.

Alison lay in Miles's arms and tried not to think how long it might be before she could lie there again. She rested her forehead against his, and the tips of their noses touched. "Already I miss you."

"Come with me. There's time yet. We may return before Mistress Phelps gives birth."

She wanted to say yes, but she knew her plan to rescue him would never work if she was at York with him, for more likely than not, she too would be arrested. Regretfully she shook her head. "I have promised Mabel I would stay close. You know not how it is when a woman approaches such a travail. It's no less frightening for all its regularity."

Miles kissed her lips and stroked her hair back from her face. Both were the gestures of a man in love. "I will miss you sorely."

"Don't miss me so much you seek out some wench to ease your loneliness," she teased.

"That would only make me miss you all the more."

"And stay away from the queen," she whispered in genuine sincerity.

"I will avoid her at all costs," he promised.

Outside the window came the plaintive cry of an owl. Alison superstitiously eased closer to Miles and put her thigh between his. "Are you certain you'll be safe?"

"I was safe at court all my life before I married you.

It's not so odd that the king has sent for me." Miles would not burden her with his concern.

"Just the same, take no chances."

"You worry enough for three women," he teased gently. "Kiss me and leave off this fretting."

She complied, hoping to find surcease in the comfort of his arms.

"You feel so good," he marveled as he inhaled the fragrance of her hair and skin. "You also taste good." He ran his tongue over the pulse that beat in the hollow of her throat.

Alison tilted her head back and savored the feel of his kisses and the way his knowing hand stroked her side and hip before reaching up to fondle her breast. She moved under his hand, urging him to touch her more freely, tempting him with all her womanly curves.

Miles stroked her nipple until it beaded under his palm. Then he lowered his head and drew it into his mouth. Alison murmured with pleasure, and he pulled gently on the turgid bud.

His hand caressed downward to cup her rounded buttocks, and he pressed her against him as his hips moved sensuously against hers. Alison smoothed her hands over the hard satin of his shoulders and back as she opened her legs invitingly.

Miles's hand rounded her thighs and traveled up to touch the soft nest of curls. She moved against his palm and his fingers found the treasure they sought. Alison whispered love words to excite him further as Miles stroked the bud of her femininity.

All her blood seemed to center in the spot he touched, then swelled outward until she felt as if she were on fire from her inner core to her skin. Love's fire heated her as Miles touched, stroked, probed. Suddenly she felt the leap of extreme awareness that signaled her fulfillment. At that moment he entered her and Alison cried out as the sensation sent her tumbling into oblivion. She rode the waves of pleasure for as long as she could make them last, then settled back with a happy sigh.

"You're most beautiful of all when you're satiated," Miles said with a smile.

"I'm never quite satiated," she returned, "just satisfied for the moment. I can never have enough of you."

She and Miles moved together with the special motions of their loving, each knowing the way to ignite the other's wildest desires. Her eyes met his as he poised above her. So much love was mirrored in their blue depths that Alison's heart went out to him. They were not two beings seeking their own pleasures, but rather one intent on giving the utmost satisfaction to the other.

Again the desire mounted to undeniable heights, and though Alison tried to hold back, she reached her peak. Her rhythmic contractions triggered Miles's release and together they let love sweep over them.

The night-filled room protected them and the feather bed cradled them as they lay contentedly in each other's arms. Once again they touched forehead to forehead, nose to nose, and sleep drifted over them.

By first light the next morning Miles was dressed and in the courtyard. The other knights exchanged pleasantries with each other and with those they were leaving behind, but silence hung between Alison and Miles. She had so many sweet words to tell him, so many silly admonitions, such as to be careful and keep dry and don't ride too long in one day. But she didn't want to send him off with a whine in his ears, and she wasn't certain she could speak about his leaving without begging him to stay.

Miles stood next to her, his arm about her waist as if he might just sweep her up onto the saddle with him. He didn't want to leave her behind, and he knew Mabel Phelps's delivery was only an excuse. She was afraid to confront the king again. He couldn't blame her, for he too was dreading days of contact with his unpredictable sovereign.

Their horses shifted and snorted expectantly in the briskness of the September morning. They smelled of grain from their morning feeding and were ready to be on their way. Their breaths made visible puffs in the frosty air.

Alison turned to Miles. There was so much to say and now the parting was upon them. If all didn't go well, she might next see Miles in chains, or worse. Her golden-brown eyes were moist from barely restrained tears as Miles bent to kiss her.

"I hear you," he whispered. "Between us no words are necessary. You'll be in my thoughts forever."

"You'll take care?"

"I swear I will return to you unharmed. King Henry has not yet begun to eat his knights at the royal feasts. You underestimate my ability to sway him. My father was a cunning man, and he taught me well. I'll be safe."

Once again he kissed her, and then looked into her eyes as if he couldn't force himself to leave her. But he had no choice, and all his men were mounted and waiting. He gave her a hug and swung up onto Excalibur's broad back. "Tell Mistress Phelps I wish her a healthy babe and a speedy recovery."

Alison nodded. "Beware of wenches while you're in York. Especially plump ones with short upper lips," she added wryly.

Miles laughed and flashed a grin. "I know the wench you mean. She'll not come near me unless there are six others in the room for protection."

"Pray six will be enough to dissuade her."

Miles was still laughing as he tightened his heels against the horse's sides and led his men at a gallop through the gate. The clatter of the iron-shod hooves on the cobblestones changed to a hollow drumbeat on the drawbridge, then was muffled to a dull thunder on the turf of the green.

Alison waved until they were out of sight, then hurried up onto the roof to watch them cantering over the hills toward the north. Although Miles had been gone only a few minutes, Alison felt bereft. True, she had never enjoyed her first husband's absences, but his leaving never caused her to feel hollow inside. She considered going down to the church and asking her mother to watch after him, but she no longer felt her mother's presence there. Besides, her mother would have been more likely to side with the king if she had any say in the matter.

Slowly she walked along the lead-covered roof. In the summer they often ate up there or used the flat expanse as a sitting area. It was a marvelous place to watch the bonfires on Midsummer's Eve. Now it seemed as barren as a desert. She looked back over her shoulder. Miles and his men had disappeared entirely, leaving only their tracks in the fields of grain.

Resolutely Alison pulled herself straighter and lifted her chin. She would not shrivel away in the face of danger. She could use these days to perfect her plan to rescue Miles if it became necessary. Purposefully she strode to the steps that led toward Miles's closet. She had maps and sailing schedules to memorize.

From the gatehouse apartment, Edmund Campbell watched Alison walk about on the roof of the castle. She seemed overly upset that her husband had gone. This was only to be a fortnight's separation. Edmund had seen wives send off husbands on year-long journeys with fewer long looks, and seldom such a sorrowful countenance. Was there something here that he was overlooking? Perhaps Miles wasn't so firm in the king's graces as Edmund had supposed.

He rerolled the foolscap he had been about to peruse and laid it on his desk. Edmund had keen instincts for ferreting out untoward behavior. Perhaps he should look around the castle before he started the day's work.

He went down the stone steps and crossed the courtyard, listening to the typical early-morning sound of a rooster crowing over his flock of fat hens scratching lazily in the dirt of the kitchen yard. From the dovecote and the gatehouse he could hear the cooing of pigeons and doves. A cow lowed in the diary, and one of the dairymaids was singing a lilting tune about a shepherd's lost love.

Edmund started up the broad steps to the hall, but he hesitated. He rarely went into the chapel, but today some sixth sense made him gaze at it thoughtfully. Since he had come to Wyndfell, he had wondered if the Catholics might use the chapel for services when the chaplain wasn't around, but he never saw anyone coming or going at odd times. Now he recalled the chaplain's door at the back. People could easily slip in and out, unseen from his apartments in the gatehouse. Since no one was around now, this would be a good time to look for any possible evidence.

Quickly he crossed the corner of the yard, and went silently up the outside steps to the chapel door. He listened briefly, then pushed open the door and went in.

The double rows of green windows splashed a marine-hued light over the orderly rows of pews. Edmund disliked the windows because green was a rare color and very costly. Plain glass would have been good enough, in his opinion. Such gaudiness smacked of papist ways.

He strolled down to the altar and cast a suspicious eye over the altarcloths and the religious tapestry behind the pulpit. All seemed to be in order. Lady Alison did an admirable job in seeing that the cloths were kept clean and mended. In view of her feeling regarding the new religion, he found that surprising.

Edmund was turning to go when a slight movement caught his eye. He had left the door open at the far end of the chapel and the draft had widened the gap of the secret panel.

With growing excitement Edmund went to the crack

and pressed against it. The panel swung back easily, revealing the dim outline of stone walls and steps and releasing the damp smell of an unaired chamber.

He looked about to see that he was alone, then took a candle from the altar and lit it with his flint. Cautiously Edmund stepped into the passage. By holding the candle aloft, he could see that the steps led to the inside wall of the battlement that connected the castle and the back wall of the chapel. Cobwebs hung like nets along the damp ceiling, but the floor was surprisingly free of dust in the middle where a person would walk.

Drawing back his lips in a satisfied grin, Edmund cautiously made his way up the steps. When he passed what he thought was the back of the hall, he peered through the small peephole and realized he could see everything that was happening there. Moving with great stealth, he passed the gallery. Here the passage branched and led, he assumed, to a concealed outer door. He followed the other fork that led back and up. There was no peephole in this door, but after a bit of exploration Edmund found the latch and opened the panel the merest crack. When he saw the master's bedchamber, he drew back quickly.

The steps circled up behind a mass of chimneys and arrived at an unused chamber, then up again to the final door. Edmund put his ear to the paneling and heard the unmistakable singsong of a man reciting the holy offices.

Exhilaration flooded over Edmund. He had found the priest! Shoving open the panel, he burst into the room.

Damion was on his knees in front of the homemade altar. His thin fingers were threaded through the black beads of his rosary, and the heavy silver crucifix dangling below reflected the light of his candles. For a moment the two men merely stared at each other. Then Damion replaced his rosary at his belt and slowly got to his feet.

Triumphantly Edmund came forward. "I arrest you in the name of King Henry of England. I will take you to York and present you to the king. What a merry bonfire you'll make!"

Damion made no reply. He lifted one candlestick and quietly blew out the candle.

"I knew one of your kind was around here!" Edmund chortled. "You're the one who has been printing the placards, aren't you!"

"Yes," Damion said in mild surprise, as if he didn't see how Edmund could doubt it.

"And you've been holding Mass right here under our noses!"

"We meet in the chapel for Mass, or in the oak grove."

"You admit it? What a fool you are not to deny it!"

"It doesn't matter if you know." Damion raised his hand and brushed back his hood to reveal his gaunt cheeks and shaved pate.

Edmund stared at him in transfixed wonder. The man had an odd glitter in his eyes that reminded Edmund of a mad boar. "Who are you?" he asked. "What are you called?"

"My name is Brother Damion of the Cistercian order from St. Benedictine on the Ouse. Can you remember that?"

"Certainly, but . . ."

Damion's lips smiled, making wrinkles in his emaciated cheeks. His eyes stayed cold. "When you see St. Benedict, tell him I am upholding the true religion and will not stop until his order is reestablished on the Ouse."

"What are you talking about?" Edmund blustered. "That makes no sense at all!"

"Just tell him." With an unexpected movement, Damion raised the heavy candlestick as he leapt forward, and brought it down squarely on Edmund's temple.

Edmund gave a startled cry before he crumbled to

the floor. Damion stood over him and watched for any movement. To be certain the steward was dead, Damion lifted the candlestick again and struck the man on his lower skull where his spine connected. Satisfied that one or both blows had been mortal, he took a cloth from his chest and cleaned the candlestick.

Going back to the altar, he knelt and relit the candle from the other one and placed it carefully on the altar. Ignoring the crumpled heap, he took up his rosary and began the recitation exactly where he had left off.

21

Damion was patient. He had learned how to exercise great control over himself through the years at the monastery, and now his mind could set aside virtually anything for almost any length of time. Otherwise, he might have found Edmund Campbell's presence quite unnerving.

Instead, he busied himself with the devotionals that made up all his days, and ate his spare meal. As night fell, Damion walked along the corridor in the wall, watching the castle's people preparing for bed.

He waited in the dark passageway until the lackeys snuffed out the rushlights and candles, and all the men who slept in the hall on the trestle tables or rushes had bedded down. When everyone seemed to be asleep, Damion silently mounted the steps. He listened at Alison's door, but heard no sound. Nevertheless, he climbed to his chamber and waited another hour to be sure that everyone was soundly asleep.

The new moon was a sliver in the sky when Damion decided to venture out. He rolled Edmund to a sitting slump, then hoisted the dead man on his narrow shoulder. Though thin, Damion was wiry and strong from his life of imposed hardship.

Taking the steps carefully, he carried his gruesome load down the passageway, exercising care that Edmund's body didn't bump against the walls and reveal his clandestine activity. When he reached the gallery, Damion left the passage and went out into the long room. At the window he paused and looked down. If he threw Edmund out, it might look like a suicide. But the windows were too deep and narrow to get the steward's body through.

Damion shifted his load to a better balance and walked down the gallery toward the solar as he had on the day he arrived. The round room was, of course, empty, so Damion laid Edmund's body just inside the door while he went in search of a shovel. He found one easily enough in the stable and returned to the solar.

Again he shouldered the body, picked up the shovel, and carried his burden to the steps that led downward into the darkness of the buttery. Although it was very difficult for him to do so, Damion took a candle from a sconce, lit it, and proceeded downward.

As he had assumed, the steps opened through an archway to a large vaulted room. Casks of wine and barrels of ale rested in wooden cradles, with aisles between as walkways.

Damion peered at the floor. It was flagstone, which almost certainly meant that dirt was underneath, not bedrock. He carried Edmund to the far end and dumped him on the floor. After flexing his shoulder, he knelt and began working loose a sizable slab of stone. When he had removed several, he started digging.

He spread his scapular on the flagstones and piled dirt upon it. When the grave was deep enough, Damion rolled Edmund into it. As an afterthought, he arranged the dead man's hands on his chest and covered his face with the man's velvet cap. Then Damion shoveled in the dirt, packing it tightly, until the flagstones again lay flat and appeared undisturbed.

After quietly murmuring the prayer for the dead, Damion carried the remaining dirt and the shovel up and out the kitchen door. He stood the shovel against the wall where he had found it, and dumped the dirt behind the cow barn. Shaking the loose earth from the scapular, Damion pulled the undyed garment over his head to cover his white habit, and walked noiselessly to the chapel.

There he found the chapel door open and the panel ajar. Obviously Sir Edmund had come this way, but for the panel to have remained open and undiscovered by anyone else all day seemed miraculous. Damion accepted this as proof that he was under divine protection. After carefully closing both doors and double-checking the panel latch, Damion went to his room for a well-earned rest.

Miles and his men had no difficulty finding the royal court in York. An abandoned abbey had been restored as a temporary lodging, and everyone they met had either just come from there or was on his way. Even without directions, Miles could have ridden straight to it.

The king had arrived in splendor with four thousand nobles, guards, attendants, and servants. The abbey was decked in brilliant pennants bearing the king's device, and great tents covered the grounds around the ancient building.

Henry was in the hall, formerly the nave. He was seated on the enormous brocaded throne which Miles had last seen in his audience chamber at Hampton Court. The nave was hung with rich brocades and adornments of every kind. Music for his entertainment floated down to the hall from a raised platform set into the wall between nave and chancel. Courtiers and knights were flirting with gaily dressed ladies as if they were at home in London. The church bells had been removed from the tower, but Miles saw several liveried men with brass horns to signal the arrival of anyone of consequence.

Evidently the trumpeters had already announced Miles, because as soon as he entered the room, Henry waved for him to draw near. "You have ridden swiftly. I like that." He clapped Miles heartily on the shoulder. "Where's your lady wife?"

"She was unable to come, your majesty. We at Wyndfell are recovering from the sweating sickness, and she also had to attend a birth in the village."

"She's taken up midwifery, has she? You want to watch that. Midwives are rarely good breeders."

"Nothing like that, your grace. This is a woman my lady wife has gentle feelings toward. The woman is afraid of dying as she almost did with the birth of her last child, and would rest easy only if Lady Alison stayed beside her."

"Women take on odd presentiments at such a time. And what of your own hearth? Any signs of a son?"

"None yet, but we've not been married quite a year."

"Betimes I believe the old teachings are correct and that a woman may breed or not as she wills it." He pointed toward Queen Catherine, who was gossiping loudly with several of her ladies. "Her waist is as small as it was when I wed her a year ago. She shows no sign of giving me a son." He spoke these last words in the same confidential manner that had, in his youth, captivated trustworthy friends. To have been privy to such personal thoughts of the king was considered a great honor.

Miles followed the king's stare. While he didn't consider Catherine's waist small, it was clearly not swollen in pregnancy. "Perhaps with time . . ."

"Pah! I have no time. By St. George! I'm fifty years old, and though you'd not believe it by my size, my health is not what it was. No, I must get another prince, and I must get one soon." He scowled at his giggling queen. "Prince Edward is well at present, but I need more sons to be sure of having one to rule after me."

His small eyes sought out Princess Mary, who was standing to one side with her arms folded across her chest. "Can you ever see her as ruler? Ha! She'd have you all in convents and monasteries! And her sister, Elizabeth, will never be more than a scholar. What good that may serve a woman, I'll never know!"

Miles wasn't sure how to reply to this, so he remained silent. Catherine glanced at him, then looked back and smiled more openly. Miles pretended to be studying one of the Flemish tapestries.

"This progress was genius on my part," Henry said after a while. "Thousands have come to give me their pledge of loyalty. I daresay York isn't the hotbed I was led to expect."

Miles relaxed a bit. "Nor have I found it so, your grace. In truth I find I like the wildness of Yorkshire. 'Tis a pity you've decided not to come by Wyndfell on your journey home."

"Not come? Who told you that? I still intend to come. I'd not miss it. I plan to arrive with a contingent of about two hundred men."

"My lady wife will be overjoyed. We only assumed, by your summoning me, that you had changed your mind."

"No, Lord Miles, I rarely change my mind." Henry again looked over at Catherine. "I sometimes alter my plans to meet new circumstances, but that's rather a different thing, isn't it?"

"Yes, your highness."

"Yes. A different thing altogether."

"Have you had word yet from King James of Scotland? I saw no clans in the tents as I approached."

The king's scowl deepened. "My nephew has played me false. He refuses now to meet with me, and even threatens to conduct raids across the border, killing and burning as he pleases!"

"Does he wish to goad your majesty into an open confrontation?"

"I've sent men to reinforce the border and ordered them to give three times what they get. I'll show that impudent pup. His mother was never like that. He must take after his senseless father!"

"Undoubtedly, your majesty."

Henry turned back to Miles. "I know you've ridden hard to get here so soon. Go see to your horses and set up your pavilion. We will talk later."

Miles bowed and took his leave, carefully giving a wide berth to the area where the queen was holding attendance. He hoped to avoid her for his entire visit, but he knew that would be nearly impossible. He had seen the way the king looked at her, and he sensed Henry was no longer blinded by love.

Trahern had found a likely spot for the tent—near the stream and sheltered by an enormous beech whose raised roots provided places to sit. By the time Miles arrived the men had almost finished erecting their golden-hued tent with the Garrett griffin emblazoned in bright green on each side. Because of the cool temperature, the sides of the tent had been lowered to form walls.

Miles helped unload the pallets and chests and soon the interior had taken on an appearance not unlike Wyndfell's winter parlor. He dispatched a knight to return to Wyndfell with news of the number of guests Alison should expect, then sat on one of the stools and began polishing his dress sword. Already he missed Alison more than he had thought possible.

The day after Miles left for York, Alison received word that Mabel Phelps had begun birthing her child. Alison was relieved for the diversion, and quickly took the basket of herbs and cloths she had prepared down to the village.

The Phelpses' rebuilt cottage and those of their closest neighbors stood out amid the older houses near the center of the village, even though they had been restored with no improvements to minimize possible jealousy. As the buildings had not been originally set in a straight line, the lane in front was still winding and scarcely wide enough for a cart. Directly behind the Phelpses' house were their vegetable patch, a crumbling barn and minute barnyard, and in the far back of their plot were a few fruit and nut trees.

Alison was greeted at the door by Mabel's eldest girl, a frail-looking lass of twelve years. The girl's eyes were round and her face pale. Alison stroked her hair in passing. "Where are the others?"

"I sent them out to the barn with my sister Fanny," the child said.

"Then you must be Katie. My, how you've grown!"

Katie smiled shyly. "I sent for Goody Smith, but she was too drunk to come."

"We won't need her," Alison said with more confidence than she felt. She had been on hand at many servants' birthings, but had never attended one alone. She was thankful that she had stayed behind, otherwise Mabel would have been tended only by this frightened child.

Alison was led to the back room, which was just off the cooking area. Mabel was lying on a rumpled bed, her dark hair making her face seem even smaller and paler than it was. The petite woman seemed to be all eyes and nose.

"Good day, Mabel. How are you feeling?"

"Not so good, my lady. The pains started in the middle of the night. I fear it will be another long one."

"You're not to be afraid. I'm here now and will see to you."

"Ira and the oldest boys are in the field. Mistress Walpole next door said she would feed them all."

"Then there's nothing left to worry about except having this baby. Katie, go put a large kettle of water to boil." Alison watched as Mabel arched against a pain but made no sound.

Alison tied the ends of a sheet to each of the square bedposts to give Mabel something to pull against, and offered her a strip of leather to bite on when the pains got too bad. She had once seen a maid crack a tooth, and since then Alison had kept some strips of leather on hand when a birthing was expected.

While she waited, she put clean sheets under Mabel along with a folded quilt to serve as a birth pad. She gave the soiled sheets to Katie to wash and hang over the bushes by the back door. Katie was glad to have anything to do that would let her escape the sight of her pain-racked mother. Through the open window Alison watched the girl washing the sheets, and wished for the girl's sake that she was less sensitive. The harsh life of a peasant was even more severe for those who were tenderhearted.

During the day, Mabel's pains became more frequent and harder to bear. Alison did what she could to comfort the woman, but only the birth would end her misery. As night approached, Alison heard Ira and the two older boys come in. Katie told them of her mother's progress, but only Ira came to the bedroom door.

"Is she doing poorly?" His voice was full of anxiousness and concern.

"She will be all right. The baby is large and is taking longer to birth than a smaller one."

Ira went timidly to his wife's side and leaned over to kiss her damp brow. "I ain't going to put you through this again, Mabel. I ain't!"

Mabel nodded, but another pain cut through her, making her unable to speak.

Alison wiped the sweat from the woman's brow as Ira pulled back and went to the door.

"I'll take the bairns next door to eat, then we'll go out to the barn and wait."

With a nod, Alison dismissed him. She didn't want Ira and all eleven of their children underfoot at this time. "He cares for you a great deal," she said when Mabel was easier.

"Because he said he won't give me another babe? He says that every time."

Alison thought a minute, then said to Katie, "You

go eat your supper, then go to the barn with the others and tell your father he's needed here."

"Yes, my lady," Katie said in surprise and relief.

By the time Ira returned, the pains were almost constant and Mabel was growing weaker. Alison hoped she was doing the right thing in having his help. She had never heard of a man at a birthing, but she needed another adult and not a frightened child. Besides, she thought this just might help strengthen Ira's resolve not to add more mouths to his brood.

Mabel cried out with the pains now, and each time her body tensed to endure the contraction, veins stood out in her thin throat. Her hands gripped the sheet rope so tightly that her knuckles were white and her hands were trembling. When Ira heard her first scream, his face went chalky white, and Alison thought he might faint.

"Go on that side of the bed and hold her up so she can push harder." Alison checked the baby's progress and nodded. "It won't be long now."

But another hour passed and the baby had not come, so Alison went into the kitchen for some peppercorns. After grinding them into a powder, she went back to the bed. She let Mabel inhale the black powder, and in a fit of sneezing the baby was finally born.

"It's a girl," Alison said triumphantly. "Here, Ira, you clean her up and wrap her in that linen towel there." Alison finished tying off the cord and handed the slippery baby to the father, who seemed to be in worse shape than the mother. Alison helped Mabel finish the birthing and changed the sheets. As she leaned close to Mabel's ear she said, "Mayhap now he will be more resolved to let this be the last."

Mabel didn't answer, but her pale lips curved up in a smile.

Later Ira walked Alison back to the castle. He was quiet all the way, but when he saw her safely across the drawbridge, he tugged at his cap as a servant to a mistress. "I'm obliged to you for looking after my wife, Lady Alison. I'm wondering if you'd take it amiss if we named the babe for you."

"I'd be honored."

Still he hesitated. Finally he said, "That's the first of my babes I've ever seen born. It was something, wasn't it! I have a feeling that little mite is going to be my favorite of them all. I just wished I'd have known all along what it was like. My Mabel, she's some woman, ain't she?"

"She's a fine woman. You have every right to be proud of her."

"I just never knew it was so hard to do something so natural." Shaking his head, he walked back into the night.

Alison sighed. Ira seemed more fascinated with what he had seen than repelled. Perhaps having him witness the birth wouldn't have the desired affect after all.

The sliver of moon that hung over Wyndfell's turrets cast almost no light into the courtyard, but the blaze from the large rush torches near the gatehouse and to either side of the door to the hall lighted her way. Alison glanced up at the dark windows of Edmund's apartments and frowned. True, she was out late, but the steward should have waited up to see that she returned safely.

Alison went into the hall and Walt came to take her basket. "Has Sir Edmund retired for the evening?" she asked.

"I've not seen him all day, my lady. Shall I go wake him for you?"

"No, no. There's no need." As Alison wearily climbed the curving steps to her bedchamber, she decided she would have a few words for Edmund in the morning. If he thought to use Miles's absence as an excuse to slack off in his duties, he would soon be set straight.

The days became a week and still Miles had no idea why the king had summoned him. No reference had been made to the trouble in Wyndfell's district, and from all the people crowding to swear fealty to the king, Henry could scarcely suspect trouble in York.

Miles decided he must go to the king and ask permission to leave. Perhaps then Henry would say why he had been called to York. Never one to put off action, Miles was on his way to the king when he received a royal summons to one of the small rooms used as an audience chamber. Thinking this message was from Henry, Miles thanked the courtier and turned his steps in that direction.

As was usual, anywhere the royal court resided, there were great numbers of people—not only the king's retinue, but flocks of people who had come merely for a glimpse of the royal family. In the throng, Miles saw a profile that looked familiar, but when he turned back to see if it was indeed Roger Bainbridge, the man was no longer visible. Miles shrugged. Although he was not aware of any particular reason for Bainbridge to be there, his presence was not that unlikely. He too was a viscount and might have similarly been summoned by the king.

He was admitted to the antechamber, and was surprised to find Lady Rochford, the queen's confidant, in the room. She smiled thinly when she saw him, and motioned for him to go through into the audience chamber. Miles hesitated, but he had no choice; this was a royal summons.

As he had begun to suspect, Queen Catherine was alone in the room, sitting on the smaller of the two thrones, her posture a studied pose of elegant boredom. When Miles entered, she smiled invitingly, her plain face almost pretty. "Good day, Lord Garrett. Since you were so long getting here, I had thought my courtier must have been unable to find you."

"There are so many people here, your majesty. I suppose he had to search for me."

"Indeed. I was beginning to think you might leave

before I had a chance to speak with you." She rose and descended the two steps of the dais.

"Oh?" Miles said carefully. "Was there something you wished to speak with me about?"

"I want you to tell me of your castle here in Yorkshire. What is its name?"

"Wyndfell."

"Of course. What a picture it conjures of a constant breeze blowing over the hills. Is it a lovely castle?" she asked as she walked closer to Miles, her eyes fixed on him like a cat stalking a robin.

"It's not grand by royal standards, but I find it most suitable."

"And your lady wife—is she content there?" Catherine circled Miles, her eyes gauging him from head to foot.

"Lady Alison is very happy at Wyndfell. She has lived there most of her life."

"Do you never long for the excitement of court?" Catherine said as she let the tip of her tongue moisten her lips. "For all the intrigue and liaisons?"

"Never, your majesty. My wife and I are uncommonly happy together."

"How dull," the queen said with a laugh. "Come now, Lord Miles, tell me all about Wyndfell and why you prefer it to court."

Miles drew a deep breath, hoping some of the queen's ladies would come in before he ran out of words. He had never been in a more awkward position.

Meanwhile, Roger made his way through the crowd toward the tent where he had been told Thomas Culpepper would be found. He had spent the week watching Culpepper, and was positive that Alison was right about his being the queen's lover. In fact, Roger was amazed at the couple's openness. They all but kissed under the king's nose.

To keep from attracting attention, Roger had dressed in the plain russet garb of a lackey. As such he could pass in and out of rooms and not have to observe the protocol required of a viscount. He found Culpepper, and when the man was finally alone, Roger went to him and gave him a sheet of folded paper.

"What's this?" Culpepper asked.

"A message, my lord."

"There's no seal. No emblem on the paper."

"I know nothing of that. I was sent by Lady Rochford and told to give this to you when no one else was standing near."

"Lady Rochford? You must be new in her service." He unfolded the paper and grinned as he scanned the page. "Can you read, lackey?"

"No, my lord. Is it important that I should? Lady Rochford asked me the same thing."

"No, no. Not important at all." Culpepper grinned and gave Roger a coin.

"Thank you, my lord," Roger said as if such a small coin were a great boon to him. He bowed and turned to melt into the crowd.

Roger suppressed a grin as he thought how easy this was going to be. Culpepper was even now on his way to a certain secluded spot by the stream. Roger took the second square of paper from his sleeve and glanced at its wording to be certain he had the correct one. This note would send Queen Catherine to meet Culpepper. The third paper was to be delivered to the king after the couple had had time to meet.

After questioning several servants, Roger found his way to the suite of rooms where Catherine was supposedly spending a few private hours. He knocked on the door and was admitted by Lady Rochford. Roger felt uneasy as the older woman's suspicious eyes studied him.

"I've a message for the queen," he said, holding out the paper.

"I've not seen you around court. Who are you?"

Roger hadn't thought to be asked his name. He stammered, "I'm new in Sir Thomas Culpepper's employ, my lady."

"Culpepper!" She took the note and read it quickly. Her lips thinned into a smile. "Come with me. There may be a message to return."

Roger hadn't expected this either, but he had to obey. Lady Rochford tapped on the interior door, and at the queen's summons, she walked briskly in, with Roger at her heels.

Miles stared at Roger, taking in his peasant clothing and startled expression. Roger turned to run, but Miles was quicker. He hauled Roger back into the room as he said, "What is the meaning of this?"

"You know this man?" Lady Rochford demanded.

"Aye. He's my neighbor and viscount of a castle, though you'd never guess it to look at him." Holding firmly to Roger's jerkin, Miles said, "Why are you dressed like this?"

"Has he a weapon?" Catherine cried out fearfully. "Is he an assassin?"

Lady Rochford held out the paper. "He gave me this."

Catherine read it and her face became pasty. "Who sent you?"

Roger looked away and refused to answer. The letter to the king seemed to be burning a hole in his sleeve. If it was found upon him, his life was as good as finished.

"I think I should take him to the king," Miles said.

"No!" Catherine and Lady Rochford exclaimed together.

"No? Why not?"

"I . . . I forgive him," Catherine stammered, crushing the letter hastily into her sleeve.

"Your majesty, this man is obviously here under false pretenses. I know him to be a wealthy viscount, yet he's posing as a servant. This could be a plot to overthrow the king. I must not release him."

Catherine's lips moved silently before she found her voice. "Yes," she whispered at last. "Yes, of course you must take him to the king." Her frightened eyes met Lady Rochford's.

Miles shoved Roger toward the door, keeping a firm grip on his clothing and arm. "I don't know what is going on here," he muttered, "but you'd better have a damned good story or you're a dead man."

Roger stumbled as they were leaving the anteroom and managed to throw down the other letter without Miles seeing him. He could only hope it would be trampled underfoot and thrown away by a servant.

Miles dragged him to the king and said, "Your majesty, this man is Lord Roger Bainbridge, Viscount of Bainbridge Castle and Wyndfell's nearest neighbor. I found him giving a message to the queen and pretending to be a servant. I thought you should know."

Henry leaned on the arm of his throne and shifted his massive body forward. "A viscount, you say? What is this jest!"

"That's it, your majesty!" Roger exclaimed. "It is but a jest!"

"I believe him not," Miles said. "I know this man and he is lying."

"What message did you take to the queen?"

"I know not, your majesty. It was but given to me and I was encouraged to dress thus to deliver it! I swear I never read it!"

"Who sent you upon this extraordinary task?" the king demanded.

"I'd . . . I'd rather not say. Not unless we can speak privately."

Henry frowned in his effort to rise. "We will go to my privy chamber."

"Your majesty," Miles said quickly, "I fear there may have been trouble at home. As I say, Bainbridge Castle is not far from Wyndfell and my lady wife may be under siege. I have mistrusted this man all along. Have I your permission to return to Wyndfell?"

"Yes," Henry said after a thoughtful pause. If Miles had suspicions about one of his neighbors, why hadn't he written to inform the king? Henry's eyebrows lifted in the unasked question, then said, "You may go, Lord Miles."

Painfully Henry made his way to his privy chamber, with Roger held securely by two of his guards. When the four of them were closeted away, Henry said, "Now. What is the meaning of this?"

Roger drew a steadying breath and said, "I dared not speak in front of Lord Garrett, for I fear he is a traitor. Had I said so in his presence, my life would have been in great jeopardy."

"What! A traitor!"

"There has been much unrest at Wyndfell. Traitorous placards have been posted. Church services are ill-attended."

"What is this you're saying!" Henry thundered.

"I believe the leader of this unrest is Lord Miles Garrett. I accuse him of treason. His lady wife is innocent, though. This I could swear to."

Henry growled low in his throat and his eyes took on a glint of fury. "I will look into your accusation, Lord Bainbridge. You may depend upon it!"

22

By midmorning Alison was becoming angry over Edmund's absence. She knew he had wanted to accompany Miles to York, and now assumed that he had gone there without permission.

"When Sir Edmund returns, he will be properly punished," Alison said angrily to Leatrice. "Whoever heard of a steward neglecting his duties like an apprentice lad running off to see the fair!"

"I would never have expected it of Sir Edmund," Leatrice said. She was still thin and drawn from her illness, but her strength was at last returning. "I don't suppose he could possibly be here and us not know it?"

"Impossible. I've asked everyone and no one has seen him."

"I don't wish to alarm you, but Walt told me some of the silver plate is missing."

Alison nodded. "I know. I moved it for safekeeping during Miles's absence." She didn't want to tell Leatrice yet that they might all be fleeing to France at any time. Leatrice's health was still too precarious for her to be burdened with such worry.

Alison crossed the hall and looked up at the apartments on the second level of the gatehouse. "Come, Leatrice. Let's see if his belongings are still there."

They crossed the cobblestones of the courtyard through a thick fog, pulling their hands inside their gown sleeves for warmth. With an unexplainable prickle of apprehension on her neck, Alison made her way up the stone steps, balancing herself with her fingertips on the cold wall of the circular stairwell.

"What if he's lying within, too ill to answer?" Leatrice asked as Alison knocked loudly on the door.

Hearing no response, Alison boldly opened the door, and they went into the suite of rooms that had always been used by Wyndfell's stewards. The heavy oak table in the center of the room was polished to a walnut hue by constant use. On its surface were several neat stacks of papers bearing Edmund's spidery handwriting.

"What do they say?" Leatrice whispered.

"It's the accounts for Wyndfell and a listing of rents due. See? This one is a bit askew, as if he was working on it but left suddenly. How odd!"

"I feel uneasy being here," Leatrice murmured. "I feel as if he's watching me."

"Nonsense. And there's no reason to whisper." But Alison also felt disquieted, so she walked briskly to the bedchamber door to mask her trepidation. As she rapped on the door, she called out, "Sir Edmund? Are you in there?"

"Mayhap we should send Walt in. After all, Sir Edmund is a man and we might be intruding at an awkward time."

"Leatrice, what could he possibly be doing that would keep him here for an entire day and a half?" She pushed open the door to reveal the empty chamber.

The room was smaller than the one where Edmund kept his accountings and met with men to conduct the castle's business. The chamber jutted partly over the gate itself, and there were two large trapdoors of heavy oak to cover the "murder holes." By rule of the castle these doors were to remain unobstructed by furniture in case it became suddenly necessary to drop missiles or pour hot water onto an invading enemy.

On the wall behind the trapdoors was a regular door that could be opened during warfare so that the knights could have access to the entire gatehouse. Two more murder holes and the guardroom were on the other side.

Edmund's bed was wide enough to accommodate a married steward, for some of them had been, but the room was too small for many children's cots. Edmund's clothing hung on wooden pegs set into the wall, and his chest stood at the foot of the bed. His riding boots, which he had rarely worn since arriving from London, were beside the bed. There was no sign of a struggle, nor of a vacating. Edmund simply wasn't there.

"His cloak is here," Alison observed. "Surely he wouldn't ride forth and not take at least that! If he went to York as I suspected, he would have taken all his clothing and bedding, not to mention his riding boots!"

"Then he must be here at Wyndfell."

"But how can that be?"

Leatrice shook her head. "It's as if he magically disappeared."

Alison brushed aside the cloth curtain to look out the narrow window. A thick fog shrouded the hollow in which the village lay, and long fingers of drifting white reached over the green toward the castle. Above, the sky was the leaden hue of an old shield. Alison let the cloth fall back in place. This did indeed seem to be of magic. "Are there any sorcerers about, to your knowledge? Any witches?"

"No, my lady. There was that witch in Wakefield, you know, but she died last spring."

"She was a white witch and not one to spirit someone away. No, he must be here in the castle."

"Perhaps he fell from a loft or out a window and hasn't been found yet."

"Whatever would Sir Edmund be doing in a loft?"

"Well, he *is* an unmarried man and some of the

maids are little better than walking-morts, especially that red-haired one. I daresay she's shown the loft to half the men in the castle."

Now that it was evident that Edmund had not left by his own volition, Alison was becoming fearful. One place no one would know to search was the secret passageway.

Alison and Leatrice went back to the hall, and Alison made an excuse to go alone to her room. Leatrice was eager to seek out the ladies so she could spread the word of Edmund's disappearance.

When Alison was alone in her bedchamber, she went to the secret panel and triggered the latch. The dank smell of confined air wafted out with the perpetual dampness. She hesitated. With Miles away from the castle she felt particularly vulnerable. Besides, she had no desire to stumble over Edmund in the dark passage—alive or dead.

Taking a deep breath, she lit a candle and entered the dark corridor. The faint light flickered over the ancient stones as she moved upward toward Damion's chamber. Somewhere below her she heard the hollow sound of water dripping, and she shivered.

Damion opened the panel at her approach, and she wondered if he had somehow heard her or if he had divined her presence. She didn't speak until she was inside the room. That same fanatical light that she had seen earlier blazed in his dark eyes, and his movements intermittently went from jittery to utterly motionless.

"Have you seen or heard anyting amiss, Damion?"

"Such as what, sister?"

Alison paused. She had the uncanny sensation that he was baiting her. "One of my men is missing. The steward, Sir Edmund Campbell."

"Missing, you say?" Damion spread his arms wide and pivoted to view the entirety of the small room. "You can see he's not here." A faint smile was on his lips, but no humor reached his eyes.

"No. No, of course not. I never thought he would be. I merely wondered if you had seen anything odd. A man riding away after sundown, for instance."

"You think he rode away? After sundown?" The smile widened.

"For goodness' sake, Damion! I have no idea when he may have left. I simply can't find him."

"Have you looked in the buttery?"

"The buttery? No. Why would he be there?"

Damion hid his mouth with his hand and turned away. "I merely wondered if you had searched the castle thoroughly. One of the king's men, is he? Do you trust him?"

"No, I don't," she replied with a sigh. "That's one reason I'm so concerned about his absence. With the king in York, Sir Edmund might have ridden there."

"You think he knows about our plan to dispose of the queen?"

"He couldn't possibly. And please don't lump me into that. You and Roger hatched that idea between yourselves."

Damion's eyes narrowed. "Are you saying you're not with us?"

"I'm not saying anything at all," she answered quickly. "I just want to find my steward."

With a shrug, Damion said, "He is no longer my concern. You must leave now. It's time for my noon meditation." He turned his back and knelt before the small altar.

Alison stared at Damion's poker-straight back. What did he mean by saying Edmund was no longer his concern? Shaking her head, she went back to the passage.

She went back to her room and automatically dusted her voluminous skirts. Why had Damion mentioned the buttery? She went down to the hall, into the serving room that led to the kitchen, through a door, and down the familiar steps to the buttery.

Alison often came here to inspect the castle's stores,

as her mother had done in her own castle. She knew without a listing which barrels contained ale, which malmsey, which canary, and so on. A glance told her no one was in the cellar room, at least no one who was visible. Cautiously she walked down one broad aisle, inspecting the room with great care.

Through the windows set high in the wall she saw the fog had been replaced by a steady rain. The buttery had the stillness of a cave and a fairly constant temperature to coddle the delicate wines. She put her hand on a butt of ale at the far end of the room and looked back the way she had come.

Obviously Damion had merely suggested the buttery as a possible place to look, since Edmund certainly wasn't down here. Alison walked slowly back, her skirt brushing the loose dirt that clung to a group of flagstones.

Perhaps, she thought, Leatrice had been right. Edmund could have fallen in some remote corner of the large castle and be lying dead. She went through the far arch that housed the steps to the solar and gallery. Walt should be sent to gather a search party.

Walt was in the gallery with two of the knights Miles had left to guard the castle. She dispatched them to find some more men and cover the entire castle and its immediate grounds. If Edmund was not found, they were to search the parks and gardens and ask around in the village.

Alison still felt uneasy, but she tried to reassure herself. After all, Edmund couldn't have dissolved like the fog. She went to join Leatrice and the ladies in the solar.

The castle search proved fruitless, as did the inspection of the grounds and village. By the next day Alison was deeply disturbed. If Edmund was gone, wouldn't the king wonder why? Or if Edmund had gone to York, despite contrary evidence, did that not prove he knew of Damion's plot and had gone to implicate Miles? Alison spent less time embroidering and more time sewing secret pockets into her riding habit to hold their jewels and gold coins.

By late afternoon she was sick with worry. Her head felt light and her stomach was queasy. Unable to face supper, she retired to her chamber, where the smell of food wouldn't reach her. She couldn't allow herself to be sick now. Not when Sir Trahern could arrive at any time with news that Miles had been arrested.

That reminded Alison of the king. With no way of knowing if the king still intended to come to Wyndfell, Alison knew she must be prepared. She normally kept the pantries well-stocked, and there were storerooms in the towers that held bags of grain and ground flour and meal, as well as dried fruits and vegetables. But special preparations would be necessary to accommodate the king and his retinue.

She got up and went down to Miles's closet. Since Edmund was missing, she would have to see to provisioning the castle for the royal visit. Along with the inventory of the castle's supplies, she found Miles's ledger of the stock that belonged to the castle's tenant farmers. She made a list of the animals they would need to slaughter, and set aside gold to purchase them the next morning. If they didn't use them all, they would have extra animals to feed through the coming winter, but if they ran short of food for the royal visitors, it would be a catastrophe.

She took the bags of gold back to the bedchamber and tossed them onto the bed. She placed the gold in her chest of gowns and locked it. Walt could take care of the purchases. He wasn't shrewd enough to act as steward, but he could manage to buy the animals.

Alison's malady was gone now and she went downstairs to look for something to eat before everyone retired for the night.

The villagers were glad to rid themselves of the surplus cows, pigs, and sheep. No one wanted to feed an animal that wasn't necessary for the family's survival. Alison sent the castle men to fish in the river above Wyndfell. Those they caught were placed in the holding ponds in the kitchen garden and were fed bread scraps to keep them alive until they were needed.

Boys were sent out before dawn and after dusk to cover the bushes with large nets and capture the birds roosting there. Soon the dovecote was full with a large variety of edible birds.

Alison sent two boys to the next town to buy a pair of swans and a peacock. Having become attached to the swans that swam on the moat and the peacocks that roamed Wyndfell's greens, she couldn't bring herself to kill them just to provide the king with a dish that he probably wouldn't eat anyway. King Henry was known to be extremely fond of artichokes, so Alison bought an abundance of the hard green vegetables and stored them on racks in the tower nearest the kitchen gate.

Spices to flavor exotic dishes and cover the taste of aging meat were purchased and added to the stores. Coloring agents such as alkanet, saffron, mint, blue turnsole, and violets were measured again and again to be sure enough was on hand for the foods that would need coloring. Almonds were skinned and blanched in preparation for the marchpane extravagance, and the head cook began planning a spectacle to delight the jaded royal eyes.

The next night Alison's stomach again rebelled against the sight and smell of food, and she remarked to Leatrice that she seemed unusually high-strung over the king's visit and Edmund's disappearance. Leatrice merely smiled and waited to see if the sickness would recur the following night. It did.

23

Alison had always loved the view from Wyndfell's roof. On clear days such as this one, she could see the swell of the hills stretching far into the distance on one side and the sweep of the lower country on the other. Wyndfell's river was like a bright ribbon of silver in the afternoon sun, and she enjoyed watching the white clouds race their shadows across the surface. A breeze was always blowing on the roof, and though it was more bracing than pleasant, it brought with it the scent of autumn.

Far away Alison saw a band of riders, and she watched to see if they would veer south on the way to Wakefield or continue on to the castle. When they passed the turn, Alison walked slowly to that side of the roof. Raising her hand to shield her eyes, she strained to discern the men's shapes or to recognize the horses they rode. When she saw that the lead horse was gray, her excitement began to build. Then, when they topped a rise, she recognized Miles, and her heart thudded in her chest with excitement.

With a cry of happiness she ran down from the roof and through the winding corridors and stairs and out to the courtyard. When she got to the drawbridge she saw Miles galloping toward her. She had worried that Miles might not return, but until now she had not realized how strong that fear had been. Tears of relief gathered in her eyes, and she brushed them away.

She waved as hard as she could, and he returned the gesture. In moments he was near enough for her to hear the creak of the leather on his saddle and see the steam from Excalibur's nostrils.

Miles was grinning as if he had been gone for a year rather than a fortnight. When his horse reached the bridge, he reined him in enough to bend down and scoop Alison up into the saddle in front of him. She held him as if she would never let him go, and didn't care that his knights were gawking at her open display of affection.

By now all the castle was alerted, and the courtyard was filling with people. Boys ran to greet their fathers and to take the sweaty mounts to the barn. Wives and sweethearts ran to their respective men, and the babble of voices and laughter filled the air.

"I missed you," Alison said, her eyes shining.

"I missed you too, love." He held her close before lowering her to the ground.

She held the horse's reins while Miles dismounted, and arm in arm they went up the broad steps. "How was York?" she asked. "Did all go well?"

"Well enough. The day we left York there was some excitement. Lord Roger Bainbridge showed up in a lackey's garb and tried to give the queen some sort of message. Naturally I questioned him, but he wouldn't explain."

"What did you do?" Alison's face was suddenly pale.

"I turned him over to the king. Why are you trembling?"

"I'm just so happy to see you. When will the king arrive?"

"I expect him in three or four days."

"So soon!"

"I must check with Sir Edmund to see that he bought the necessary supplies. Most of the king's retinue can lodge in the castle, and the rest can camp on the green where we held the tourney."

"You mean you didn't see Sir Edmund in York?"

"No. Why should he be there?"

"Well, he isn't here."

Miles stopped and stared at her. "Are you saying you sent him to me at York? For what reason?"

"I sent him nowhere. He simply disappeared. I assumed he must have followed you."

"He left without permission?"

"Yes. He's been gone since you left."

"God's bones!" Miles frowned back at the gatehouse. "I would never have guessed it of him. Deserting the castle while I was away!"

"I never trusted him," Alison affirmed. "There was always something underhanded about him."

"Who has been looking after the castle business?"

"I have. I purchased the supplies for the king's visit, but I've not had time to collect the rents." Alison was appalled that Lord Roger had been caught. If he confessed to the king and implicated her, she was done for. "Are you certain the king will arrive in three or four days?"

"Preparations were being made for his departure when I started home." Miles frowned and shook his head. "Sir Edmund gone. I can't believe it!"

"I can't believe what has happened either."

He drew her into a private niche in the shadowy recess of the hall. Bending his head, he kissed her passionately. Alison laced her fingers through his hair and returned his kiss with all the love in her heart, hoping desperately to find refuge in his embrace. The anxiety over not knowing what Roger might have said was robbing her of her breath.

"God, I've missed holding you," he sighed as he pressed her close and nuzzled her neck.

"Miles, don't ever leave me again. I love you and have missed you so much. I've scarcely been able to sleep with our bed so empty."

He grinned and kissed the soft flesh of her neck just beneath her earlobe. Her pulse was racing wildly. "It won't be empty tonight, love. I promise you that."

Nearing voices told them that others were entering the hall, and their brief, private moment was over. Regretfully they stepped out of the niche, though they still held hands.

"Why did the king send for you?" she asked.

"He never said. I have no idea why he wanted me to come there, when all the while he still planned on coming here to visit Wyndfell. Lately he's seemed to be rather erratic."

A small frown puckered Alison's brow, but she smoothed it quickly. "Whatever it was, I suppose it didn't amount to much if he never mentioned it." But her mind was working fast. Roger had been foolish enough to get caught, and that was certain to throw suspicion on this area, even if he had confessed nothing. If he had told about Damion and the insurrection, it was a moot point whether Edmund had somehow discovered Damion and gone to tell the king in person. The king might be coming here to arrest them all!

Alison felt faint. What other answer could there be? She wasn't at all sure they could escape now. But Damion would have mentioned being discovered by Edmund. Or would he? Maybe Damion wanted to ensure that the king would come to Wyndfell.

She squeezed Miles's hand and excitedly said, "I must tell the cooks to begin preparing for the king's visit. We have very little time as it is."

Miles nodded and watched her move swiftly toward the corridor that led to the kitchen. He knew she had great reservations about giving King Henry her oath of fealty, but he was sure that when the time came, she could at least give lip service to the pledge. Miles was tired of the whole matter and looked forward to the departure of the king and a return to the more peaceful life, with Wyndfell's affairs as his highest priority.

Alison nervously moved through the main kitchen,

ordering the servants about like a general preparing troops for battle. A steer was killed and butchered in the kitchen yard, along with the first of the hogs. Pots of steaming brews were cranked over the fire by the long arm of the rachyncroke and balanced on three-legged blandreths. Strainers and sifters of strong horse hair, made in graduated sizes and degrees of fineness, were used to prepare the hippocras. Birds were killed by piercing the nape of their necks with a quill and were carefully skinned so they could be reassembled later as a spectacle food. Although there were smoke vents in the tall, domed ceiling of the kitchen, so much preparation was under way that a thick cloud of smoke had been trapped near the peak as if it were a thundercloud about to burst.

The cooks went about under the watchful eye of Grace, the chief cook, who made certain the four humors of the foods—hot, cold, moist, and dry—were balanced one against the other and that spices and herbs were added to promote digestion and health. The foods, when prepared, would be placed in a cool cellar under the tower nearest the kitchen. The finishing glazes and sauces would be prepared the day of the feast itself. Until the king and his many followers left, the kitchens would be in use day and night, so Alison dispatched several yeomen to guard against the increased risk of fire.

All the while Alison had been seeing to the preparations, her mind had been racing in search of some logic and reasoning. The fact that the king let Miles return could have indicated that Roger had in some way satisfactorily explained his odd behavior and admitted nothing. But Sir Edmund was still missing, with no plausible explanation.

Miles supervised the rent collection and double-checked the amount of livestock Alison had bought. In his spare moments he finished drawing up the plans to enlarge the castle. As the modifications were rather extensive, he would have to get the king's permission, and what better time to obtain it than when the king and his retinue were crowded into Wyndfell?

Miles found Alison in the herb garden and pulled her to one side to show her a large sheet of foolscap.

"Not more trouble!" she exclaimed. Her thoughts were still heavily laden with her concern that Damion might have resumed his writings.

"No, no. Look. I've finished the plan for enlarging Wyndfell. See?" He led her through the inner gate and pointed at the flower gardens. "The new wing will be here."

"Are you certain it's a good idea to destroy the gardens?"

"We will move them back farther so that they are out of the way. I'll send a message to my stewards in Wales to grow cuttings of those roses I told you about."

"But Wyndfell hasn't been altered since the reign of Henry VI!"

"What difference does that make? The solar you use as a ladies' parlor was once the master's chamber. You can tell by the way it's placed near the gallery—which was probably the old hall."

He drew her farther out into the garden and pointed to show her the older section. "See? This is where the castle once ended. Our hall and sleeping wing were added later."

"I like our hall."

"So do I. The addition I plan will give us a new, more expansive gallery and a new chamber, as well as more comfortable lodging for our attendants."

She nodded. " 'Tis awkward having to pass through Leatrice and Trahern's chamber and that of my ladies to leave our room." At last she smiled, letting go of her worries in favor of this diversion.

"Exactly." Miles spread his drawing over a bush and said, "Our present chamber will become the primary room for guests. We can have much more company if we have a guest wing. I propose to put the new gallery here . . . with glazed windows, not just tapestries," he added temptingly. "And three big fireplaces. You know how cold you got last winter in the drafty old gallery."

"That's true."

"There will be a fireplace in our chamber, of course, and one in the anteroom here."

"Where will our attendants sleep?" she asked as she studied the plan.

"Leatrice and Trahern will have this chamber across from ours. The others will sleep here, with the unmarried ladies along one corridor and my men along the other."

Alison said, "Our chamber will be above the new gallery? That makes the new section shorter than the one we have now."

"No, there will be other chambers above these so that the roof is even, and there will be crenels along the battlement as there are on the old section—if the king gives his permission."

"Surely he will. It's a lovely plan."

"It seems to be the only way to expand. The other three sides are surrounded by moat, and naturally we can't fill in the courtyard."

"Of course not."

Miles smiled at her. "The top level of rooms will be the new nursery suites."

Alison returned his smile, not telling him that she might be pregnant. Leatrice had said she was sure of it, but Alison wanted to be certain before she told him, lest he be disappointed if she were wrong. Nevertheless, her hand glided unconsciously across her slender middle. She was almost positive. If fortune was with her, she could tell him in a few days.

"I meant not to disturb you," Miles said, reaching out to caress her cheek with an intimate touch that bespoke his love. "I know how busy you are."

"I'm never too busy to speak with you," she said softly.

"I wanted you to see these plans before I spoke to the king. Your agreement is important to me."

"I like your ideas for Wyndfell. Do you think the king will give his permission?" Alison had gotten so involved with the discussion, she had completely forgotten her concern over what the king might know of the insurrection activities here at Wyndfell, but her own question revived the whole issue.

"Why not? He knows I am loyal to the crown, and he assumes you are, as well."

"I suppose," she replied slowly—but if Henry was so sure of their loyalty, why had he summoned Miles to court and not given him a reason? Alison wasn't very confident of the king's trust in her. That he had not yet asked her pledge of allegiance didn't mean that he wouldn't. And if she stood by her convictions and failed to give him that pledge, she would likely be condemning Miles as well. Alison looked up at the window of Damion's cell, set against a backdrop of blue sky and shifting clouds. Behind that window was a man actively plotting the overthrow of Henry's queen.

As they walked back around the castle, a man in the king's livery rode into the courtyard. Miles acknowledged his bow and took the roll of paper the man held out. As he silently read the royal document, Alison tried to swallow past the lump in her throat. She studied Miles's face for some indication of the contents, but his features were implacable.

Looking to Alison, Miles impassively repeated the message. "The king will arrive tomorrow. Most of his retinue will go from York directly toward London in the queen's company. The king will visit here with a troop of two hundred, as he told me in York."

Alison tried to hide her relief. For a fleeting moment she had thought it was the order for their arrest or news that the entire entourage of four thousand was about to descend upon them. She had had nightmares of Wyndfell's entire green being turned into a mound of mud and litter and of her castle being packed to overflowing until every morsel of food was eaten. Of Miles she asked, "Does it say if they will arrive early or late?"

The messenger, a haughty young man, said, "They are camped about fifteen miles from here. I would expect them by midafternoon. If there's aught else ye want to know, you can just ask me."

"That will be all. You may go to the kitchen for refreshment," she ordered coolly. It was a mystery how such an impudent young man had come to be a royal messenger. Or had he been chosen purposefully to show disrespect to them before the king's arrival, like the sort of game a cat would play with a mouse before devouring him?

When he was gone, she turned to Miles with a nervous laugh. "I seem full of foolish fancies. I find myself worrying that the king has some hidden motive for sending such an impudent messenger." She hoped this was merely one of the breeding fantasies of which she had heard women speak.

"There's nothing to fear. I suspect the young lad's just a bit full of himself. This is probably his first errand away from the watchful eye of someone at court."

"That's not entirely reassuring. We still don't know why the king is coming."

Miles tried to comfort her with a hug. "Don't fret so. Think how grand our castle will look in a few years when the additions are finished. That should chase the worry from your mind."

She tiptoed up to kiss him and noticed the faint lines of concern at the corners of his eyes. She wasn't the only one who was fearful of this visit. "I must see to the maids," she said, and briskly walked away.

Miles watched her go and wished he had been able to reassure her. Unfortunately he wasn't so certain that this was in fact to be an amiable visit. With the king's behavior so unpredictable, Miles didn't know what to expect. He decided to double the number of men on village patrol for the king's visit to ensure that Henry would see no sign of unrest.

After gathering a good supply of bread, cheese, fruits, and a pitcher of ale, Alison made her way up to the gallery, where she entered the secret passageway. She had dreaded telling Damion of Roger's capture and the king's upcoming visit, but she could delay no longer. Damion was in his room as usual and nodded to her in greeting.

Putting the food and ale on the small table, Alison said, "I recently learned that King Henry will be arriving at Wyndfell tomorrow for a visit, and since I may not be able to slip up here very often, I have brought extra food for you. Do you need anything else?"

"No. The king will be here tomorrow, you say? And the queen?" Damion's composure was totally unexpected. Alison had thought he would at least raise his voice in objection.

"You're not to try anything, Damion. Not here at Wyndfell. Thank goodness the queen will not be with him."

"Don't take that tone with me, sister. You forget whom you are addressing."

"I am addressing my brother! I refuse to let you put us in further danger with some half-baked scheme. The plot you and Lord Roger planned failed most miserably. Lord Roger was caught trying to deliver a note to the queen and was taken before the king."

Damion's stoic silence was unsettling, so Alison didn't mention her fear that Roger might have confessed. Instead she crossed Damion's small room to the door that led to the servants' corridor and made sure it was locked. "I will house some of the king's men on this floor, but if they hear you, they will assume you are one of my servants, unless you are making a noise that would arouse suspicion—like chanting a hymn."

"I'm not a fool, sister."

"I'm sorry I spoke so abruptly, Damion. It's just that I'm so worried. The king's visit seems odd in that he summoned Miles to York for no reason, and now he plans to visit Wyndfell with a troop of soldiers rather than the court."

Damion's dark eyes flickered with interest. "Why would he do that?"

"How should I know? Perhaps Lord Roger broke when he was questioned and told the king of your whereabouts."

"Lord Roger wouldn't do that!"

"He would to save his own neck. I know Roger better than you do," she retorted.

"He would become a king's man?" Damion's voice was dangerously cold. "He would do that?"

"How am I to answer that?" she snapped. "He has always looked after his own interests. And that's not all. Sir Edmund is still missing. I think he has gone to tell the king about the trouble here."

Damion smiled. "No, he hasn't."

"What makes you so certain? I've searched the castle from top to bottom. My men have scoured the parks and fields and village. He isn't here!"

"Have you looked in the buttery?"

Alison stopped her agitated pacing and turned to face Damion. "The buttery? You mentioned that before! Why do you say he might be there?"

"Because I know for a fact that he is."

She stared at him, then said, "Nonsense. I searched the buttery days ago. People are in and out of there all the time."

"Not at midnight, they aren't."

"Damion what are you saying?"

The monk moved silently to the basket of food and looked inside before he answered. "Sir Edmund found the secret passage."

"He what!"

"You can imagine how surprised I was. He broke in upon me during my prayers."

"He came here! He saw you? Then he must have ridden directly to the king!"

"No, sister, he rode nowhere, directly or otherwise. I found it necessary to silence him . . . forever."

Alison stepped back, aghast. "You killed him?"

"With the candlestick there." His voice was devoid of emotion, as if he were discussing an abstract theological point. "After everyone went to bed, I carried him down to the buttery and buried him under the flagstones near the rear of the room."

"You didn't?"

"Of course I did. What else could I have done?"

Alison stared at her brother. He was telling her he had killed her steward, yet he sounded as if this was of no importance. She edged toward the secret panel. "You must leave here, Damion. I can't harbor a murderer!"

He wheeled on her, his eyes like black firebrands. "You call it murder! Can it be that you too have crossed over to the king's camp?"

"No!" Thinking fast, she said, "I'd never do such a thing. It's only that you may not be safe here. What if someone saw you?"

"No one did. If I had been seen, you would have heard about it by now. And I'm not leaving. Not with the king on his way to this very castle."

Her hands and feet felt suddenly icy, and Alison wondered if she was about to faint. The pit of her stomach knotted and she hurried toward the secret panel. "Very well, Damion, stay here. But I pray you, please be quiet!"

"I will," he said in an amiable tone that was at odds with his former manner. "For now, at least."

Alison let herself into the passage. The stairs seemed unusually black, even with the glow of her candle. Damion must have taken each of these steps as he carried Edmund's dead body down to the buttery. Superstitious fear pricked her skin, and she was afraid at every turning that she might meet Edmund's ghost.

When she reached her chamber she thankfully stepped into the daylight that filtered through the tall, narrow windows. For a moment she leaned back against the secret panel, wishing she could lock Damion in forever, but as the panels all opened into the passageway, even moving a heavy chest in front of it would not block his way.

Shakily she blew out the candle and placed it on a nearby corbel. Damion was telling the truth about killing Edmund—she had very little doubt about it. Might he also try to kill Miles? Or the king himself? How had she gotten herself into this predicament? She longed desperately to tell Miles and let him help her out of this coil, but she dared not. If Miles knew of Damion's presence in the castle, he would be certain to oust him, but how would he ever convince the king that he knew nothing of the monk? Perhaps, she considered, Damion would be less apt to cause trouble in his upper cell than if he was roaming openly across the countryside. His clothing alone proclaimed his priesthood, and he would never put it aside.

She felt drawn to the buttery, and with a morbid curiosity she went downstairs. At the gallery she paused and looked down the long room. Taking a deep breath, she went to the steps at the far end and slowly descended to the buttery.

The cool air wafted about her and she paused again. In front of her was the main aisle, lined by casks of wine and huge butts of ale. Her body moved forward rigidly. As she had done so often, she passed the oak barrels, her mind automatically clicking off their contents as if that would protect her from thinking about what might await her at the far end.

When she reached the last of the kegs, she stopped. Now that she knew where to look, she could see dirt embedded in the flagstones' shallow indentations—dirt that should have been worn away over the centuries.

She knelt and brushed her fingers over the stones. They *had* been moved! She could tell by the way one rocked slightly when she pressed upon it. Cold sweat trickled down her spine. Damion had been telling the truth. Sir Edmund Campbell was buried beneath her feet!

A door slammed, and she leapt up as she swung to face the steps, her hands trembling and her eyes large in her pale face.

"Pardon, my lady. Did I startle you?" the yeoman said. "I come to draw a flagon of charneco for the cook. Shall I come back later?"

"No, no! I mean, you're not disturbing me. I was only rechecking the amount of perry and metheglin." She patted the barrel closest to her and said briskly, "I see there is plenty." She strode briskly to the steps that led to the gallery. When she was out of sight on the landing, she leaned against the wall and tried to draw her breath into her aching lungs. Would anyone else notice the irregularity in the stones? She asked St. Ruan, the patron saint of Wyndfell, to watch over the buttery and over Wyndfell's inhabitants.

By suppertime Alison was as nervous as a thief, and even the servants were openly staring at her. Miles put his hand over hers as they waited for the servants to place their food in the winter parlor. When they were gone, he said, "Calm yourself, love. 'Tis the king, but you act as if we were being visited by the devil himself."

"Is there a difference?" she whispered back in case one of the servants was near.

"You're making too much of this."

Alison frowned at him and forced a potrous into her mouth. When her stomach rebelled against the layers of egg, cheese, and honey topped with brown mustard, she pushed her plate away and took deep breaths.

"Are you ailing?" Miles asked in concern. "You ate no supper last night either."

"I've been nibbling on food in the kitchen as I oversaw the preparations," she lied. "I seem to be full."

"Can't you at least try some of this farsed chicken? It's your favorite."

She shook her head resolutely.

Miles leaned nearer with a broad grin. "Are you certain you have nothing to tell me? Some secret, perhaps?"

"What? No! I have no secret," she exclaimed in alarm, thinking of the buttery.

He drew back in surprise. "I only thought perhaps . . ."

She drank a sip of perry, recalled where the casks stood, and rose hastily to her feet. "Excuse me," she mumbled as she ran for the door.

Miles chuckled softly as he cut off a thick slice of the cherry-stuffed chicken. She might say she had no secret, but he had seen many women at court who were in the early stages of pregnancy. The lack of privacy had made everyone aware of each other's business. Besides, he knew Alison's body as well as he knew his own and she was thickening in a way that wasn't suggestive of overeating. He hoped she, too, would soon be positive enough to tell him they were expecting a baby. He drank his perry and wondered if the babe would be born in late winter or early spring.

24

Alison had taken her bath, and sat combing her hair as Miles soaked in the barrellike tub. He soaped his long arms and wiped a cobweb of bubbles over his chest. He had already washed his hair, and it was starting to dry into a sleek black thatch.

"You look so pensive," he observed as Alison drew her comb through her long auburn hair. "I wish you wouldn't worry so."

Alison's eyes moved from the round hand mirror to the nearly invisible crack that distinguished the secret panel. "I'm not worrying," she denied. "Do you think the king will stay long?"

"Probably not too long. Prince Edward is in London, and he's prone to winter colds. I imagine the king will want to be near him before snowfall. Besides, traveling in the snow is very difficult, especially on the queen and the other ladies."

"It could snow almost any day now," Alison said hopefully. "I believe it's colder tonight than it was last evening."

"I only wish I knew where that lowborn steward went. Henry will probably ask for him and I'll have to explain that he's disappeared."

Alison's rhythmic strokes stopped, and she gazed at Miles's reflection in the mirror.

"He's put me in a difficult position. Walt hasn't the brains to look after the castle accounts, and I have more than enough to do preparing for the royal visit."

"Aye. We both do." She wondered if she had taken enough food and ale to Damion. He ate and drank little these days. Most frightening of all was his admission of murder, and how the fanatical light had sparkled in his eyes when he had told her. She was afraid of him! Her own brother! And him a priest! When Miles spoke, she jumped.

"Will you wash my back?" he repeated.

"Gladly," she answered. Kneeling beside the tub, she took the linen cloth and lathered his broad back. She loved doing this. The water made his muscles gleam, and the trails of soap rippled over them in lazy-flowing rivers. "I love touching you when you're wet and soapy. My hand slides over you so easily."

She looked around their chamber. "I will miss sleeping here during the visit."

"Once the new wing is built, you will like that chamber even more. We will use this one only for guests and not have to move out when someone of higher rank visits." He put a dab of soapsuds on her nose to make her smile. "What color bed hangings and coverlet will you make? Green, like our griffin?"

"Green is so expensive! Perhaps yellow. Or red."

"I like red. But this new addition won't beggar us, you know. If you want green cloth, we can afford it."

"I know, but I saw a chamber at court that I fancied. It was as red as a pigeon's blood and embroidered with white, silver, and gold."

"I know that chamber."

"I could embroider griffins and unicorns onto the bed hanging."

"We might even purchase a rug from Turkey to put on the floor."

"On the floor! Now, that *is* extravagant. We'll drape it over a chest or hang it on the wall."

"The king has rugs on the floors of his privy chambers."

"He is the king. We aren't. The rug goes on the wall where it belongs."

Miles put his wet arm around her and pulled her against the edge of the tub. "You should have married a poor man, with your penchant for saving money."

"I wasn't always wealthy, you know. When I was a child, there were times when my stepfather hadn't enough revenue to properly feed and clothe us."

"All that is behind you now. As my viscountess you'll never lack for anything."

"I love you, Miles." She kissed his damp lips and breathed in his soapy aroma. "I'd love you even if you were truly a poor man."

He released her and stood up so she could rinse away the last of the soap with ladles of warm water. "You make a lovely chambermaid," he commented as she rubbed him dry with a square of coarse linen.

She smiled and brought him his chamber robe, then went to Leatrice's chamber door and motioned for two of the maids to come in.

In well-trained silence the two girls bailed the water out of the tub and tossed it out of the window. When the tub was empty, they put the pails inside it and carried it back to its storage place in the cellar below the older kitchen.

Miles put another log on the fire and slipped out of his robe. The pegs in the wall were full, so he lifted Alison's riding habit to another hook to make room, but the weight of the habit surprised him, and he almost dropped it. He looked over at her in astonishment. "This is as heavy as my armor. Why is that?"

Alison took it from him quickly and hung it on a peg. "It's not so heavy. It simply has numerous lengths of velvet in it."

"Had I realized the weight, I'd have bought you a larger horse rather than your little Spanish jennet."

"It's not so very heavy," she repeated, although it

was easily twice the weight of a gown that had no gold coins sewed into the hem and seams. If flight became necessary, she would gladly tolerate the inconvenience of its weight.

To distract him from the riding habit, she pulled off her robe and hung it over the velvet gown. Her nakedness had the result she had hoped for.

"God's bones, but your body is lovely." He admiringly ran his hand over her shoulder and down to cup her breast.

She went to the bed and climbed in. As much as she enjoyed his lovemaking, she felt no inclination for dalliance this night. Worries seemed to press upon her. Also, her queasiness at supper had become full-fledged nausea by the time she reached the garderobe. She felt well again now, but since she was rarely ill, she was upset over her body's rebellion. As Miles rolled onto his side facing her, she turned over and closed her eyes to sleep.

Miles's arm circled her, and he drew her back against the warmth of his flesh as his hand began to caress her breast.

Alison's eyes opened. "Are you not tired? I know I am," she hinted.

"I'm not too tired to love you." He nuzzled in the hollow of her neck where he knew she was particularly sensitive.

Alison shrugged away. "I'm sleepy."

"Go to sleep if you like," he said with a grin as he moved lower to take her nipple in his mouth.

She frowned and sighed to let him know she really wasn't in the mood for this. He continued licking and teasing her nipple as if she were as amorous as he was.

"Miles," she said, pushing against his shoulders.

He looked at her with twinkling eyes.

"I can't go to sleep with you doing that."

"No? Have you ever tried?" His hand explored the curve and peak of her other breast.

"Be serious. We have a long day ahead of us. I must

finish overseeing the last of the banquet, and be sure the chambers are aired and clean. You have dozens of things to do as well."

"Yes, that's right. But we will do none of them before tomorrow." He returned his mouth to her breast and tugged gently. He drew his hand lower to seek out the secret bud that was her seat of pleasure.

When his fingers found the treasure they sought, Alison moved restlessly. This was beginning to feel wonderful, but she didn't want to back down. "I'm tired, Miles."

"Then lie back and let me give you pleasure."

She gazed up at the fabric medallion where the bed hangings formed a roseate. She would show him, she decided. She *would* go to sleep. She closed her eyes and tried to ignore the insistent probing and teasing of his fingers and lips, but all thoughts of sleep escaped her, as she tried to guess where and how he would touch her next. Against her decision to relax, her body pressed against his hand in remembered response, and she had to bite back the moan of pleasure that rose in her throat.

Resolutely she overrode her growing responses and pretended to be on the brink of sleep. Miles shifted so that he knelt between her legs, and in one fluid movement he became one with her. Alison's eyes flew open.

"Did I wake you?" he laughed. Slowly he began to move deeply within her, stirring to life all the fires she had tried to quell.

Alison couldn't help laughing at him. "Have you no shame?" she asked in a pretended affront. "Do you ravish a woman even when she says you nay?"

"I do when it's so obvious that only her lips are denying me. As you can see, your body was more than willing."

"My body is a traitor."

"Would you have me stop? I will if you command it." He caught her nipple between his thumb and forefinger and rolled it gently to a firm bud. "Would you rather sleep?"

"No," she sighed as she gave herself up to pleasure.

Slowly Miles brought her to the point of tingling excitement where the slightest touch or movement made her tremble on the brink of completion. She murmured his name as if it were a love charm and moved her hips in a way that she knew gave him delight. Finally, breathlessly, they let their bodies claim the trembling prize. As one they reached their ecstasy and their souls spun and tumbled in sheer love and pleasure.

When they could speak again, Miles kissed her forehead. "Will you not sleep much better now?"

"Yes," she said, snuggling closer.

He ran his hand over her stomach and said, "Soon we will have to temper our lovemaking."

"What!" Her head jerked up so she could see his face. "Why do you say that?"

"I shouldn't have mentioned it. I know wives like to tell their husbands in their own time, but I couldn't hold back. When were you planning to tell me we are expecting a babe? When you hand it to me in a swaddling cloth?"

"I was waiting until I was certain. I was afraid I might be mistaken and you would be disappointed."

He smiled tenderly. "You're not mistaken, sweetheart, nor will I be disappointed. I can tell it's true, whether you can or not. There are certain changes in your body that confirm it."

Alison lay back on his shoulder and put her hand on her stomach. "It's not moving yet."

"Give it time."

"How do you know so much about this?" she asked suspiciously.

"There were many ladies at court, and their husbands—the young ones at least—were very vocal in discussing such matters. The older ones just shrugged it off as one more babe in the house."

"Will you do that? See our later children so dispassionately?"

"I doubt I will ever see anything dispassionately if it has to do with you," he laughed softly.

She smiled. "I hope the first is a boy to carry on the name of Garrett. A girl can come next."

"I need a son, as all men do who have titles and lands to hand down," he agreed. "But I confess to a yearning for a girl."

Alison looked at him in surprise.

"A girl, you see, has no pressure to share your politics or to be practiced in chivalry and accounts, and doesn't have to be trained her entire life to rule in her father's place. A girl is to be loved. Only that."

"I never thought of it like that."

"And I'm telling you now, Alison—there will be no talk of sending our sons away to be nurtured," he said firmly. "They will stay here with us, and we will teach them all they need to know. Court is especially no place for a boy." He shook his head in the darkness. "You'd never guess what I learned in the back rooms of court, nor how young I learned it."

"Our sons will stay here," she agreed. "And so will our daughters. We won't betroth them when they are practically babies, and send then to their future husbands' castles. Everyone will say we're spoiling them unbearably, but they will grow up in Wyndfell's safety."

Miles stroked her stomach, and a smile lit his eyes when he imagined the tiny spark of life in there. "I fear we will be doting parents, my love."

"I hope so. Our children will have all we missed ourselves. Seclusion from the jades at court and two parents to love them."

He kissed her nose and cuddled her into the hollow of his side. Gradually sleep overcame them, and unknown to the other, their last conscious thoughts were that they would somehow placate the king.

* * *

The next morning Alison moved through her chores at a frantic pace. Every time someone came upon her unexpectedly, she jumped, thinking it was an announcement of the king's arrival. The usual hum of voices and movements through Wyndfell had become a constant undercurrent of sound. In the kitchen the chief cook shouted and cursed at everyone, and tempers matched the heat of the ovens.

Alison had the sheets and cover stripped from her bed and the feather mattress turned. The king would, of course, bring his own linens. The maids spread the richly embroidered coverlet over the bare mattress in preparation.

An argument broke out in the buttery, and Alison hurried down to break it up. Everyone was nervous about the visit, and this wasn't the first altercation she had had to set straight.

She sent the men on their way, and her eyes went to the end of the long central aisle. She tried her best to stay away from the buttery these days because even the thought of the shadowy spot at the rear of the room rekindled her fears.

Raising her eyes as if she could see through the ceiling to the upper room, she wondered what Damion was doing. A coldness crept over her, and she tried to tell herself it was the damp chill of the underground room, but she knew it wasn't. She couldn't let him roam freely with the king in the castle. Besides, he might well be planning some coup that would destroy them all.

How could she fasten him in the cell? There was no lock on the secret panel, nor could the latch be dismantled quickly and silently. Even if it could be broken, the panel would likely open more freely rather than remain shut. She considered nailing the door closed, but quickly rejected the idea. Not only would Damion force open the panel before she could drive a nail deep enough to secure it, but there was no justification for the Viscountess of Wyndfell needing a hammer and nails from the smithy. Not to mention the noise hammering would make.

Against the far wall were some long poles that were used to lever the large casks of ale into their wooden cradles. Alison went to the poles and held one horizontal to the floor to judge its length. The panels all opened into the passageway, and the interior walls were rough, unhewn stones, the backsides of the finished walls. She could wedge a pole between the panel and the wall and Damion couldn't get out at all. Later she could think of a way to safely release him.

Before she could lose her nerve, Alison crept up the stairs and through the servants' corridor to the outer door to Damion's chamber. Very quietly she secured the door by slipping a peg through the outside latch, then hurried back to the buttery for the pole she had chosen. She went upstairs with the pole partially concealed in the folds of her skirt. If anyone noticed what she was carrying, he asked no questions.

Fortunately the antechambers were empty and so was the bedchamber. Alison hurried to the panel, grabbed a candle, and let herself into the dark tunnel. Still concealing the pole she climbed the stairs, her heart pounding. If Damion suspected anything, he would be uncontrollable. Mentally she went over the amount of food and ale she had brought him. Given Damion's love of fasting and his frugal habits, he should have plenty.

At last she reached the small landing at the top of the steps. Pausing, she wondered where Damion was. She would gain nothing if she fastened the panel, only to discover he was below her watching the activity in the hall or gallery.

She put her ear to the rough wood and held her breath. After a long wait she heard a movement on the other side. To be certain, she made herself wait until she heard another sound. He was definitely in the room.

Silently she placed one end of the pole in the crevice

between two stones and pulled the other end tight against the panel. Although she had made very little sound, Damion's footsteps came toward the door. Alison clasped her arms about herself as she heard the familiar click of the latch being released. Damion pushed against the panel, but the pole held firm. Alison heard a most unpriestly string of curses as she went back down the steps.

Henry and his retinue arrived in midafternoon to a fanfare of trumpets. When Alison heard the dreaded noise, she lifted her skirts and ran down the corridor to the turret steps. Mustering all the decorum she could, she descended to the hall, her face calm and her bearing regal.

Miles was waiting for her in the hall, and smiled encouragingly as he offered her his arm. Alison placed her fingertips formally on his wrist and tried to return his smile as he led her to the wide entrance. Walt opened the door, and they stepped out into the sunlight as the king rode through the gatehouse.

They bowed low and curtsied as Henry dismounted and laboriously made his way up the steps. "Welcome to Wyndfell, your majesty," Miles said.

"Ha! So this is the castle that has stolen you away from my court," Henry replied in a booming, jovial voice.

"It's not as grand as Hampton Court," Alison said, "but you're every bit as welcome here." She thought a small lie might not hurt to preserve the king's good humor.

"Well said, Lady Alison." Henry gave her that same scrutinizing stare that she found so unsettling, then preceded them into the hall. As soon as his foot touched the rushes, the musicians in the loft struck up a lively tune written by the king himself. Henry grinned in appreciation.

Miles motioned for the cupbearer to bring forth the jeweled chalice of wine. Other servers hurried to pour out measures for the noblemen and gentry as they entered the hall.

Alison smiled until her jaws ached, and the din from so many voices made her ears hurt. She thought, with longing, of Wyndfell's usual state of relative peace and quiet.

When carts arrived, she gave orders for the king's belongings to be taken to the master's bedchamber. The rest she left to be delegated by Leatrice and Sir Trahern, who knew exactly where to put each of the retinue according to rank.

"What a pity Queen Catherine didn't come with you," Miles said when the king had taken a long draft of wine.

"She hasn't much stomach for traveling and was eager to return to London. My men and I will be able to overtake them before they reach Leicester."

"Then I fear your visit will be a short one," Miles observed.

"Yes. I expect it will be." Henry studied Miles's face as if he were reading his mind. "So, Lord Miles. Have you aught to tell me about the area?"

"Nothing I've not mentioned before, your majesty. It's very quiet here. Aside from peddlers and an occasional traveler, our days seldom change from one season to the next."

"Nothing to report?" Henry asked in a probing way.

"We did have a tourney," Alison put in quickly. "It was the first ever held here at Wyndfell, as far as I know." She described the jousting in great detail to avert the king from his questioning. "My lord husband was champion of the day despite an injury. But he is healed now."

"Someone bested you?" Henry exclaimed in disbelief.

"No, your majesty. He raised his lance at the last moment in an effort to wound me, but I kept the saddle and took him on the next charge."

"A villainous thing to do! Who is this blackguard?"

"Lord Roger Bainbridge. You met him at York, as I'm sure you recall."

"Bainbridge," Henry said thoughtfully, stroking his beard. "Perhaps I shouldn't have released him so quickly."

"He was released?" Alison asked. She hadn't seen him since he left for York.

"Yes, I sent him back to his castle. Did he not return?"

"I suppose he must have," Alison replied. "We have very little contact with Bainbridge Castle."

"As I'm sure you recall, Lord Bainbridge had planned to marry Lady Alison before you betrothed her to me," Miles added. "While there isn't exactly bad blood between us, neither are we friends."

"I see." Henry pursed his lips thoughtfully. "Yes, I see how that could cause ill feelings between the two of you."

"Come and sit down, your majesty. After your ride you must be hungry."

"I'll have a servant bring in a bowl of fruit. Wyndfell's apples are most delicious," Alison said, taking the opportunity to hurry away. The king's overwhelming presence frightened her, and at the same time she was in awe of him. Was he indeed her father or not?

She sent for the bowl of fruit and paused in the stone-seated window to catch a breath of fresh air. The press of humanity in the hall stifled her, and she hoped she wasn't about to become nauseous again. As she leaned toward the window to gulp in cool air, she saw a lone rider approaching the castle from the northeast. She leaned forward in shock. Even though the back wall soon obscured him, she had no trouble recognizing Roger.

In the days since he had returned from York, Roger had avoided Wyndfell. He even stayed away from the oak woods where he usually met Damion. But he marveled at his freedom, for the king had neither detained him for further questioning nor arrested him. Henry evidently believed his accusation of Miles.

For days Roger had planned and schemed. Miles had foiled his plan at York and had almost gotten him in serious trouble, but when he accused Miles of being a traitor, the king let him go, saying he would look into the matter. Roger realized, however, that if the king began an intensive investigation, he might discover the true culprits. Somehow he had to find a way to ensure that Miles was the only one implicated, and that he was removed forever. If he could prove Miles was a traitor, Henry would probably reward him with Alison and her rich holdings. In truth, Roger was more interested in increasing his own wealth than in restoring Catholicism in England. Especially as he had also observed the king's failing health and had heard rumors that the sickly Prince Edward was unlikely to survive childhood. The next in line would be the Catholic Princess Mary. And if that failed, from all he had seen at York, Roger knew the queen would soon make a fatal slip, and her infidelities would be made known.

Roger finally reached a plan. He would have Damion draw up another of his placards, showing Miles stabbing the king in the back, with the queen cheering him on. Roger could then take the placard to the king, saying he had found it on the inn wall. Surely Miles would be arrested on the spot. Henry was ever ready to believe the worst in regard to his queens.

With that in mind, Roger rode to Wyndfell. He approached from the back, carefully avoiding the king's guard patrol. He tied his horse to a bush and swiftly let himself in through the secret door. As he passed the hall he could hear the riotous merrymaking that always accompanied the king.

At the top of the steps he paused. Someone had placed a pole in such a position that the panel couldn't open. With a frown, Roger dislodged the pole. As if Damion had been waiting for the pole to move, the panel swung open. Roger went into the cell as he asked, "Who did this?"

"Who else knows of this passage?" Damion countered with a growl. "It must have been Alison!"

"You don't know for certain? Perhaps Lord Garrett found out you're here and blocked you in. The king has arrived. Mayhap he means to turn you over to him!"

Damion's lips drew back from his large teeth. "Yes! That seems more reasonable. It must have been him!"

"I have a plan," Roger said. "I want you to draw up a placard—"

"It was Lord Garrett! I know it! He found the passage as Sir Edmund did!"

Roger stared at him. "Campbell was in here? Then perhaps he did it. Alison has always said she felt he was loyal to the king!"

"It was his ghost then," Damion said in a gravelly voice.

"What do you mean?"

"Sir Edmund Campbell is dead. I killed him myself!"

"You didn't! You killed him?" Roger gasped. "You should never have done that!"

Damion jerked around with his nervous quickness. Bright fires of fanaticism lit his dark eyes. "You say I shouldn't have killed him? Are you also a traitor to our cause?"

"I?" Roger took a step back. He wished now that he had left the pole in place; Damion looked and acted as if he were a madman.

"Yes! I see it now! You want me to draw up a placard so you can take it to the king!"

"Well, yes, but I meant to—"

"You would betray me to that murderer of the true religion!"

"No, no. You misunderstand! I only—"

"Traitor!" Damion bellowed as he rushed toward Roger.

Roger was completely unprepared for the attack,

and he fell beneath the furious onslaught. Everything happened so quickly he scarcely felt the razor-sharp knife when it sliced through his throat.

Damion staggered to his feet, his knife dripping from his hand. Great red splotches stained the unbleached linen of his habit and scapular. His teeth were drawn back in a parody of a grin, and he mumbled a barely coherent prayer for the dead as he cleaned the blade on Roger's jerkin.

Damion grabbed Roger's wheel-lock pistol and tied the pouch of balls and powder to his rope belt. A noise on the steps caused him to whirl like a trapped beast, and he bared his teeth as Alison appeared in the secret doorway.

"Damion, did Lord Roger—" When she realized what she was seeing, she fell back in fright.

Damion gave a growl and plunged past her down the dark steps, shoving her against the stone wall. Alison stumbled and cried out as the floor rushed up at her. When she opened her eyes again, she was on a level with Roger's limp body, and she stared in shock at the wide scarlet pool that was spreading across the floor.

Suddenly she leapt to her feet and started back the way she had come. Although she was afraid of catching her brother, she was more fearful of letting him run loose. Every panel she passed was unlatched, and she had to carefully resecure the latch on each one before moving on. Each room was filled with voices, and she couldn't believe Damion would be so foolhardy as to let himself be seen by the crowd in the castle. Only the last door, the one that led outside, was still fastened. Cautiously she opened it, but Damion was nowhere in sight. She saw only Roger's horse, munching unconcernedly on the bush.

Alison shut the door and secured it. The passageway again was drenched in darkness. Her heart was hammering so hard she felt as if it might burst. Was it possible that she had somehow run past Damion in the twisting corridor? There were corners where one wall of chimney met another that could hide a man.

Trembling from head to foot, Alison silently climbed the steps. At the first secret panel she hurriedly slipped through into the chapel, unconcerned that she might be seen coming through a wall. She had to get out of the passageway that seemed populated not only by Edmund's and Roger's ghosts but also by the madman who had killed them both. Damion was insane, and more dangerous than an injured bear.

Systematically she went from room to room, checking to see that each of the panels was well shut, while surreptitiously searching for any sign of Damion. No one showed any indication that a bloodied priest had run by, so she checked the last of the panels and hurried back to the safety of the crowd. All the while she was wondering frantically where Damion might be, and how she could explain Roger's body. She decided the time had come to confide in Miles.

25

Miles was still talking to the king when Alison returned. Nervously she waited for a break in the conversation before she discreetly asked, "Miles? May I speak with you a moment?"

"Of course. What is it?"

The king turned his probing eyes toward her and Alison faltered. "I . . . that is, I wouldn't want to bore his majesty with domestic talk."

"Nonsense," Henry boomed. "Is something amiss?"

"No, no. Nothing. It can wait." Alison couldn't insist on speaking to Miles alone without giving offense to Henry. She would just have to wait and hope the king would decide to speak to someone else.

"I was about to tell his majesty about our hopes of enlarging Wyndfell," Miles said.

"Enlarging it?" Henry asked.

"As you can see, we are pressed to house your retinue. It was the same during the tournament. With your permission, I propose to add another wing of bedchambers and a gallery on the garden side."

"Do you wish to surround your parapets with battlements?" Henry asked thoughtfully.

"With your permission, your grace."

"For what reason? Battlements are primarily for

reasons of defense. Do you expect a siege or a war from some quarter?" Henry smiled chillingly.

"No, no. Nothing like that. I merely meant to have the outline of the roof a uniform shape."

"I see." Henry gave Miles his peculiarly unnerving stare. "No other reason?"

"No, your majesty. We are at peace. Is there a chance of an impending war that I've not heard of?"

"One never knows. It wasn't so long ago that Yorkshire tried to rise up against me."

"Surely that will never happen again, but if it should, then battlements would be to your benefit, for I could more easily defend the castle."

Henry looked unconvinced. "I suppose it would depend entirely on which side you supported."

Miles gazed at Henry in astonishment. "Surely your majesty knows I'm loyal to the crown!"

"Of course! Of course!" Henry replied with sudden joviality. "I was jesting, Lord Miles."

Alison tried not to bounce from one foot to the other. She had to get Miles alone. Obviously the king was suspicious, if not already convinced, that Miles was a traitor. She looked about the crowded room and wondered again where Damion was. She must have somehow passed him in the secret passageway, but she dared not go back and look. She tried to subtly convey to Miles that she needed to speak with him at once.

Miles glanced at her, and she jerked her head almost imperceptibly. When he looked back at her, she rolled her eyes toward the window seat. He didn't take the hint.

Alison tried to reassure herself that Damion wouldn't dare enter a room where he might be seen. Especially not with his cassock stained with blood. She tried to deduce what he might do, but she couldn't guess. Damion's thought processes were no longer logical.

"I will consider your request to expand Wyndfell," Henry was saying. "However, for now I will make no decision, for I would rather be enjoying myself."

Miles smiled and said, "Wyndfell is at your disposal, your grace. We have hired a team of acrobats for your amusement. Shall I call them now?"

"Delightful! I've always enjoyed acrobatics, but you must watch with me."

Miles motioned for two of his yeomen to bring the chair usually reserved for himself, and when the king was seated, he signaled the acrobats to come forward. The crowd pushed back to form an arena in the center of the hall, and the four men and two women, clad in brilliant blue and red satin, came forward. After bowing and curtsying to the king, the leader of the troop called out a command in Italian and the act began.

While all eyes were on the performers, Alison slipped away. She had to find Damion. Once more she searched the castle, beginning on the roof and working her way downward. As before, she found no sign of him, and all the secret panels were securely closed. She glanced through the kitchens, which were filled with a frantic activity, but he was not to be found.

Very apprehensively she descended to the buttery and looked about. It was eerily silent after the throngs above, and gathering dusk was gradually displacing the little light that crept in at the high windows. Alison forced her feet forward. Shadows were thick at the back of the vaulted chamber, and a man could easily hide behind any of the large butts of ale.

She dared not call Damion's name, and she tried not to break the heavy silence as she walked with great trepidation down the long aisles. This seemed the most natural place for him to hide, and she was terrified that he might leap out at any moment. She wondered what she would do if he did.

"Alison!"

She jumped and cried out as she whirled to face the sound.

"Alison, what are you doing down here?"

"Miles! God's bones! You frightened the life out of me!" Alison pressed her palm to her waist and tried to draw in steadying breaths despite the wild hammering of her heart.

Miles came to her and she reached out to touch him. The buttery didn't seem quite so frightening now.

"Why are you down here instead of watching the acrobats? Is there some problem with the servants?"

"I wish that's all it was! Miles, I have to tell you something that I know is going to upset you."

"Are you ill? You look as if the world may be ending. You aren't about to lose the babe, are you!" He put his arm around her, concern etched on his face.

"No, nothing like that. I'm fine. Oh, Miles, I don't know how to tell you!"

He led her to a narrow bench under a window and sat down beside her. "Can it not wait? The performance must be almost over, and dinner is soon to be served."

"No, it can't wait!"

"Trouble in the village? It can't be another of those damned placards. I have men posted all over the village to see that none show up."

"In a way it's about the placards," she said, seizing the opening. "I know who was making them. It's a priest by the name of Brother Damion."

"I knew it!" Miles said triumphantly. "No one but a priest could write in such a hand! But how do you know this? Have you seen him? Where is he?"

Alison moistened her lips before she continued. Her mouth was dry with fear. "He's my brother."

"What! You never mentioned having a brother."

"We were never close, and I thought he would spend his life in St. Benedictine's monastery. I saw no reason to tell you."

"You should have told me. No wonder the king is suspicious."

"He has no reason to know about Damion. He was a child of my mother's marriage, not her liaison with the king."

"Isn't St. Benedictine the monastery that was closed a short time back? The name is familiar."

"Yes, it was. Damion came here, as he had nowhere else to go."

"Here to the village, you mean."

"No, here to Wyndfell."

"He came here? When! Where did he go?"

"Actually, he didn't go anywhere. As far as I know, Damion is still here."

Miles's expression was dark and forbidding. His eyes bore into hers as he tried to sort out her meaning. "He has been living here? In Wyndfell? That's not possible."

"Yes, it is. There is a secret passage. He's been living in one of the upper rooms that's never used."

"A secret passage?" Miles asked incredulously. "Why didn't you tell me?"

"At first I thought he would be here for only a day or two. But he needed refuge and I couldn't put him out. Before I realized what was happening, he and Lord Bainbridge had begun stirring up another rebellion."

"And you never told me? But why?"

"I was afraid."

"Of what? Of me?"

Alison didn't answer. How could she admit that she had been afraid of his reaction?

"Never mind that. At least I know now, and I can deal with it. Where is this Brother Damion?"

Alison moved restlessly. "I don't know exactly. I think he's still here in the castle."

"What do you mean by that? Surely he wouldn't show himself with the king here!"

"There's a bit more to it. I also know what happened to Sir Edmund."

"That blackguard's returned? Where is he!"

"He never left. He's . . . over there."

Miles looked quickly in the direction she pointed, but saw only the blackness of the back corner. "Where?"

"Damion killed him when Sir Edmund accidentally

discovered him. He buried him at the far end of the center aisle. Beside the perry."

Miles stared at her without speaking.

"You see, Damion has become crazed."

"Tell me you're making all this up!" Miles felt her forehead. "Are you running a fever?"

"No, no. All this really happened just as I said!"

Miles shook his head in shock. "There's an insane killer loose in Wyndfell! And the king is here as well! Do you realize the trouble we're in?"

"Yes, I do. That's why I needed to speak with you."

"You say Lord Bainbridge is also in on this. I will have him arrested at once. Surely that will convince the king that we have no part in this."

Alison was silent as she bit her lower lip.

"You *aren't* a part of it, are you?" Miles demanded.

"No. Somehow I ended up in the middle. I've tried to dissuade them from their schemes."

"Good! We can somehow force Lord Bainbridge to tell that to the king."

"I'm afraid there's more."

"More?" he asked suspiciously.

"Lord Bainbridge is also dead." She pointed toward the ceiling. "Up there. I just found him."

Miles's mouth dropped open, and he could think of no adequate words. "What happened?" he finally managed to ask through clenched teeth.

"I don't know. I had barricaded Damion in his room after I learned he killed Sir Edmund, but evidently Lord Bainbridge opened the secret panel and freed him. They must have argued and Damion killed him. As I said, Damion has gone quite mad over the past months. He was bending over Lord Bainbridge when I went up to see if he was still fastened in. Damion pushed past me and ran down the secret passageway. I've looked for him, but I can't find him."

"Mayhap he left?"

"I think it unlikely. Roger's horse is still tied to the bush beside the outer entrance. If Damion fled, I should think he would have taken the horse. Besides, he's . . . rather bloodied. How far could he ride in a monk's habit with blood on it? No, I think he's still here in Wyndfell."

Miles sat silently for a long time, his face a dark mask of concern. Then he got up and went down the central aisle to where the butts of perry were stored. "Here?" he asked.

"Here." Alison pointed down at their feet.

Miles knelt and ran his fingers along the lip of the flagstones where the dirt was definitely looser than around those beside it. With a heavy sigh he stood up and regarded Alison in the fading light.

"What will we do, Miles?"

"I'm not sure. If you were to guess, what would you say Damion will do next?"

"I'm afraid he will try to kill the king."

Miles raised his eyes in the direction of the hall. "I think so, too. We have to stay near the king at all times."

Alison nodded. "I wish I had told you all this before now."

"I do too," he said with barely concealed exasperation. "I do too."

When they reached the hall, the acrobats were finishing their performance with a human pyramid that reached almost to the war banners that decorated the hall's ceiling. They landed lithely on their feet amid enthusiastic applause and shouts. Henry showed his appreciation by thanking them in fluent Italian and tossing each a gold coin.

Miles stationed himself at Henry's side, his eyes searching the crowd for Damion. As soon as the acrobats cleared the floor, Miles motioned for the servants to begin setting up the long trestle tables in preparation for dinner.

"Marvelous acrobats," Henry said enthusiastically. "There's nothing like an Italian troop when it comes to feats of balance and tumbling."

"They came highly recommended, your grace." He tried to scan the people without seeming nervous, and at the same time to appear to be giving his entire attention to Henry. A secret passage at Wyndfell! He would never have guessed it. He wished he had thought to ask Alison where the panels were located. And what was he to do with Lord Bainbridge, lying dead on the upper floor?

The king was seated beneath the embroidered baldaquin in the chair of honor. Miles and Alison, as owners of the castle, sat to his right, with the other nobles of highest rank seated to either side on the dais. All the others took their places according to rank down the double row of tables covered with snowy linen cloths and sanapes. Sir Trahern and Sir Robert of St. Giles rode into the hall on their gaily caprisoned horses to oversee the serving of the meal and to be certain no one's chalice became empty.

As they ate, a group of musicians, high above in the loft, played intricate music on lute, viol, cittern, and rebec. Between courses the diners were entertained with games of draughts and tables, as well as with madrigals and rounds sung by three boys with angelic voices.

Miles and Alison partook sparingly of the feast as most of their time was spent looking about the room. While the king was busy with a game of tables, Miles leaned near Alison and whispered, "Is there an entrance into the hall from this passage?"

"Over there," she murmured. "Behind the panel with the tapestry of Diana."

Miles looked hard at the tapestry she had indicated, but that panel seemed no different from any of the others.

Custard lumbarde was brought in, followed by canelyne. The beef dish tasted dry in Miles's mouth, but he suspected the problem was within himself and not the food. Henry seemed to find no difficulty in eating it.

A servitor ladled the joutes into glass drinking bowls.

Miles sipped the thick borscht and nodded his absent-minded approval before the servitor and his assistants moved on.

There were too many strangers here, Miles thought. Although he knew some of the men from his days in court, a number of them were new faces. If he were Damion, he would steal clothing and mingle with the crowd. How else could he hope to get near enough to the king to murder him? One man near the end of the table drew Miles's attention. He had heavy, dark features and a treacherous scowl. When he ate, he hovered over his platter as if daring anyone to approach it.

Miles nudged Alison. "Is that the man we spoke of?"

"Where!"

"Down there on the right. The dark one."

"No, no. He looks nothing like Damion," she whispered back. "Damion resembles Sir Robert in coloring and height, but is very thin."

Miles nodded. Medium height, brown hair, and thin. The vague description was better than nothing.

A cockentrice was brought out on a platter borne by two men. The front half of a rooster had been attached to the back half of a suckling pig. The bird's feathers had been replaced after it was cooked and the pig half had been gilded with a saffron pastry. The hooves were painted gold, and it was nestled in a bed of parsley. The cook had done well with the familiar dish, making it look quite lifelike. Henry beamed with pleasure and had the carver cut him a generous portion of both bird and beast.

A ball of pastry, a good yard across, was wheeled in by four servitors. It was decorated like a nautical globe with the continents painted in green on a sea of blue. Mermaids and sea monsters in red and yellow cavorted around miniature galleons and flotas under full sail. Behind it came four dwarf-size figures of marchpane representing the four seasons depicted by the four ages of man.

Henry roared his approval and slapped Miles on the

shoulder as the spectacles came to a stop in front of him.

Suddenly the globe of pastry burst open and a wild-looking man clothed in hides jumped out. Miles was on his feet in an instant, but Alison pulled him back down as she frantically shook her head. The "wild man" grabbed colored balls from inside the broken globe and began juggling to shouts of encouragement.

Miles sank back in the chair and tried not to show his relief.

The banquet lasted far into the night, and Miles was glad when the king finally signaled he was ready for bed.

Miles lit the king to the master chamber and aided the king's men in preparing their royal master for sleep. He handed Henry a silver cup of sack and stood by while he drank the syrupy mixture. Then he bade the king good night and bowed out of the chamber. At the door to the last antechamber stood the king's burly chamber guards. Both the men's and ladies' antechambers were filled with his soldiers. Miles breathed a sigh of relief. At least the king would be safe until morning.

Miles felt reassured until he reached his temporary chamber, where Alison was pacing as nervously as the lions in the Tower of London.

"There's a secret panel in the king's bedchamber," she said without preamble.

Miles felt his spirits plummet.

26

Damion hid in the deep niche behind the chimney in the passageway until he was certain Alison had left. His thin lips drew back to expose his crooked teeth, but he held in his laughter. Even as a child his sister had been no good at seeking games.

He had listened to the barely perceptible click as she refastened the panels he had left ajar. When she didn't return, he decided that she must think he was in the castle proper mixing with the crowd. Carefully he left his hiding place and returned to his cell. Roger lay exactly as he had fallen, and as Damion stepped over him to get into the room, he felt a remorseful sensation that he quickly suppressed. He wouldn't allow human weaknesses to sway his noble cause.

Damion examined the stout pole that Alison had used to barricade him in, puzzling over it momentarily before throwing it out the window and into the moat. He didn't care if anyone saw it. In a few hours he would be away from Wyndfell forever. Whether he left as a crusade leader or a martyr made little difference. In the end they were the same.

Damion looked down at Roger. He regretted that Roger had turned on him. Perhaps Roger was the culprit who had fastened him in, and not Alison or Lord Miles. In retrospect, Damion thought it highly unlikely that a woman would think of locking up a man, much less be daring enough to do so. True, he had not known many women, but his mother had been obedient and shy, as were the nuns in the church. No, it must have been Roger.

He knelt beside his former friend, his lips moving in a silent one-sided conversation. He had developed this habit in the monastery, where silence was the rule. He never considered how odd he might look with his pale lips moving and Adam's apple bobbing but no words coming out. In his silent discourse, Damion told Roger how sorry he was for having to kill him, and he humbly asked Roger's pardon. After long minutes of waiting, Damion felt a satisfaction that he interpreted as Roger's forgiveness and blessing.

Now that peace had been made between them, Damion no longer felt the weight of guilt. There were things to be done. He was a priest, and he had vows to observe. One of the seven Christian virtues was proper burial.

Naturally Damion thought first of the buttery, but he rejected that idea immediately. Lord Roger's rank had to be considered. A viscount couldn't be buried beside a mere steward. Besides, with so many extra people in residence, the chance of being caught in the act was too great. No, the thing to do with Roger was to return him to Bainbridge Castle.

Dusk had fallen by this time and night was quickly approaching. Drawing Roger to a sitting position, Damion pulled him over his shoulder. Slowly he stood, shifting the body until he gained his balance. Roger was heavier than Edmund had been, and Damion was still weak from a recent fast.

The secret passageway was as black as the inside of a well, but Damion was as familiar with the twists and turns as he had been with his monastery's winding corridors. When he stepped out into the night, he paused in the cool breeze. The scent of rain was in the air, and in the far distance he saw a dull flash of lightning. In the dusky half-light he saw the bulk of a horse that he recognized as Roger's. As carefully as possible he draped the body between the tall pommel and the back of the saddle. The horse shied nervously but was too well-trained to refuse the burden.

Damion untied the animal and led it down the back slope of Wyndfell's green. He skirted the village but paused at an outlying cottage. A busy housewife had evidently finished her wash late that day and an assortment of clothing was still drying on the bushes. Damion looked down at his own bloodstained garments that gleamed white in the dark. As much as he dreaded putting them aside, he knew he must to avoid premature capture. With reverent ceremony he removed all his clothing, retaining only the hair shirt which he had worn since his early days in St. Benedictine's.

He folded the garments and laid them over Roger's body, then dressed in the peasant's garb. After years of wearing the loose skirted tunic, Damion felt strange in the linen shirt and jerkin. He pulled on a coarse russet gown and belted it with the rope girdle he had worn with his habit. He hung his black rosary around his neck beneath his clothing.

The two miles to Bainbridge Castle went slowly, for the horse was unaccustomed to being led, especially with the deadweight of a man dangling over his back. At last Damion saw the square bulk of the castle. The horse, sensing home and the promise of food, picked up his pace.

At the top of the knoll, Damion tied the reins to the saddle's pommel and touched Roger's head in a last benediction. Damion was glad he no longer felt animosity toward the man. He didn't want hate to stain his conscience.

Damion led the horse forward and slapped the animal's hip to send him down the slope and through the gates. In a few minutes the castle's courtyard was alight with torches, indicating to Damion that Roger's body had been discovered. Damion nodded his satisfaction. They would see to Roger's proper burial. He turned and began to retrace his steps to Wyndfell.

"What the hell do you mean, there's a secret panel in our bedchamber!" Miles demanded as loudly as he dared.

"Hush, hush! There is one. I swear it."

Miles paced the width of the chamber and came back to Alison. "The king is sleeping in there!"

"I know!"

Miles thought quickly. "The king has guards on the chamber and antechamber doors. I must guard the secret one."

"I can't let you go in there alone! Damion is dangerous!"

"So am I right at this minute. Come show me how to enter this passage."

Because the castle had settled down for the night, Alison took a candle and led him down the servants' stairs and away from the crowded hall and gallery. All the royal servants, as well as Wyndfell's staff, were sleeping in the large rooms.

She avoided the kitchens and crossed the pantry to go outside, where soft rain made the courtyard smells more pungent. In one of the barns a cow lowed sleepily, and in the chicken shed she could see the hens roosting on long poles as if they were so many headless balls of feathers.

They circled to the garden gate and Alison found the hidden door by running her fingers over the wall. "That's odd," she said. "Roger's horse was tied there. I meant to free him in hopes that he would go home, but I forgot. Do you think he broke free?"

"More likely Roger was only wounded and rode him home."

"He was dead. I'm sure of it." She pushed the door open and they stepped into the musty blackness. "I brought you to this door because it is at the farthest end of the passage from Damion's cell. We can search for Damion as we go up."

The small light flickered on the stones and steep, narrow steps carved from the native rock. The steps quickly disappeared into a cobwebbed blackness.

"You come here often?" Miles asked in amazement. He knew knights proven in combat who would be hesitant to venture farther.

"Come, Miles, we must hurry if we're to guard the king."

"Not we. You're going back to the chamber and go to sleep."

"I'll do no such thing!"

"I insist!"

"How will you find the correct panel to the king's chamber without my help?" she countered.

"Very well. You can show me, then leave."

"And come back down this passage alone after all that's happened? Don't even think it."

With a sigh, Miles nodded. She had a point there. "I don't like it, but I suppose I must agree. But if Damion shows up and there is fighting, you must promise me that you'll run to safety."

"I promise," she lied. Her hand closed on a fist-sized rock.

Alison led Miles up the winding steps. She was afraid to speak lest Damion or someone on the other side of the wall might hear her, so she didn't point out the various panels or tell him where they led.

On the small landing outside the king's chamber, she paused and pointed. Miles put his lips beside her ear and whispered, "Show me where you saw Lord Bainbridge."

Alison climbed higher, her steps faltering as they neared the upper room. Miles moved past her and, taking the candle, held it high. The room was small, as it was designed for a menial servant, and it held only the barest of furniture. An altar had been improvised with candlesticks that Miles had seen before in the chapel. A pool of dark red-brown had soaked into the floor's dry wood, but there was no body.

"He was here!" Alison affirmed, pointing down at the dark stain.

Miles nodded. The stain looked a couple of hours old, maybe more, but it was most definitely a new one. "He must have only been injured. Where else could he be?"

"In the buttery?" she asked in a voice filled with dread.

Miles went to the panel and examined the stone steps, but found no blood there. If Roger had been wounded severely enough to lose that much blood, he would still be bleeding when he left. Miles looked again at the large dark stain on the floor. That was a lot of blood for a mere wound, no matter how deep it was.

"Go out that door and into the servants' corridor. You'll be safe there," Miles said firmly.

"We have no idea where Damion may be. I'm not leaving you."

"You're a stubborn woman, Alison. It's one of your less-endearing traits."

She managed a weak smile. "I only wish I had told you sooner. But whoever would have guessed it would come to this? I know I've gotten us in a terrible mess, and I don't blame you for hating me. I just hope that someday you'll be able to forgive me."

Miles looked astonished. "Hate you? Alison, I don't hate you. I'm just very concerned. I'm not sure how we'll get out of all this."

"You don't hate me? But—"

Miles put his finger on her lips to silence her. "Hush now. We've got work to do." Together they went back down to the landing outside their bedchamber and sat on the cold stone floor. Beyond the panel they could hear the sawing cadence of Henry's snores. Miles reached for Alison's icy hand and drew her closer.

He kissed her forehead, then her lips, and encouragingly smiled at her. "Lean on my shoulder and try to sleep," he whispered.

"Sleep! Here? I couldn't possibly!" Alison was much too frightened to sleep. She wanted to be happy that he didn't hate her for what she'd done, but her fear was blocking all her other emotions. Then it occurred to her that he had only said he didn't hate her. He hadn't said he would forgive her or that he still loved her. But then he did kiss her. What was she to think?

"Take it easy, Alison. Just rest, then. We must look as if nothing is wrong in the morning." He put his arms protectively around her and pulled her head down to his shoulder.

"I'll rest for a little while." Her thoughts whirled from one worry to the next at an exhausting pace. After a few minutes she said sleepily, "I may doze off a few minutes. If anything happens, wake me right away."

"You'll be the first I'll tell," he said wryly.

"If nothing happens, wake me anyway. We should take turns watching, for you must be rested tomorrow too."

"All right."

As he held her against his body and cradled her head on his shoulder, he felt her body relax into a restless sleep. Miles had no desire to follow her example. He had always been very uneasy in close quarters, and the idea that a madman could lurch out of the darkness and attack them was a powerful stimulant. Remaining as still as possible so as not to disturb Alison's sleep, Miles watched the candle reduce itself to a thick stub in a puddle of pale wax. During those long hours he had ample time to consider the events that had led them into this quagmire.

He wished that she had come to him sooner, but he understood her fear that he would be angry with her. How could she have known that he would be willing to help her out of this predicament? Once they were free from this life-threatening dilemma, he intended to convince her that she could come to him with any problem. With one hand on his wheel-lock pistol and the other securely around his wife, Miles peered into the darkness, hoping Damion had fled Wyndfell Castle forever.

When Miles heard Henry call for his morning attendants, he stretched his cramped muscles and awoke Alison. Silently they made their way down to the courtyard and up to their unfamiliar chamber. After washing up and changing into clean garments, they wearily headed out to meet the new day.

At their doorway, Miles paused. "I fear for your safety more than for the king's. It's possible Damion killed Roger because Roger could identify him. As can you."

"I don't think he would hurt me," she replied, but her doubtful tone belied her words.

"He's a madman. You can't know what he might do. Here, take this." Miles took his wheel-lock from beneath his cloak and checked it over carefully to be sure it was loaded and that the flint was dry before he handed it to Alison.

"Miles! I have no idea how to use this!"

"All you have to do is pull back this lever, point it, and pull the trigger. Remember, it is accurate for only a few yards, but I think it will protect you better than a knife."

Alison looked at the weapon with trepidation. "I could never use it. You keep it and I'll stay close by you."

"I have my sword. If your life is in danger you'll be able to use it."

Reluctantly Alison put the pistol in a beaded velvet bag and suspended it from her waist along with her pomander and the velvet pouch containing her scissors, needle, and eating knife. "It hangs so heavy!"

"No one will notice. Do you recall how to fire it?"

"Yes."

"As soon as everyone is gone and there can be no

questions asked, I'm going to seal that damned passageway forever."

"I'll help you," she said firmly.

When Damion returned to Wyndfell, he went to the stable loft to sleep. He curled up in the corner farthest from the door and pulled some hay over him for warmth.

As was his habit, Damion awoke before daylight. At first he couldn't understand why he was wearing a peasant's clothing, but then it all came back to him. Today was the day he would rid England of a scourge and the persecution. As he stood and brushed the straw from his hair and clothes, he decided that he should kill Alison as well. She was the only one left who could identify him, and if he was fortunate enough to escape after killing the king, he didn't want to remain in hiding forever, though it might be necessary.

He checked Roger's pistol and reassured himself that the powder had stayed dry inside his jerkin. He would go to the castle and mix with the crowd until he was close enough to fire at the king. As he ran away, he might be lucky enough to stab Alison in passing. Now that she had turned traitor, she would be keeping close to the king. That was the way of traitors.

Silently he went down the ladder to the stable and listened at the half-open door to the head groom's living quarters. Damion could hear the man splashing water on himself as he lustily sang. Damion's hand touched the bald pate of his tonsure. He had almost forgotten that. He needed a cap.

Carefully he looked through the doorway. The groom was in a tiny alcove off the main room, his clothing around the corner was hanging from pegs. With great stealth, Damion was able to reach a shapeless velvet hat with a yellow plume, and as an afterthought he took a broad leather belt, leaving his knotted rope in its place. That way it was a trade and not a theft.

Damion knew all this would come to light later when his heroic story was reported to the pope.

Several kitchen maids were in the side yard ladling hot porridge for the servants and slicing thick slabs of bread and pale cheese. After his fast, Damion was not only hungry but also rather weak. If he was to accomplish his task, he would need strength.

He sat at the end of the trestle table and nodded to the man beside him. The man, who wore Wyndfell's insignia on his breast, asked no questions, thinking Damion was one of the royal servants.

A maid poured Damion a liberal amount of ale, and as he drank it down, he felt it warm his chilled body. He was strongly reminded of the monastery and how the monks gathered at this same time of day to break the night's fast. He had to watch himself closely so he wouldn't give the silent signal for more bread or cheese. Damion missed St. Benedictine more with each passing day.

When his hunger was abated, Damion gave a silent thanksgiving, then left the table without ever speaking a word. He crossed the courtyard and went boldly up the steps to the door. Drawing a deep breath, he went inside and was at once swallowed up in the crowd.

Alison stayed as close to Miles as was possible without arousing suspicion. Miles, in turn, didn't stray more than a yard from Henry.

"Did you sleep well, your majesty?" Miles asked when the breakfast things were being cleared away from the crowded hall.

"I've not slept so well in months. The country air is like a balm to me." Henry slapped his thigh and added, "Even my leg is giving me no trouble."

"I'm glad to hear that. If you need a potion for it, my physicians and the apothecary will fetch whatever you require."

"Tell me, Lady Alison, how goes it with you? You seem overly pale and silent today."

"She has reason to be, your grace," Miles answered quickly. "She's with child."

"So! By St. George, that's always good news for a husband. Mayhap I'll hear it myself one day soon."

The look in Henry's eyes didn't match his jovial tone. He had not mentioned Catherine a single time, and Leatrice had said there was a rumor of his displeasure with her.

"Tell me when the babe is born," Henry said. "I'll send a christening gift."

"Your majesty is too kind," Alison said, dropping a curtsey.

The king had been given the solar as an audience chamber, and the crowd slowly followed him as he made his way up the stairs from the hall. In spite of his assurance that his leg gave him no pain, Henry moved slowly, and had to pause several times before he reached the next floor. Whenever he hesitated to rest, those attending him gossiped and made jokes among themselves as if they took no notice of how long the ascension was taking. Thus the king was able to convince himself that no one was aware of his limited mobility. The progress down the gallery also took a while, and Alison could hear the air puffing in and out of Henry's laboring lungs.

"There aren't many chambers like this," Henry observed, as if his slow pace was deliberate so he might better admire the long room. "I've only seen one other, and it is at Hampton Court."

"King Francis built one at Fontainbleau several years ago," Miles added. "I expect such chambers will become more popular in years to come. As you know, it's a perfect stretch for exercising during foul weather, though it must have been too long and narrow to make a good hall. Certainly it's much drier than an open cloister."

"You say you propose to build another such chamber?"

"Yes, your majesty."

"I would avoid putting it on the south side. 'Tis well known that the south wind carries pestilence. The east wind is much more temperate."

"Does that mean I have your permission to build?"

Henry gave him a chilly smile. "It means I, too, have an interest in architecture. I've not yet decided to give my permission."

Alison saw they were approaching the secret panel in the wall, and she felt her mouth go dry. What would she do if it suddenly burst open and Damion ran out? She touched the weighted bag and hoped she would be able to save the king without killing her brother. When they passed the panel without incident, Alison breathed a bit more easily. Once Henry was in the solar, he would be much safer, as it had only one entrance, and would be guarded by his soldiers.

The solar's theme was unicorns, and in addition to the depiction of the solid wall of two rearing beasts, allegorical tapestries of the mythical animals hung in the round room. One tapestry had been pulled back to let sunlight stream over the throne that Henry had brought with him. Alison was glad for the fresh air as the throng began to fill the moderate-size room. Henry lowered himself into the large throne, emitting an audible sigh of relief. A servant placed a stool and pillow at his feet and lifted his ulcerous leg onto it.

Alison looked up to find Henry watching her. Again she was drawn, and at the same time repelled, by his frightening charisma, as if she were a moth and Henry the flame. Why did he stare so at her?

After a thoughtful pause Henry said, "Lady Alison, it occurs to me that you've never given your oath of fealty."

The impact of the king's words came so swiftly and unexpectedly that Alison reflexively winced and grew nauseous. With all that had happened, she had completely forgotten that dreaded oath. She looked to Miles, and there she found the courage to do what she knew she must. "I believe you never asked for it, your majesty," she said in a clear voice. "I assumed since you hold my lord husband in such high regard, there was no need for my oath."

"I'll bargain with you, my lady," Henry said with a faint smile. "Your oath of allegiance to me in return for my permission for you to enlarge Wyndfell."

Alison moistened her lips nervously. Everyone's eyes were upon her and shyness swept over her. She lowered her eyes to collect herself and found that she was staring at a pair of sandal-shod feet. For a moment she was confused, for all the others wore warm leather shoes with colored hose. When she realized what she was seeing, she gasped in horror, but couldn't speak. Her wide eyes were frozen on Damion.

As if he had been waiting for her to see him before he made his move, Damion stepped forward with a pistol in his bony hand. Before anyone else realized what he was doing, Damion pointed the gun at the king and drew back the lever to cock it.

From Alison's terrified expression, Miles knew that Damion must be in the room. Not bothering to discern which man Damion might be, Miles threw himself in front of Henry.

The gun discharged, filling the room with the stench of gunpowder and shouts and shrieks from all the crowd. As if she were watching movements underwater, Alison saw Miles crumple, and the king arise, then drop back onto the throne. As bright blood flowed from Miles's side, she found she was holding the wheellock from her bag. Damion lurched toward her, and as she saw the flash of a dagger, she pulled back the lever and fired point-blank into Damion's chest.

All the room erupted into turmoil with half the people trying to run out and more trying to rush in. Henry's guards thrust people to one side and forced their way in as Alison dropped the pistol and knelt beside Miles.

He was pale, but when she lifted his head, Miles

opened his eyes. He managed a smile. "I'm not dead, love. Don't look so frightened."

"You're bleeding!"

"I would be faring much worse if I hadn't put on my leather tourney vest." Miles gingerly put his hand over the wound. "It feels like a mere flesh wound." He looked past Alison to where Damion lay. Already the guards were rolling him onto his back to identify him. Damion's cap fell off, revealing his shaved tonsure.

"A priest!" Henry exclaimed. "He meant to kill me!"

As Miles got to his feet and put his arm about Alison, Henry stared at them. "You would have given your life to spare mine!"

"I have always been your loyal subject, your grace. Of course I would have died for you."

Henry slowly got to his feet and put his hand on Miles's shoulder. "Such loyalty will not go unrewarded. I give you my permission to build and fortify Wyndfell as you desire, and I hereby decree that you and all your heirs will henceforth be addressed as earl. Let it be so noted that as of this moment you are Lord Miles Garrett, first Earl of Wyndfell."

Sir Trahern stepped forward to help steady his friend and master. Miles grinned from Alison to Trahern and back to the king. "I know not what to say, your grace."

"You have made words unnecessary. Take him away, Sir Trahern, and have my royal physicians see to his wound." As Miles started out, with Alison right behind, the king spoke up again. "Lady Alison, wait. I would have a word with you in private." Henry motioned the murmuring throng to leave, and she was left alone with him.

Alison dared not speak. Her heart was hammering, and she longed to go with Miles and see for herself that he wasn't badly injured.

Henry took Alison by the wrist and led her to the window, where she was illuminated by sunlight. "Tell me, Lady Alison. Did you shoot this villain to protect me or because he shot your husband? And how came you to be carrying a pistol?"

Alison lifted her chin defiantly. "Miles and I had reason to fear an attempt would be made on your life and perhaps on myself. For that reason he insisted I carry a gun for my protection as well as for your own. I told him I could never shoot anyone."

"But you did."

"He threatened someone dearer to me than aught else in the world. My husband."

Henry studied her honest eyes and chuckled wryly. "You have a great deal to learn about courtly wiles. Anyone else would have lied and said the bullet was to stop my would-be assassin."

Alison made no reply.

After a moment Henry lifted his hand and touched the firm curve of her cheek. "Such loyalty is rare in a wife."

"I love him," she replied, not daring to draw away.

"How like them you are," he marveled as if to himself.

"Pardon, your majesty?"

"You have your mother's eyes and mouth, but I also see my mother in the shape of your face and in your figure."

Alison's lips parted in amazement.

Henry patted her cheek awkwardly. "That's the most I can say, and mayhap it is too much. Go now and see to this precious husband of yours."

Alison curtsied and turned to hurry from the room.

"Wait!" Henry called as an afterthought. "I find myself wondering—would you have given me your oath of fealty?"

Alison flashed her brilliant smile at her father. "You have but to ask me, and I will give it to you."

Henry nodded. "It's no longer necessary. Tell me, child. Where is your mother buried?"

"In the church in the village."

"I may perhaps ride that way before I leave. And fret not about your husband. Lord Miles didn't move like a man severely wounded. Go, go. I can tell you must see for yourself. And not a word about what has passed between us, for I must deny it."

"Yes, your majesty." Alison dipped another curtsey and flew from the room.

As he watched her go, Henry leaned his bulk against the ledge of the sun-splashed window. His crown had rarely weighed as heavily on his spirit as it did at that moment. He gazed down the green to the village and picked out the unmistakable shape of the church where Eleanor lay. Behind him Henry heard people flocking back into the solar, and his rare moment of solitude was over. He put aside his regrets that no wife of his had ever been as loyal to him as Alison had been to her husband, and slowly returned to his ornate throne.

Alison found Miles in a nearby chamber, sitting on a stool with the king's physician looking him over. As she entered, the physician turned to her and smiled. " 'Tis but a slight wound. Lord Garrett will not even be bedridden."

Alison rushed to Miles and embraced him as tears of happiness coursed down her cheeks.

A broad smile crossed Miles's face as he pulled Alison closer and held her securely in his arms.

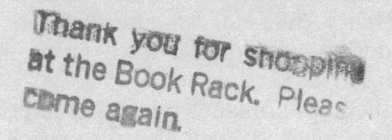

About the Authors

Lynda Trent is actually the award-winning husband-and-wife writing team of Dan and Lynda Trent. Not only is it unusual for a husband and wife to become coauthors, but Dan and Lynda are living the kind of romance they write about. After dating for only a short time, they were married in 1977, and then began together a new career for them both.

Formerly a professional artist, Lynda actually began writing a few months before she met Dan, when she put down her brush and picked up a pen to describe a scene she couldn't get onto the canvas. The paints dried and the picture was never completed, but Lynda continued to write.

Dan, also a native Texan from Grand Prairie, worked for seventeen years for NASA in Houston before turning to writing full-time. The Trents have written a total of twenty-novels, and when asked how they manage to write together, Lynda says, "We only use one pencil."

SIGNET ⬤ **ONYX** **(0451)**

SWEEPING ROMANCE by Catherine Coulter

- **MIDSUMMER MAGIC by Catherine Coulter.** He tantalized her with wild kisses and the promise of love ... Frances Kilbracken, disguised as a mousy Scottish lass was forced to marry the rakish Earl of Rothermere. Soon deserted, she shed her dowdy facade to become the most fashionable leading lady in London and to ignite her faithless husband's passions. (400577—$3.95)

- **MIDNIGHT STAR.** British heiress Chauncey FitzHugh had come to San Francisco to ruin Delaney as he had ruined her father. But her desire exploded for the man she had sworn to hate.... (142977—$3.95)

- **FIRE SONG.** Marriage had made Graelam the master of Kassia's body, and now he must claim her complete surrender with the dark ecstasy of love.... (140001—$3.95)

- **CHANDRA.** Lovely golden-haired Chandra was prepared to defend herself against anything ... except the sweet touch of Jerval de Veron which sent the scarlet fires of love raging through her blood.... (142012—$3.95)

- **SWEET SURRENDER.** The handsome American had paid heavily to possess her exquisite body, and Gianna, able to resist him no longer, begged to be released from her fierce desire.... (142004—$3.95)

- **DEVIL'S EMBRACE.** The seething city of Genoa seemed a world away from the great 18th-century estate where Cassandra was raised. But here she met Anthony, and became addicted to a feverish ecstasy that would guide their hearts forever.... (141989—$3.95)

- **DEVIL'S DAUGHTER.** Arabella had never imagined that Kamal, the savage sultan who dared make her a harem slave, would look so like a blond Nordic god, or that his savage love could make her passion's slave.... (141997—$3.95)

- **WILD STAR.** Byrony knew that Brent Hammond was the last man in the world she should want. Yet the moment she felt his warm, strong arms embrace her ... she knew she was his for the taking....(400135—$3.95)

- **JADE STAR.** Beautiful Juliana DuPres knew she should give herself to her husband Michael—body and soul, but the painful memory of her abduction by the brutal Jameson Wilkes would not allow it. When Wilkes' threat again becomes reality, would her beloved Michael be there to turn her overwhelming terror into tingling desire...? (400348—$3.95)

Prices slightly higher in Canada

Buy them at your local
bookstore or use coupon
on next page for ordering.

⊘ **SIGNET** Ⓑ **ONYX** (0451,

Heartfelt Passions

☐ **SAPPHIRE AND SILK by Leslie O'Grady.** One night of passion became a lifetime of love. Sensual young Aurora Falconet must surrender herself completely to the handsome Nicholas Devenish, an eighteenth century English Lord. How can Aurora ever claim his attention, when the most beautiful ladies surround him? (400410—$3.95)

☐ **WILDWINDS by Leslie O'Grady.** She met with a man's desire in a place where passion meant peril ... now that she had come back to Greg Chatwin, the handsome, arrogant man who had fled years before.
(149546—$2.95)

☐ **SECOND SISTER by Leslie O'Grady.** Winner of the Romantic Times' Best Historical Gothic Award. Beautiful Cassandra Clark arrives at her unknown mother's Victorian mansion, where her innocence is shattered. She falls into the brooding hands of her half-sister's domineering husband. "Titillating suspense!"—*Romantic Times* (145615—$2.95)

Prices slightly higher in Canada

Buy them at your local bookstore or use this convenient coupon for ordering.

NEW AMERICAN LIBRARY
P.O. Box 999, Bergenfield, New Jersey 07621

Please send me the books I have checked above. I am enclosing $_____
(please add $1.00 to this order to cover postage and handling). Send check or money order—no cash or C.O.D.'s. Prices and numbers are subject to change without notice.

Name_____

Address_____

City _____ State _____ Zip Code _____
Allow 4-6 weeks for delivery.
This offer is subject to withdrawal without notice.